DARK WATERS

Also by Toni Anderson

Dangerous Waters

The Killing Game

Edge of Survival

Storm Warning

Sea of Suspicion

Her Sanctuary

DARK WATERS

TONI ANDERSON

Montlake Romance

The characters and events portrayed in this book are fictitious. Any similarity to real persons, living or dead, is coincidental and not intended by the author.

Published by Montlake Romance
PO Box 400818
Las Vegas, NV 89140

ISBN-13: 9781477805039
ISBN-10: 1477805036

To my daughter, Jamie,
who is brilliant, beautiful, and kind.

PROLOGUE

No one gave ex-cons the benefit of the doubt. Hell, his wife had made that clear the day she filed for divorce. Davis Silver stared at the numbers on the screen and it suddenly all made sense. All that benevolent "second chance" baloney blown out the hole.

These guys had reeled him in and made him a believer. Gifted him with that vastly underrated commodity—hope. Now these *bastards* were going to get away with stealing millions in charitable donations made to injured vets if he didn't act soon. And *he* was the fall guy. The mark. The dupe. The asshole who'd believed in them.

He'd been so pathetically grateful to be hired as an expense accounts manager and kept on in this dismal economy. Not only was he an ex-con, he was decades older than the college grads who were so desperate to find work they'd accept payment in beer. *Should have known.*

He'd noticed an anomaly in his activity logs—not something a guy like him would ignore or take for granted. So he'd started following money: numerous small under-the-radar amounts, from business accounts to shell companies and then to five separate offshore accounts in Ireland. Transfers done using *his* access codes, and he'd bet his ass if he dug deep enough, the accounts would also be linked back to him.

He was *not* going back to prison.

No way.

He checked his e-mail—more reflex muscle memory than conscious thought—stalling for time while his brain figured out what to do next.

This whole deal had been one long con setting him up for the big fall. He'd put in four years of dedicated service—all those extra hours, the all-nighters during tax season. All the obsequious, sycophantic fawning. He ground his teeth. He could have fallen asleep over the keyboard and barfed all over the boss at the annual Christmas party and they still would have kept him on.

Sixty million US dollars and change.

His neck grew hot and he undid the top button of his white shirt. Strain made his fingers ache. He stretched them out. No *way.* He was fifty years old. No way was he going down for this. Last time he'd survived the joint because of one man. Next time he wouldn't be so lucky.

The cubicles were dimly lit. It was late on a Friday night in the heart of downtown Chicago. Everyone else had gone home to loved ones or off to happy hour at Ernie's. The boss's office was upstairs, but Davis had seen him leave at five with Kujo, his head of security, whose real name was Kudrow. Kujo suited him better.

His eyes scanned the account numbers. What could he do? He took a screenshot and printed it out. An elevator dinged and his head shot up to look over the top of his cubicle. He blew out a sigh of relief when Rosalita, one of the cleaning crew, threw him a cheery wave before she started to vacuum.

Sweat ran down his sides despite the arctic blast of the AC.

Were they watching him? He glanced around, but cameras could be hidden anywhere. He had to act fast. If he left the money in place, it could be gone any second and, as a repeat offender, he'd go down for a damn sight longer than last time. No one would believe a word he said. His gaze caught a photograph on his desk and his heart gave a squeeze. *Anna*. His beautiful daughter. She'd never forgive him.

What could he do?

And, with a flash of insight, he knew. He knew exactly what to do. Shut down the organization and expose them for the frauds they were. He pulled up directions to the nearest FBI field office and printed them out. He checked the time on his monitor and feigned a yawn. Yawning men did not steal every penny from their crooked bosses' offshore accounts. It took fourteen seconds to type in the numbers he'd memorized. A split second of hesitation before he pressed "enter" and "confirm" to become a multimillionaire.

It was a pity money didn't buy the important things like love, happiness, or reputation.

He moved the money again, sideways this time, breaking the chain and putting it beyond the grasp of these heartless thieves. And if someone in law enforcement used their brains and figured out who'd set him up nine years ago? Well, maybe it was time. He took a second screenshot. Printed it out. Insurance, in case the feds didn't believe him. Then he deleted the browser history, logged out, and closed down the PC. With shaking hands, he stuffed the two screenshots into a manila envelope and added a sticky note briefly explaining what he'd found. Then he scribbled an old but familiar address on the front. Dug out his wallet and rifled through the pockets until he found a couple of stamps. He couldn't take anything with him other than what he normally carried, but he surreptitiously slipped the photograph of Anna into his jacket pocket. Then he sauntered out as if he didn't have a care in the world. He was just another exhausted drone going home after a long week in the office.

"Good night, Rosalita," he called as he pressed the call button for the elevator. "Have a great weekend." *Enjoy it because you're probably about to be out of a job.* Inwardly he winced, but this wasn't his fault. He was catching bad guys and it felt great to be in the driver's seat for a change. He tapped his foot, waiting for the doors to open. Then he got in and concentrated on the burnished metal of the steel wall. There was a vague hint of his reflection. Blurry. Indistinct. He scratched his scalp. Balding.

Life hadn't quite gone as planned.

Katie...

He swallowed the memories. His breathing was over-loud, raspy in the closed metal box. He tried to relax his face. *God.* After an eternity, he landed in the lobby and hurried out through the huge glass doors of the twenty-story building in the heart of downtown Chicago. He headed to the nearest "L" station.

He was boiling under his jacket, shirt sticking to his skin like warm wet tissue. His stomach growled. He placed a hand on his belly—plenty of time to eat in protective custody.

There was a mailbox on the corner of the street. He opened the flap, dropped the letter in, and hovered on the curb at the crosswalk. He turned in time to see two men run out of his building. They pointed at him and his blood hit his toes.

How the hell did they know so fast? Someone must have tried to move the money and realized it was gone.

He felt smug for about half a second.

Oh, shit. Frantically, he searched for a cab or a cop. Nothing. He looked back over his shoulder—they were only a hundred feet away, hands diving under jackets as if they were reaching for guns. He dashed into traffic, dodging a blue truck and a bus. Horns blaring. Across another lane and brakes squealed. Shouts. The awful crunch of metal on glass as someone got rear-ended. *Sorry.*

He scrambled in his pockets for his metro pass and ran into the Clark/Lake station. He grabbed his cell in his other hand and dialed 911 with ice-cold fingers as he ran full speed.

"Nine-one-one. What is your emergency?"

"Someone is trying to kill me." He had no doubt they would kill him just as soon as they got those account numbers out of him.

"Where are you, sir? What's your name?"

"Davis Silver." Ex-con. Thief. Righter of wrongs. First-class idiot. "I work for the Holladay Foundation. Someone's been stealing from the company so I took it back before it disappeared forever. I want to come in. I need police protection."

"Did you just say you stole money from the Holladay Foundation? Are you confessing to a crime, sir?"

"No! Yes." *Just help me!* There was no time to explain. His feet felt pinched from running in cheap, too-tight shoes. He dashed through the turnstile. Headed for the subway. He searched for the next train arrival as he ran. Two minutes. Fear poured over his skin in a crackling wave. He swallowed as he heard sounds of pursuit behind him. Two minutes was too long. Why couldn't it be like in the movies when two trains arrived at once and he darted between them at the last minute? He looked up, still talking to the emergency operator, searching for cameras. "I need assistance. I'm at the Clark/Lake 'L' and someone is trying to kill me." He waved at the cameras and something whipped past his ankles. He hopped.

Shit! That was a bullet.

The distant rumble of a train shook the ground. *Hurry.*

He hung up as he hit the platform and ran, dodging behind the big square columns. His heart pounded as people scattered. He pulled up behind the last column, sank to his haunches in the grime. Clutched his hands to his chest almost in prayer. *Anna.* He had to explain this to Anna. Desperate, he speed-dialed her number. Swore when it went to voice mail.

Sweat pooled on his skin as he spoke into the phone. He could feel his pursuers creeping closer and closer. He squeezed his eyes closed. Oh, sweet Jesus, what if they went after Anna? She had to get out of there!

"Dammit. I've done it again." Screwed up her life. Quickly, he told her where to run. Whom to trust.

Someone grabbed him by the shirtfront and hauled him to his feet. He dropped the phone, which landed with a clatter on the pavement. Wind and noise thundered through the tunnel as he stared into the cold black eyes of a predator.

Those eyes told him he was going to die.

Slowly.

Painfully.

No cops were going to rescue him. No feds would shake his hand or thank him for his service. He was going to be beaten and tortured. Then he was going to hand over those account numbers and die. They'd frame him just like they'd always planned. The same way someone else had framed him and stolen his life, his family, all those years ago. His actions had barely made them break a sweat. But a cornered man with nothing to lose was the most dangerous.

Some primal force had him driving both fists up into the man's iron jaw. Surprise earned him enough freedom to stagger away, but momentum kept him going—straight into the oncoming train. The whole world went black.

Rand's lips tightened and he picked up the cell phone from the worn-out floor and pocketed it while catching the eye of his partner. The situation had morphed from a shitfest to a total Charlie Foxtrot. He and Marco faded in separate directions, keeping their heads down as they exited the station. The General wasn't going to be happy, but they couldn't exactly put Davis Silver back together again.

Where was the envelope?

Davis had had it leaving the building, the little weasel, but not during the chase so he must have dropped it or mailed it. Hopefully it contained details about where he'd stashed the money. Sixty goddamned million swiped from right under their noses. Petrie was trying to trace it. From the sweat on the guy's brow when he'd screamed at the computer in the office, Rand knew he wasn't feeling optimistic about his prospects.

The General was not someone to screw with and neither was the US government.

He walked swiftly down the street, away from the offices in case some would-be hero decided to follow. Rand could get the fuck out, walk away, and sink himself into some dirt farm in Mississippi. But after all these years of blood, sweat, and bullets, where was the fun in that? He'd earned his money the hard way. Five GSWs to various parts of his body, a knife in the gut, malaria, dysentery, and a broken ankle from a piss-poor landing in the African jungle. Definitely earned every fucking penny.

He pulled Davis Silver's cell phone out of his pocket and scrolled down to see who he'd been calling. Nine-one-one and a woman named Anna Silver. Wife? A muscle twitched in his cheek. He pressed redial and cocked his head to one side as it went straight to voice mail. He stared into the street for a moment before heading into a coffee shop and getting himself an espresso while he did a quick Internet search on her name and number.

Cauldwell Lake, just outside Minneapolis.

He slugged back his coffee and checked his wristwatch. They needed to know where Davis had funneled their money; otherwise they could forget their plans of early retirement. Never trust a goddamned thief.

CHAPTER 1

Anna let Peter take her hand and swing it gently as he led her up her curved garden path. It was dark, but her porch light shone with welcoming warmth. School had broken up and she was more than ready to start summer. She loved being a teacher, but without a much needed summer vacation she'd be a total raving lunatic.

They'd been to the movies to see the latest romantic comedy. The story line had been comfortably predictable, mildly amusing. Peter didn't seem to mind chick flicks, which was a bonus, although she wasn't really sure their relationship was going anywhere.

He was cute, though. Auburn hair cropped short enough to disguise the natural wave most women would envy. Guileless blue eyes and a smattering of freckles. He wasn't particularly athletic or tall, which suited her fine because at twenty-six years old and five feet three inches she didn't need towering height or abs of steel—at least not outside the movies.

The evening breeze swished her cotton dress around her knees. The scent of roses drifted heavy and succulent on the breeze. A robin sang.

She sighed. It was perfect. “Thank you for a wonderful evening.”

“It was my pleasure.” He raised her hand to his lips and gave her a look that told her he really wanted to kiss her somewhere else entirely.

Maybe it was time to take a chance. What the heck. They’d dated for six months and she’d been taking it slow, even by her snaillike standards. But experience bred caution, and she was exceedingly cautious. She took a step closer. His eyes widened as she wrapped her arms around his neck and leaned up to press her lips to his. His arms tightened for a moment before he returned her kiss.

There were no fireworks, but that was OK. She didn’t want uncontrollable passion—she didn’t want uncontrollable anything. She opened her mouth under pressure from his firm lips and tried to calm her pulse that pounded for all the wrong reasons.

Sweat on his palms seeped through the thin cotton of her dress, then his fingers dug into her skin. She pulled back, uneasy.

“Anna, come on. Let me in.” His voice was deep and gruff. He dove for her lips again and crushed them in what was probably supposed to be an ardent kiss, but was wet and full of hard enamel.

Fighting for calm, she tried to gentle the exchange, but he was having none of it. His hand cupped her bottom through her skirt, bunching up the material, exposing her legs to the summer breeze. His knee pushed against hers. She grabbed his biceps, digging in her nails in a message to slow down and back off. His hand rose to smother her breast.

No, no, no. She clamped her lips and legs shut. He groaned, oblivious, consumed by lust, which might have been flattering had she reciprocated. His scent enveloped her. His heat washed over her, making her nauseous. Willing herself not to panic, she tried to turn her head away, but he used his other hand to grip her chin and then pushed her up against the door, his arousal obvious against her stomach.

For a moment fear made her freeze. Her heart hammered, lungs imploded as she struggled to escape. She finally tore her mouth free, blood sharp on her tongue, and shoved against him. "Let go of me, Peter. Now."

He released her immediately and took a step back. A flush rode his cheekbones, confusion and frustration rushing over his features. "We've been dating for months but we don't…that is… we never…" He ran agitated fingers through his springy hair. "We don't make out, let alone have sex. So I thought maybe you were waiting for me to make a move. You know, take charge."

"No." Revulsion curled around her body like a constrictor. "You thought wrong."

"Sorry." He grimaced, then his lips curved into what was supposed to be an endearing smile. "I've messed up, haven't I?"

Shudders ran down her spine. She wrapped her arms around herself and wished she was someone else. Someone stronger. Someone unbroken. "You need to leave."

"Is it because I can't have kids? You said it wasn't a problem but—"

"It's me, OK, Peter?" Her voice was loud. Shrill. "It's *all* me. So just get your perfectly normal butt off my deck and leave me alone."

"You're overreacting." His expression darkened and he moved forward an inch, but she shoved her palms against his chest and forced him back. "I made a mistake, Anna. You have to give me the chance to make it up to you."

She turned her face away. "I want you to leave."

He frowned and she thought she saw anger in his eyes. She braced herself for violence, but all she got was mild censure. "I'll call you tomorrow and we'll talk about it, when you've had a chance to calm down."

Because she was unreasonable…

Rage shot through her, so intense she started to vibrate, but she held the fury inside. She didn't want to antagonize or fight, she wanted him gone. He hopped down the two steps and walked backward, almost tripping over the brickwork. "Just sleep on it."

Sleep on it?

He went through the arched gateway and closed it gently behind him. The arch was covered by a pink climbing rose that flowered all summer long and brought a beauty to her life—a beauty she'd always craved. That rosebush and the white picket fence had made her fall hard for this little house, and she'd bought it on the spot. It was amazing how easily the darkness could force its way back to destroy the peaceful illusion she'd worked so hard to create.

"Good night, Anna. See you tomorrow," he called.

As if she didn't know her own mind.

"*No one will believe you. They hate you so much they'll just laugh. You weren't even any good.*" Memories echoed inside her head.

Peter climbed into his silver Volvo and drove slowly away.

Was she being too harsh? Cruel?

Probably. But she'd rather have a reputation for being a cold-hearted bitch than be with a guy who stuffed his tongue down her throat because he thought she needed him to *take charge.*

With shaking hands, she unlocked her door and stepped inside, then slid the deadbolt home. She slipped out of her pink high-heeled sandals and dropped her keys on the side table. The house was empty. Frigid. Or maybe that was just her.

Unable to settle, she picked up her cell, which she'd left charging, and saw that her father had called. She didn't want to talk to him.

Leftover emotions mixed with scrambled memories from a time in her life she worked hard to forget. Peter had brought it all crashing back like a bucket of water to the face. It wasn't like she'd never had sex. She'd *had* sex. It was just a long, long time ago.

Damn.

She walked into the kitchen and poured herself a large glass of white wine and took a big gulp. Gazing out the window, she watched the shadows of her secluded back garden. Shadows didn't scare her.

She spent a lot of time pretending to be normal. It was how she coped. But that didn't stop memories of a night that should have been one of her happiest of her adolescent life, turning into an awful twisted nightmare. It had been bad enough with her father getting arrested for stealing a million bucks and causing a scandal that had put their family in the news for months. But one night of violence had ripped away her defenses and left her raw and bleeding. A few days later, she'd tried to end all the pain and anguish by going for a midnight swim in a storm-tossed ocean. Luckily, she'd been rescued by a fishing boat. Unluckily, she'd been locked up in a psych ward for a week.

But she hadn't needed a psychological evaluation to cure any suicidal tendencies. That startling revelation had crashed over her head along with the first wave. She'd been in pain but she hadn't wanted to die. There were other ways of running away and, over the years, Anna had perfected them all.

The doorbell rang and she jolted away from her memories. Putting the wine on the counter, she grabbed her phone so she could dial 911 if Peter had come back to claim something he thought he was entitled to. The sight of two uniformed cops on her doorstep made her stop short. In an instant she was catapulted back to that awful day when she'd been seventeen and the police had arrived to arrest her father.

They'd ripped her life apart and she was still trying to put the pieces back together.

She opened the door. "Can I help you, Officers?" Her voice sounded high-pitched and frightened, and she stiffened her spine.

The older guy's mouth tightened, steeling himself for something. "Anna Silver?"

She nodded, standing back to let them inside.

"Daughter of Davis Silver?"

Oh, God. What's he done this time? "Yes."

"I'm afraid we have some bad news."

Her lungs stopped working properly and she had to breathe deep to draw out enough oxygen. The cops looked out of place in her floral living room, with its satin throw cushions and white couches. The older guy cleared his throat and the younger one refused to meet her gaze.

"Chicago Transit Authority contacted us earlier. There's been a terrible accident, ma'am. Your father died."

The world whirled as the floor rushed up to meet her. She grabbed the back of the couch.

"Are you OK, ma'am?" Helping hands maneuvered her onto the sofa.

Was she all right? Of course she wasn't all right. The younger one fetched a glass of water, but she put it straight down on the floor when her hand shook so much it spilled over the lip. Her father couldn't be dead. There had to be some mistake.

"What happened?" she croaked.

"Your father fell under an 'L' train, ma'am."

She flinched. The cops exchanged a harried look.

"Police are investigating claims he was being chased on the platform."

She covered her mouth. This couldn't be happening.

"Was your father in any trouble, Miss Silver?"

Her eyes snapped to his. "Not that I'm aware of."

"Is there anyone you can call to sit with you?" the older guy asked, at the same time edging toward the door.

"I'm fine." She rose shakily to her feet. She just wanted them gone. "You're very kind, but I'm sure you have a lot of important things to do."

"As long as you're sure you'll be all right," the younger one said.

Anna laughed, and it came out as sharp as broken glass. Cops had never been this considerate. Maybe they didn't know who her dad was. "Will someone be in touch about the arrangements…?"

"About his body?" The older one wrote a number on a piece of paper and handed it to her. "Call this number. Someone there will be able to help you with those details. I'm sorry for your loss."

"Thank you for coming in person." She held herself together as she showed the officers out and then closed the door. Her father was dead? She'd talked to him yesterday. He'd called her tonight. He couldn't be dead, the idea didn't seem real.

Her mother…

Oh, heck, she didn't want to be the one to tell her mother.

Her mom had shut down when her father had been arrested nine years ago. Turned in on herself and stopped functioning as a human being, let alone a parent. For a short time Anna had become the adult, and then Ed Plantain arrived on the scene and picked up all the little broken pieces of their lives. Ever since her mom married Ed, she and Anna had been drifting inexorably apart, like big lonely land masses going in opposite directions.

And it was all so damn unfair.

They'd had a good life before her father stole that money. Sure, they'd been poor, but Anna had never really cared. But her dad had constantly promised he'd one day give them the world, shower her mother with diamonds and buy Anna her own computer. Her mom hadn't wanted diamonds, she'd just wanted a car that ran. Money had caused the only real friction they'd had in their house and, in the end, it had blown the family to smithereens.

How would Katherine react after years of hatred? Would she let go of some of the vitriol that poured from her when anyone mentioned his name? Somehow Anna doubted it. She might be the one person in the world who gave a damn that he was gone.

She picked up her phone with fingers as spongy as cotton wool and checked her voice mail. Her heart cinched painfully when she heard his voice. "Anna, I'm in big trouble. But I didn't do anything wrong, I swear it." *Papa?* He sounded panicked. His breathing was rough as if he'd been running. "I'm on my way to the FBI offices, but they're too close. I'm never going to make it. They're gonna kill me. They're going to be looking for their money. I mailed you the printouts, but they don't know where I sent it. *You* know. Take the information to the feds."

She squeezed her eyes shut and held the phone so tight it was a wonder the casing didn't crack. What had he been involved in? Something illegal?

"You need to get out of there until things quiet down." The fine hairs on the nape of her neck stood upright. "Dammit, I've done it again." *Please, no, Papa.* "I love you. And I'm sorry for everything. There's only one person I trust besides you, you know that, right? Go to him, tonight. Tell him I'm cashing in those promises we made one another." He was yelling now, and she pulled the handset away from her ear even as there was a rushing sound—her heart thundered when she realized it must be the train that had killed him—and then nothing. The white noise went on for another twenty seconds before it was cut off. The next message was a hang-up from him. She laughed hysterically, then pressed a hand to her stomach as it knotted tight. Bile started to sting the base of her throat. She bolted to the bathroom and heaved up wine and popcorn and her normal life. After five minutes with nothing left in her stomach, she washed out her mouth and pulled her hair back from her damp forehead.

She stared in the mirror at her red-rimmed eyes and wondered how, after she had constructed her life to minimize trauma, this could be happening all over again. Only worse this time because her father was dead.

And she might be in danger.

Brent Carver lay in bed listening to the surf outside his open window. The rhythmic pounding pulse helped calm the ragged unsettled feeling that clawed inside him. Sometimes it even let him sleep. Not tonight.

He shifted restlessly, sweat damp on his skin. The west coast was getting a blistering-hot summer that had him thanking God he wasn't stuck in that shithole prison, sweating it out with a few hundred of his least best friends. He sat up in bed and swiped irritably at his too long hair.

Gina had liked it long.

Damn.

He'd spent the past year trying not to think about Gina, or her murder, and yet memories snuck past his guard all the time. Her smile, her giving nature, her unwavering dedication to his undeserving ass. When he'd broken things off with her, he'd hoped she'd finally move on. Find herself a man she could marry and have babies she could spoil. But things hadn't worked out that way, and no one regretted it more than he did.

He whipped back the covers and padded naked to the open window that faced the Pacific. It took a moment for his heartbeat to stop hammering. A moment for the burn in his chest to ease. At nearly forty years old, he'd spent half his life in prison and would never get enough of breathing in the fresh clean air of freedom.

The dark water before him stretched like a smooth satin sheet all the way to the horizon. But the calm tranquility was an illusion that disguised deceptive currents and gigantic swells, cold depths and wicked storm surges.

That ocean called to him—it always had. This sliver of coast was what he'd missed locked up in his cell for so many years. Not peace. Not serenity. Not pissing in a private bathroom. Huge rollers crashing home. Elements clashing like titans in his backyard. The abandon. The wildness. The energy. Prison had squeezed the need for that energy into a tiny corner of his mind and tortured him with it in his dreams. When he'd gotten out, he'd spent two days just staring at the ocean. *This* was where he belonged. *This* was where he needed to be. And no one was ever going to take it from him again. Being caged, being imprisoned, had almost wiped him out of existence, and the worst thing was—it was his own damn fault. He'd taken a life and gotten what he deserved.

He'd been out four years now, but the smells, the memories, the sense of watching his back, were ingrained, tattooed on his brain like most cons wore ink. He'd found his salvation in a talent for painting, enough of a talent that he could afford a kick-ass mansion anywhere in the world. But he'd returned here, to the small remote strip of land on the western edge of Vancouver Island. The scene of the crime and the only home he'd ever known.

Maybe he should buy a yacht, learn to sail. But that sort of aimless wandering didn't appeal, and his parole officer probably wouldn't approve either. He rubbed his aching neck muscles and headed downstairs for a drink. He'd finish that last piece for the exhibition.

Exhibition.

He shook his head in disbelief. Some fancy-schmancy museum in New York was giving *him* an exhibition. He opened the fridge and pulled out a beer and popped the top. His agent had worked some serious magic, wrangling that mother. Only trouble was the gallery wanted the elusive and mysterious *B.C. Wilkinson* to turn up in person to the opening. His agent had even taken care of a passport and special visa requirements.

Yeah, right. He snorted. No fucking way. Still, Brent had learned years ago that it was easier to do what he wanted and beg forgiveness later. Not that he dealt much in forgiveness. Gina's image smiled sweetly inside his head, but she was dead—stabbed to death by a homicidal maniac last year—and thinking about her wouldn't bring her back.

His fist tightened around the neck of the bottle and he resisted the urge to hurl it at the wall. Prison had taught him iron control—he just hadn't realized how much he'd need it on the outside. He headed onto his back porch, buck naked and glad of the fresh ocean breeze that cooled his overheated body. His nearest neighbor lived a quarter of a mile away, out of sight, over the bluff.

This region was too remote for passersby, and anyone with a boat would moor it in a sheltered cove, not at the mercy of Barkley Sound's treacherous grasp. The moon was cloaked behind restless clouds that billowed like smoke across the sky. He was just about to sit his ass down when he saw a shadow flitter near the woods.

He had *visitors*?

No fucking way.

In prison he'd received enough death threats to take serious precautions with his safety. When some of the local thugs had been arrested last year, he'd let down his guard and thought the danger was over. He'd obviously thought wrong. What if it was his brother, Finn? Or the cops? He pressed his lips together. Finn knew better than to spook him and the cops had no reason to be sniffing around.

Something was going on.

No one made social calls on Brent Carver—no one without a death wish. He lived on a peninsula that, due to the rugged terrain, was only accessible by boat. There were about thirty locals living on this side of the inlet, but they were more likely to hand-feed rabid wolves than drop in for a beer.

Did his visitor know he was out here?

Leaving the bottle on the deck, he carefully slipped over the side of the porch and melted into the night. It was pitch-black in the woods, but he'd grown up here and knew every tree and hollow. He made his way along the side of the shed and ducked into the forest. Over the last year, he'd gradually stopped listening to the scanner for signs of trouble, stopped keeping firearms in the house. He'd gotten soft, but not stupid. Silently he dropped to his knees beside a massive Sitka spruce that was technically on his neighbor's property. If she found out about his little cache, she'd be pissed. He swept dirt and dead needles off the top of a waterproof box he'd sunk into the ground, and removed his SIG Sauer. He replaced the lid and covered it as best he could in the dark. He got his bearings, and found the tree where he'd hidden his ammo. He grabbed a magazine and headed up to the road, circling around. He inched down an old trail and came up behind where the shadow had been.

Darkness cloaked the clearing where his house sat but his night vision was sharp. And damned if the woman—put a man in prison long enough and he could spot a female blindfolded at twenty paces—wasn't climbing his porch steps shining her flashlight around the place like a laser show. Maybe she was a thief? Maybe someone had figured out Brent Carver was B.C. Wilkinson and sitting on a shedload of very expensive artwork? Then she knocked on his back door.

What the...?

He rubbed his hand over his brow. He was stark naked except for his gun, and now some woman was standing on his deck? He hoped to hell she wasn't a Jehovah's Witness, because she was about to have a *come-to-Jesus* moment.

But she could still be armed and dangerous. He'd pissed off enough bad guys in the joint to be wary of anyone turning up in the middle of the night. Hell, no one visited here, period.

"Hello?" She pressed her ear to his door. "Mr. Carver?" she said louder. Her shoulders sagged when no one answered.

He didn't recognize her voice. He moved fast and silent across the clearing, padded up the stairs just as she reached for the doorknob.

"You're trespassing."

She jolted, her hand going to her heart as she spun to face him. "Oh, my God. You scared me."

Never admit fear.

"I don't like visitors, lady."

Her flashlight dipped and then shot back to his face, almost blinding him. She swallowed, taking in his lack of clothes and keeping her eyes north of the hot spots. "You're naked."

"I was in bed." He didn't know why he needed to explain himself.

Her voice came out like gravel. "I'm looking for Brent Carver."

"I'm looking for peace and quiet. Looks like we're both screwed."

"You're Brent?" Her free hand slipped into her bag, and he grabbed her wrist and pinned her against his door before she could get the drop on him. She went ballistic and tried to whack him with the flashlight. He jerked it out of her fingers and threw it behind them. She felt tiny and delicate, crushed between him and that solid piece of oak, although her lungs were in full working order.

Shit, his ears hurt.

"No one will hear you, so you might as well stow it." She jammed one hand against his chin, squirming like an eel, then went for gold by trying to knee him in the nuts. He deflected the attack and pressed her tighter against the door, wedging her there with his body. She barely came up to his chin but fought like a wild thing. "Want to tell me who you are and why you're knocking on my door in the middle of the night?" He concentrated on making sure he didn't injure her while he tried to check out what she was going for in her purse.

She scratched sharp fingernails down his arm, drew in a breath to scream even louder. Her breasts pushed against his chest, which would have worked for him in a big way if she wasn't so goddamn terrified. Sonofa-*fucking*-bitch.

Why me?

He had nowhere to stick his gun so he removed the pocketbook from her fingers and stepped back, keeping a wary eye on her bloodthirsty knee. She stood there stunned, trembling, and breathing heavily. He didn't think it had anything to do with his dazzling good looks.

"You bastard." Her chin snapped up. "You aren't Brent Carver."

He cocked a brow. "What makes you say that?" He searched her bag, more by touch than sight in the darkness. A cell phone, wallet, keys, tampons, tissues. No gun or shank.

"He's a respectable painter. He's not some nutcase who runs about in the middle of the night, waving around a gun, *among other things*," she muttered darkly. "Attacking innocent, defenseless women."

The scratches on his arm stung enough for him to snort out a laugh at that. Her eyes narrowed. He watched moonlight flow over her features, fine boned and delicate, except for the tight clench of her jaw.

There was no obvious threat in her pocketbook, but it didn't mean he should let his guard down. He needed clothes. For some crazy reason, he was getting a little turned on by Miss Prim and Proper telling him who and what he was. It was probably being naked and within a hundred yards of anything two legged and female, but he didn't want to scare her any more than he had already. He wasn't a hound. Nor was he under any illusion about what she thought might happen when he grabbed her. Someone had jumped him in the shower once and lost their eye for the trouble. Hell, most people thought he was evil incarnate and that was the way he liked it. He reached past her and opened the door. "Inside. Now."

"I'm not going anywhere with you." She tried to dodge aside.

He grabbed her by the shoulders and forced her across his threshold. "You want to meet Brent? I'll take you to him." Her eyes were so huge with fear she looked like she'd been electrocuted. But she'd come to him, she had to play by his rules.

CHAPTER 2

"Get your hands off me!"

An elbow in the gut made Brent let her go. Jeez, she was a touchy little thing. He rubbed his stomach. It wasn't like he was creeping around her place while she was nude, because he was damn sure she'd be crying bloody murder and he'd be waving at everyone from the back of a police cruiser. This was *his* property. It was nighttime. He'd been in bed. Kind of.

"I don't even know what I'm doing here." The tiredness in her voice hit him differently than her anger had.

"That makes two of us." He opened the door to the laundry room just off to one side and snagged a pair of clean jeans from the top of the basket. Resting the gun and her bag on the washing machine, he kept his eye on her as he pulled the jeans on and zipped his manhood back into place. Then he dragged a black T-shirt over his head, grabbed his gun and her pocketbook, and skirted past her into the living room. He didn't turn on the light.

She hovered uncertainly in the hallway near the kitchen before following him through the moonlit house to stand beside the couch opposite.

Hair brushed her shoulders in a dark mess. Eyes, wide and bright as a spaniel's but not as full of terror as before. Hands were tightly clasped, betraying nerves she was trying hard to conceal. She wore a blouse, edged with silver ribbon that glinted in the darkness, and shorts that hit mid thigh and showed off a pair of very fine legs. The sneakers on her feet were the only concession to trekking through the wilderness.

"What do you want with good old Brent?"

"None of your business. Where is he?"

She looked vaguely familiar but he couldn't place her. "I'm his PA. Persuade me you need to talk to him and I'll wake him."

She shifted her feet. "It's personal. I'd rather talk to him."

Stubborn, that was for damn sure. "No one talks to Brent unless they go through me first." Hell, he *should* hire a PA to deal with all the bullshit that came his way, but then he'd be stuck with someone in his house 24-7 and he'd rather not deal with people, period.

He watched the internal struggle play out across her features. Dark eyes narrowing over a cute snub nose, her sweet bow of a mouth thinning, the delicate line of her throat rippling as she swallowed her frustration.

Stymied.

He smiled grimly.

She leaned forward an inch. "I'm…er…in trouble—"

"Pregnant?" No one was pinning a paternity suit on his ass and he'd sure as hell remember doing hers.

"Don't be an idiot," she snapped.

Ouch. He absently rubbed his sternum. She started pacing the hardwood. "Although maybe *I'm* the idiot. I've come all this way on nothing more than one of his stupid whims." She wiped her hands over her eyes. "Brent's probably as trustworthy as my father was—"

"Was?" he interrupted sharply. "What do you mean *was*?" His mouth went dry because he suddenly knew where he'd seen her before. And he knew who her father *was*. He tried to swallow, but the muscles in his throat tightened like a noose.

Her eyes shimmered in the night, so young, so beautiful. Anna Silver. Her father had been his cellmate for five long years and had read her letters out loud to him so often Brent felt like he knew her inside out. But he didn't. She was a stranger.

"He died." Her voice cracked but he made no move to comfort her. A huge cavern of darkness opened up inside him, trying to consume him whole.

"I think he was murdered."

His head jerked up. "What?"

She nodded toward her purse, which he handed back to her. "Last night I received a voice mail from him. That's what I was trying to show you when you slammed me against the door."

"I barely touched you," he snarled.

"You had no clothes on! And have a gun—"

"You're damn lucky I didn't shoot you. Christ knows, I'm starting to regret it myself," he muttered the last. He tried not to think about Davis. It hurt. Like losing Gina all over again. "Ex-cons aren't the sort of people you drop in on, especially at"—he glanced at the clock on the stove—"two a.m. How the *hell* did you get here?" He dragged his hand through his hair. The water taxi closed hours ago.

She looked away from him. "I flew into Vancouver late last night. Contacted a pilot I've used before who flew me into Victoria on his floatplane. I got a few hours' sleep and then drove up here. When I got to Bamfield, I borrowed a rowboat to get across the inlet, and tied it to the public dock. I figured I'd return it before anyone noticed it was gone." She kept rubbing her thumbs over one another, actions that belied her no-nonsense attitude. "Dad wrote to me once describing the house and exactly how to get here."

Brent was intimately acquainted with how much Davis liked to write to his kid. But she was talking about hours of driving on rough logging roads in the Canadian bush at night. Anything could have happened. His stomach churned just thinking about it.

Moonlight flooded the room as clouds shifted across the sky; everything turned bright cold monochrome.

"It wasn't that hard. Now go and wake Brent Carver so I can figure out what to do next." The edge to her voice was back as if she were clinging to her temper by the thinnest of margins.

"I'm Brent."

Something flashed in her eyes. "Oh, please. I'm not stupid."

Brent figured there were all kinds of stupid, and went over to the kitchen drawer where he kept his wallet. He tossed it to her, not wanting to get too close in case he gave in to the desire to throttle her.

"If you're lucky," he sneered, upper lip curling because he'd rather bait her than think about her father, "I'll show you my etchings." She was pissing him off and he wasn't known for his charm or patience.

She took out his driver's license and squinted at him through the darkness. Damned if he was putting on a light so she could examine him more thoroughly. That thought brought a hot wave of sexual awareness bolting though his blood, and sweat broke out across his back. *Great.* Because twenty years of frustration wasn't torture enough.

She pursed her lips and stared him down. Not bad for a rookie.

Then it hit him. Davis was dead. His best friend was gone. His throat stretched taut as emotion crushed him. He strode to the window to stare at the sea that glistened with silver ribbons, anything to avoid dealing with the tsunami of grief that wanted to demolish him.

Davis had barely survived his first week in prison. Despite Brent being more than a decade younger than Anna's father, he'd already been in jail for fourteen years when Davis had arrived, which made him vastly more experienced when it came to staying alive. He'd taken pity on the older guy, stood up for him, and taught him how to survive in a place where weakness meant years of humiliation or death. In return he'd found a friend in a place where they didn't usually exist.

The sound of Anna's breathing was louder than the surf. She was fighting for control, trying to manage what would likely be one of the worst days of her life, and he was being an insensitive prick.

"Why do you think he was murdered?" he asked gruffly.

He heard a rustle as she dug for her cell. The electronic ding as she turned it on.

"*Anna, I'm in big trouble.*" Davis's voice punched him with memories. Five years in an eight-by-ten cell surrounded by Brent's canvases and the smell of paint as they dissected each other's lives from top to bottom, and watched each other's backs. "*But I didn't do anything wrong, I swear it. I'm on my way to the FBI offices, but they're too close. I'm never going to make it! They're gonna kill me. They're gonna be looking for their money. I mailed you the printouts but they don't know where I sent it.* You *know. Take the information to the feds.*"

What the hell had Davis gotten mixed up with?

"*You need to get out of there until things quiet down. Dammit. I've done it again.*" He sounded like he was crying now and it was noisy as fuck in the background. Brent's fists clenched. "*I love you and I'm sorry for everything. There's only one person I trust besides you, you know that, right? Go to him, tonight. Tell him I'm cashing in those promises we made one another.*"

Shit—anyone else he'd have told to go to hell, but *Davis*? He cleared his throat. "Any idea what he was talking about?"

Huge shadowed eyes met his and she shook her head.

"And he's definitely dead?" The words sounded callous and harsh, spat out into the quiet room.

She swallowed twice before she answered. "Cops said he fell under a train at a subway station. Someone said they thought he was being chased." A glistening streak bisected one cheek, but he'd never have known she was crying from her rock-steady voice.

He went over and grabbed his cell. "Play it again."

Her lips tightened but she did as he asked. He recorded the message, then took the cell out of her hand and pulled out the SIM card. He strode over to the kitchen sink and ran the card through the garbage disposal.

She made a sound like a strangled warthog. "What the hell?"

"Until we figure this out, it's better if the bad guys can't track you. I'll buy you a new phone. Does anyone else know you're here?"

She shook her head and wrapped her arms tight around her waist.

"Did you use your credit or debit cards anywhere?"

"Only to book my flight to Vancouver. After that I paid cash."

"And you didn't tell anyone where you were going? You're sure of it?"

"No one in the world knows I'm here."

Brent blinked as she bolted for the door. *What the…?* He went after her. Slapped his hand on the solid wood when she tried to wrench it open.

"Leave me alone!" She frantically tugged on the doorknob.

"Jesus, lady, calm down." Hysterical females were not his thing. She was stronger than she looked and he had to put some effort into keeping the door shut. But her eyes held raw panic that told him she was genuinely terrified he might hurt her. And she should be—she should be scared of a man with his reputation. She yanked so hard on the door handle he budged an inch. Not bad, considering he weighed at least a hundred pounds more than she did and was probably a good foot taller. He wanted to ease away but knew if he did, she'd run into the wilderness at night where anything could happen to her, and this wasn't just some anonymous stranger—this was Davis's daughter. He was stuck and he was pissed. He didn't placate, he didn't soothe. But he did keep his word.

"I can't believe I listened to anything Dad said—"

"Why wouldn't you listen to him?"

Eyes flashed. "My father was a liar and a thief who never gave a damn about how his actions affected others."

"Are you fucking nuts? The guy was set up."

"Oh, please." She stopped tugging long enough to argue with him. That figured. "He stole a million dollars and got caught and never had the guts to own up to it."

"You're wrong." Anger had him gritting his teeth. He gripped her shoulder, applying enough pressure to make her stop fighting with the damn doorknob. She quivered under his fingertips. Davis had asked him to keep her safe. He wouldn't let the man down. "You're the only thing he ever truly cared about."

"Well, he had a funny way of showing it."

The scent of her engulfed him and those huge frantic eyes made him want to tell her everything was going to be all right. But her dad was dead and he knew from experience it would never be all right again.

The two of them stood close in the darkness. Too close. The hollows of her collarbone and graceful line of her neck called to something primitive inside him, and he had to force himself not to react. She'd grown from the pretty teen he'd seen in photographs into a pretty woman—maybe even beautiful. But her oval face was punctuated by that stubborn jaw that would have told him she'd be trouble even if she hadn't landed in his lap in the middle of the night. Harsh gasps made her breasts stretch the thin fabric of her shirt, but as her expression once again morphed into fear, he worked very hard not to notice.

Fear wasn't the same as weakness. Everyone in jail was intimately acquainted with the difference.

"Look." He held his hands aloft and stepped back. "You can leave any time you want. I don't want you here any more than you want to be here, *but...*" Her bottom lip stuck out just enough to set off a chain reaction in his body that ended at his dick. *Off-limits, partner.* "Your dad was the only friend I had in prison and more like a father than my own."

Maybe now wasn't the time to bring up his biological father. There were bad people in the world, and closing your eyes and pretending they didn't exist was for fools and children. Judging from Anna Silver's expression, she already knew that. Unfortunately she was more scared of him than the guys who'd gotten her dad killed. He had to change that if he was going to help her.

"I'm not going to hurt you. You've been traveling for hours. You're tired." Christ, he wasn't good at this shit. He went and grabbed his handgun and pressed it into her palms. She flinched. "It's loaded. Do *not* shoot me. This should make you feel safe enough to rest until we figure out what the hell he was into."

Her mouth dropped open and he tipped up her chin to close it. There was a weird kick in his gut from the physical connection. When was the last time he'd touched another human being that didn't involve handcuffs?

Forget it. Not important.

"There're spare bedrooms upstairs, take the first on the right. Stick a dresser in front of the door if you need to, get some sleep. But do me a favor—do not call anyone. Don't e-mail anyone. Definitely don't use your credit card in town. We'll figure out this mess in the morning."

"How do I know I can trust you?" She took a step back and weighed the gun with both hands. It was his turn to sweat.

"Hell, I didn't say you should trust me. But I'm wealthy enough that I don't need to sell you out to the bad guys." He grimaced. "A bonus in my circles, believe me."

He turned away from the overemotional female who'd invaded his space. She looked deceptively slight, but was as thorny as a blackberry briar. He didn't want her here. No one stayed in his house. Except Davis, who'd come to visit most summers and had been one of the few people Brent could tolerate for more than thirty seconds at a time. Not even Gina had stayed more than a few hours before he'd sent her away. *Christ.* He closed his eyes, wishing he could turn back the clock and change things, knowing it was futile.

Since Gina's murder he'd lost his faith in knowing who he was. He just knew he wasn't the heartless bastard he tried so hard to portray. He couldn't chase this woman off until he'd figured out whether or not she was in real danger. But she sure as hell couldn't stay here without him going bat-shit crazy.

Davis had sounded genuinely terrified in that message and now he was dead. If it were a coincidence, the timing *sucked.*

He opened the door.

"Where're you going?" she asked, suspicion loaded into every syllable.

"To make sure the rowboat you borrowed gets back safely to the right dock and no one suspects you're here. You have a rental car?"

She shook her head. "I stayed at my mom's house in Victoria and borrowed her VW to drive up here. I left it outside the bar. My bag's in the trunk."

His brows rose in question.

"I didn't talk to her. Mom," she clarified. "She and my stepfather are on a cruise to Alaska. I left a message on her voice mail to tell her about Dad."

Now that was cold.

She grimaced. "Told her I'd make the arrangements and come home soon for a visit. She won't miss her car for at least a week."

He held out his hand for the keys.

She went back to her bag, dug them out, and dropped them into his palm. "Don't ditch it in the sea."

He laughed, which felt strange. "I have a garage on the other side of the inlet. I'll squeeze your car next to my truck." Staring at her in the darkness was like remembering a dream. "I'm sorry about your daddy, Anna," he said softly. "He was a good man."

She caught his hand and he jolted, the coldness of her skin at odds with the heat of the connection.

"Not many people thought so." She squeezed, then let go. Then her face started to crumple—from exhaustion or tears he didn't know, and he wasn't about to stick around to find out.

He went out the back door and headed down to his motorboat. The moon hung high above the water of his little bay, constant, and yet never the same. A big old spotlight for trouble.

Well, trouble had come to this cove many times before and he was still standing. But life was a damn sight easier to deal with when you only had yourself to worry about. He looked back at his house, and saw a light go on upstairs as he started the motor on his boat.

Anna Silver.

A complication he didn't need.

The sooner he got rid of her, the better.

More than twenty-four hours and the woman was still in the wind. Rand had driven to Minneapolis to search her place. Photos showed a dark-haired, pretty little thing. Pity she hadn't stuck around. She could have entertained him while they waited for the mailman. Now he was back in Chicago with the rest of the team, hunkered down in the boss's office for a crisis meeting. Rand didn't remember a time that a crisis hadn't involved automatic gunfire and fucked-up intel.

"Did you track her phone yet?" Hank Browning was the top guy—on paper at least. The gray-haired, stocky individual was the figurehead of the charity, a former general, ex–Special Forces soldier who'd paid his dues in the jungles of Colombia. His reputation was akin to that of the drug lords he'd targeted and he'd earned every bit of it. Bobby Petrie sat at a desk with four monitors all flashing information at him. Pretty boy Petrie was their IT guy, a whiz at hacking communication systems and moving money, but an irritating little shit when things didn't go his way. Kudrow managed operations, domestic and international, from home base here in Chicago. Rand was the leader on the ground—Vic and Marco, his foot soldiers.

They were a tight group—considering their occupation, they had to be. And, with the exception of Petrie, they'd worked together for nearly two decades, serving in three wars and countless conflicts in the venerable US Army. These men were as close to family as Rand was ever going to get.

"I'm trying to locate it," Petrie repeated between gritted teeth. "If these guys gave me some space, I might have more success. You try cracking this shit with some asshole breathing down your neck."

Kudrow hauled their resident geek to his feet by a fistful of shirt and hoisted him until they were nose-to-nose. "We're not the ones who lost the money, *asshole*." He flung him away like a rag doll.

"And I'm not the one who lost Davis Silver." From where he was sprawled on the floor, Petrie shot Rand and Marco a sneer.

Kudrow swung his rage in Rand's direction, but Rand didn't let his expression change. It was a game of chicken, and if he blinked, he lost. He never lost.

After a long moment, Kudrow pressed his lips together and visibly checked his anger.

"Think Davis planned this?" Rand asked.

Kudrow shook his head. "We had someone go through his personal effects at the morgue. No envelope. Just a photo of his daughter and directions to the nearest FBI field office. We're fucking lucky he didn't get there."

Petrie turned back to his screens. The General pinched the bridge of his nose, then said, "His phone message said he mailed those account details to his daughter."

The old man was starting to panic. He'd lost his edge, which was a damn shame for someone who'd been such an inspirational soldier. When the General had retired from the army six years ago, he'd been asked to do a little side work by some friends on

Capitol Hill and, using the charity as a smoke screen, they'd all done very well for themselves. Or had. Until Davis had ripped them off.

Rand hated anyone getting the better of him.

"We'll keep checking the mail at her place and his place. As soon as that envelope arrives, we grab it. Done deal." Kudrow tried to reassure them all.

"I just want to retire with my wife to fucking Florida. Is that too much to ask?" The General paced behind his desk. "If the cops believe this guy's story and start an investigation, this whole organization falls apart."

"Not if we don't report the theft," Rand spoke up. He widened his stance, folded his arms over his chest. "With no crime to investigate, the cops will lose interest. All the legitimate donations to the charity are intact." Petrie had covered the trail of the laundered money, which was what he'd been doing when Davis Silver had spotted his access codes being used. They should have made sure he'd gone home like all the other drones. They'd gotten sloppy and now they were paying the price.

And they were all FUBAR unless they recovered that money.

"What if he didn't mail it to her house? Where the hell *is* she? If she gets the info and takes it to the feds, we're all screwed." The General smacked the table.

"Any idea who the guy Davis trusted is?" asked Rand. There was nothing in her house to suggest a name. He'd done a quick search and snagged her hard drive, but needed to go back and dig deeper if they didn't find her in the next twenty-four hours.

"No idea." Kudrow shook his head. A tic played with the man's right eye as he shoved his fingers deep into his receding hair. They'd been friends once, but too much death and disappointment had honed their relationship into something tougher, more durable. "I can't believe this. Fucking cheese eater."

Davis should have just kept his mouth shut. Shoulda, coulda, woulda.

"What else do we know about Davis Silver? Does he own property anywhere?"

Kudrow snapped open a file. "He spent five years in prison in Canada for stealing a million bucks from the city—swore he didn't do it. Wife divorced him and remarried before he was even convicted." Kudrow snorted—he had three ex-wives. "He has one kid—a fucking elementary school teacher—who has so far outwitted a team of former elite soldiers."

"Maybe she isn't what she seems," said Petrie.

"Yeah, maybe she's a covert Russian agent with government training." Kudrow's expression of disgust made Rand's spine tingle. The guy was close to snapping and he needed to be ready for whatever the hell happened next. "Of course she's what she seems! She has twenty-seven grade-three pupils starting September fifth. I have a list of their names. She drives a VW Beetle and shops in fucking Ikea. She's a schoolteacher who's made us look like a bunch of assholes."

"We know she flew into Vancouver." Petrie tried to calm his boss down. "Then she dropped off the radar."

"Cool it. She's just a schoolteacher," Rand reminded them quietly. "We'll get our money back." They'd taken out warlords and heavily guarded government ministers, but his colleagues were suddenly pissing their pants like raw recruits over one untrained female? Women were good for one thing and that didn't include getting in his way. "How'd Davis get this job anyway?" Rand asked.

"I hired him." The General's thick eyebrows bunched. "Prison warden heard about the fact we hired ex-cons, Davis Silver had dual nationality, and he wanted to help him out. Gave him a personal recommendation and I thought he might prove useful." And he had—all the way up to stealing their money and falling under that train.

Kudrow's brows wedged into a deep furrow. "We need to run deeper background checks on both of them if we're going to find the girl."

The General surveyed his troops and Rand automatically stood to attention. He hit each of them in the eye with a bullet-hard gaze. "I know we all have a little cash stashed away, but not enough to disappear from Uncle. There is no backup plan. There is no extraction strategy for this situation. That sixty million is *ours* and we earned every goddamned penny." He adjusted his shirt cuffs. The man always looked more comfortable in camo gear than a suit. "And just in case any of you get cold feet, know this..." Rand stilled. "*If* you run, *if* you talk to the feds, or betray this organization, I will hunt you down, I will find you, and I will kill you. Clear?"

Silence bounced around the room.

No one discounted the man just because he was a good twenty-five years older than the rest of them. But it didn't mean Rand would make it easy for him if it came to that. A small smile curled the edge of his lips as he acknowledged the challenge.

"As a fucking bell, General," said Rand. "Don't worry about a thing. I'll hunt down the woman." The thought heated his blood. Not that she had a chance against a man like him, but at least she wasn't completely dumb. She had a good head start. It always made things interesting.

"Goddamn elementary school teacher." Kudrow shook his head again. "Take Marco with you."

"Enjoy Canada." Petrie smirked.

"Dump your personal phones and vehicles—I don't want any electronic trace of you anywhere outside this office." Kudrow's jaw was clenched so tight it looked like it might crack.

Rand caught an untraceable burner phone Petrie tossed him. Kudrow handed them ready-made false identities they used on jobs, a wad of cash, and a credit card associated with—he looked at the papers—Benny Tacon. *Shit.* Who the hell thought up that alias?

Rand headed out the door with Marco on his heels. Hunting was what he did best, not sitting around watching Petrie type and moan like a girl. He didn't like people fucking with him, and he was in the mood for a little fun, a little payback. Anna Silver was just the girl to provide it.

"So the dead guy called nine-one-one before he fell under a train?" Jack Panetti asked his contact at the Chicago PD on the phone. *And you guys didn't think this might indicate foul play?* Jack had been a detective before he'd become a PI and sometimes wished he was back on the force. That was always before he climbed into his Mercedes convertible or took off on a week's vacation just for the hell of it. He had offices in Los Angeles, New York City, and Denver—where he was based because he liked the mountains—eight assistants, and a country full of people doing stupid-ass things.

Life was good.

"Security chased him because the guy was caught with his hand in the till. He called nine-one-one and made out like he was some sort of whistle-blower," the sergeant out of the 1st District told him. "But he was just an ex-con who couldn't do an honest day's work. They grabbed him, but the asswipe ran right into the path of that train. It's all on video."

Jack had seen the video. No doubt Davis Silver had been terrified of the people chasing him. The question was why. And why had those so-called "security guards" disappeared?

"I bet whoever gave him a job is going to regret it," Jack said as he sat in a supermarket parking lot across from Davis Silver's apartment, watching puffy white clouds float across a blue sky. He'd gotten a phone call in the middle of the night and headed out straightaway. Some clients demanded personal attention. Brent Carver was one of them. Usually Jack steered clear of ex-cons, but for some reason he couldn't put his finger on, he didn't mind dealing with Carver. Maybe it was just his money? Jack grimaced and hoped he hadn't sold out to the dark side.

"Giving an accounting job to a guy who'd already swiped a million? Yeah. But no one got fired this time, because the bright spark who hired him just happened to be the boss of the whole deal, claiming they specialized in giving ex-cons a second chance." The cop laughed. "If it had been some dumb-ass in HR, they'd be out on their ear."

Jack heard the derision in the guy's voice. "Did they say how much he took?"

"Nah. Said it was negligible and they wouldn't report it, given the guy ended up as a smear on the metro."

"Did they find anything unusual on the body?"

There was a weighty silence. "Who'd you say your client was, Panetti?"

"You know I don't reveal names." Jack prided himself on never giving up a source and always giving clients their money's worth. "I do, however, happen to have tickets to the Bears season opener. And, if you get me names and addresses for those security people, I'll see what I can do about Super Bowl tickets." Carver could afford it.

There was a grunt, but Jack knew he had the guy. "I'll see what I can do. But you didn't hear it from me." The cop hung up and Jack leaned back in the seat of his rented Buick. He looked up at the building where Davis Silver had lived. An unremarkable, squat, square redbrick apartment complex. Jack had grown up in something similar.

He was about to get out of the car when he noticed another car parked on a side street with someone inside watching the building. Not wanting to raise any flags, he headed into the store and bought himself something for lunch. He went back to the car with his plastic bag in hand and pulled the tab on a can of soda, getting the license plate as he chugged the cola. He climbed in his car, and paused for a moment after starting the engine. The other guy got out of the car and walked swiftly to the front entrance of Davis's building. He held keys, but caught the door just as the mailman left the building.

Jack surreptitiously took a picture, then reversed out of his spot and drove around and past the entrance as the guy came out again, heading back to his car. Jack went around the block again, but when he glanced at where the other car had been it was gone.

He parked and went and looked at the buzzer buttons. V. BERNSTEIN. He leaned on it.

"Who is this?"

"Mrs. Bernstein? I was a friend of Davis's and I'm hoping to talk to you for a moment?" Hopefully this was Viola, the name he'd gotten from Brent of the woman who had collected Davis's mail whenever he was away.

The door buzzer rang and he figured he'd give her a lecture on building security that she could pass on to the super—just as soon as he was done. No point in shooting himself in the foot.

CHAPTER 3

Anna slitted open one eyelid and saw a lethal-looking handgun on her nightstand. How on earth had her life come to this? Sunlight poured through the windows, burning red when she closed her eyes. Her mouth was parched, and she forced herself to sit up, to look around.

The room was Spartan but elegant. Solid, hand-carved wooden furniture, eggplant-colored bedcovers, and a lone picture of the ocean on the wall.

The sound of that same ocean drew her to the window and she looked out on a sea that glittered with blue fire all the way to the horizon. Tall snowcapped peaks dominated the hinterland to the north, with rocky outcrops covered in straggly trees surrounding this secluded little cove. She pulled on some clothes, shoved the empty dresser out of the way, and made her way down to the beach.

No sign of Brent Carver anywhere. Thank goodness.

He was a lot bigger, brasher, and younger than she'd expected. Her father certainly hadn't mentioned washboard abs or that intense probing gaze, but then again he wasn't likely to, was he?

For just a moment last night, there had been a dark, hungry look in his eyes that had damn near scared her to death. That's why she'd panicked and almost run. But he'd been right, she'd needed rest, and he hadn't hurt her.

Yet.

She shouldn't have come. Grief and uncertainty had driven her onward, without any real plan and with nowhere else to turn. But with the clarity of a good night's sleep, she realized she should have gone straight to the cops even though they'd never believed a word she'd said in the past.

Instead she'd run.

Now she stood at the end of the world—a place so isolated and remote, it had taken a full day to get here. There were more accessible desert islands. She was exhausted after her trip. Mentally wiped. And grief welled up like fresh blood in a deep cut. She needed to figure out what was going on so she could take back control of her life. She breathed in the scent of the ocean and tried to find her equilibrium, but it just brought back even more memories that she'd rather forget. At least she had time to regroup while she figured out if her father had been paranoid, delusional, or just plain crooked.

The faint tinge of iodine mixed with salt on the breeze. After a moment she slipped out of her sandals and hiked her skirt up to her knees, wading into the water. It kissed her skin with a bright, cold lash, jump-starting all the nerves that had still been asleep.

She hadn't been back in the water since the day she'd almost drowned. She'd been a good swimmer once, but that whole time in her life—the rape, the impulsive suicide attempt—had stripped her emotionally to the bone, and she'd avoided all reminders. Today, for the first time in years, she wanted to dive into these cold waters and wash away her worries. Unfortunately, she knew from bitter experience it didn't work.

She waded back out of the surf and turned to look at the log cabin. It was more of a mansion than a cabin, gleaming like burnt honey, situated high enough to avoid the worst storm surges—maybe even a tsunami. Brent Carver had obviously done very well for himself with his paintings. She'd known he was private, almost reclusive, and hid his identity from the world. Her father had talked about him often—full of glowing admiration, but with no real details about his appearance, she realized. Her imagination had conjured a man she was comfortable with, an older gent, someone who was almost frail. This guy was nothing like she'd imagined. He wasn't kind or old or frail. He wasn't safe.

A bald eagle swooped through the air and landed in a tree high above her head. He stared at her with a beady eye that suggested she didn't belong here.

"Tell me something I don't know."

"Talking to yourself?"

She jumped. Brent Carver moved as swift and silent as a cougar out of the shadow of the trees. She stared into his bright blue eyes, more than a little disconcerted to realize just how handsome he was in daylight. Tall and rangy, he had rugged features and a bold straight nose. Lines of experience etched his face, but a dimple cut in and out of his cheek and, combined with the vivid sparkle in those eyes, it was hard not to stare. Plus, he was shirtless and the torso she'd worked so hard not to ogle in the moonlight was once again on full display with wide hard pecs and those smooth blocks of muscle pulling taut across his abdomen. She hadn't known that sort of muscle tone existed outside men's underwear commercials.

Her eyes shot back to his face. Wet, sunbaked blond hair, unshaven scruff darkening his jaw, and a full bottom lip that would have most normal women drooling. She wasn't normal, but her pulse took a leap anyway.

"Anna." He cocked a wary brow.

Water glistened like diamonds all over his chest. Wet board shorts clung to him like a second skin. He'd obviously been swimming. She whipped her eyes back up again as her cheeks heated. Not her type. Definitely not her type—but he had her mouth watering with basic female appreciation because, while she might be screwed up, she wasn't dead.

Brent Carver was *not* someone she was comfortable with. Sexy as hell. Oozing testosterone. Definitely not her type. She voted team beta in every way. "I always pictured you as the same age as my father."

He lifted the other brow.

"Dad talked about you in his letters." They'd written to each other every week after he'd gone to prison. Being arrested had forced him to grow up. It had been painful to see him lose his childlike spirit even though it had been his own stupid fault.

Guilt rose up. Guilt and grief, and terrible swirling regret. She closed her eyes and tried to remember good times. Cleared her throat. "He told me how talented you were. Said you were going to be famous one day."

"Famous? I never wanted to be famous." His mouth thinned into a stern line.

"You seem to enjoy the trappings." She swept her hand at the private beach and massive house.

"I've always lived here." Words were drawn out reluctantly, like he'd forgotten the art of conversation. "I just wanted a house that would withstand the squalls."

"This is where you grew up?"

"Yup."

Anna stared around. It was beautiful, but..."Don't you ever get lonely?"

"Hell, no."

"You don't find it a little isolated?"

Thick brows crunched over his eyes. "Not isolated enough, apparently."

Ouch. She turned away and cinched her arms over her chest. "I apologize that I dumped this on you."

He moved closer. Only a step, but it made her senses spring to life and the muscles of her feet flex as if preparing for flight.

"Your father was right to tell you to come to me. I'm just not real good with people."

"No kidding." Her voice shook. Brent Carver's rugged maleness was something she didn't trust. That was why she dated guys like Peter. Too bad she couldn't trust them either. "I probably overreacted, coming here." She eased away from him. She felt stupid and irrational, and she was never irrational. She was calm and levelheaded and always in control.

"Losing your dad is a good reason to overreact." Sympathy softened his voice and it stroked over her skin like a caress. "For what it's worth, I think you did the smart thing to disappear when you did."

Something in his voice made her tilt her face toward him. "Why?"

He bent down and picked up a white shell. Polished the smooth surface with his thumb. Eventually he met her gaze.

"I spoke to a law enforcement friend of mine last night."

"You have law enforcement friends?"

"Wild, huh?" The wind blew his hair in his eyes. Sand dusted his bare feet. He looked like everyone's fantasy castaway. He bent over and picked up his smartphone, which nestled on top of a towel, behind a log. "You ever seen this guy before?" He held out the phone with a picture of a lean, fit-looking man with short, black hair on the screen. He wore a gray suit. There was a time stamp on the bottom that was about five seconds before her father's message had been sent.

"No. Who is he?" Her fingers shook as she handed him back the phone.

He draped the towel across his shoulders. "One of the guys who chased Davis into that subway station. The other one wore a ball cap and glasses, not so easily identifiable. This asshole actually grabbed hold of your dad."

"There was a hang-up after that message he left me." Her stomach dipped.

"They must have taken his phone. They know he called you." He cleared his throat but his voice remained gruff. "Just after that photo was taken, your dad broke away and fell under a train that was pulling into the station."

Blood drained from her head and she swayed. Brent caught her elbow, holding her firmly on her feet. He let go of her arm as soon as she was steady.

"He wouldn't have suffered. He died instantly," he told her.

Bitterness welled in her throat. "Is that supposed to make me feel better?"

"You bet your ass it is."

Her hand went to her mouth to hold back sobs as grief rammed her. Her father was dead, and no matter how much he'd hurt or frustrated her in the past, she'd always loved him. Hot tears blurred her vision.

Great.

She spun away, drawing in huge gasps of air, fighting the onslaught of emotion. Why now? Why not yesterday when she'd been alone for hours? Why not in bed? Why here in the presence of a stranger who'd been closer to her father than she'd been?

Brent didn't reach for her. He just stood there, watching her fall apart. Intimidating, scary, and grim, but perceptive enough to know she didn't want to be touched, especially not by a man just as dark and tortured as her father had been. Score one for Brent Carver.

She wiped her cheeks. Stared at the waves that crept up the rim of the beach. Felt as hollowed out as the shell he'd held in his hands. "I need to bury him."

"The cops are investigating his death. The coroner's gonna want to keep the body for a while."

She felt sick. Cold eased into her bones and she shivered despite the heat of the sun. Her relationship with her father had always torn her to shreds, the shackles of love and distrust pulling equally hard in opposite directions. During high school, writing to her dad had become a way of dealing with her life, an escapist fantasy where she got to be in control. By the time she left home to go to college, her letters had become a habit and almost a diary that helped her cope—a way of communicating with a man she loved but would never trust again. In the end, her letters had been less about her father and more about herself, and that too felt like a betrayal.

Their letters had created the illusion of closeness. She'd known it was an illusion because when her father was released from prison he'd felt like a stranger. And even though she wanted to rebuild those bonds, she could never bring herself to really trust him. That realization had created a distance between them that her father had been unable to breach, no matter how hard he tried.

Now he was dead, and with that bleak reality came a sudden need to honor him. "I have to give the police that voice mail message."

"No," said Brent.

"I have to."

"*Fuck*. No, that's the last thing you should do." Brent propped both hands on his head as if to contain his frustration. "Davis wasn't the sort of guy to scare you for no reason. He loved you. You were the only thing that mattered to him in the whole damn world."

"Then why couldn't he keep his hands off other people's money?" It was impossible to keep the bitterness out of her voice.

He opened his mouth to speak. Cut himself off. Scowled. "Listen, Anna, the cops don't care about *why* things happen, they only care about the goddamned law. Your daddy talked about moving money—we don't even know whose money. What are the chances they're gonna believe Davis did it for the greater good unless we have proof?"

Nausea swirled in her stomach. She knew what it was like when the authorities suspected you of involvement in a crime. That was another reason why her mother could never forgive her dad, because she'd been humiliated by the cops and the press.

Being treated that way by people who were supposed to protect you shattered your belief in the justice system. "I don't want to go through another scandal."

"Whoever he took the money from is going to want it back. From the look of that guy in the subway, they're not going to ask nicely." The wind tossed his hair in his eyes again and he shoved it impatiently away from his face. "All we need to do is find the letter he sent you and deliver it to the cops. Going to them before we have that evidence is only going to make your daddy look guilty and possibly put you in danger."

She stared at him, feeling like she was about to come apart at the seams. But she wasn't the only one suffering. Fine lines of fatigue etched Brent's eyes; a touch of crimson stained the whites. He hadn't slept much last night.

"Any idea where he might have mailed this thing?" he asked, quieter now.

Her brain turned slowly. "My house, my school?"

"We need to check them out, but we have to assume the bad guys will be doing the same."

"How would they know what he said to me on my voice mail?" she asked, confused.

Brent picked up another shell and tossed it into the sea. "Bribery, hacking. There are ways of getting into your voice mail messages."

And criminals always seemed to know about them. Her teeth started to rattle. "This can't be happening." She was a teacher. The daughter of an ex-con.

"It's OK." He took a step forward but didn't touch her. His expression was flat, but there was a fervency in his eyes that made them glow. "As long as no one knows you're here, you're safe."

For some reason his reassurance helped. Her brain slowly engaged the problem. "There was a lady in his building—Viola—who picked up his mail when he wasn't there. Maybe he mailed it to himself?"

"Already on it." He nodded. "But he said *you'd* know where he sent it."

The pressure felt like it was going to explode her skull. She pressed her hands to the side of her head. "Maybe my mom's house? Or my grandmother's old house, but I rent that out to students." Her grandmother had died six months ago and left her the property at her father's insistence. Anna had flown back for the funeral. It was the last time she'd seen her father alive.

She'd been a lousy daughter.

She clenched her jaw and narrowed her gaze. "I didn't see anything at Mom's when I was there yesterday, but it wouldn't have arrived yet. They're the only places I can think of, right now."

"Make a list. We'll figure out a way of checking them, safely, from a distance."

"I could call the school."

"No phone calls." Brent shook his head. "I don't want anyone tracing you to Bamfield. And the only way to know for sure is to ask them, face-to-face. I have a PI I've used before. I called him last night and asked him to see if anything turns up at Davis's apartment, and see if he can dig up anything on the company your daddy worked for."

The energy drained out of her and she shook her head. "I can't just sit around for the rest of my life, just waiting…"

He grunted. "You still a teacher?"

"Why?" It was disconcerting he knew that much about her. She knew very little about him, except he was an artist and he'd been in prison. Although, maybe that was enough.

"Kids broken up for the summer?"

She nodded.

"So you've got time to figure this out." His eyes held patience and an unexpected kindness. There was another long pause. "It might be safer if you never went back."

"What do you mean?" Shock froze her in place.

"Life changes." He shrugged. "You can disappear. I'll set you up with a new name, new job. You don't *have* to go back. It's an option you need to consider."

But she had responsibilities. A house and career she loved. "If I run away, the people responsible for my dad's death will never be punished."

Brent's expression was guarded.

"What if it were your father?" asked Anna.

Something indecipherable shifted in the depths of his eyes. "Then I'd want the bastards to pay."

"OK, then." She started up the beach.

"Where do you think you're going?"

"Back. To Chicago and Minneapolis."

"No!" A frustrated groan came out of his mouth. "Jesus H. You're not listening to me." He grabbed her arm. "You can't go home yet."

"What do you mean, *can't*?" She tried to jerk out of his hold, but he was strong as hell.

"Because it's stupid to rush headlong back into danger without—"

"Don't call me stupid." She twisted until she was free.

"Then don't act like a damn fool." His voice bounced around the cove. The eagle took off with a giant flap of disgust.

She stabbed her fingernail in his breastbone and jabbed him with each word. "Do. Not. Yell. At. Me."

He winced and carefully removed her nail from his chest. He towered over her and his face hardened into a mask of bitter fury. He should have terrified her.

Why didn't he terrify her?

"Sorry." Even with the drawn-back upper lip he looked shocked by his own words. "But you can't just waltz home as Anna Silver without putting yourself in danger. You have to assume they're watching the airports and borders."

She shook her head. "This isn't Watergate. Who the hell do you think we're dealing with?" She started to brush past him. This was insane. He was insane.

"My PI checked into the company your dad worked for—the Holladay Foundation. They raise money for injured vets."

Please don't be stealing from wounded soldiers, Papa.

"The head honcho is a senior military guy, and former advisor to the White House. If he's involved in something dodgy, he has a hell of a lot to lose."

And a lot of connections.

She stopped moving. *Dammit.* Her teeth chattered. She was so out of her league it was ridiculous. "What do you think I should do?" She didn't like asking for advice. Especially from an ex-con. Her father's buddy. She didn't like relying on him for anything, but she didn't have the first clue how to deal with something like this.

"Look, let my PI guy ask around for a few days. In the meantime we can sort you out some false ID, which should slow down the bad guys when you go back to the States. Your daddy said you could trust me, remember?" He smiled, and it looked like a deliberate attempt to put her at ease. The tired lines disappeared. Dimples cut into his cheeks, making him appear years younger. It was like being smacked in the face with sunshine and rampant sex appeal. His gaze drifted absently down her body and an unwanted answering heat fired in her veins.

And just like that, she was caught in the web of another silver-tongued snake-oil salesman, the same way her father had charmed her mother after yet another row about money. And with that body and those dimples, Brent Carver would be devastating to any woman foolish enough to fall for him. But despite her body's instinctive reaction to that rugged masculinity, she was immune. She nodded curtly and walked away, leaving him on his incredibly beautiful, isolated beach. Alone.

Brent fired up the boat's engine and motored around to the mouth of the inlet, past the lodge that sat high on the ridge, and dropped his speed below seven knots to reduce wake. He maneuvered around a couple of kayaks and a hapless rower who was heading to the store, and angled toward the marine station dock on the east side of the inlet. He tied up in an empty slot and gave a nod to the new dive master who'd taken his brother's place last summer when the latter had fallen in love and gotten shot.

Brent didn't know which was worse.

He ambled up the steep gravel path, passing students who carried heavy-looking buckets, and headed into the marine station. He nodded to the secretary, who eyed him like trouble but didn't call the cops. Things must be looking up.

"Is he in?"

She nodded, and the authoritative tilt of her head had him moving past her with a small salute. He knocked, eased inside, closed the door after himself, and leaned against it. Thomas Edgefield, director of the Bamfield Marine Science Center, looked up from his desk, gray eyes widening in surprise.

"I need a favor," said Brent without preamble.

Thomas's brows rose. Tall and gaunt, he looked like the sort of man who'd be a pushover, but he had a titanium core and had shown such dogged determination to solve his wife's murder and children's disappearance that Brent knew better than to underestimate the older man. Plus, Brent owed him.

"What can I do for you?"

"I need one of your cabins. I can pay."

Thomas swept a hand through his thinning hair as he blew out a tight breath. "When?"

"Now?" He couldn't rest with someone in his space. Anna would be safe here as long as she didn't go around spouting off her real name. He frowned. He should have told her to start using an alias.

Thomas grimaced and shook his head. "We're full up. Just about every physiology prof in Canada has descended on us with not only their entire labs, but their families too. It's like Disney World."

Brent stared up at the ceiling. "Well, shit."

"Who's it for? Because I have a spare room in my house..." The same spare room he'd opened up for Brent's younger brother, Finn, who'd been a badly beaten, undersized thirteen-year-old when Brent had been arrested. There were some things you could never repay, and looking after his kid brother was one of them. A cloying sense of failure started to press down on his chest. He didn't want this man to always be clearing up his mistakes. And, thinking about it, he couldn't risk that the bad guys might track Anna down and hurt not only her, but someone else in the process. He couldn't let Anna stay at Thomas's house alone. With Davis gone, she was his responsibility. Whether he liked it or not.

Sleep was overrated. "Doesn't matter."

Thomas opened his mouth to argue but Brent shook his head. "Forget it. It was a stupid idea." He cleared his throat. "I never did thank you—"

"Thank me?" Thomas looked confused.

"For taking care of Finn when I was arrested."

There was a pause. The phone rang but Thom ignored it. "You don't need to thank me, Brent. You gave everything you had to protect that boy. After what happened to Bianca"—his voice got rough talking about his first wife, who was murdered thirty years ago—"I was grateful someone was out there protecting others from violence. I just wish someone had been there to save you..."

Brent planted his hands on his hips and frowned down at the man. He wasn't that shit-scared sixteen-year-old anymore and this wasn't what he'd come to discuss. Frankly, his battered dysfunctional heritage was something he spent most of his time trying to forget.

Thom avoided his eye, but kept talking. "To be honest I was glad to have someone around to look after." His lips drew back on one side. "That sounds terrible—"

"No, I get it." Sometimes, when you lost everything, you had to take comfort where you could find it.

"Laura likes her painting, by the way," Thomas said softly. Laura Prescott was Thomas's girlfriend and Brent's lawyer. An unlikely ally for a man like him, but a good person to have in his corner. As a thank-you for her help last year, he'd painted her an enormous canvas he could barely get through his double doors.

"Does she have a wall big enough to hang it on?" He opened the door back to the secretary's office.

Thomas laughed and followed him out. "If she doesn't, she'll probably build a new house. It's a good thing she isn't attracted to—" He cut himself off.

"Ex-cons. You can say it, Thom. Not like everyone isn't thinking it." He gave Gladys a pointed stare. She sniffed and looked away.

"I was going to say artistic types," he muttered under his breath, obviously still trying to keep Brent's alter ego a secret. "Anyway, I always thought what you did was more in the line of self-defense than—"

Brent held up his hand to cut him off. He did not want to talk about it. Thomas looked upset, obviously wanting to say more, but Brent wasn't looking for absolution. And when had he gotten so soft that he cared what other people thought? But he knew when. Last spring, when Gina was murdered, and these people had helped him through the second worst day of his life.

"You going to marry her?" he asked Thom.

Gladys's chin jerked up then, and her eyes brightened. If anyone deserved a Happy Ever After, it was Thomas Edgefield.

"You think I should?"

Brent laughed bitterly. "I'm the last person you should be asking for romantic advice."

Thomas followed him outside and they both looked across the inlet to the other side of Bamfield. "I was thinking about it, but…" He shuddered and, despite the heat, huddled deeper into his V-neck sweater.

"It's hard to let go of the past sometimes." Brent understood.

"What if I'm bad luck?"

Brent pressed his lips together, because wasn't that one of the reasons he guarded his privacy so fiercely? Not just because he didn't like people—which he didn't—but because he was terrified that getting involved was sure to get any friend—or lover—killed.

But he'd sacrificed his soul years ago and didn't deserve that sort of happiness. Thom did.

"I'm pretty sure if any of us has earned the love of a good woman, Thom, it's you." And he strode away because he didn't want to think about love or what it did to people when it all went pear-shaped.

Rand figured Vancouver was everything they said and more. It had ocean, mountains, enough Oriental restaurants to satisfy a horde of invaders—everything a guy could want, minus a cute, petite brunette who held his balls tightly in her sweet little hands.

Anna Silver was putting him to a lot of trouble. If she got hold of that envelope before he did, she'd have the power to put them all inside. That was not going to happen.

"You seen this girl?" He'd given the local transportation people some bullshit about being US cops with no jurisdiction in this country, looking for a woman who'd kidnapped her children. It was a good way of garnering sympathy from a largely male workforce, but they needed to be careful to avoid the attention of the Canadian Border Services Agency.

A grease monkey stripping down an engine of a Cessna glanced at the picture of the woman, paused, and shook his head.

"Were you here Friday night, Saturday morning?" The man shook his head again and went back to his wrenches. The place stank of motor oil and avgas, manual labor, and a lifetime of drudgery.

He curled his lip.

Petrie had found no record of the girl on any passenger manifests out of Vancouver International Airport. Rand and Marco were canvassing the car rental companies and smaller regional airports. Boundary Bay was only a short hop from the international airport, and Rand had a feeling about the place. Unfortunately no one was giving them jack.

She could have jumped on a bus and headed to downtown Vancouver. The chances of finding her without a money trail were about a million to one.

He walked to the hangar door, looked out at the flat delta that surrounded them. Called Kudrow. "Give me something to work with. I'm pissing in the wind here. Fucking Canucks don't know a damn thing about anything."

"Here's something." He could hear the excitement in the other man's voice. "Davis's ex—Anna's mommy—still lives in Victoria on Vancouver Island. It's where the teacher grew up and where Davis committed his crime."

He felt a tingle low in his spine. She'd bolted for home. "Got an address for me?" He motioned for Marco to join him as he memorized the address, then hung up. He headed back inside the hangar and into the manager's small office. "We need a flight to Victoria. Any chance one of your boys can give us a ride?"

The grease monkey followed him inside, listening in on the conversation. "You find that girl you're looking for?"

Rand gave him a smooth smile. "Was the damnedest thing. She's been spotted on Vancouver Island."

The grease monkey's eyes slid away and Rand knew the fuck-chop had lied to him. "I'll give you twice the going rate if we can leave in the next thirty minutes."

The manager's eyes lit up. "Andy here can take you."

"Sorry, boss, I'm going to have to order another part for the Skyhawk."

"I thought you said you were almost done?"

"I just noticed a crack in the prop and we don't have a spare in the warehouse." Andy, the grease monkey, backed away a few steps and refused to meet his eye.

Rand and Marco exchanged a look. If leaving a trail of bodies in their wake wouldn't be a problem, this guy's neck would have been snapped. Unfortunately they'd questioned too many people, and had been caught on several surveillance cameras. If they got nowhere in Victoria, Rand would come back and work on the bastard until he spilled more than his guts.

"There's another pilot heading to Victoria via Nanaimo in fifteen minutes. You can catch a ride with him." The boss shouldered past his employee and Rand followed him out. Excitement started to spread along his nerves. Most soldiers balked at taking human life, but it had never bothered Rand. Murder was easy to hide in a war zone, but in a civilian world it was more of a challenge. He wasn't worried. He knew how to escape and evade, and he had no intention of ever getting captured.

CHAPTER 4

Katherine Plantain hurried to dress for breakfast. She shimmied into new linen pants and wondered if the neighbor's teenage son had remembered to cut the lawn. She checked her wristwatch: 6:50 a.m.

They'd agreed no cell phones on this vacation, but she'd nurtured that lawn back to life after Ed had removed one of her prized azalea bushes last fall. Damned if all her gardening efforts were going to waste for the sake of a thirty-second phone call. She turned on the phone and noticed she had a message from Anna.

She smiled, then sighed. Thoughts of Anna always brought a pang. She'd failed her in so many ways and had no idea how to make it up to her, or how to fix things. But Anna didn't need fixing and she'd made it more than clear over the years that she didn't want her mother's help. She'd made herself a good life in the States. Had a successful, fulfilling career. Except for that one blip, Anna was the most sensible, most levelheaded person she knew. They all knew who to blame for the blip.

Anna was OK now, and she was also fiercely independent. Katherine put her phone to her ear and listened to the message.

Her knees dissolved. She sank to the bed as her muscles turned to smoke.

Davis was dead?

She expected to feel relief, happiness even, but the image that flickered through her mind was him on his knees the day he'd proposed, and the look of love that had captured her already ensnared heart when he'd begged her to marry him.

Ed stuck his head through the door and she jumped.

"I thought we'd agreed no cell phones?" he chided sternly.

"I was just reminding Nate to mow the lawn." The lie tripped off her tongue without conscious thought. She struggled to form the words to tell Ed about Davis's death, but they dissolved, unspoken. A cold wave of something that felt a lot like grief washed over her and pinned her in place with the weight of iron. Her lips refused to move.

She just needed time to process the information, *then* she'd tell Ed. First, she needed to call Anna back, to see if she was OK.

His lips firmed.

"Fine." With shaking hands, Katherine deleted the message and turned off the phone. "I won't call him. See?" She went to stow the cell in the side of her suitcase, but Ed shook his head and held out his hand.

"Hand it over. We're on a technology-free vacation."

She wanted to roll her eyes, but felt a familiar sense of numbness closing in around her. There were pay phones on the ship, she'd call Anna later. "Fine. But if that grass is d-dead"—she tripped over the word—"I'm ordering new turf when we get back."

Ed tucked the phone into his satchel and shook his head. "Who would have thought when I married you that you'd turn into a gardening fiend?" He slipped his arm around her shoulders and kissed her brow.

She leaned against him and waited for his presence to calm her. But it didn't. Instead there was an unexpected pain that she could never reveal to the man who'd saved her when the man she'd loved had ripped her existence to shreds. Being dead didn't change the betrayal or the grief, but it sank the knife that little bit deeper.

Tired of her confinement, Anna broke out some cash and decided to hit the convenience store. Chocolate might not cure all that ailed her, but at least it would give her a temporary high that wasn't dangerous or illegal.

The reality that her father was dead was beginning to sink in. She would never get the chance to repair their relationship. Never get the chance to kiss him good-bye and tell him she loved him—that she'd always loved him.

There was a pain in her chest, just under her heart. It ached.

The sky was clear blue and the trees a dense impenetrable green as she followed the gravel road back the way she'd come last night. The air was sweet with grass pollen, bushes dripping with ripening huckleberries and thimbleberries.

Could she really be in danger in a place like this?

The idea seemed surreal. Staying with an ex-con was surreal. She tried not to think about the fact she was being forced to rely on a man about as trustworthy as her father.

Brent was not the man she'd expected to find, and yet he was exactly the kind of person she needed to help her through this mess. And her father had trusted him. That bond had gone deep.

She walked past the Coast Guard station and turned right along the boardwalk to the store to buy a cold drink. Two men sat on a bench outside the store, watching her curiously. Another guy in crisp black pants and a pale blue uniform shirt stared at her with eyes the color of coal. His face was handsome but harsh. She avoided his gaze and picked up a basket from near the door. The men's interest unnerved her and she felt the back of her neck itch as if they were talking about her.

She loaded up with chips, chocolate, and cookies. Decided she needed to at least pretend to be an adult and grabbed bread, cheese, and tea bags. Then she pulled a couple of steaks out of the freezer, picked out two large potatoes, and a bunch of sad-looking broccoli. The idea of preparing a meal appealed to her innate need for control. Brent didn't want her here and she didn't want to be here, but at least she could show some basic appreciation for him not throwing her out on her ear. And not raping and murdering her in her bed last night.

She gritted her teeth.

She was sick of being wary of men, of living with the weight of the past strapped around her neck like a giant anvil. All these years later and she was still trying to shake it loose. What would it take to finally move on? To be free of the past?

The guy behind the counter rang up her purchases. "Visiting friends?"

"Uh-huh." She could see speculation in his eyes, but he didn't venture any more questions. An older woman, hauling a shopping bag that looked far too heavy for her to handle, called out a good-bye to the guy. Anna eyed the wine section and figured she'd never be able to manage her purchases as it was, then grabbed a bottle anyway. She had all day to walk the half mile back to Brent's house, and wine would help her get through the meal without succumbing to insanity. Anna counted out her cash and asked for a box to carry everything home.

She hefted her purchases and headed outside. Pretty houses were scattered along the inlet, backed by ubiquitous evergreen forest. Small boats were moored at a variety of jetties and docks of all shapes and sizes. A floatplane bobbed on the water, and a fancy cruiser chugged out of the inlet with a group of fishermen huddled on the deck, sporting big grins of excitement and anticipation. A dark wedge of rock above the water told her the tide was receding and with that came the fresh scent of seaweed—not unpleasant. Massive plate-size starfish glittered in rock crevices, and she could see shoals of tiny fish darting beneath the timbers of the dock.

This was a cute town for a short visit.

She rested her groceries on the railing to watch a seal pop its head out of the water and then disappear again. This is what her father had loved about this tiny community. This, and his best friend Brent.

Perhaps she was finally ready to admit that there was a tiny part of her that was actually jealous of their relationship. A small immature slice of her soul that wished she'd been as close to the man who'd raised her as his prison cellmate was. The fact that the gulf between them since he'd gotten out of prison had been her fault didn't make it hurt any less.

Hot grief surged up inside and a warm knot formed in her throat. She'd avoided seeing him lately. Told him she was busy with work and canceled at the last moment when she'd been due to visit. Had she subconsciously been punishing him? Or had she just been terrified he'd finally figure out what had happened to her when he'd been locked up, and do something stupid that would get him thrown back in prison? Dark feelings tangled inside her. She should have talked to him. Should have spent more time with him.

Anna drew in a long breath and tried to let it go. Regret would get her nowhere. Her father was dead and she needed to figure out why.

The cry of a seagull drew her back to the scene in front of her. Across the water sat an impressive array of buildings in all shapes and sizes, including a scallop-shaped one that faced the sea.

"That's the Bamfield Marine Science Center."

Anna jolted. She hadn't realized she had company. The older woman from the store stood stroking a small tabby.

Anna had to forcefully clear the frog in her throat to speak. "Looks impressive."

"It is impressive." The woman plopped her bag on the boardwalk, juggled a small bunch of tulips, and stuck out her hand to shake. "I'm Laura Prescott."

Anna shook her hand quickly. A boat was motoring over from the other side of the inlet. She squinted. It was Brent. She eyed her heavy box and then leaned over the railing, putting two fingers in her mouth to produce a sharp whistle to get his attention. When he looked up, she waved frantically. All eyes swung in her direction and she felt highly conspicuous.

"You know Brent Carver?" the woman, Laura, asked her.

"Yes. It was nice to meet you." Anna winced as she hefted her box and walked down the narrow gangplank toward Brent, tying up against the dock. When she got down to the boat, he took her groceries with a frown.

"I've got plenty of food." He eyed the massive bars of chocolate and smiled. It disturbed her. "Hop in and find a life jacket." He picked up a large wrapped canvas. "I just need to mail something." He loped up the gangplank and said something to the woman who'd been talking to her. To Anna's surprise, Laura started down the gangplank and headed for the boat. Anna took her bag and helped her climb in.

"I never learn. Every single time I buy more than I can carry. I'll be getting a car next, just for this side of the inlet." The woman huffed as she settled herself onto one of the seats.

"You're a friend of Brent's?" Anna asked carefully. She couldn't see him offering a ride to anyone who wasn't.

Laura snorted. "Not exactly." Her gentle smile turned cutthroat. "I'm his lawyer."

Anna's eyebrows rose. Brent was now banging loudly on the door of a small red building—the post office—beside the store. The guy leaning against the railing in the pale blue shirt said something to him. The exchange didn't exactly look friendly.

"The old bat who runs the post office just locked the door because she saw Brent coming up the ramp. She wouldn't know kindness or compassion if it bit her on the butt," Laura muttered under her breath. At Anna's confused look, she added, "Brent finds it hard to get served in the local shops. Mind you, he doesn't exactly make it easy for himself. And Cyrus Kaine has a stick up his ass when it comes to my client."

Anna guessed Cyrus Kaine was the guy in the blue shirt.

"He's the Coast Guard captain." Laura nudged Anna's arm and the boat rocked. "Better hope we don't sink, because Cyrus might not rescue us if we're with Brent." Her eyes shone with delighted amusement. "Although, he has an eye for a pretty girl so you'll probably be all right."

Brent strode down the gangplank with a carefully blank expression on his face, belied by the fire in his eyes.

"And you are…?" Laura asked pointedly.

"Anna."

"Anna what?" Laser-sharp eyes bored into hers. Everything inside Anna froze.

"Anna Karenina. Drop it, Sherlock." Brent climbed into the boat without using his hands and stowed the canvas down the side of his seat. He gave Laura a pirate's grin. "Anna is a personal friend of mine and that's all you need to know."

He made it sound like they were lovers, which made sense since she was holed up in his cabin, but she blushed from the tips of her toes to her hairline.

Laura eyes sparkled. "Known each other long?" She wasn't put off by his briskness or his tone. Anna had a feeling Laura wouldn't be put off by much.

"Years." He looked surprised by the word that had escaped, and Anna realized he thought he knew her because of her father. His eyes shot to hers, knowledge alive in their depths. Then a terrible sense of foreboding stole through her. Had her father shown him her letters? She might not have told him everything, but she'd sure as heck told him a lot more than she wanted a stranger to know. Especially a sexy ex-con like Brent.

She looked away, concentrating on the blast of the ocean breeze as they headed around the point and out into Barkley Sound.

Laura held tight to a bunch of tulips that probably wouldn't survive the wind. The ride was bumpy and had Anna gripping hard onto the sides. She'd lived by the sea all her young life, but had never been much of a boat person. They motored past Brent's home, which looked magnificent from the water, and around a corner to a much smaller and more modest cottage on a hill above a short sturdy dock built into the rocky edge of a secluded beach.

Brent docked and tied up the boat. "I don't know why you had Finn rebuild your dock when you don't even own a boat."

"Maybe I just liked having your brother around for some decent company," Laura said with enough snide in the remark to make Brent smile.

"If you wanted decent company, you shouldn't have moved to Bamfield."

"I didn't know you had a brother," Anna cut in, surprised.

"Makes me wonder what else you don't know about our illustrious skipper," Laura said ominously.

Brent's features tightened even as he lifted Laura's groceries out of the boat. He gave her a hand out. "For that, you can carry your own bags up the hill." He shot Laura a sweet smile that wasn't at all sweet and jumped back in the boat with Anna.

"Yeah, you're bad to the bone." Laura sniffed. "Better watch out. Any more good deeds and you're going to ruin your bad-boy reputation." She stood and watched them as they motored away and around the corner, out of sight.

"She seems nice," Anna commented.

Brent grunted. Then he seemed to realize grunts and snorts weren't part of normal conversation. "Laura hasn't lived here long, but without her help last year I'd probably be serving another life sentence for murder."

"Another?" Her voice came out muffled, as if she were drowning.

But he heard, and stilled.

"Who did you kill?" she rasped.

His eyes became hooded, and his expression went blank. "My father."

This was not how he wanted Anna to find out she was bunking with a killer. Why the hell hadn't Davis told her? It wasn't like he claimed to be innocent. Unlike 95 percent of the prison population, he took full responsibility for his actions. Although in fairness, most of the inmates were so high on drugs and drink they probably couldn't remember their crimes—or didn't want to.

But he'd owned up to his. Owned it. Paid the price. Would always pay the price.

"What did Davis tell you I was in for?" he asked carefully.

She looked like she wanted to throw herself out of the boat. He'd be glad to get rid of her except Davis had asked for his help and Brent kept his promises, even to a woman who thought her father was a common thief and was right now looking at Brent himself like he was about to turn psycho. It made him want to shake some sense into her, but that would probably give her a goddamned heart attack.

White knuckles gleamed as she gripped the side of the boat. A frown knotted dark brows over eyes that were as green as the moss on the north-facing trunk of a pine.

"He said you'd beaten someone up," she whispered. "He never said the person died."

He concentrated on steering the boat toward the dock. What the hell was he supposed to say? *Sorry?* "Sorry" was too simplistic. Words were worthless without trust, and he'd already warned her not to trust him.

"What did you do with the gun I gave you?" he asked.

Her nostrils flared, that old fight-or-flight reflex kicking in at the sight of a predator.

Anger and self-loathing traveled his veins—something he was used to and was sick of. This was why he pushed people away. "I don't want to hurt you." he explained patiently. "I'm trying to figure out a way to make you feel safe."

"I left it in the bedroom," she admitted in a low voice.

"Not real useful."

"Well, I'm obviously not very good at dealing with convicted felons." Her eyes flashed. "You'll have to excuse me."

"Hey." He much preferred anger over fear. "You came to me, remember?"

"I didn't know you were a killer."

He went still inside. He didn't know why hearing those words from her lips made a difference. But it did. The wash of the ocean against his small cruiser was the only noise, the silence so taut with tension he couldn't stand it any longer. Him, a man who once spent six months in solitary and enjoyed every damn second. The irony wasn't lost on him. "Your father sent you to me…"

"But Papa wasn't exactly trustworthy himself, was he?"

How'd he get caught in this mess? He lived on the edge of nowhere and barely answered his phone, let alone talked to people. And yet here he was doing his damnedest to help his best friend's daughter—a woman who didn't believe in a man so noble he wouldn't even take money from a rich fucker like Brent. So why would Davis steal it from someone else? He wouldn't.

He was supposed to fix this mess? No fucking way.

"Why did you kill your father?" she asked.

Pain pierced his chest. He narrowed his eyes and swallowed. He was done getting bitched at. Her mouth tightened at his silence. He took up the ropes and stepped onto the dock, securing the boat only yards from where he'd cradled his daddy in his arms as the bastard bled out. The memories returned like a grim dose of reality. He could see every detail. Smell the thick cloying tang of his father's blood. See the drunken confusion in his eyes. Feel the impotence of that young foolish boy who'd known his father was dying, who'd worried his little brother wouldn't make it either, and had realized there wasn't a damn thing he could do about any of it.

Love was too simple an emotion for how he'd felt about his father. Hatred would have given him an easy way out in a situation where there was none.

He stepped back into the boat and placed his canvas and Anna's groceries on the creaking wooden boards before climbing out again. She didn't move. He didn't care.

"Where was your mother?" Her face had lost its waxy paleness and an angry red stained both cheeks.

He'd been about to stride away. Her question stopped him cold.

"She left when I was a kid." He had a distinct memory of his dad saying he'd rather strangle him and his brother, Finn, than let her have custody. Ironic? As a dead guy's winning lottery ticket.

He tucked the grocery box under one arm and watched her shaking fingers try and fail to undo the zip of her life vest. She staggered off the boat and he caught her arm to stop her from falling on her face. There was an intense flash of awareness, hot enough to make his skin crackle, quickly replaced by distaste—on her part anyway.

He was used to the looks and whispers. He'd never pretended to be anything he wasn't, and wasn't about to start now. But a small part of him wished things could be different—not a thought he usually allowed himself because it hurt too fucking much. He placed the box and canvas on the dock. Took hold of the bottom of her life vest and yanked down the zipper. He tossed the vest onto the deck of his boat while she watched him like a raptor, that bottom lip of hers thrust out at a belligerent angle.

This shouldn't be a problem for him. She shouldn't be a problem. He was an expert at shutting down so nothing touched him. That was how he'd endured so many years in an institution that told you when to eat, when to sleep, when to wash. Don't stare someone in the eye for more than half a second, but never back down if someone tried to stare you out. Never look at someone's possessions, never touch their stuff, don't talk back to the guards unless you wanted to get beat down and stuffed in the hole.

And yet, somehow, he was failing to shun all the emotions that this slip of a *girl* was stirring up in him.

Probably because, through her letters to her father, he'd allowed himself to fall just a little in love with her when she'd been a teen struggling with a shitty situation—and now she needed his help even though she didn't want it and he'd rather jump off a cliff into boiling waves below.

A flurry of emotions crossed her features and he tried to reconcile this flesh-and-blood woman with the fantasy version he'd created all those years ago. Anna Silver...He'd ached for news of her, reveled in her achievements, itched to help her through her one shocking stumble. She'd had all the teenage experiences he'd missed, all the angst and joy of growing up on the outside. All he'd had was a paint box, four walls, and eventually, a man who liked to talk about his kid.

Getting rid of this real and judgmental Anna Silver would be a good thing. Except the itch that had kept him alive on more than one occasion was now scratching a hole through his skin.

"Look," he growled when she showed no sign of moving. "You don't have to stay here." She was still looking at him like he was going to knife her on the spot. But his crime, and his life for that matter, was none of her damn business. She should be grateful he was offering any help at all. This whole situation was driving him insane. "There's a friend of mine you can stay with if that makes you feel better. He's old and respectable and won't slit your throat if you piss him off." His teeth ached from clenching his jaw so damn tight. Why was he expected to swallow the condemnation she kept throwing at him?

Because he deserved it, a small voice whispered inside his head. He deserved punishment.

"I'm a convicted murderer. I get that it might freak you out. But that guy in the photograph from the train station? I bet my ass he's a killer too. Military grade."

She flinched. She was hurting from the death of her father, but he didn't have the time or patience for dealing with tender feelings. She wasn't a kid anymore. He turned toward the house he'd built out of the ashes of his childhood. "There's nothing I can do to change my past. There's nothing I can do for Davis, except help you find your way out of this mess. But if you decide you don't want my help?" He looked back over his shoulder into her troubled green eyes. He gave a sharp nod. "That's your business. You can leave any time you want."

And he walked away. Because he didn't need Anna Silver's approval or forgiveness. He just needed to be left the hell alone.

Brent Carver was a killer.

Well, what the hell had she thought he'd done? Stolen somebody's piggy bank? He *looked* dangerous. With those eyes and that body, he looked frickin' deadly.

But he didn't feel dangerous.

Why would a boy kill his father? Could it have been an accident? Assisted suicide? But the way Brent said "convicted murderer" suggested something more threatening. Had he been drunk or stoned? Had it been self-defense? Or a premeditated act of evil?

Anna didn't know what to do.

Her fingernails bit into her flesh. The sea breeze sandblasted her skin until she was so cold she could barely stand. Could she stay with a man who'd taken a life? Someone who'd murdered his own father?

She already had.

She'd arrived in the middle of the night and taken him by surprise. And although he'd been naked with a gun, he hadn't hurt her. He'd manhandled her until he'd figured out she wasn't a threat, and then he'd backed right off.

Would her father have suggested going to Brent if he wasn't a good guy? They'd shared a cell for five years. You might be able to fake it for a few weeks or months, but for eighteen hundred days? Though her father wasn't exactly known for his good judgment, and her mother's sucked too. She loved her parents, but they'd both shattered her trust as a teen. You couldn't repair that. Once it was gone, it was gone forever.

From their short conversation, Laura seemed to trust Brent. And, even though she'd only spent a few minutes in her company, Anna figured Laura was a smart and savvy woman.

Seaweed swayed gently in the tide, a thick fringe of underwater green. The gentle motion calmed her. Her feet took a couple of small steps off the dock and onto the sand. Her stomach growled. She hadn't eaten much in days, but she needed answers, not food. Brent Carver wasn't going to give her any, so she needed to find some other way to figure him out. She placed one foot in front of the other and slowly climbed the steps to the house. She kicked off her sandals and padded barefoot through the entranceway. She looked around with fresh eyes.

This was the home of a murderer.

The space was bright and open. Uncluttered and immaculate. Had he learned that in prison? Full of natural beauty. Open. Airy. Definitely a reaction against the small confined ugliness of a prison cell.

She thought of her father's dreary little apartment. He'd found his redemption in being given a trustworthy position again. What had happened to change that? Or was he telling the truth about being set up?

She felt sick and conflicted about her father's death. Was he a victim or the perpetrator? Either option filled her with dread. She didn't want to be the center of another scandal, didn't want to have to rely on this forbidding stranger for help. But what if her father had been telling the truth? What if someone had chased him and scared him so badly he'd fallen under that train?

Didn't he deserve justice? Bad guys should not get away with doing bad things. But that reasoning made her a hypocrite of the worst kind, because she'd never reported her own assault. Had been too frightened of the consequences. Her stomach cramped.

She slid her hand over the smooth granite surfaces in the kitchen. The steaks were defrosting on a platter and everything else had been put away in the cupboards and refrigerator. Nothing left out on the counters. No trash sitting waiting to be thrown out. Not a single envelope or junk mail flyer in sight.

It could be a show home, she realized.

There wasn't a smidgen of personality anywhere, and maybe that was a sign that she should get out as fast as possible. She helped herself to a glass of water and gulped it down. She wandered through the living room and spotted the huge canvas above the fireplace.

Now *there* was emotion.

It was such a simple picture: three bands of color—bone-white sand, gritty purple ocean, darker teal sky. The sea looked calm, but there was a brooding element to the painting, an energy that was almost tangible.

Her father had given her a painting of Brent's. It hung above her bed as gentle and soothing as a lullaby. Staring at that scene felt like going on a vacation and had kept her company on many a lonely night. This one above his stone hearth spoke of an impending storm. Of fury waiting to strike.

A shiver ran over her skin.

She moved on, looking for some clue to the truth of Brent's personality. Something substantial. Something she could trust. A huge flat-screen TV hung on the wall that formed the stairs. The furniture was dark and masculine—dark blue couches with black cushions. Almost everything was made of polished wood, stainless steel, or glass. Nothing to tell her who Brent Carver really was, except for the torment-soaked canvas on the wall.

All this rigid structure contrasted strongly with the passion she saw in his paintings. The same way his stoic expression battled the fire in his eyes. What did it mean? That he controlled it? Disguised it? What was he hiding?

Was it any of her damned business?

She prided herself on having good self-preservation instincts. More importantly, nowadays she listened to them—which was why Peter was history. It worried her that the instincts that should have been sending out five-engine alarm bells were curiously silent in Brent's presence.

Was she stricken numb with grief? Did that handsome face and ridiculously honed body blind her to reality? Why didn't she sense the danger in him?

Why had he killed his father? Something terrible must have happened, but what?

Her father's actions had driven her to the edge of despair, but she'd never wanted to hurt him. Her brain spun with unanswered questions.

Did she stay or go?

Go where?

She didn't know, but that was no reason for inaction. She wouldn't be a victim just because she didn't have options. However, she didn't want to run around like a headless chicken and get hit by a frickin' train either.

Tears stung but she blinked them away.

She spotted three photographs in what looked like solid silver frames tucked on the edge of the hearth of the wide stone fireplace. She walked over and stared down at them.

A thick lump wedged in her throat.

One picture showed a black-and-white image of two boys goofing around. Brent, looking so young and skinny, mischief dancing in that gorgeous young face as he mugged for the camera. He held a much smaller boy in a loose headlock. The younger boy, who must be his brother, if the family resemblance was to be believed, stuck out his tongue as he grappled with his big brother. Such an innocent depiction of boyhood happiness. There was another photograph—her father—making a snow angel in the sand. She picked it up and held back sobs as she looked at his handsome face smiling at the camera. She didn't know the last time he'd looked that happy. The third photograph showed a shy-looking teenage girl. She had short dark hair and a pretty smile.

"That's Gina."

She jumped, almost dropped the frame.

"We were childhood sweethearts." His voice was brusque.

Emotions were churning through the room in a thick undercurrent. "You still have her photograph? You must have really loved her."

His eyes were stark against his tanned skin. "She waited for me the whole time I was inside." There was something in his voice that gave away some terrible tragedy.

Anna stared at the photograph and tried to steel herself. "What happened?"

"She was murdered. Last spring. I broke up with her because she wanted things I couldn't..." He cleared his throat. "Anyway, she got involved with someone else and ended up dying because of it." His expression darkened. "Bad things happen to people around me. Maybe you should leave."

A full body shiver took hold of her. This man exuded menace. He'd killed. People around him died. Her silence sounded like a condemnation and his expression hardened. He started to turn away.

"What happened to your brother?" She needed to know. The boy in the picture looked like a live wire.

"The one person left alive in those photos, you mean?"

"You're alive," she pointed out.

A veil fell over his eyes.

Something else he'd learned in prison? Give nothing away? Lock himself inside his mind where no one could touch him? She'd learned that trick too.

"Finn found himself happiness with the love of a good woman." A cynical smile formed at the edge of his lips. That smile said he didn't believe in love. Neither did she.

"You ever think you'll be happy? Truly happy?" Up until a few days ago she'd thought she was happy. Now she wasn't sure she even knew what it meant. Her father's death had shown her all the fault lines in her life, fault lines that snaked back to the day he'd been arrested for theft.

His smile grew icy. "I've got money in the bank and the greatest view in the world. Why wouldn't I be happy?"

"That's not an answer." She touched a finger to the cheek of that girl in the photograph and Brent flinched. "Do you have a new girlfriend?" Murderer or not, she didn't want to complicate this man's relationships. Staying here would do that and he'd suffered enough.

"Christ, no. I prefer my own company." He padded to the fridge and pulled out a beer. "You staying?" he asked as if he didn't give a damn. But she could see the rigid, unbending line of his back, and the stiffness of his shoulders.

He'd loved her father. He'd loved that girl, Gina, and he loved his little brother.

It was enough. "For now."

CHAPTER 5

Katherine stood ready to serve the volleyball. Ed was watching her with what he probably assumed was encouragement, but what she felt as pressure. Her shorts were too snug, her hair kept getting in her eyes, and Davis was dead.

Anna wasn't answering her phone. Katherine had called twice and left a message. Now she needed to tell Ed. Except then she'd have to tell him she'd lied, and that was the one thing he never tolerated—lies. She was trapped by her own duplicity, and if anyone knew how being lied to hurt, it was her.

Katherine had grown up in a household where her father had repeatedly cheated on her mother. Davis had always been overly romantic, trying to prove he'd never betray her that way. Instead, he'd stolen and gotten arrested. She'd known she shouldn't have fallen in love with the man, known it and done it anyway. She and Anna had both paid the price.

She batted the ball over the net and scored a point. Their opponents were a couple they'd met at breakfast the previous morning and started spending time with—the Montgomerys. Harvey was OK, but his wife, Barb, was a little sharp for her taste. She did everything with a competitive air that set Katherine's teeth on edge.

You really must see the pyramids before they're gone.

Well, yeah, that would be nice.

Katherine served an ace. Harvey was nice but wore a Rolex with the relaxed carelessness of the filthy rich. That sort of wealth unnerved her. Reminded her of Davis always telling her that one day he'd give her the world. Her mouth went dry. He'd never cared about appearances or if she ate two donuts for breakfast rather than a bowl of bran flakes, but he'd wanted to give her diamonds.

They'd struggled to make ends meet. Struggled to pay the mortgage and car repairs, and to send Anna to a decent school. She'd nagged him terribly. Some days Katherine wondered if everything had been her fault, that he'd stolen that money just to stop her nagging.

Poor Davis.

"Come on, love," Ed urged.

She jerked back to the present. Wiped her brow and batted the ball but it went wide. Ed looked angry for a moment but hid it. His competitive streak was starting to irk her. After eight years of marriage, she should be used to it.

Harvey hit the ball toward her and she returned it with an easy dig. Barb blocked it by pounding it straight in her face. Pain exploded in her nose.

"Sorry," said Barb.

Katherine covered her face with her hands and felt arms curl around her shoulders.

"Are you OK, love?" Ed. Always, Ed.

Her nose stung but she nodded.

"Let's have a look at you..."

He gripped her chin and she forced herself to hold still. He was just trying to help. Most people liked being fussed over.

"Nothing Malcolm needs to fix, that's for sure."

Malcolm was her stepson. A neurosurgery resident in Seattle with the ego to match.

Ed kissed her cheek and rolled the ball back to the opposition. He did not like to lose.

Harvey caught the ball and picked it up. "Are you OK? Do you want to stop?"

Both Barb and Ed looked staggered by the suggestion. They'd play to the death.

She smiled at Harvey, whose eyes softened. "I'm fine. Thank you." And then she got into position because she wasn't going to be outdone by someone who took pleasure in another person's pain. If she could just stop thinking about the past she'd be fine. She kept her eye on Barb. She wasn't big on forgiving or forgetting and that probably made her a bad person. But life had stopped being all sunshine and roses the day Davis had been arrested and she'd been interrogated for hours in a sweaty horrible police station surrounded by prostitutes and junkies.

Perhaps if she could reach Anna, she wouldn't be so upset over Davis's death. Who would have thought that after all these years he'd still have the power to hurt her?

Rand went slowly through the mail. Flyers and a meter reading card, a credit card bill that he pocketed to examine in detail later, a couple of begging letters from charities. No manila envelope that would put an end to this goatfuck.

Marco came down the stairs with a shake of his head. Lucky for the Plantains they were currently on an Alaskan cruise, which Petrie had discovered courtesy of hacking into their e-mail accounts. Unlucky for Rand and Marco, Anna wasn't here either.

Someone, probably a well-meaning neighbor, had piled the mail up on a table beside the front door. They needed to be careful someone didn't walk in and catch them here, unless it was Anna. She could walk in anytime and he'd be fucking ecstatic.

It had crossed Rand's mind that if you knew the right people you could do a lot of disappearing with sixty million. Even though she was squeaky-clean on the surface, Anna had access to all the right people through her father's prison connections.

He called Kudrow. "She's not at the mother's house. Nor is the envelope."

Kudrow swore. "Nothing at her place or Davis's apartment. Where the fuck did he mail it?"

If Rand knew, he wouldn't be standing here like a spare part. "Any luck tracking her phone?"

"Nothing. She ditched it."

He didn't bother asking if Petrie had found the money because he'd have already heard if he had. They were running out of options. He scratched the back of his neck. "Where'd Davis serve his time?"

There was a shuffling of paper. "Wilkinson Prison."

"Any details on the mother or stepfather?" He knew they were away on a cruise but didn't know when they were due back.

"They get back next Sunday night. Petrie put a tap on the mother's and stepfather's cell phones just in case Anna reaches out to them." Kudrow swore. "Davis Silver is as much a pain in the ass dead as he was alive. No wonder she left the prick."

Rand rang off without saying good-bye. Davis had been a thorn in his side since this began, but at least he'd shown some balls. He rubbed his chin in memory of the uppercut Davis had delivered just before he'd fallen to his death. He walked into the living room, and saw a photograph of Anna looking miserable in her graduation gown. Picked it up and kissed the cold smooth glass.

He liked women OK. Naked. On their hands and knees. Or backs. Legs spread. Mouth shut. Or not—depending on his mood. He didn't like the feeling he was running out of time. He didn't like some bitch having access to his cash or holding the key to his jail cell. Frustration was starting to work its way through his body and mind, bringing with it an anger that would only be assuaged by reducing sweet little Anna to a bloody mess. And it was true that maybe he'd learned some of his finer dating skills in countries where women's rights were as advanced as clockwork computers, but that's what you got for Uncle Sam turning him into a soldier rather than throwing his ass in jail.

The sun was slipping down the horizon as they ate in silence at the massive breakfast bar that doubled as a dining table. Anna figured Brent didn't hold many dinner parties. The silence was awkward. Uncomfortable. Brent looked like he'd rather be slopping out cells than sitting opposite her and sharing a simple meal.

What had his family life been like growing up? Had they sat together for meals? Talked over school homework at the kitchen table? What kind of man had his father been?

Brent's expression told her nothing. His plate was wiped clean but she didn't know if that was another remnant of prison life or if the food actually tasted good. She couldn't eat more than a couple of bites. Instead she took a big gulp of wine to moisten her throat.

"What was it like?" she asked finally.

"What?" He stilled and then warily his head came up. "Prison?"

She nodded.

Brent pushed his plate away. "It was hell."

"But you were allowed to paint?"

A fleeting smile cut into one side of his cheek. Damn, he was handsome. She dated people who looked ordinary. Nice. Reliable. She didn't hang out with people who looked like they could hold their own with Hollywood bad boys.

"After a rough start, I managed to get my high school diploma and then sat on my ass for two years with nothing to do except cause trouble." There was a glint in his eye that suggested she didn't want to know the sort of trouble he'd caused. "At the start I wasn't exactly a model prisoner." He leaned back in his seat, crossing tanned strong-looking arms. "They finally figured out that letting me paint kept the insanity levels manageable. By the time your dad arrived, me and the warden had figured out a compromise. Did your father never talk about any of this?"

"The only thing he ever said was he'd rather die than go back inside." Her eyes rose to meet his. "And that, without you, he wouldn't have lasted a month." She realized suddenly that her father hadn't exaggerated. Brent Carver might be a killer but he'd saved her father's life—that's why Davis trusted him so much. "Thank you." The words tied knots in her throat as she struggled to get them out. "For looking out for him when he was just a stranger to you."

"I may have stopped him from becoming someone's fuck buddy"—her eyes widened at the shocking imagery—"but you're the one who kept him sane."

"Were you ever…raped?" The reality hit home. That it could happen to anyone, even someone as strong and intimidating as Brent. No one should have to suffer that kind of degradation.

Slowly he shook his head. "They tried a couple of times." His eyes darkened. "I was too big, too volatile, and too damn violent to be worth the risk." He cocked a brow. "They knew I'd kill them if I ever got them alone." His honesty was compelling and she found herself leaning forward, drawn to him despite herself. "I had nothing to lose back then, and wasn't exactly known for my forgiving nature." Echoes of brutality flickered through his gaze. She shivered, imagining all the things he'd done to survive that terrible place. "You kept me sane too."

His words shocked her.

"Oh, God." The kitchen clock ticked in time to her pulse. "He read you my letters, didn't he?"

"My favorite was the time you put ice cubes in your stepfather's gas tank when he dumped your cat at the humane society."

Her hand covered her mouth. She'd forgotten about that. Damn, she'd hated Ed that day, even though Ginger had shredded his favorite leather recliner.

"And the time you did an English assignment on *To Kill a Mockingbird*."

She shook her head. "I don't remember that one."

"You told your dad that if Atticus Finch had been alive, you'd have married him and made a good mother to Jem and Scout." He eyed her carefully. "Your dad was quiet for days after that one."

Her stomach churned.

"You didn't come see him very often."

"No." She bit her lip. The guilt just kept on building. She'd really been the worst daughter. "I went every Christmas, but it was so hard seeing him in that place and not being able to take him home." It had been awful, even after she'd gotten used to the security measures and probing stares of both the guards and inmates. "Mom wouldn't come with me so I'd go with Gran." That had made it slightly easier, having someone's hand to hold. "Writing letters was easier."

"They meant a lot to him." He looked out of the window. "Every time you wrote, he'd read and reread those letters endlessly. Hell, I can still recite some of them in my sleep."

She clamped her eyes closed. This man had been privy to her innermost teenage thoughts. He knew almost everything about her. Embarrassing. Humiliating. Worse…

He turned back to face her. "Why'd you do it, Anna? Why'd you try to kill yourself?"

Inside her chest her heart imploded. She'd never told anyone the answer to that question and even though she knew he'd understand, she couldn't describe the shame and disgust that had led to her near drowning. Her hands shook, but she swallowed the rest of her wine anyway. She went to pour herself another glass, but Brent covered her hand with his much larger one.

"Don't," he said.

The touch of his hand sparked a reaction through her body that she didn't want to recognize. She licked her lips and his eyes flicked to them.

Was that desire? Her stomach flipped. She didn't want him to desire her. She didn't want to think about him that way either. She wasn't who he thought she was, and he was exactly the sort of man she couldn't handle.

She pulled her hand away, his honesty deserving at least some of the same in return. "I wasn't thinking straight. I don't think I consciously wanted to die." She paused for a long moment, but he didn't interrupt. "I just put myself in a...*difficult*...position." The Pacific. At night. During a storm. The waves mocked her as they broke against the beach outside. She still wasn't brave enough to be completely honest.

His chest swelled as he inhaled. "Why?" He watched her like the answer actually meant something.

"Didn't *you* ever think about ending it all?" she countered.

Dark history shrouded his eyes and she wanted to know his secrets, but he wouldn't tell her any more than she would tell him. Not the whole story, never the whole story, where the truth lay.

The phone rang and Brent leaped at the distraction. Anna cleared plates and shook her head at herself. She needed to find conversation that didn't revolve around death or prison. Trouble was, they didn't exactly have a lot in common, and small talk seemed puerile.

"Send it to me via a secure account."

Anna's head shot up.

"Yeah, see if you can find out who's doing the surveillance. I need to know exactly what we're up against."

Anna poured herself a glass of water and watched Brent put on coffee as he talked into the phone. He hung up without a good-bye.

"News?" she asked.

He clenched his jaw. "The private investigator I hired spoke to that woman in your daddy's building who he was friends with—Viola Bernstein. The guy also paid the rent for the next few months so you don't need to worry about it."

She hadn't even thought about that. "I'll pay you back—"

"No."

"I can't take money from you."

He looked at her like she was crazy. "Why not? You think you'll owe me?" He stalked closer, so much bigger than she was. "Don't you get it yet?" Pain and fury burned in his eyes. "Yes, I thought about killing myself. *Often*. Getting out of that insane asylum any way I could. You know what saved me in the end? Your daddy saved me. So if you think I wouldn't give my last cent to help him and you, you're mistaken."

She sucked in air. "You don't even know me."

"I know you more than you want to admit, and you don't like it," he said bitterly. "Welcome to my world."

She averted her gaze because, despite what he thought, he didn't know everything. Her father wasn't the only liar in the family, and the truth still cut her to ribbons. She should have moved past it by now. She had moved past it—it was just that her father's death had stirred up the memories.

Sure…and she had a normal sex life and a regular boyfriend.

"Anna." His voice dropped, his expression serious. "Davis was a good man who showed me I could also be a good man. He gave me back hope." He hooked her hair behind her ear, his fingers just brushing her skin. He loomed over her, but she didn't feel like he was going to attack her. It felt more like he'd die to keep her safe.

A spark of want shot through her. Her breath hitched and she swallowed hard. Dammit, she didn't want this physical attraction on top of the mess her life had become. Men like Brent Carver were off-limits to a woman as careful as she was.

"What did the PI have to say?" Her voice was breathy, but the words had the desired effect and he backed away as if suddenly aware he stood too close and might intimidate her, given his less-than-Boy-Scout history. And although she was hyperaware of him, it wasn't because he'd killed someone. It was because of something else she hadn't felt since she was a carefree teen. Something she thought had died the night of her high school prom.

He grabbed himself a coffee. "Want one?"

"Yes." And like that they moved on. "Please." As if the heat and connection and pure weight of emotional baggage between them evaporated. It left her confused and off-balance and grateful.

He poured her a cup and went over to his laptop and opened it up. Clicked on his e-mail provider and then opened an audio file.

They listened to the 911 tape.

"*I work for the Holladay Foundation. Someone's been stealing from the company so I took it back before it disappeared forever. I want to come in. I need police protection.*" The words echoed around Anna's brain. Why hadn't the police protected him? Why hadn't someone saved him?

"I should phone the police and find out what they're doing to investigate his death," she said.

Brent sipped his coffee, sprawled in the chair in a corner of the kitchen where he kept his computer. "My PI spoke to the cops. They're treating it as an accidental death. Said security from his firm chased him when they found out he was stealing, and Davis jumped under the train rather than get caught."

"Don't you think that's possible?" All the energy sagged out of Anna and she sat on a bar stool looking down on Brent. "That he panicked and ran and then made up all this stuff about someone being crooked?" Because her father would rather die than go back to prison.

He looked at her from beneath dark brows. "Doesn't explain why security people from the foundation have been staking out your dad's place waiting for the mailman."

Her eyes widened. "Except if it is their money, they've every right to want it back." She crossed her arms over her chest. Crap, she'd been so stupid. "I need to go home."

He held his hands wide. "Why? What the hell changed? That phone call just told you Davis thought his bosses were stealing from the charity he worked for. He said he thought someone was going to kill him."

"He was lying, Brent," she said bitterly. "The same way he lied when the cops knocked on our front door all those years ago and hauled him and Mom off for police questioning. The same way he lied in court." She locked her jaw. Shame tasted bitter on her tongue.

Brent climbed to his feet. "I can't believe you don't believe in your own father—"

"Said the man who killed his?" Anna was incredulous. "Don't judge me." She shoved against his chest to gain a little space, but it was like pushing a house. He didn't move.

Panic bit and she shoved harder. "The evidence was all there, he set up those offshore bank accounts—"

"Anyone could have framed him."

Disbelieving, she stared at him. "His codes were used to make the transactions. He didn't have a single alibi for the times when the money was moved—"

"He was a scapegoat, a patsy—"

"And if you believe that you're the biggest fool in this room!"

"Oh, I'm *definitely* a fool." He scowled. "Having done time, Davis made an even better patsy second time around, except he caught on. Stopped them in their tracks."

"Oh, please. No one is that unlucky."

"Seriously?" He looked at her like she'd started speaking dog. "What planet are you from?"

Fury lit a flame under her skin. She crossed her arms and glared at him.

"So why aren't the police investigating his death? Why the desire to sweep it all under the carpet in a neat tidy package?" he asked.

"You think there's a conspiracy?" God, he was unbelievable.

"I'm guessing there's a lot of cash involved."

"I need to contact them," she insisted, picking up the phone.

His hands covered hers, his whole body shaking. "And what if they're dirty? How do you know who to trust?"

A terrible thought struck her. "How do I know you aren't deceiving me and keeping me here for reasons of your own?"

Brent reared back as if she'd slapped him. His eyes flashed with pain and his expression shut down.

Oh crap. Anna put her hand to her mouth. "I didn't mean that." But he backed away from her as if she were contagious.

He started to walk away, but she didn't want him to go. Not like this. She grabbed his arm but he jerked free.

"Brent, I didn't mean—"

"Yeah, you did. But you're wrong about me and you were wrong about your father." His eyes were glacial, and a frisson of fear snaked down her spine. "Your father didn't steal that money nine years ago, and I'd bet my ass he didn't steal it this time—or if he did," he interrupted when she was about to argue, "he did it to stop being set up again. And if you'd ever got your head out of your adolescent ass long enough to think about anyone else but yourself, you might have figured it out years ago."

The jab slid home like a blade. Then he was gone, and she was left alone in the starkly beautiful house with only the seductive sound of the sea for company.

Jack Panetti pulled out a cheeseburger and fries and bit into dinner. Most of his cases were getting photographs of spouses cheating, or workers reshingling their roofs while claiming disability. This was different. Brent Carver had asked him to check into the company Davis Silver—deceased—had worked for. On the surface the company seemed legit. Hank Browning was a former four-star general who'd cleaned house down in Colombia. Now he ran a foundation to raise money for injured veterans. A good and worthy cause.

But there was something fishy about their operation.

For one, the numbers didn't add up. Of course, there were overheads, rent, staff to pay, and anonymous donations that made it hard to track, but from what his computer guru told him the numbers seemed off. Then there was a warehouse they rented for no obvious reason. Then the people Browning employed for "security." Ex-soldiers. Mercenaries.

Why wouldn't a charity helping injured soldiers have ex-military on staff?

But something was tugging his tail, and rather than stretching out in his massive bed at the luxury hotel he was booked into and ordering room service on Brent Carver's tab, he was eating junk food while staking out Browning's head of security in the burbs.

Nice house. Nice neighborhood. No red flags. But his instincts were screaming.

Juice dripped down his chin as he took another bite of his burger. A car drove up the guy's driveway and two men got out and hurried inside. Jack wiped his chin, got out his binos, and wrote down the plate number.

A dog began barking, so he started his engine. Time to head out before someone called the cops about the strange man parked on their street. He tossed down his burger wrappings and froze when someone opened the rear door, got into the car, and tapped a pistol against his skull.

"Let's take a drive."

"Who the hell are you? Get out of my car!" Jack went with innocent indignation but knew he was screwed.

"Move it unless you want to become another Chicago statistic."

Jack curled his lip in self-disgust. He tried to see the guy in the mirror. Nothing but a dark shadow.

"Take the expressway." The guy sounded older, definitely not a kid or a routine carjacker. He'd been made by the people he was following and he hadn't been made since his early undercover days with the boys in blue. These guys were professional soldiers with something to hide.

Jack put on his blinkers as sweat trickled down his back. He sped up, hoping to attract the attention of a cop.

"Slow down, speedy." The metal of the gun grazed his ear.

And then all his prayers were answered as he saw a patrol car in the rearview mirror.

"Don't do anything stupid and you might get out of this alive." The voice was flat and devoid of emotion.

Suddenly Jack knew this man was going to kill him. How the hell had an investigation into one man's supposed accidental death turned into a life-and-death situation?

The cop car drew level and the guy lowered the pistol and leaned against the backseat. Jack gripped the wheel so hard his knuckles hurt. Tension grew to a snapping point. The cop pulled past. Just as the guy in the backseat started to relax, Jack jerked the steering wheel hard left and hit the cop car side on.

Jack saw the cop's look of incredulity a moment before he turned on his turret lights.

"You stupid fucking asshole." The guy in the back barely raised his voice. "Drive."

But Jack was jamming on the brakes, undoing his seat belt, and bailing out the door. He rolled, heard a series of squealing brakes and the crash of metal as he crawled like a maniac to the side of the freeway. Streetlights illuminated the scene as he lay panting. Old bullet wounds ached. He mentally weighed his cuts and bruises to reassure himself nothing was broken. Then he turned to see what was going on.

His rental car had come to an ugly stop at the side of the road. The cop had pulled up at an angle in front of it, lights dancing across the tarmac. Jack lay on the ground, hands on his head, offering no threat to law enforcement. He wanted this bastard in custody.

The cop got out, shot him a look, then approached the vehicle with his gun drawn. The next moment, he was jerking on his feet, pounded by impact as the guy in the car shot repeatedly through the steel door.

"Holy mother." The cop fell to his knees, blood spraying the concrete behind him. Horrified, Jack realized he'd just gotten the man killed.

His stomach clenched. Sirens wailed in the background. Cars pulled over all around him in a monster jam. The door to his rental opened slowly, and he saw the guy's face for just a second before Jack got his shit together enough to stand up and start running. The bullet hit Jack in the back, a single flash of excruciating pain before he slammed face-first into the blacktop.

Brent paced his studio. Anger threaded through his veins. For all the things he'd done. For everything he couldn't undo. For being stupid enough to let her words hurt. He picked up his palette and daubed some black into the center of it, then slammed the palette down, paint splattering across the floor. His teeth clenched so hard he thought his jaw would break. *Fuck.* He whirled and put his fist through an unfinished canvas that had shown a serene lake scene, but was now as damaged as the rest of him.

He let out a tight breath and rolled his shoulders. Flexed his fingers. Tried to rein it in. How could someone who'd been so sweet as a teenager turn into such a bitch? Hell, she was as dark and cynical as most cons.

At least inside, people knew better than to ask about your crime. Do your own time and keep your nose out of it. His heart pounded even thinking about being inside. Prison was a nightmare—being locked up. His ribs squeezed tight against his lungs. He never wanted to go back, but at least he knew the rules for being inside.

Outside—anything could happen. He'd learned to expect the unexpected, but accusations, like the one Miss Prim and Proper had thrown at him, hurt. *Fuck.*

He concentrated on his work. Added black to the pine forest on one side of the canvas. And stood back to survey the effect.

Christ. He stepped forward and scraped off as much as he could and slammed the palette once again onto his worktable. He had to finish this piece for the exhibition, but since Anna had arrived, he couldn't concentrate, couldn't *think* about his work. And usually it was all he thought about.

Immersing himself in his art had been his only escape from the confines of prison, and nowadays painting was an anchor in a world he didn't even pretend to understand.

He was fine in this house, on this beach. He didn't want to go anywhere else. Didn't need anything or anyone else.

The sound of the back door opening and closing had him jerking his head to see out the window. He tensed as he watched Anna walk down to the end of the dock and sit with her toes dangling in the water.

There was no breeze tonight. The sea was flat calm, like some lazy seductress extending a languid hand in an invitation to play. The last rays of the sun slowly disappeared, and he looked off at the boiling horizon and narrowed his gaze at the streaks of purple and blue that gathered like bruises on young flesh. The calmness was deceptive. The lack of energy was a lure for the unwary. A storm was coming. A big one. He looked back at Anna—the expression on her face was unguarded, desolate, and played the fiddle on his heartstrings.

She pissed him off but…hell, he was attracted to her. Admitting that made his mouth go dry. He liked how she moved, how she ate, how she didn't flinch away from him even though she was obviously nervous. He wanted to dig deeper, to uncover the core of who Anna Silver really was.

But she was also the daughter of his best friend, a man who'd entrusted her to his care. She was a twenty-six-year-old schoolteacher and he was older and rougher than sin. Even if she had been interested in him, he couldn't pursue it. He respected the memory of his friend too much to sully his daughter. Hell, he barely slept at night, let alone functioned in the normal world.

The last woman he'd been involved with had ended up on a slab in the morgue.

He watched Anna watching his ocean. Watched her as she slowly absorbed the rhythm of the waves against the shore. All the anger and resentment fell away from him. Peace fell over her features and he knew, with gut-wrenching certainty, that he'd do anything to keep it there.

CHAPTER 6

"Good morning, how can I help you?" Warden Rick Pennington picked up his telephone on the second ring.

Rand was calling from Anna's mom's place where he and Marco had holed up overnight. "I'm afraid I have some bad news I wanted to pass on to you on behalf of Davis Silver's family. He was an inmate with you from—"

"I remember Davis," the man interrupted. "What's happened?"

Rand put on his deepest voice. "Terrible accident in Chicago. Davis was tragically hit by a train and died instantly." Marco sniggered and Rand shot him a look. *Shut the fuck up.* "His daughter, Anna, is organizing a memorial service on the island after the funeral, but didn't know if he had any friends from his time in prison who might like to attend."

"Only Brent." *Brent*—Rand wrote it down and Marco did an Internet search on it and Wilkinson Prison. "That's too bad about Davis. He was one of our success stories." The warden cleared his throat. "How about you tell me the details and I'll pass them on to the people who were close to him in prison?"

Rand fed him a line of bullshit and hung up.

Ding. They got a hit. Brent Carver. Lifer. Served twenty. He'd grown up in a tiny community on the west coast—Bamfield—and had been out of prison for the last four years.

"Let's get some wheels, Marco, and track this bastard down." Maybe this was the guy Davis had sent Anna to. All he knew was he was done sitting around with his thumb up his ass waiting for something to happen. "We're gonna need some equipment."

The boys in Chicago were busy running damage control after one of them killed a cop and shot some PI who was nosing around too close for comfort. Rand would handle getting the gear they needed himself. He had his own contacts. They were elite soldiers used to operating in hostile environments under pressure, not undertrained, underequipped cops.

Rand had no intention of doing time for his crimes—goddamn, he'd gotten medals for some of them in the past. If Anna was with this Brent character, he'd set it up so the guy went down for Anna Silver's murder. It seemed like poetic justice, and after all the shit Davis had put him through, he was looking forward to a little payback.

The distant sound of a phone ringing had Anna blinking away the grit in her eyes as she lay in bed. She fought to surface through the fog of exhaustion and tried to figure out where she was.

Then she remembered—the edge of nowhere with the last man on earth she should trust.

She squinted at her wristwatch on the dresser: 9:00 a.m. Wow. She'd been awake for most of the night and had finally drifted off when the sun started to lighten the eastern edge of the horizon. The phone carried on ringing. She staggered out of bed and onto the landing. Brent's bedroom door was closed. She hadn't seen him since she'd accused him of keeping her here for his own reasons and he'd told her to grow up. He was right. It wasn't like he'd keep her around because she was such great company or anything. And he didn't seem to want to hurt her despite her being a royal pain in his butt ever since she'd arrived.

Sheesh. Talk about being paranoid. She ran to the kitchen, but just as she was about to pick up the receiver it stopped ringing. Rats.

"I need coffee," she told the empty space. Exhausted, she fixed a pot, and was just filling a cup when Brent came down the stairs, freshly showered, wearing a shirt—albeit unbuttoned—and a pair of clean, well-worn jeans.

Although he might be wearing more clothes than usual, there were still plenty of hills and valleys visible beneath that open shirt, and every one of them looked like an adventure.

She averted her eyes, wishing she were someone else. Someone with the courage to enjoy looking at a fine physical specimen of a man without blushing. Although, crap, couldn't he be just a little out of shape? He made her aware of all the soft places on her body that no gym was ever going to fix.

She braced herself. She'd acted like a brat last night. "I need to apologize for what I said." Her gaze hit his feet and she blinked. He wore socks—a first in their short acquaintance.

"Forget it. I have to go out. Don't answer the phone." He shot her a scowl.

Forget it? How could she?

"Aren't you curious to see who was calling you?"

He looked at her like she was crazy. Then he grabbed a cup of coffee and an expression of bliss crossed his features as he took a sip. "Damn, if you didn't talk so much, I'd keep you around for your coffee and your cooking."

"Yeah, I always wanted to be someone's housekeeper." She lifted an unimpressed eyebrow, but felt a weird sliver of pleasure at his words. No one had ever offered to keep her around before. Not for any reason. She wasn't an easy person to get along with. Ironically, neither was he.

He grinned and all those body parts that had been dormant for eons started to jiggle for attention. Crap—this was not what she needed.

"Where are you going?" Anna crossed her arms over traitorous nipples. Her nightshirt hung to mid thigh and she wasn't wearing anything except panties underneath.

"I have a meeting in Port Alberni." His expression didn't encourage questions.

"I want to come too."

"No."

"Why not?" she asked.

He blew out an exasperated breath. "Look, I'll be back by dinnertime. You just enjoy the rest."

That was what normal people did. Relaxed on the beach, built sand castles, and enjoyed the view. She paced the kitchen floor. "I'm already bored out of my skull."

"You've only been here two nights." He sounded incredulous and it made her smile.

"I have nothing to do." God, she hated being a whiner, but being idle was driving her crazy. All her books were in Cauldwell Lake. Her garden. Her home. She'd had e-books on her phone, but that was toast. This summer she'd planned to redecorate her office. Summer was her time to get things done, and yet here she was trapped doing nothing, with no end in sight, and she couldn't settle.

"You'd never have survived prison." His shirt matched his eyes and the effect was mesmerizing.

"That's why I don't break the law." She didn't want to be mesmerized. He had beautiful everything but it didn't change the fact that he wasn't the sort of guy to fall for.

"Fine, come with me but"—he ran a frustrated hand though his too long hair—"in case you've forgotten, you're supposed to be in hiding." He went into the laundry room and pulled a ball cap off a peg, and dusted it off by slapping it against his thigh with a *whack.* "Wear this." He tugged it over her hair. "You've got five minutes to get ready. As much as I hate this guy, I can't be late."

She dashed up the stairs, making sure her shirt didn't ride up and flash the guy. "Who is it?" she called.

"My parole officer." He followed her and she knew she was blushing even though he couldn't see anything. Or maybe he could because his eyes gleamed when his gaze met hers at the top of the stairs. She closed the bedroom door and hurriedly pulled on a denim skirt and a blue shirt that didn't match her eyes. Brushed her teeth, took a swipe at her hair, and grabbed her pocketbook. When she came out of the bathroom she noticed the handgun was missing off the bedside table. Brent must have removed it—which was fine with her. She didn't like guns and wasn't sure she could actually shoot another human being anyway. She met him coming out of his studio carrying two huge canvases wrapped in bubble wrap and brown paper.

"Is that a bribe to keep you out of prison?"

"If that's what it takes." A line cut down one cheek as he grinned.

She sighed. She needed to stop making him smile.

"If you must know, Miss Sarcasm, they're original pieces for an exhibition someone's running of my work in New York City."

She noticed a slight tinge of scarlet touch his cheeks. "Impressive stuff." She let him lead the way down the stairs.

He looked back over his shoulder and she told herself not to fall for the charming rogue persona. "People are crazy, what can I say?"

"Some more than others," she agreed. He laughed and her heart gave a little tumble. She didn't tell him she had one of his paintings over her bed at home and that it was better than therapy when it came to helping her relax.

Half an hour later, they were rumbling along the dusty gravel logging road in Brent's truck. It was royal blue with rust around one wheel arch and a foot-long crack in the windshield. Not what she expected from a wealthy painter.

Brent's brooding silence and tight features didn't invite idle chitchat. They hit a rut that had her airborne and he thrust his arm across her chest in an old-fashioned protective gesture that had her flinching away from him. A flush burned across his cheeks.

"Sorry," he said, giving her an unreadable look from under his lashes.

"It's OK." She wished she didn't automatically freak when a guy touched her. Not just with him, but men in general. She noticed something different about his profile. "You shaved."

He rubbed his chin. "Usually I can't be bothered, but I try not to look like a Neanderthal for the people who can put me back inside."

"So if you break the conditions of your parole, you go back to prison?"

"Yup." His shoulders tensed. He obviously didn't want to talk about this.

"What about your gun?" Anna asked.

"What gun?" Brent deadpanned.

The gun was a parole violation. She'd probably known that but it hadn't registered until now. The fact he'd given it to her at the cabin was an even bigger sign of trust than she'd realized. He'd handed over the power to put him back inside, and from what she knew, that was the last thing he wanted.

"How long are you on parole for?" What she really wanted to know was why he'd killed his father. Brent didn't seem like a bad person—maybe a little scary, but not evil. So what had caused him to take a life?

His lips turned down. "For the same amount of time my dad's dead. Forever." He made it sound like he deserved every minute, and yet…there was something about him that made her want to believe in him—or she was the biggest fool to ever walk the face of the earth.

"If you could go back in time," she asked quietly, "would you change what you did?"

The tension in the cab stretched as taut as a fifty-pound shark on a ten-pound line.

"No," he said finally.

Her stomach clenched.

That simple word reminded her of all the reasons she needed to be careful around this man, at a time when she was just beginning to relax her guard.

Brent sat in the parole officer's waiting room in Port Alberni and stared at the institutional green walls and matching linoleum. This place was nothing like prison, but it held the same tinge of fear and grimy unease that was a constant reminder of that demoralizing institution. Prison was meant to be punishment, but knowing he'd killed his father had been punishment enough. The rest had been torture.

The guy opposite had a nervous tic and way too much energy than was sensible while visiting your parole officer.

Brent held his gaze for a second and moved on. The other guy did the same. Not a connection, just an exchange of information. *Don't fuck with me*. The secretary opened the door. "Mr. Carver."

Brent stood and walked into the office. Anna had gone to pick up a bunch of supplies from Walmart. He certainly didn't want her in this soul-sucking place. The secretary sat back down with a smile, but the parole officer didn't even look up as his pen whizzed across paper.

Until last year he'd been down to reporting every three weeks, which had been bearable. After Gina's murder, even though he'd had nothing to do with her death, they'd upped it back up to weekly. Pain in the ass.

"Anything to report, Carver?" The guy's abrasive tone irritated Brent, but he'd dealt with worse over the years.

"No, sir."

The guy slowly raised his head and gave him a gimlet stare. "How's the painting?" He made it sound like Brent did finger painting for elementary students. Although it must grate like a horsehair jockstrap to know the con you were in charge of could earn more by doodling on a napkin than you made in a week.

He gave a slow nod. "Got a big exhibition in the States next week."

A cruel smile played on this guy's lips. "Pity they won't let you in."

Jerkoff. "Oh, they'll let me in." He leaned back and crossed his arms over his chest. Noticed the secretary checking him out from under her lashes and gave her a wink. "They already gave me a visa, but no way in hell am I going to New York City. Or missing my appointment with you." This was a great excuse to feed his agent. *Goddamn parole officer won't let me go—*

"If it's to further your career, I'll sign off on the visit."

Now *that* was twisted. Why couldn't he have his old parole officer back? She'd been strict but didn't like to pull the legs off spiders. "I don't want you to sign off on it. I don't want to go to NYC."

Perspiration glistened on the man's shiny forehead. "Fortunately, I get to make the rules, not you, Carver."

"And what happens if I don't like your rules?"

The pen paused as small eyes gleamed. "You can always issue a formal complaint, but we both know how that would turn out for you."

Not good.

Shit.

Anger welled up, but Brent forced it down. *Never show reaction.* Although this guy wasn't the same as a guard, he had the power to send him back. Brent wasn't ever going back. He took his slip of paper and folded it neatly into his wallet.

"You have a nice couple of weeks." Brent saluted. *Jackass.* He smiled at the secretary and left whistling, just to piss everyone off.

He went out the front door and climbed into his truck. He drove over to Walmart and parked. Anna came out, looking as bright and pure and shiny as a newly minted coin. He touched his horn and she started walking over. His cell phone rang. It was probably his agent, so he answered because he'd just shipped his last canvas and was sick of the guy hassling him.

"Brent?"

The voice of the warden from the prison where he'd spent twenty years of his life shot through him like a knife that pinned him to his seat.

He cleared his throat. "What can I do for you, Warden?" They'd played chess and he'd even given the guy a few pictures over the years. Without the cooperation of the Prison Service, he wouldn't have been able to paint, and Christ knows what he'd have done then.

"I've got some bad news for you"—Brent's heart started pounding and his hands started to shake. *Shit.* And just like that he was catapulted into mind-numbing terror—"Davis Silver died a few days ago."

Davis's death. This was about Davis's death. He didn't have to go back to prison. Brent managed to get hold of himself.

"I received a call from the family."

Brent frowned. Had Anna called the guy even though he'd told her not to?

"Saying they are going to organize a memorial service here on the island. I have some details…" The warden kept talking, but the details sounded off.

She hadn't had time to arrange anything. They didn't even know when the body was going to be released.

"Did you happen to mention my name to whoever was calling?" he asked.

"No." Then there was a pause, a cough. "Well, I might have said, 'Brent'…"

Oh, for fuck's sake. Combine the prison and "Brent" and they had him.

Anna climbed in the truck and smiled. Some of the shadows had lifted from her eyes. The sun had kissed a little color into her cheeks, lightened streaks in her hair to dark gold.

She was beautiful. And someone was after her.

He scrubbed a hand over his face. He was about to drag her back to ugly reality. He'd have shielded her if he could.

"I appreciate the information, sir. When the family calls again, you be sure to tell them I'll be at the memorial service." Anna's eyes widened and she opened her mouth to speak. He put his finger on her lips and the touch shot a flare through his body that had him hard in a heartbeat. *Shit.* They didn't have time for distraction, not even the ones that would feel like heaven if either of them were ever foolish enough to go for it. His brain kicked in. "When did they call? Maybe I can catch them?"

"First thing this morning. I tried calling you at home, but then something came up in the courtyard." Which usually meant a fight. "Caller ID said they were phoning from the ex-wife's house."

Brent blew out a breath of relief. Maybe they were still there. Maybe they'd get lucky and Finn's fiancée could pick the guy up for B&E before he even hit the highway.

"Is there a problem?" The warden's voice grew suspicious.

"No, sir." Brent forced a little gruffness into his tone. It wasn't hard, given his best friend was dead. Davis had been a good man with a soft heart who'd never belonged in prison. No way was Davis a thief, and now that he was dead, Brent was suddenly determined to prove the guy was innocent. "I guess I'm in shock. You know how close we were in prison."

The man seemed to buy it and rang off with the promise to call again with more details when he knew them.

There was a long beat of silence. Hot sun pressed through the windscreen. There was a good chance his carefully constructed refuge was no longer safe. If it were just him, he'd have gone back, set up an ambush, and waited for the bastards to show up. He looked at Anna. He couldn't risk it. *Sonofabitch.*

"What is it?" She fidgeted with her skirt.

That guileless green gaze of hers was so direct, so honest. *Davis's daughter*. Even though he didn't want to be forced out of his home, Anna was his priority. Above all else, he had to keep her safe.

"They've found you."

Her eyes flared with shock as she looked around and he handed her the ball cap from earlier and adjusted it over her hair. Curled a lock behind her ear. She sat completely stunned. "I'm sorry." He'd promised her safety, and his arrogance had almost led the enemy right to his door.

"How?" She swung to look at him.

"Called the prison from your mother's house pretending to be family arranging a service. Warden gave them my first name. It won't take them long to find me."

"I can't believe Papa was right. I can't believe someone actually followed me."

"I'm guessing that there is a lot of money involved." For once he wished Davis had been lying. He shook his head. "Doesn't matter. We need to get out of here." They needed to find the evidence Davis had mailed to Anna and end this thing. Why the hell hadn't he just sent the evidence to the cops? He didn't like the idea of Anna being in danger and it was more than basic concern for a fellow human being. It was fast turning into something he couldn't afford—not for any woman. He was a loner by nature. Preferred it that way.

"Here's what I want you to do." He gave her a list of things to buy. Burner phones, clothes, travel stuff. She left the car with another wad of cash and he watched her as she entered the building.

Then he dialed a number and did something he'd never before done in his whole life. "Finn."

"What's up?"

Words dried up on his tongue.

"Brent, you OK?" The concern in his brother's voice cut through him. For years Brent had tried to push him away, but Finn had never given up on him. Christ knew, he didn't deserve him.

"I need your help."

"About damn time." Finn's tone turned grim.

It still didn't feel right. "I've got someone after me." He gave Finn Anna's mom's name and told him what the warden had told him. "If they aren't there, I'm pretty sure they'll be coming for me at the cabin tonight." Nighttime was always the best time to launch an attack.

"I'm surprised you bothered to call." Finn knew he usually took care of business himself.

Brent's lip twitched. "I'm trying to be a law-abiding citizen. Anyway, that's not the problem. The problem is, I'm not actually there at the moment. I was wondering if Holly's colleagues at the major crime unit would scoop up these scumbags?"

Holly was Finn's fiancée—Royal Canadian Mounted Police Sergeant Holly Rudd—whose father was the top cop in British Columbia. She and Finn were getting married in September and although he'd never say it out loud, Brent admired her spunk and appreciated her dedication to his brother.

"Who's after you, Brent?"

"They aren't after me. They're after a friend who got caught in someone else's cross fire. She hasn't done anything wrong." He didn't want to get his brother tangled in anything illegal, and until Brent had evidence Davis was innocent, Brent couldn't prove the guy had altruistic motives for moving that cash. "These guys are players. Maybe ex-military. Probably armed. Definitely dangerous. Your people need to take care." He didn't want any dead cops on his conscience.

Finn was silent on the phone. "Freddy Chastain is based in Port Alberni for an investigation. I'll sound him out, then talk to Holly."

Brent gripped the phone. "I just need the place standing when I come home." He didn't care if it was riddled with bullets, he just needed four walls and a roof.

"Where you going?"

He didn't want to go anywhere. "I have that exhibition in the States."

"I thought you weren't going to make that," Finn said cautiously.

Brent snorted. "My *parole officer* thought it would be good for me." It was a great excuse for B.C. Wilkinson to leave Canada, even though the thought of leaving the island crawled around his belly like fire ants.

He made arrangements to meet Finn in Victoria where his brother had opened his own scuba diving school and ran ecotours during the off-season. Hopefully the cops would find the guy who was asking questions sitting around Anna's mother's kitchen table, and put an end to this shit.

One thing was certain, his peaceful life was screwed until this was over. He thought of Anna, and how her world had once again been shattered by bad guys who played fast and loose with other people's lives. He remembered the letters she'd written as little more than a child. She was innocent. She didn't deserve any of this and he'd do his damnedest to make it go away. Even if it meant venturing into the world he'd done his best to avoid all these years.

"Suck it up," he told himself and dialed his PI.

It was answered on the fourth ring. "Chicago PD. Who's speaking?"

Shock rocked through him. It was turning into a hell of a day for the unexpected. Brent cleared his throat. "I was trying to get through to Jack Panetti—maybe I have a wrong number…"

"You are…?"

Shit. If he hadn't used his own phone to call he would have already hung up. "Name's Brent Carver. Jack Panetti is doing some work for me."

"Regarding?"

Nice try. "Just trying to track down an old girlfriend."

The heavy pause. "Mr. Panetti was involved in the fatal shooting incident of a police officer last night. He's in the hospital."

Fuck. "He gonna make it?"

"I hope so." The voice grew barbs. "We're trying to figure out if he's a victim or part of it."

"Jack's a straight-up guy."

"So we hear."

Christ. Jack had been in Chicago looking into Davis's firm. What were the chances of this shooting being unrelated?

"Did you catch the shooter?" Brent asked.

"Not yet. You have any information, we'd appreciate it, Mr. Carver."

"Sure thing." He hung up and dialed Jack's secretary, who was already at the hospital in Chicago. Jack was stable, but hadn't regained consciousness yet. He'd sideswiped a police cruiser and then thrown himself from a moving vehicle. The shooter had murdered the cop, shot Jack in the back, and run like a motherfucker.

Brent sat in his truck in the Walmart parking lot as a feeling of dread settled around him. What the hell was going on? Exactly who had Davis ripped off? People who killed cops weren't the sort you wanted on your tail. The stakes were getting higher, and slap-bang in the middle was the woman walking toward him with tired eyes and a worried expression. She climbed in, pushing the bags into the back.

Her smile faded. "What is it?"

He watched the way her lips parted and wished that was all he had to worry about—lusting after his best friend's daughter.

"Someone killed a cop last night. Same guy shot the PI I hired to check out your dad's firm."

"Is he OK?"

"He's alive."

Her pupils widened until her eyes were completely black except for a tiny rim of emerald. "I need to go back, don't I?"

"You could head to Tahiti or Australia. Take a year off." Fear and frustration ramped up the tension in the cab. The electricity that snapped between them shorted out his nerves.

"I can't run away from this forever," she said quietly.

He watched her for a long moment, his mouth so dry he could barely speak. "Then, yeah, we need to go back."

"We?" Sunlight glistened in her hair. "You're coming with me?"

He wanted to put his hand over hers. Knew it would be a mistake. He wasn't the touchy-feely type unless you counted sex, which seemed like a long-forgotten memory. But he kept his promises. Always. He put the car in gear and took Highway 4 to Nanaimo. "I promised Davis if anything ever happened to him, I'd look out for you."

"I don't need a babysitter."

"No, but something tells me you might need someone to watch your back before this is over. Right now, I'm it."

She crossed her arms over her chest, which unfortunately distracted him from his driving and he nearly ran a red light. He slammed on the brakes and they both lurched forward. Another example of weakness getting you killed. And Anna Silver might prove to be the biggest weakness of all.

"Do you want me to drive?" she asked, the whole schoolteacher vibe doing it for him in a big way.

He shifted uncomfortably. *Fuck*. It wasn't like he could admit the truth—that he'd been distracted by her pert breasts outlined in fresh cotton. *Nice, Carver*. She was fourteen years his junior and made driven snow look dirty. Sick bastard.

He cleared his throat. "We have to go to Victoria to pick up those travel documents I mentioned, and I asked my brother to get his fiancée to check your mother's house. See if the bastards are still there." He had a plan but he needed help. He just wished he could stash Anna somewhere nice and safe until it was all over. Trouble was, if they'd found him in his remote corner of the Pacific Rim, they could find her anywhere on the island. She had more chance with him than alone. And right now that was the only thing that mattered.

CHAPTER 7

Katherine couldn't see over Ed's shoulder. He had his camera glued to his eyeball and was in full paparazzi mode as he shoved his way to the front railing at the stern of the massive cruise ship. She shivered under the bleak sky and wished she'd worn socks and sneakers rather than sandals. She tried to inch her way forward as another rush of air signaled a whale had surfaced not far from the bow, but even when she danced on tiptoes her view was blocked by a solid wall of shoulders. Someone grabbed her arm and drew her in front of them next to the railing—Harvey.

"Thanks." She smiled up at him, surprised by the expression of joy on his face.

"You can't miss this." A sparkle lit his eyes.

Another whale broke the surface directly below them, so close Katherine couldn't control a shiver of pure awe that wracked her body. She held back her hair with one hand and stared, rapt.

"She's looking right at us," Harvey whispered in her ear.

"She?" Katherine questioned, unable to look away from that intelligent black gaze.

He laughed. "Looks too smart and sensible to be a male, but I'm no expert."

The brisk sea breeze numbed her skin, but she wouldn't have missed this for anything. She was grateful for Harvey's warmth at her back. The contact was innocent, but she knew Ed wouldn't approve. She frowned, gripping the railing tighter. Come to think of it, Ed didn't like her being friends with any man. He even had strong opinions about which women she spent time with. The vague feelings of disquiet about their relationship had been growing stronger lately, at times morphing into flat-out resentment. She wasn't the type of woman to cheat, so why treat her like she was? He'd been treating her that way for years, she realized. It had taken her a long time to notice because she'd been so emotionally shattered when they'd gotten married. She'd been desperate to hide from the world and avoid conflict of any kind.

It was a time she'd never have gotten through without Ed, but lately…

She shrugged it off. Davis's death had hit her a million times harder than she'd expected. She needed a little time to get her head back on straight, that was all.

A strong odor blasted her, and she pulled a face and turned with a raised eyebrow to Harvey.

"Not me," he told her with a laugh. "Whale breath. It was how the whalers knew there was a whale around, even in a thick fog."

"Ew."

"But worth it?" he probed intently.

She turned back to the enormous creature, so elegant and powerful. So magnificent and threatened. Their vulnerability suddenly made her sad. "Definitely worth it."

The whale disappeared, and then breached farther away from the ship—a thirty-four ton ballet dancer in all its glory. Water splashed up in great waves. The whale did it again and again, dazzling them with its exuberant glee.

Davis would have loved this. The thought made her heart hurt.

Katherine's eyes grew misty with wonder even as she shivered from bone-numbing cold. It was so beautiful. So majestic. They were so free and so hunted. She'd never given them much thought really, but now their plight called to her in a way it never had before. Harvey was jostled against her by the crowd. Her teeth chattered. He slipped off his jacket and draped it over her shoulders, the thick material holding his warmth and keeping the wind at bay.

"Thanks." She tugged it gratefully around her body.

A plume of water hissed about twenty yards to their right as the humpback once again moved closer. A sleek black back appeared, a small hump, and then the long smooth curve of shiny body. It seemed to move in slow motion, uncaring of the massive ship and the infinitesimal passengers. The tail fluke glided slowly up into the air and hung suspended for a moment before disappearing beneath the waves. Gone.

"Got it." She heard Ed shout with triumph.

She gazed helplessly after the whale, wondering why she suddenly felt so bereft.

The crowd continued to stare at the flat water, but the whale had moved on and after a few minutes people started to disperse. "Where's Barb?" she asked, turning slightly toward Harvey.

"Decided the shops were more exciting than the wildlife." His voice deepened, and there was an edge to it that suggested he was angry. She heard Ed calling her name and pressed her lips together. She should go. He hadn't seen her standing beside Harvey, and she was a little ashamed at how much she wanted to slink off in the opposite direction.

Just because she was in a mood didn't mean she should spoil his vacation. Ed worked hard and deserved a break.

Harvey watched her closely.

"I better go," she said, suddenly feeling awkward.

"Yeah." His eyes searched hers for something she couldn't name. "I'm going to stay here and see if our friend reappears."

She slid the jacket off her shoulders and handed it back. A weird gripping sensation took hold inside her chest. "I'd better go find Ed."

His expression went carefully blank. "Yes, of course."

She headed to where she'd seen her husband go inside the ship looking for her. At the doorway, she glanced back and Harvey was staring off over the pewter waters of Alaska's Inside Passage, lost deep in thought.

A stab of envy pierced her.

Harvey was doing exactly what she wanted to do. Spending some time alone, staring at the beauty of the ocean, and remembering a past she'd tried so hard to forget.

The sun was low on the horizon by the time Brent drove down a quiet street in an area of Victoria that Anna was unfamiliar with. He pulled into the parking lot. An elegant blue and gold sign above a leafy hedge declared the large square building RCMP headquarters.

"What are we doing here?" She gripped the dash as her mouth went dry. She didn't want to deal with the police any more than she'd wanted to deal with the disreputable-looking character who'd taken her photograph earlier and made her a false driver's license and passport. She especially didn't want to deal with cops with those falsified documents tucked in her purse.

A tall, good-looking guy opened the back door and climbed in, followed by a serious-faced woman in full cop regalia.

Anna turned to confront the newcomers. Her heart thudded. *Crap.*

Brent twisted in his seat and lifted an eyebrow. "I didn't realize this was going to be a family party."

"Stow it. She's already pissed at you for getting involved in a *situation*," the blond guy said without heat. The face had broadened and matured, but Anna recognized the boy from the photo. Brent's younger brother, Finn.

She started to defend Brent, but he silenced her by dropping a hand to her thigh. The touch sent a lightning shock of awareness through her system that left her mute.

"Who's coming after you?" the cop bit out. She looked pretty damn scary with her steely gaze and rigid air of authority. "I want them off the streets before you end up back inside."

"I don't know who it is." Brent pulled smoothly out of the parking lot and headed west, following signs for Douglas Street. "In case you're wondering, Anna, that's my brother Finn and his sweet fiancée, Holly Rudd, supercop." Brent introduced them grimly.

"Anna Silver?" Holly's sharp eyes assessed her.

"That's right." Anna hunched her shoulders, automatically defensive around the law.

"I spoke to the warden," said Holly. The cop hit Anna with the brightest gray eyes she'd ever seen. They were beautiful, but also clinically cold. Her wide mouth thinned. "I'm sorry about your father." If anything, her expression grew sterner. "But if whoever called the prison this morning is after you, and therefore Brent, I want to know why."

"I really don't know what's going on." Anna's stomach swirled uneasily. This was getting much bigger and more complicated than she wanted. What if her father had stolen that money? Now she was involving Brent's family? Cops? She shrank in her seat.

Holly raised unimpressed brows. "After Brent's call I sent two plainclothes officers to check out your mother's residence. No one was there."

Finn's mouth took on an uncompromising line.

Holly turned her attention to Brent. "Freddy Chastain has your place staked out. He doesn't have enough resources to cover the town, the logging road, and the house, especially with no tangible threat, so he concentrated on your cabin. He better not find anything out of order."

"He won't," said Brent mildly. Anna figured it was more for her benefit than Holly's. He knew she'd be worried about the handgun, but he must have concealed it, maybe even brought it with them in the truck. The thought made her hands start to shake.

"I'm so sorry for everything." This was not what she'd wanted when she'd gone to Brent for help. She shot him a glance, but he wasn't looking at her, he just gripped her thigh like he owned it and carried on driving. A slide of something sexual shimmered, just inches from his large warm hand. A warm wave of arousal that rushed over her body. *Where the heck had* that *come from?* Because she didn't lust after guys like Brent unless they were on the big screen and therefore safe—and that self-revelation sat like a lead ball in her stomach.

"Do you know who these people are or what they want from you?" Holly asked again.

The pressure on her leg increased a fraction. She swallowed hard as liquid desire hit dry, dusty erogenous zones. The timing sucked. What else was new?

"I, um, no." She squirmed in her seat. God, what was wrong with her? "After the police told me about my father's death, I received a voice mail message from him. He told me to get out of town, so I went to Brent's." As if they were old friends rather than complete strangers.

He doesn't feel like a stranger anymore.

No kidding.

"And your father claimed to have taken money from the charity he worked for because he thought someone was trying to steal it and set him up?" Holly had obviously listened to her father's 911 call, and her father's story sounded ridiculous even to Anna.

"If you know that, you know as much as I do." Except this supposed evidence he'd mailed to her. *Damn you, Papa.*

"US authorities aren't investigating the firm at this moment." Holly's voice was flint. "I spoke to Chicago PD, and they say they have no grounds except the word of an ex-con who stole money and then committed suicide rather than face his actions."

They'd reduced her father to less than nothing. Anna sank lower into the leather. "So what do you want from me?"

"Is this about money, Anna?"

"Leave her the hell alone," Brent snapped.

"Your daddy dies and you turn up on the island. Brent calls Finn for help for the first time in his life?" She gave her a flat cop stare. "I think you're not telling me everything I need to know, and if you get Brent involved in anything illegal, I will hang you out to dry."

A fierce sense of injustice rose up inside Anna. She hadn't done anything wrong, and yet this woman was attacking her like she was a criminal. She'd been here before and it reinforced all the reasons she'd kept her personal nightmares to herself. Brent's hand tightened on her thigh, almost bruising in intensity. She welcomed the pressure. It grounded her.

"You're making me wish I hadn't called you," Brent said dryly, looking at his brother in the rearview.

"You can't do everything alone, bro."

"Actually"—Brent's voice dropped two octaves and she felt it rumble through her bones—"I can."

"This could land you back in prison—" Holly began.

"We haven't done a damn thing wrong." Brent snarled.

"Stop it!" Anna pushed his hand aside. "I truly don't know what's going on. I don't even know if I'm really being followed or if anyone will turn up at Brent's house looking for me or if this is just some big misunderstanding or a hoax or someone trying to scare me. I don't know. But I do know I didn't ask for your help." There was a brief awkward silence when all she could hear was her own hoarse breathing. "This isn't Brent's problem. It's mine. I don't want to cause friction between you." She could only imagine the complexity of their relationship, given the circumstances.

They sat in silence for about three whole seconds.

Finn leaned forward between them. "You caught a live one, Brent."

Brent's fingers tightened on the steering wheel, but he held his silence.

Holly snorted. "She should have more sense than to get tangled up with the Carver boys. Unlike some people," she muttered darkly, and both Finn and Brent shot her a look.

They were passing Beacon Hill Park, heading toward mile zero on the Trans-Canada Highway. They waited for a horse and cart carrying tourists to pass on by and then turned down Niagara Street.

"It's just up ahead," Anna told Brent quietly. He pulled up a few houses away from where her mother and stepfather lived. It was gorgeous, all quiet and leafy in the heart of the old city. Deep shadows grew as the sun slid ever lower into the Pacific.

"You grew up here?" Finn asked.

"No." Their house in Fairfield had been repossessed. They'd been destitute after her father went to jail. Without Ed, Anna didn't know what would have happened to them. "We moved here when Mom and Ed got married. He was a widower."

They got out of the car. Holly took the lead heading down the side of the large Victorian, with its blue painted siding and red trim. There were balconies and even a widow's walk on the roof. It was a gorgeous heritage home. Anna had never been comfortable here though, and had spent as much time at her grandma's as possible.

No one was on the street. Everyone was probably eating dinner. "If the neighbors hear about any of this, my mom will die of mortification." Although maybe worrying about what other people thought shouldn't be such a big deal.

"We were discreet," Holly said. "I had someone come look for fingerprints on doorknobs and light switches to run through the system, but whoever was here cleaned up after themselves." Holly shot her a thoughtful look and slowed so Anna could lead the way.

Her heart pounded. This whole situation was beyond crazy. She kept wanting to close her eyes and pretend none of it was happening. Unfortunately, life didn't work like that.

She pulled her key out of her purse, opened the door, and stepped inside the cool interior of the house. The hallway was neat and spotless as always. She stood to one side as everyone traipsed inside. The house was quiet. Real quiet. She ran her hands across the dark oak paneling.

"Do you mind if I look around again?" Holly asked politely, poised on the balls of her feet. Since Anna's outburst, the cop's demeanor had softened considerably.

Anna didn't think it would matter much whether she minded or not. "Anything to get my life back."

Holly headed upstairs and Anna wandered into the formal living room and frowned. Everything gleamed. Not a speck of dust dared show its ugly face in this house. She rubbed her hands over her arms as goose bumps formed.

"What is it?" Brent asked quietly. The last rays of the sun shone through the windows at an oblique angle, highlighting the immaculately polished surfaces and sparkling glass.

She stared around at the leather chesterfield and the baby grand piano. "Something's different."

Brent stood beneath a huge portrait of Ed and her mom that hung over the fireplace. His expression twisted. "She didn't waste much time after your dad was arrested."

She shrugged. Her mother had needed someone to look after her. "We'd known Ed for a couple of years. Mom had been friends with his first wife and had helped them out when she was dying. I guess it felt natural to lean on him when it was her turn to need support." Once Ed had come into their lives, everything Anna had ever known had shifted on its axis. She'd grown up fast.

Brent pointed to graduation portraits on the piano. "You have a stepbrother?"

Revulsion spiked. "He was a year older than me in high school."

"I take it you two didn't get along?" he asked. The guy didn't miss much.

"Not really." She didn't look at the photo. "He lost his mom and then his dad got married soon afterward, it must have been hard for him." She'd always tried to put herself in his shoes even though they didn't fit.

"My heart bleeds."

Her lips curved into a reluctant smile. "He left for college soon after the wedding." She glanced at the stack of mail, almost sure someone had gone through it since she'd been here on Saturday morning. She fingered the edge of an envelope. "I haven't seen him in years. He works down in Seattle and we don't do the family get-together thing."

Brent was staring at her hard, but she refused to meet his gaze. Holly came back into the room, Finn at her back like flexible body armor. Anna watched them, intrigued.

What was it like to love someone like that? Like you'd die for them?

Her mouth went dry. The thump of her heart felt hollow. Ed doted on her mother, but he never let her think for herself. Finn and Holly were both obviously very independent people and yet they operated as a team. It wasn't something she'd observed before, but then she tended to surround herself with single people, and avoided the couples and family scene.

"See anything out of place? Any clues as to who these jokers may be?" Holly's eyes were sharp, but her tone was sympathetic.

"You do know who my father was, right?" Anna questioned suddenly.

Holly nodded and her eyes grew somber. "Kids aren't responsible for their parents' actions." Her gaze darted to Brent.

What did his father do? Abuse his wife? Abuse his children?

"I want you both in protective custody—just until we figure out what is going on," Holly finished.

Anna's mouth dropped open. Brent crossed his arms over his chest. Finn eyed his brother like he was going to tackle him.

"It won't be for long, just until we track these people down and find out what they are up to. You can stay at our new house, which isn't far away." She looked at Brent with a beady eye. "Which you promised to visit months ago."

Brent rolled his eyes. "Fine."

Finn relaxed. Then Brent squinted again at the horrible graduation portrait of her that her mother insisted stay on display. He moved his head to one side and back again, brows crunched together. "Is it my imagination or is that an impression of lips on Anna's photograph?"

The patina of the piano was a glossy black, the glass in the frame spotless, so that smudge was obvious with the angle of the fading light. Holly went over and peered closely. "Looks like someone kissed the glass."

Ice eased through Anna's veins.

Holly pointed at the faint imprint. "How likely is that to be the person we're looking for as opposed to your mother?"

She choked out a laugh. "My mother and Ed are OCD when it comes to cleaning. No way would either of them leave a smudge on the glass."

"Can I take it for evidence? Just in case?" A spark of excitement lit Holly's gaze as she pulled out her cell.

"Burn it, for all I care." Anna nodded. Shivers laced through her spine and her teeth started to chatter. Who would kiss her photo? Why?

Warm hands closed over her shoulders. "I'm going to take Anna outside. She looks green."

Holly nodded absently. Finn watched them through narrowed eyes.

Anna found herself maneuvered out the front door. Brent closed it softly and then started jogging away from her.

"What's going on?" she asked as she chased after him.

"No way is anyone locking me up. And I'm not real good at relying on others to solve my problems for me."

And that's what she was, a problem.

They were at his truck and he opened the door. "Stay here. Finn and Holly will take good care of you."

Anna's hands closed around the door handle and she climbed in beside him. The idea of sitting around doing nothing while he put himself in danger and searched for answers made her nauseous. "He was my father. I'm the one who got you involved in all of this. I'm not letting you take all the risks."

Brent pulled away from the curb just as Finn sprinted down the driveway. Anna closed her eyes against the fury in Finn's eyes. The last thing she'd wanted was to cause division between Brent and his brother because she was pretty sure, now her father was dead, Finn was the only person in the world Brent had left.

Rand stood in the woods and eyed the huge log cabin with envy. *This* was the sort of lifestyle he was after. Not some apartment in the Windy City, staring down drug dealers and gangbangers. Just as soon as he got his money back, he was gone.

Good choice of hideout, Ms. Silver. Luxurious and remote.

Getting here had been an adventure, but this was the end of the line and there was nowhere left to run. Fog hid the moon, drifting over the canopy of the trees with ghostly threads. It was quiet in the bush—so quiet even the sound of his own breathing seemed loud, although he knew no one else would be able to hear it. He held his sidearm down by his thigh as he watched the back door from the woods. He and Marco had waited for over an hour—caution and darkness their best allies for an attack. The sun had finally dropped below the horizon, leaving a thick, dense absence of light surrounding them.

He wore camouflage and had night vision goggles—overkill for tackling two civilians, but Rand went with what worked for him. He wasn't screwing this up, not with Kudrow and the General both frothing at the mouth for whatever information the girl had, and time running out.

Since the last US administration change, General Browning had not only done black-op jobs for the government, but also a little freelance work on the side. For four years they'd been running a clandestine mercenary operation, using the charity as a front to hide their activities and a means to launder their money before funneling it to offshore accounts. Davis had stumbled across them moving the latest payment from a Saudi sheikh who'd asked them to do a little destabilization work in Yemen. Didn't take much to spark a fire in that tinderbox.

Rand wanted that money back. Damned if anyone was taking what was rightfully his.

But Anna Silver couldn't get killed in the cross fire. They needed her alive until after they got those account numbers, and he had plans for her. The idea had had him hard as rock all day.

Over the years he'd found the least willing women were usually the most fun. Sometimes Marco joined the party. Sometimes he hunted alone. It all depended on how Rand was feeling and whether or not he was in the mood to share. He hadn't decided whether to share Anna or not, yet.

Marco had circled around to the side of the property that faced the sea, skirting the shoreline. Rand waited for his all-clear signal. There was a light on upstairs, but no activity around the house for the last thirty minutes. It was only 8:00 p.m. but with the fog it felt later. Much later. Maybe they'd gone to bed. Maybe the prick was fucking her right now.

He almost stepped forward, actually raised one foot. Then a rustle in front of him and off to his left had him freezing in place, and melting to the forest floor. What was that? A bear? A squirrel? He turned very slowly and spotted a figure lying prone in the trees. Black fatigues. Assault rifle. WTF? Suddenly he was aware of potential eyes all around him.

Cop? Spec Ops?

Shit, this was an ambush? Anger screamed through his bloodstream.

He wanted to warn Marco, but first he needed to gain a little breathing space. He faded back through the forest, carefully checking others weren't close by. He approached the figure silently from behind. The guy was focused front and center and never heard him coming. Rand snapped his neck with a barely audible crack. He took the earpiece out of the dead man's ear. Listened in as others moved into position. Clicked his own comms rapidly to get Marco's attention, but it was too late. Lights flooded the area and Marco started shooting. He watched his man take a bullet even as Rand slipped back into the shadows and away from the action.

He hit the other side of the road and arrowed south through thick forest, then into the water before adrenaline stopped beating the fuck out of his heart. Slogging across the narrow inlet in full gear kept the fury building. The cops had been expecting them. Someone had tipped them off. The warden, maybe. Or Anna Silver had gone to the cops from the get-go and fed him a thin trail of crumbs. Setting him up.

The water was cold. Clothes heavy. Weapons waterlogged. He didn't remember the last time he'd had to work this hard to find his quarry. *Bitch.*

And now Marco was shot and captured, and chances were they'd know he had an accomplice. Anger seared his veins.

She'd made him look stupid. *Shit. Fucking shit.* He couldn't believe this. He sluiced water out of his hair and pounded through the waist-high seawater up onto the shore, intent on putting as much distance between him and Carver's house as possible. The throb of helicopter rotors punched the air. He set his jaw.

How many cops were out there? Had they found their dead buddy yet?

The whole op was a total clusterfuck.

He and Marco had stolen a truck to drive to Bamfield. Switched plates in the metropolis of Port Alberni. They'd left their belongings in a hotel room in Victoria and he needed to retrieve them before Marco was identified. Identifying him wouldn't be simple because their prints were not on file—unless Marco wasn't dead and tried to make a deal. *Fuck. Fuck. Fuck.* He couldn't believe a schoolteacher had done this to him. He jogged onward along the road, ready to dive into the bush if a car came. About three miles out of town, he spotted a house up ahead, to one side and buried in the woods. He slowed. Secluded. He figured he wasn't far from the logging road that led south. There was a car in the driveway. He could steal it, but it would get reported too damn fast and they might be able to set up a roadblock and trap him on the road out.

A dead cop meant there'd be a roadblock all right.

A redheaded woman crossed the window, serving a plate of food to a man as he sat at the table. Rand's stomach growled.

Rage contracted down to a fine point as he considered his options. His heartbeat slowed. Focus was what had kept him alive in more situations than he wanted to count. He watched the house as the man and woman ate their meal. He even let her clear the dishes. Then the guy started pulling on a jacket.

Rand pulled his ski mask over his face. Gripped his pistol and wondered if they had beer. He sure as hell could do with a beer right about now, though he couldn't risk dulling his senses.

The guy headed outside and Rand slipped behind him as he opened the car door. He hit him with the pistol and the man dropped like a rock. Rand dragged him over rough gravel into the bushes, then tied his wrists and ankles with fishing twine from a rod and reel propped on the deck. He stripped off one of the man's socks and stuffed it in his mouth, and wrapped twine repeatedly around his head until he was confident the poor sap wasn't going to be making any noise. Then he hitched him between two trees. This sucker wasn't going anywhere without help. Hell, he should be thankful he hadn't just slit his throat. A cold smile played the corner of his mouth as he turned back to the cabin. His breath was hot and tight in his lungs. He walked up the steps and quietly opened the door. Warm air hit him with a welcome blast against his damp clothes. The place was shabby and rustic, but comfortable. It felt safe.

He turned the lock as the woman called, "You were quick. What did you forget?"

She came out of the bedroom all smiles and rosy pink cheeks. He raised the gun. It was useless, but she didn't know that. She stopped dead and lost all color. Her eyes darted to the window.

"He's not going to be able to help you."

Her eyes widened and then flashed with anger. "What did you do to him?" She took a step toward him and raised her hand as if to strike him.

He slapped her hard and she hit the ground. He liked the sight of her down there, a lot. Anger morphed into something else. Something primal and ruthless. Ancient and animalistic. He dropped to his haunches, lowered his voice. The imprint of his hand was stark red on her milk-white flesh. "Where are your car keys?"

Her eyes flashed to the key rack. "Over there. Just take it and get out."

Little bitch. He grabbed her by the hair and twisted her around so she was bent up in an uncomfortable arch and had to grab onto his wet shirt for balance. He could feel the revulsion in her touch even as she defied him, but he knew how to break her.

"Where's the bedroom?"

She started punching him and he slapped her so hard her head bounced off the linoleum.

"We can do this the hard way or the easy way," he told her, because he *was* doing this even though he didn't have much time, just to ease the pressure in his balls and siphon off the fury that pounded his blood. "If we do it the easy way, your old man need never even know." He held her gaze, and understanding filtered through the confusion and fear.

First, her husband wasn't already dead. Second, she wasn't getting a choice in this and fighting would just make it worse. The emotion leaching from her gaze was fascinating to watch, but Rand didn't have time for any long-term observations. She nodded slowly and climbed jerkily to her feet. He gripped her wrist as she led the way to the bedroom, although she panicked at the doorway with the bed just feet away.

He subdued her easily and dropped her to the floor. He started peeling off his wet clothes, thankful to be out of them. Taking an extra five minutes wouldn't harm his escape plans and right now his dick was so hard it felt like a lead weight between his legs. He pulled her up, pushed her on the bed, and dragged her jeans down to her ankles. She thrashed and he smacked her again, dazing her with the impact. "Keep still."

Finally, she lay unmoving and he did what he needed to do. When he was finished, he pulled on her husband's dry clothes that were too short for him in the arms and legs, but at least were dry. He made her get dressed and forced her into the car at gunpoint. "You and I are going for a drive. If the cops stop you, I'm your brother visiting from Victoria and you're driving me home. If you do anything to raise their suspicions, I will kill them, and then I will strip you naked and make what just happened look like a fucking romantic comedy. Understand?"

Her eyes were bleak as she nodded at him. She started the car and turned onto the main road.

Yep, he sure as hell knew how to break them, but he was pissed this was just some redheaded stranger rather than the brunette he was chasing. He didn't like anyone jerking his chain and he really didn't like people shooting his buddies.

CHAPTER 8

Sitting in the passenger seat of Brent's truck, Anna had her knees drawn up to her chin, the neat denim skirt pulled tight over her legs. He liked the girly clothes she wore, not that it was any of his damned business.

"How do you know Holly won't stop us getting on a plane?" She bit her bottom lip and he had to drag his eyes back to the road.

"She might go to the airport, but she won't risk anything that might put me back inside because that would not go down well with her fiancée. Not that she wouldn't bust my ass if she found out I broke the law," he added. He'd made a few calls when they'd been getting Anna's "other" passport. "But that won't matter, because we aren't leaving through the usual channels." And he was pretty sure Finn would know that. He'd hurt his brother by rejecting his plans to help, but he'd spent a lifetime not trusting others and wasn't about to change now, even though part of him wanted to. But he couldn't do it. Not even for a brother whose unfailing loyalty he'd done nothing to earn and didn't deserve.

In darkness, the inner harbor was lit up like a Christmas tree. They'd taken a quick detour to Brent's agent's Victoria offices to collect his travel documentation, and although the guy hadn't been there, his secretary had been ecstatic to help him with all the paperwork he'd needed done on short notice. Brent drove to the wharf and saw Anna's surprise when he pulled into a parking space and cut the engine. He hoisted the bag of goodies she'd picked up that morning out of the backseat.

"Let's go."

The place was still bustling with tourist frenzy. Too many people. Too much noise. He blocked it out. Concentrated on Anna. Her scent. Her smile. Keeping her safe.

She followed him, somewhat hesitantly.

He didn't blame her. The situation was fucked up. Cop-killing bad guys had tracked them down after he'd assured her they couldn't, and he'd just ditched the one offer of protection she'd had. Maybe it wasn't such a great idea, going back to the scene of the crime, but it was the last place anyone would expect them to turn up. And hell, he needed to figure out where Davis had mailed this evidence, needed to talk to Jack Panetti if and when he woke up. Jack must have been pushing someone's buttons. He needed to figure out whose.

When Holly connected the dead cop in Chicago to Davis—which she would sooner or later—there was no way she'd let him or Anna out of her sight. He'd be eating, sleeping, and dreaming Mounties. And no one was locking him up—not even for his own good.

They strode along the wharf, past the million-dollar boats in their prime berths, toward the jetties where the floatplanes bobbed incongruously on the water. They passed a city cop patrolling the wharf, and Brent tugged Anna closer and rested his arm across her shoulders. He shortened his stride so she wasn't forced to rush to keep up. Her muscles felt rigid as tempered steel.

"Relax," he breathed into her hair. A strand caught on his lips and he had to force himself to move his head away and not just stand there inhaling her scent like a fool.

Brent led her to where a bright red seaplane was tied to the end of a short pier. The pilot stood at the end of a gangplank, his eyes licking at Anna like candy. Brent's fingers tightened on her shoulder and then he let go. She wasn't his. But she was his best friend's daughter in one hell of a mess, and deserved to be treated with respect.

He nodded to the other man. It had been a few years.

"Never thought I'd see the day you left the island, Carver." There was a lingering touch of Australian in his accent.

"You sure this piece of shit flies?"

The pilot aimed a grin at Anna, though anger shimmered in his eyes. "Charming as ever, I see." He held out his hand to shake Anna's. "And who might you be?"

Brent laid a cautionary hand on Anna's lower back as she shook the pilot's hand. "Nice to meet you," was all she said. He tried to figure out when he and Anna had learned this silent form of communication. The fact he couldn't keep his hands off her even in the most innocent of situations told him he was in trouble, but thankfully she was sensible enough for both of them.

The pilot gripped her small pale hand for an extra second. "You're here because you want to be here, right? This guy isn't abducting you?" His eyes were worried.

Brent took his hands off Anna and turned his back on them both. *Sonofabitch.*

"I wouldn't say I want to be here, but Brent's helping me," Anna said softly.

He whirled back to face them. "Ready now, or you want me to pass a lie detector test before you let me on board?"

"Hey, I'm just trying to do the right thing, mate."

Brent rolled his eyes. He didn't want small talk or questions or reminders of the sort of man he'd once been. Although he'd never once gone after the little guy. Nor had he ever touched a woman in anger. But you didn't spout your weaknesses to people who might use them against you.

"Just need to finish the preflight inspection and we're good to go."

They climbed aboard, stowed what luggage they had, and sat in the bright red leather seats. Brent secured his harness, leaned back his head, and stared up at the ceiling of the small tin box they were about to take to the skies in. Every muscle in his body tensed and his hands gripped the end of the armrests so tight it hurt.

"Is this the first time you've flown?" Anna asked quietly.

He jolted at the sound of her voice, wishing the taste in his mouth wasn't fear. "Never went anywhere as a kid and didn't want to explore once I got out." Or maybe he was just too chickenshit to face the world. He sat up straighter. He didn't like that option.

"Do you trust him?" Anna leaned past him and tried to catch sight of the pilot outside.

Brent shrugged the stiffness out of his shoulders. "I'm paying him good money and he'd think twice before he crossed me. That's as much as I trust anyone."

"Are most people scared of you?" Anna's eyes were wide, but he couldn't read them.

In prison, he'd specialized in keeping out of trouble by being a hard-ass. It had kept him alive. "Sixteen-year-olds who kill their fathers are given a wide berth even in prison." The words had their usual bitter aftertaste.

Bright green eyes bored into him. "You loved him, didn't you?"

He felt like she'd shot him in the stomach. *Christ.* "Yeah," he admitted grudgingly, "I loved him."

"So why did you kill him? What did he do to you?"

He shrugged.

Her expression turned hurt before it turned angry. He grabbed her hands to hold them still and blew out a big breath, giving up the battle to keep it all a secret. Who gave a shit anyway? It didn't change anything, and if anyone deserved the truth it was Anna.

"It wasn't me. Not that night," he spat it out as if it were a curse.

"Your brother then," Anna guessed.

Blood chilled in his veins from the memories. The idea of striking a child was shocking to most, but it had been commonplace when he'd been growing up. Even now it hurt to think about what his brother had endured. "When I was little, things were OK, but then Dad lost his job driving logging trucks and started drinking heavily. He started hitting Mom and I couldn't stop him."

"But she left you there with him...?" She sounded incredulous.

"He didn't hit Finn or me until after she ran away. I don't think she'd have left us if she'd known what was gonna happen." Maybe that's just what he liked to think, and he hadn't realized he was still that naive. "She did what she had to, to survive. It's what we all did."

"No one ever tried to help?"

"People weren't so up on issues of child abuse or domestic violence back then. Plus, people liked my dad. Me and Finn were both a bit wild." He had tried to ask for help once and got told to stop telling tales. That miserable bitch still ran the post office.

"So the night you killed your father, he was assaulting Finn?" She searched his face. She had the kindest, greenest eyes. The softest looking mouth he'd ever seen. *Christ. Don't think about her mouth.*

Cold sweat broke out over his back. He started talking. "After Mom left, the sonofabitch transferred all the hate to Finn, and if I got in the way, he'd dish me up some fun times too. I'll never forget the first time he punched me—felt like I'd run smack-bang into a Douglas fir." His voice dropped. Hell, he didn't want to drag all these memories back to the surface, but maybe it would be enough to take his mind off the thought of flying and be enough to let her trust him. They were going to have to trust each other now to get out of this situation alive.

"Usually we got out of the cabin Friday and Saturday nights because that's when he drank. We'd sneak home after he'd collapsed somewhere unconscious. For years we had it down to a fine art, but then I started dating Gina and wasn't watching out for Finn the way I should have been." He gave a bitter laugh. "Discovering sex short-circuited my brain." *Christ.* If only he'd known. "Finn must have fallen asleep watching TV and Dad caught him. I walked in just as Finn told him to go fuck himself." Thirteen years old and the kid had already been broken and bleeding. "You wouldn't know it from looking at Finn now but back then, he was a hundred-pound weakling. Our daddy was more your brick shithouse variety." Brent had inherited his height. He shook his head remembering the screams, and the even more shocking silence. "I thought Dad had killed him for sure that time, so I picked up a bottle—I was big for my age, and a hell of a baseball player—and hit him over the head to make him stop. Just once, but it was enough." The carnage from that night was forever imprinted on his senses.

Anna sat frozen, but he didn't look at her. "I knew I'd hurt him, but he didn't want me to leave him. Made me hold his hand until..." He flexed his fingers and she took his hand in hers.

Saliva pooled in his mouth. His insides were already wobbly at the thought of flying—now he felt like he was about to throw up. "Finn was too beat up to go for help, so I just held Dad until he stopped breathing, and then I carried Finn to the Coast Guard station and waited for the cops to arrive." He let go of her hand and jammed his fingers into his hair. "I was drenched in his blood. Looked like something out of a slaughterhouse. Finn was airlifted to the hospital and I was hauled off to jail."

"It sounds like self-defense." She sounded angry on his behalf. Some people had been. But not the jury or the judge.

"Prosecution said otherwise. Dad rarely hit me." He slanted her a look. "Usually he couldn't catch me. I didn't lie about any of it on the stand."

"How could you love a man like that?" she asked quietly.

Brent tried to swallow but couldn't. If there was any real shame in his life it was this. It felt like a betrayal of his mother's and brother's pain. "When he was sober, he treated me like his best buddy.

He taught me how to fish, how to drive a car and a boat." Maybe he hadn't loved his father, maybe he'd just loved the memory of the man he'd once been.

Something moved in her eyes. Some shadow of pain that jolted him.

"Anyway, unless you start thrashing kids with rebar, you're probably safe from my dark side." A flash of horror swept over her features, followed by pity, which pissed him off. To counter it he let all the sexual heat he'd been feeling since he'd met her show as he slowly dropped his gaze to her mouth. "But I can't promise anything else." Because he was done pretending the awareness that had simmered between them didn't exist.

She didn't look away like he expected. She held his gaze, searching his eyes for something he didn't understand. And when she finally did look away, he felt hollow and a little bit lost.

After hours of traveling on two different aircraft, Anna handed over her new fake passport to the hotel receptionist in Chicago. Hannah Sylvester. Not so very different from her real name, but Brent said it should be enough to slow them down on computer searches—whoever the hell *they* were—especially if they weren't expecting her to come back to the scene of the crime. They were staying at a pretty fancy hotel. Big marble entrance with a dandy waterfall in the center.

The clerk took a quick look at her face and typed rapidly into her computer. It was 3:00 a.m. and Anna was barely conscious. "We have a suite reserved for Mr. Smith." The woman glanced at Brent, who sat in the foyer wearing a bulky Chicago Bears sweatshirt they'd picked up at the airport, black ball cap pulled low, lips sucked in, eyes hidden behind massive black glasses—the sort blind people wore.

Her heart hammered as she handed over a credit card in B.C. Wilkinson's name—he was incorporated—and signed as his new personal assistant who'd been authorized via his agent the previous day. The different identities didn't faze the receptionist. Apparently the rich and famous often traveled under assumed names and got damn good service.

"I hope you enjoy your stay." The woman handed back her documents and Anna slipped them into her purse. Her palms were damp, despite the AC being set to "morgue."

She walked back to Brent, grabbed his steely arm, and helped him to his feet.

"Tell me again this isn't illegal?" she hissed.

"A misdemeanor at worst," he whispered back.

Blood drained from her face. "I shouldn't have got you involved. If we're not careful, this whole disaster will get you locked up."

He cleared his throat. "Technically, *I'm* not the one traveling under a false identity." He grinned suddenly and she caught his eye over the glasses as they strolled toward the elevators.

"Oh, crap." Her career flashed before her eyes. Although she understood the necessity of deception if she wanted to find out the truth behind her father's death, she wasn't good at this. She was good at teaching kids math and penmanship, and how to resolve conflict without violence. She was still holding Brent's arm when they got inside the elevator, thankfully alone. Awareness prickled her skin and she went to withdraw her hand, but Brent caught her fingers and trapped them on his arm.

"Cameras," he mouthed.

She hung her head. There were butterflies in her stomach, a swirl of fear and attraction that left her feeling sick and dizzy. The elevator stopped and they got out. Slowly. She bit her lip in frustration as they walked unhurriedly along the corridor toward their suite. She wanted to rush Brent inside, but he was exhibiting a patience beyond her.

It took three attempts to get the keycard in the slot and by then the bellhop was there with the luggage they'd picked up in the airport. She gritted her teeth at the need to put on this calm, cool charade, but they didn't want to draw unwanted attention to themselves. They needed to be able to walk around Chicago in relative anonymity with a safe place to hide out if necessary. The whole stupid situation was getting to her, and she just wanted to go home and get on with her life.

Her father had said she'd know where he sent the evidence, so why didn't she? What if he'd accidentally sent it to the wrong address? What if the post office lost it? She could be doing this evasion dance for years.

No way.

Brent pulled her inside the sitting room of the suite, his arm warm against her side.

"Could be worse," he whispered in her ear. "We could have been forced to share a twin bed at the Motel Eight."

An unexpected curl of desire threaded its way through her body but she ignored it. Smiled sweetly. "But then people might say I slept my way into the job and we couldn't have that sullying your brilliant reputation, now could we?"

He pushed the blind-man's specs back up that perfect blade of a nose. "I could cope with a little sullying," he muttered irritably.

She helped him rather forcibly onto the couch. Ignored his grunt of protest as she turned and tipped the bellhop and ushered him out of the room. Then she locked the door and leaned against its cool surface as Brent ripped off the glasses, hat, and sweatshirt.

"Motherfucker was hot."

She gave him a long look. Wished he wasn't so rough, ready, and unexpectedly honorable. "You curse too much."

"Yes, ma'am." He ran a hand through his hair. His face was pale. He looked tired.

She softened. Damn, she felt like the Arctic, defrosting a little more each day.

On paper his background was vicious. Awful. Even knowing the reasons behind why he'd killed his father didn't change the fact he'd only survived prison by being one of the toughest men in an arena that bred violence. None of these facts went together with the man who was going out of his way to protect her. He'd killed, but didn't seem cruel. Was reclusive and hated to travel, and yet had come all the way to Chicago to help her. He was a complicated man who'd shown her nothing but consideration and deference since this whole thing started. She didn't know what that made him, but it definitely wasn't a monster.

She knew monsters.

He had hidden depths—unexpected pockets of kindness, compassion, and humor. And he worried her because he was astute enough to figure out her secrets. Considering she'd pushed and prodded him until he'd told her about the night his father died, she didn't know if she was entitled to secrets anymore. But she'd spent years pretending the events of the night of her high school prom had never happened. It was almost impossible to just bring them up and blurt them out.

Despite her fatigue, she paced the floor.

Brent's dim and distant past was irrelevant. She was more worried about his future in this dangerous game they'd started playing. "I should call the morgue."

"I should check on Jack Panetti's condition."

The shooting freaked her out. These people definitely meant business. Why the hell had her father moved—or stolen—their money? Why hadn't he just gone to the cops? But she knew why. He was an ex-con. They wouldn't have believed him.

"Do you think we should go to the hospital?" she asked.

"Yeah, but let's get some rest first." She watched him unwind that hard-toned body. "Remind someone to shoot me before I get old, huh?"

"That might not be a problem." God, had she really dragged him into this mess? She stared at him with wide eyes.

"It was a joke." He squinted at her with concern. "Hey, I was kidding."

She swallowed and nodded. But suddenly *that* wasn't the problem. He was the problem. His eyes sizzled. He moved like liquid sin. One hundred percent unadulterated alpha male. Tall, dirty blond, and deadly. Every time that brooding, grim face broke into a smile, her knees gave way.

What was happening to her? She hadn't felt this gritty sort of lust since she was sixteen. She crossed her arms over her traitorous breasts. Crap. Why was she feeling it now? A woman with her history? Hiding out from killers? With a man who'd spent twenty years in prison?

She sure could pick 'em.

He took a step toward her and she backed up, tripping. He froze.

"Anna." Even the way he said her name was sexy, and she didn't think he did it on purpose. He frowned fiercely. "You don't need to worry. Relax, I'm not going to attack you."

The words brought a vivid memory to life. She swayed on her feet and he reached out to catch her. The rapid beat of her heart and jagged timbre of her breath reminded her about the power of flashbacks, and though they'd faded over time, they never completely disappeared. His hands were big and comforting on her shoulders.

"What is it?" He sounded confused as he led her to the sofa.

No wonder.

Where was the smart capable woman she'd grown into? Where was the heart of steel that had gotten her through every day? Acting like the idiot girl she'd once been was humiliating, pathetic, and she didn't want to be pathetic anymore.

"I just got a little dizzy, that's all."

She could tell he knew she was lying. He thought he knew everything about her. She saw the exact moment he figured out he was wrong.

"I don't want to talk about it." She didn't like the edge of desperation that tightened her vocal cords.

He clenched his jaw, relenting even though she'd pushed him for his secrets. His bangs fell in his eyes and he dragged his hair back with impatient fingers. "Where are those scissors? This hair is driving me bug-ass crazy."

Changing the subject and letting her breathe. A warmth filled her that had nothing to do with lust or fear. He was a good man. No wonder her father had loved him.

He went and pulled out his overnight kit—in a plastic bag of supplies she'd bought from the airport. Then he brandished an electric razor. "I *could* go bald."

"Don't you dare." He was joking. She hoped.

He grabbed the scissors instead and walked into the bathroom, picked up a blond lock of hair, and snipped. "Why not?" He snipped again.

Anna shook her head. "Give me the scissors."

He held them out of her reach. "I don't know about that. Last time anyone cut my hair…" His voice halted as his brain caught up with the memory.

"Gina?" Anna hated the expression of grief and loss that moved over his features. This man deserved peace, not to be dragged into a situation with people who had no qualms about killing. He had too much to lose—but so did she. Her only other option was to go to the cops and she didn't trust them.

She took the scissors out of his hands and circled him awkwardly.

He sat on the toilet lid. Caught her wrist. "You ever done this before?"

She shook her head.

"Just don't hit an artery, we'll be fine." His humor was unexpected and her tension eased.

He released her and she edged closer, trying not to touch him with her body as she picked up that first lock of hair. It was soft and slid between her fingers like a ribbon of silk. She snipped. Tentatively to begin with, she took a good three inches off the length until it was short and spiky on top. He looked silly with the sides still long and she smothered a laugh.

Brent eyed her narrowly. "You won't be laughing when it's your turn." His eyebrow quirked.

"Over my dead body."

"That's what we're trying to avoid."

She touched her hair. The idea of cutting it off made her feel physically ill. "It would feel like a loss of identity." She sucked in a breath as his eyes slowly met hers. She read the understanding in their depths, and shame welled up inside her. Prison had stripped him of his identity. It had stripped her father of his identity too. She hadn't had a clue how difficult it must have been until now—she'd been too busy feeling sorry for herself.

"I'll wear a hat to start with, but I will cut it or dye it if you think I need to." She held his gaze for another moment before he closed his eyes with a nod.

Such a sign of trust that she felt a little shift in the region of her chest. Her hips brushed his side, intimately familiar in this small space. She held rigid for a moment and then got over herself. She wanted to do a good job, didn't want him to look stupid or be humiliated. He'd been there many times, and Anna was damned if a simple haircut would take him there again.

When she was done he scrubbed his hands over his head and neck, getting rid of stray hairs. "Not bad for your first time."

It was seductively ruffled, darker at the roots but still with those sun-bleached tips—he could have walked straight off a modeling job.

"We're not going to be able to walk around unnoticed," she realized suddenly.

He grinned and she banged her elbow on the wall. "Because I'm such a handsome fuc—" he cut himself off. "Devil," he finished with a grimace.

He was kidding *and* trying to watch his language. *A double whammy.* Warm feelings bombarded her, leaving her feeling helpless. But she was serious. He was too big and too gorgeous to pass by unnoticed. "You need to wear a wig."

"No fu-rickin' way." He stood and bumped into her.

Her knees hit the edge of the tub and crumpled.

"Whoa." He steadied and turned her so her back was to the wall.

Every particle of oxygen disappeared from the tiny room. His eyes glowed. The heat of his hands on her arms was a searing brand that sizzled along her nerves like a solar flare. Her lips parted and his gaze dropped to her mouth. She trembled as he moved closer. The whole world seemed to hold suspended in time. Brent's eyes darkened and his nostrils flared. His hand tightened for a split second before he dipped his head and kissed her, softly. The wall at her back stopped her from falling over in shock.

His lips were warm and firm. The kiss a cross between Prince Charming reverence and Indiana Jones adventure. He didn't close the gap or invade her space. Just stroked his lips over hers while gently holding her upright. No full frontal assault. No hello-happy-to-meet-you erection jammed against her stomach.

It was a beautiful kiss. Sweet. Possibly the most perfect moment of her life.

He pulled back, looking as stunned as she felt. Her heart pounded as they stared into one another's eyes.

Oh.

God.

She touched her mouth.

She'd kissed him. A man just as dark and tortured as her father had ever been. Worse, she had the awful feeling she could do a lot more to Brent Carver if she let herself.

It wasn't fear of physical assault that scared her anymore. It was the emotional pull she felt toward him, the knowledge that she *could* fall for him and she didn't want to. Love was an emotion she didn't trust, and although sex was a million miles from love, she couldn't risk it. She couldn't risk dropping her armor just to satisfy a physical urge. Because something about this man spoke to her on a level she hadn't even known existed until he'd kissed her.

"Let me go," she whispered.

He released her and his face went white. "Anna, I'm sorry—"

But she wasn't listening. She raced out of the bathroom, into her bedroom, and slammed the door.

He let her go.

CHAPTER 9

Brent and Anna sat outside Davis's redbrick apartment building in the sedan he'd rented. A nearby YMCA and a midsize supermarket provided enough general traffic that no one noticed them sitting there waiting. He and Anna had spent the morning scoping out the office building where Davis had worked, and then they'd visited the site of his death. Brent had stood staring at the tracks, feeling ill as the trains had rushed headlong through the tunnels, passengers streaming on and off at the stop, going about their normal lives, unaware that a man had died there just a few short days ago. Anna had been very quiet, contemplative, ever since.

In the afternoon they'd stopped by the hospital but there were too many cops to even risk getting close to Jack Panetti and, according to Jack's secretary, the guy was still in a coma. They'd each checked their e-mail in an Internet café downtown. His agent was still driving him bat-shit about this exhibition. He'd told him he'd be there. The guy would just have to trust him. After a few hours' rest at the hotel, where both he and Anna had retired to separate rooms, they were back in enforced confinement, staking out Davis's building. He cracked his window, swapping the plastic new car smell for the taint of exhaust fumes. He was hyperaware of the thud of his heart. Of the flow of traffic. Of the quiet tick of Anna's wristwatch in the thick, strained silence. His stomach growled. Breakfast had been a rapid affair of festering indigestion and they'd skipped lunch, too raw to even think about food.

This was why he didn't do people.

Kissing Anna? He was such a damn fool. A woman so wrong for him on so many levels it wasn't even funny. So what if she'd tasted right? They weren't compatible in any way except the horizontal.

And now he was thinking about them in bed together and his jeans were so tight he was sure every drop of blood had diverted south. If it were just sex, it wouldn't be a problem. He could definitely do uncomplicated sex, but everything about Anna screamed *complication.*

It was obvious she had issues. He'd seen it in her eyes last night when she'd stumbled away from him in a panic and pretended to be dizzy. Hell, he'd recognized the lies before they'd even left her tongue. But he'd let her get away with the "I don't want to talk about it" bullshit because she'd looked fragile enough to break.

Something bad had happened to her at some point, but he hadn't pushed. He desperately wanted to know everything there was to know about Anna Silver, the same way he'd craved her letters when he'd been stuck in that hellhole. But he understood the need for privacy—hell, he craved privacy. It wasn't his business. But more than curiosity burned along his nerves.

Which left the concept of "just sex" six hundred feet up in the air.

It was dark. Streetlights glowed on the charcoal tarmac. Red brick turned into burnt orange. The temperature had ramped up and a storm was building. It was hot, humid, and oppressive, and reminded him so much of prison he was half choking on city smog and memories.

He hated the city. Could feel the walls touching the edges of his soul.

He slid a glance at her profile. Sweet. Beautiful. Not for the likes him. He'd destroy her, the same way he'd destroyed Gina. It was never going to happen.

Although, the idea Anna might be genuinely interested in him was laughable. He wasn't just an ex-con, he was a *lifer*, a murderer. Sure, women liked the outer package. He'd have to be blind not to notice the way women looked at him. But he knew better than anyone that beauty came from within. And he sure as hell wasn't beautiful on the inside. He was a dark mess of seething anger and pressurized fear.

The anger he'd harnessed. The fear he buried deep so he wouldn't get destroyed.

A car drove by and pulled up around the corner. They both tensed and then relaxed again as a mom and two kids trailed out. No one else appeared to be watching the complex, but Brent believed in being extra careful where Anna was concerned. Usually he pushed people away, but they were stuck in this mess together until they found whatever it was Davis had sent her, and he couldn't afford to piss her off. She was prickly enough to go off on her own, and he'd never forgive himself if she got hurt. Memories of Gina tried to rush him again, but he refused to let them in. Maybe if he could keep Anna safe, it would grant him a little redemption for failing Gina so terribly.

"Let's go," she said.

"Not yet."

She pushed open her door and he rolled his eyes. No patience. It had taken him five years in hell to learn patience, and it was a gift he took from his time in prison. Another had been Davis.

He followed her across the street. Checked out the surroundings without being too obvious about it. She walked up to the door and unlocked it. Her old man had given her a key to his apartment because that was how he was—trusting and open.

Brent shook his head. Why couldn't she see her father had been telling the truth all these years?

They checked the mailbox, which was empty.

Anna led the way to the elevator and they rode up to the fourth floor in silence. She was wearing black pants and a black button-up shirt that dipped into a low vee at the front. *Cat burgling clothes*, she'd told him when she'd bought them in the hotel boutique earlier that day. They were tightly fitted, and the sweat on Brent's brow was from more than the brewing storm. She'd morphed from schoolma'am into sexpot, and both looked good on that tight little body.

Fuck.

He was torturing himself.

They walked down the characterless corridor to a wooden door that needed a fresh coat of varnish. Anna's hands shook as she put the key in the lock. He wanted to help her, steady her hand, but the idea of touching her was a bad one and he intended not to do it again—ever.

He liked his life. He was happy. OK, maybe *happy* was a bit too upbeat for him, but he was fine. Better than fine. He scanned the corridor and then looked at Anna's profile as she caught her bottom lip in her teeth.

Those full lips bare of makeup did terrible things to his libido. But the woman herself didn't mesh with his need for peace and quiet, because from whatever angle you looked at it, Anna was complicated. She gave off strong *don't touch me* vibes that he not only respected, he was grateful for. Except for that damn kiss...

She finally got the key into the lock and opened the door. The place smelled stale and musty. They stepped inside, and Brent longed to open a window but that might give them away.

"Don't switch on the main light," he warned as he closed the drapes. Using the light from the open doorway he found a desk lamp and turned it on. Closed the door and bolted it from the inside. Every muscle in his body contracted. He rarely locked his doors at home. Even the thought had him strung tighter than razor wire on prison walls. He distracted himself by looking around the small cramped space. There was no stack of mail waiting for their perusal.

"It's not much bigger than the cell we shared," he commented. The inside of his skin itched. He'd have gone insane living here. He needed to see the vast stretch of ocean just to breathe.

There was a small TV set in the corner, a sagging orange couch. A cheap wooden coffee table, polished until it gleamed. Magazines stacked in neat piles on the shelf beneath it—travel magazines and photography. Davis had been interested in both while in prison, and had sworn he would pursue these two loves when he got out.

It hadn't happened.

His best friend might have left jail, but he'd recreated it here in this one-bedroom fleapit.

"This place is a hellhole," he said.

Anna looked at him with eyes as dark as a winter forest.

Brent picked up a battered paperback off the shelf. "I offered to buy him a house, but he wouldn't let me. It would have been a good investment." Anguish tormented him. "I flew him out for a visit every summer." Davis hadn't ever wanted to go anywhere else. A garrote tightened around his throat. He'd let him down. The man he owed everything and he'd let him down.

Anna picked up a jacket that had been draped over the end of the sofa, and stroked the material. "He never liked charity."

So why would he steal? Brent wanted to scream, but clamped down on it. She didn't want to hear it. But why would a man who wouldn't accept help from anyone steal other people's money?

He wouldn't.

Brent knew—Brent had always *known* that Davis was innocent, although he'd have been lying if he said he hadn't been grateful for the man's company in prison. The warden had been content to leave them be—two model prisoners who were actually doing well in a system that wasn't designed for lifers mixed in with the general prison population.

Davis had been punishing himself by living here. Brent's gut tightened. Because of Anna. Because of what she'd been through after his arrest. Photographs of her were everywhere—some he recognized from the cage, others were new.

He looked up as she started opening drawers in the desk. A box he recognized sat next to a laptop. An old shoe box that Davis had painted vibrant red using Brent's supplies, in a quiet rebellion against institutional green. Brent walked up beside her, brushing her shoulder as he leaned forward. They both jumped, but he bent over his task and removed the lid. She froze as they stared down into a neatly stacked pile of letters, tied with a length of brown string. The prison address was printed in neat schoolgirl handwriting on the front of the envelopes.

"He kept them all this time?" She reached out an unsteady finger and then pulled back.

"I told you they were his lifeline in prison." He picked one up and opened it. Grinned as the memories drifted over him like snowflakes. "Your first Avril Lavigne concert. I remember it well. Did you wear heavy eye makeup and skinny jeans?"

"Maybe." She hooked her hands into her back pockets, frowning. "I sent him the CD."

"I know." His tone was droll.

"You don't like Avril Lavigne?" She sounded shocked by the idea.

"Let's just say it was better for everyone when Avril had a little accident in the break room."

Her eyes narrowed. "I sent him her second CD when that came out too."

He grimaced. "What can I say? Prison is no place for a woman." Her lips pressed together as he put the letter back. He doubted the information they were after was in that box.

He stared around the place in disgust. "I had no idea he was living like this."

Big eyes met his. "I visited a few times, but we'd meet in the city or at the art gallery for lunch. I don't remember the last time I came to the apartment." Guilt made her voice fade away.

Brent set his jaw. He knew Davis and Anna's relationship hadn't been easy after the man had gotten out, but frankly he'd have been surprised if it had been. Prison changed a person. People moved on. He, on the other hand, was a gutless wonder for not taking care of the man he'd called friend. Too chicken to leave his little beach hideaway. Christ, he'd thought he couldn't hate himself more than he already did. He was wrong. "I'm going to search around, see if he hid some notes about what was going on at work. You check the laptop."

She just stood there looking desolate. Tiny. Big dark eyes drenched in regret.

Families were ripped apart every day. He knew this from vivid personal experience. Hell, look at his relationship with his brother—still damaged. After his arrest, he'd purposely tried to alienate Finn because he hadn't wanted to drag him down to the gutter with him. Finn had been saved by Thomas Edgefield. Anna had her mother, but after the woman remarried, he knew she'd put more effort into making things work with her new husband than making time for the teenager who'd fallen apart.

The knowledge left him aching with regret, even though there was nothing he could have done to help the girl Anna had been. He wasn't the sort of man to save people. He just did his damnedest to survive.

Brent turned away. The walls started to press in on him, so he started searching. Fast. He checked all the obvious places and then started on the places cons used. Behind light fittings, along the backs of pipes, inside the mattress and bedposts. He started tapping on the walls. He had some custom-made hidey-holes in his place although he now stashed most of his arsenal in what was technically Laura Prescott's backyard.

He'd gone to prison for murder at age sixteen, and he'd earned his tough reputation in the worst way. At the time he'd had nothing to lose and no hope for the future. But as he got older that reputation stuck, and there was always some badass wanting to prove Brent Carver was really a pussy. Survival had been one of his main priorities when he'd gotten out, and bending a few rules had seemed prudent. Now he wanted it over. He wanted his past far behind him. May as well wish for the moon or front row seats at the Victoria's Secret Christmas Show.

He really needed to call Finn and ask if they'd caught the suckers who'd followed Anna to the island, but he couldn't face him yet. Didn't want to hear the accusation—or worse, hurt—in his brother's voice.

"There's nothing here." Anna hung onto the door frame and leaned into the bedroom. "What are you doing?" she asked as he held the mattress aloft. That schoolteacher voice of hers sent a bolt of something primal down his backbone and he tried to shake it off. He needed to get laid. Find some woman who didn't mind a casual and impersonal relationship. *In exchange for what, asshole?* Money? He hadn't sunk that low. So he may as well get used to abstinence. Again.

Ignoring Anna's question because it was obvious what he was doing, he dropped the mattress and decided to call Finn. He used one of the burner cells.

Finn answered on the first ring with a vehement, "What the fuck are you involved in?"

Dread coiled inside him. "Why?"

"You were right about someone coming to your place. Freddy caught one bastard walking up the front steps about to knock on the door with a semiautomatic." His brother's voice was tight with fury.

Shit.

"But they missed his partner, who took out one of the ERT guys and then escaped after assaulting a local man and abducting his wife."

"Who?"

"Mitch and Megan Teague."

Brent felt like they'd ripped out his insides. "Is Megan all right?"

"Sonofabitch is sly as a fox. He dumped her in the bush twelve miles west of Lake Cowichan. He made a call from a gas station that effectively turned the manhunt into a search-and-rescue operation and stole another car—you know how many gravel roads are out there. We lost him, but we're canvassing all the island hotels and airports looking for someone who might fit his description."

But he'd be long gone and they both knew it.

"Megan get a look at him?" He remembered Megan Teague as a tiny redheaded kid who'd followed him around when he was a young teenager. Cute with freckles and a spitfire temper.

"We don't know." Finn's voice grim.

"Did he hurt her?" Brent's voice dropped to just above a whisper.

"She's not speaking."

Anna stepped closer. "What is it?" she asked quietly.

But he couldn't tell her. Another cop had been killed and a young woman traumatized. And if he hadn't gone to see his parole officer yesterday morning, if the warden hadn't called him straightaway—chances were, despite his promise to keep her safe, Anna would be dead. Nausea rose up in his throat and he had to force it back down to concentrate on what Finn was telling him.

"You can't fuck with these people, Brent."

"I'm not." Sweat broke out across his back. "I swear I'm not. I don't know who they are or what they want. I haven't broken any laws, Finn."

"Good to know." The voice had changed. Holly, cold and pissy. "I've got a dead cop and a lot of angry colleagues. I need to talk to you, Brent."

"You *are* talking to me."

"A man is *dead*. A man with a pregnant wife and a toddler at home. You think I won't haul your ass into jail if that's what it takes to catch these people?" Fury vibrated down the phone line and he could almost hear it being traced.

He sat on his friend's bed and thought about what Davis would do in this situation. Anna sat next to him. Her hands shook even though she couldn't hear all the conversation.

"All I know is Davis is dead and Anna turned up on my doorstep a couple of days ago. Davis left a phone message telling her he'd mailed her evidence about someone stealing money, but he didn't say where he'd sent it. Once we find whatever the hell it is, we'll take it straight to the police."

He could hear Holly's brain working. "That's everything?"

"Yeah." Pretty much. Except the dead cop in Chicago and his PI with a bullet in the back. He toyed with telling her that, but then it wouldn't take her long to figure out where they were and he didn't want to get dragged off to jail. Not even for his own good.

"Is Anna telling the truth, Brent? Are you sure you can trust her?"

"Absolutely." He looked at the woman at his side. Hell, yes, he trusted her. He'd honed his instincts on murderers and criminals. Every emotion showed in those big green eyes, from uncontrollable fear to pissed-off attitude to random flashes of physical attraction. Yup, she'd be a shitty poker player, but he trusted her. If there was anyone he didn't trust, it was Holly—wearing the same uniform as the people who'd arrested him all those years ago. But he was working on that and so was she.

There was a long silence. His stomach was tied in knots. What if she insisted they turn themselves in? The seconds ticked by like a bomb countdown. Was she waiting for the trace to finish? He almost hung up at the thought. Trust was so damn hard.

"Whoever killed that cop last night was a professional. We have roadblocks set up, but from what Finn tells me, the chances of finding him are slim to none. He's after Anna, Brent."

"Without that evidence she'll never be safe. As soon as we find it, we turn it over to the nearest cop shop and everything will go back to normal." Or as normal as it got, anyhow.

"You'd be safer in protective custody."

He wasn't convinced, not when these people were so determined to find Anna they'd already killed two police officers who'd gotten in their way. If he voiced his doubts, Holly would take it as a personal challenge and he wasn't about to put the woman his brother loved in danger. It was bad enough risking Anna. "Then no one's searching for whatever the hell Davis sent Anna. That's the key to catching these assholes—you know it is."

"Fine. I'll start asking more questions at the place where Davis Silver worked. Keep me informed. If you need my help, call. Here's your brother again."

"You need to get your ass back here, bro," said Finn.

"I need a couple of days, max."

"Anna needs proper protection."

And he wasn't up to the job. Good to know.

"Just don't get shot. It hurts." Finn had been shot last year. "And don't fucking die."

Brent didn't laugh. Visiting his brother in hospital last year was another life experience he could have done without. "I'll do my damnedest not to." He rang off, met Anna's serious gaze.

"They went to your house?"

"Killed a cop."

Her hand went to her mouth. "This is crazy."

He didn't mention Megan or her husband. "Our best chance of getting out of this alive is to find this evidence Davis sent."

"You could just walk away. This isn't your problem." Her eyes glistened.

"Davis was my best friend. I made a promise. I'm not letting him down." He took her fingers in his and squeezed. "I'm not abandoning you, Anna."

There was a knock on the door and they both launched to their feet. It was nearly midnight. The apartment was only dimly lit from a couple of lamps, but maybe someone had heard voices or him knocking on the walls. His heart jackhammered. They were four floors up. If this was the bad guys they were screwed. He crept to the front door and used the peephole, cell phone in hand, ready to dial 911.

A little old lady with purple hair stood outside gnawing tangerine lipstick. Tension leached from him in a wave. This was probably the old lady Davis had talked about. The neighbor he'd befriended.

Anna stood next to him. Brent leaned down and whispered into her ear. "Old broad at twelve o'clock. Want me to take her out?" He slanted her a cool smile and Anna glared at him as she opened the door. Brent stayed hidden. No point giving away any more information than necessary.

"Can I help you?" Anna asked politely.

"You must be Anna, dear. I was so hoping I'd get to meet you." The old lady grabbed both Anna's fists in her gnarled hands and pumped vigorously. "I was so sorry to hear about your father. He was such a *good* man. Tragic. Just tragic."

Anna's mouth was opening and closing, trying to find a gap in the conversation.

"I was wondering when you'd come to sort out his things." The old lady shuffled inside, and Anna was no match for old age or purple hair.

The lady squinted tiny eyes at Brent. She barely reached his navel. "And I recognize you, young man. Davis's friend." She nodded and her chin wobbled. "He'd be pleased to see you helping Anna out. Such a difficult time, going through everything." Her voice broke for a second, and Brent tried to interrupt but she didn't let him.

"I'm happy to help if you need me. You must let me know when the service is going to be."

"They haven't released his body yet, but I will be sure to tell you as soon as it's arranged." Anna got in a few words.

"Dreadful." The woman seemed to run out of adjectives. "Some people from his office are trying to look through his mail."

"They say why?" Brent shifted away from the wall.

"They gave me some baloney about Davis having mailed something from work accidentally. Something *very* important." She rolled those tiny eyes. "Why would he mail himself anything from work? He'd just carry it home."

Unless he didn't want it on his person when bad guys caught up with him. Unless he wasn't intending to go home.

"I spoke to a nice young man who claimed to be a private investigator. He told me he thought these people were dangerous and I had to be careful. But I told him I was too old to worry about any of that." She waved neon-colored nails at him. "I survived the Nazis as a small child in Berlin, and things don't get any more dangerous than that."

Maybe so, but Brent still wanted to wrap her up and send her away somewhere safe. "Did they find what they were looking for?"

The old lady smiled coyly. "I've lived in this building for twenty years, young man, and I know the mailman pretty well. We decided he'd put Davis's mail in my mailbox until his next of kin arrived. And now you're both here."

"I'm not next of kin," said Brent.

"He listed you both as next of kin when he moved in. Said you were the son he'd never had." The old lady tapped his hand and Brent felt like he'd been kicked in the gut. His eyes burned. Contempt was always easier to deal with than affection.

"You'd better follow me," she said.

Grabbing their stuff and turning off the lights, they locked up and followed her across the hallway into an apartment that had probably last been decorated twenty years ago when she moved in.

The lady—Mrs. Viola Bernstein—handed Anna a thick wad of letters and flyers. "I thought about sorting through the junk mail but then figured it was your business, not mine."

Anna whipped through all the pile and pulled out all the letters. But nothing looked like it had come from Davis himself.

"Thanks so much for being there for him, Mrs. Bernstein." Anna's expression spoke of remorse and guilt. He knew exactly how she felt.

"If there's ever anything you need, you let me know," Brent told her.

A smile dragged back those scary lips to reveal glowing dentures. "Now you mention it, my garbage disposal isn't working. How about I put on a pot of coffee and you see if you can get it unclogged? Usually Davis would do it for me but..." She shuffled off, still talking.

Not quite what he had in mind. Brent leaned down to whisper in Anna's ear. "If she knew I was a convicted killer she wouldn't be so keen to get me in her kitchen."

"I don't know." Amusement tugged the corner of Anna's lips. "She looks more dangerous than you do. And who knows what she's trying to get rid of in her garbage disposal."

"Ugh. Thanks for the visual." He rolled up his sleeves, squared his shoulders, and headed into the kitchen. "Don't leave me alone with her," he growled over his shoulder.

"Scaredy-cat," she whispered as she followed him. She started opening envelopes at the small kitchen table. He took the wrench from Mrs. B's arthritic fingers. May as well do a good turn. Christ knew, he had plenty to make up for.

Music blared and a disco ball glittered overhead. "You don't dance?" Katherine asked Harvey, who grimaced. She'd avoided him after the whale-watching episode. It had seemed intimate and somehow wrong even though it had been completely innocent.

"Sorry, I'm being rude sitting here with you while your husband is partnering my wife. Would you like to dance?" he asked politely but with obvious weariness.

Katherine smiled. "No. Thank you. My feet are killing me." She flexed them beneath the table. *Darn heels*. "I'm enjoying the rest." She didn't like dancing. Davis had loved to dance and his betrayal had ruined the act for her, although she danced with Ed to keep him happy. She bit her lip. She did a lot of things she didn't enjoy to keep Ed happy.

"What is it?" Harvey's voice grew quiet and he leaned closer.

She drew back in shock that she'd let her thoughts show on her face. "Nothing. I, uh, had some bad news this week, that's all. I'm a little shaken up." Why was she telling him this? She shot a nervous look to Ed, but he and Barb were lighting up the dance floor with a two-step.

"And Ed doesn't know?"

Her eyes flashed back to Harvey.

"Don't worry, I won't say anything." Kind eyes crinkled, then grew sad. "Barb is my second wife. My first wife died of cancer six years ago today."

"Oh, I'm very sorry."

He nodded. "Melanie would be pissed to see me now." His eyes were on Barb as she flitted around the dance floor. "It isn't even as if the sex is any good, you know?"

She choked on a sip of wine.

"Sorry." He laughed. "Are you OK?"

She nodded, dabbing her mouth with a napkin.

He looked relaxed and more attractive than he had a right to be. "TMI?" He scratched the back of his neck. "Something about you seems to make an honest man out of me."

Her laugh was sharp and bitter. "That's ironic, because my first husband went to prison for stealing a million dollars from the city." She slapped her hand over her mouth. She never mentioned Davis. Never admitted what he'd done to her and their daughter. *Anna*. She still needed to talk to Anna. She couldn't reach her.

Harvey gave her a long stare. "Do you love your husband?"

Which one?

"Pardon me?" They'd shared a highly moving moment with the whale, but no deep dark secrets. And the subdued male interest in his eyes made her doubly wary. "I really don't think that's any of your business."

"Because I watched you with him and although you listen to him, defer to him even, I don't sense any great affection and certainly no lust—not on your part anyway."

Lust? Her brain screeched. She didn't think much could shock her, but this man's words hit her like a bolt of lightning from a clear blue sky. "I-I don't think that is any of your business."

He put his hand over hers on the white tablecloth. Electricity burned her skin. "I didn't mean to upset you or annoy you. I'm not some creep who's coming on to you." She squirmed in her chair. She was *married*, for heaven's sake. He squeezed her fingers and let go. "Just that watching how you are with Ed made me see my own marriage in a different light. You made me acknowledge things I'd been trying to ignore." His lips broke into a sad smile. "Now I figure I'd better do something about it while I'm still young enough to enjoy my freedom."

She sat aghast. "You're going to leave Barb?"

His face grew serious. "Please don't tell her."

"I'm hardly likely to, now am I?" The conversation made her extremely uncomfortable and hit a little too close to home. She started gathering her things. "Can you tell Ed I have a headache, please?"

"Katherine, please don't go," Harvey spoke with quiet desperation.

She paused. "Is telling me that you're leaving your wife supposed to make me jump into bed with you?"

"Don't you want more from life than what you have right now?" he countered.

"Like a tawdry fling with a man I barely know?" she snapped. Her head throbbed as if it was about to explode.

"That isn't what I meant…this isn't about sex." He looked angry, but she didn't care.

Men.

She stood, knocking over her chair, desperate to escape the stuffy hot lounge. Harvey's intimate conversation and a barrage of unwelcome questions made her want to keep running and never stop. But she was trapped on this damned ship.

And, OK, she wasn't deliriously in love with Ed, but they were settled and secure. When Davis had left her bankrupt with no hope of getting a job in the city, Ed had been there to help her out. He'd been the only friend to stick by her. You didn't forget that sort of loyalty.

She hit the deck at the front of the ship and stared up at the night sky. Pulled an enormous breath deep into her lungs. Then she felt like a fool.

Harvey was rich. Did she really think he wanted to go to bed with *her*?

She was an idiot some days—most days, it seemed.

Her heart squeezed as she remembered what it felt like to fall in love and then to find out your lover had betrayed you. Wasn't that what Harvey was about to do to Barb? Even if she was a horrible person—and she was—did it mean it was OK to just discard her like a piece of trash?

Isn't that what you did to Davis?

Her throat felt like she'd swallowed barbed wire as she held back despair.

She couldn't bear the thought of going back to the room she shared with Ed, so she started walking, letting the chill night air that flowed off nearby glaciers cool her overheated skin. She walked and found the space to grieve for a man who didn't deserve it.

CHAPTER 10

They were heading onto the street when Brent grabbed Anna's arm and started marching her forcibly toward their car.

Ouch. "What's the matter?" she asked.

"Someone is in a jeep back there, watching the front door of the apartment complex." There was the sound of an engine starting, and Brent swore under his breath and dug out the keys. "Move it."

She swiped the keys from his fingers. "I'll drive."

"What…?"

She climbed into the driver's seat while he gaped at her.

"Get in." She adjusted the seat closer so she could reach the pedals.

He got in fast. She put her blinkers on and pulled out. Stopped for a cyclist. Brent looked at her like she'd morphed into an alien species.

"What?" she asked pulling out sedately into the flow of traffic.

"If those guys are the people I think they are, you need to release your inner Indy 500 driver and ditch the schoolteacher."

Her cheeks felt hot. "I told you, I'm not made for breaking the law."

He looked over his shoulder. "Well, look on the bright side. You'll be too dead to be arrested if these guys catch up with us. Why the hell did you insist on driving?" He sounded pissed and angry, and hurt unwound in her chest.

"Because," she said with deliberate slowness, "if I get caught I get a ticket. If you get caught breaking the law, *you* go back to *maximum security.*"

He rechecked the mirror. "Better that than dead—although maybe not. Drive!"

She slammed her foot on the accelerator and took a turn, then another, until they'd almost gone in a full square.

Brent kept looking behind him. "Not bad. Did you see that on TV?"

"*Hawaii Five-0.*" She pulled out onto the main highway. "One of those rare shows that's just as good with the sound off." She swore when she saw the dark jeep cut back out on the street behind them.

"What do we do now?" This sort of excitement was not something she was equipped for. *Thanks, Papa.*

Brent leaned forward. "If they shot a cop, they aren't going to worry too much about injuring innocent civilians." Anna looked around at the minivans and cars full of people on the road even at this late hour.

"They can probably trace the tags on this vehicle if they get close enough to read them. But from the way they're hanging back, I don't think they know we spotted them. Maybe they figured we just got lost back there." He gave her a look. "Try not to let them get close enough to see our tags."

Anna bit her lip and nodded. It meant getting off the freeway. Now. She took the next exit and kept going into the burbs, turning into a supermarket parking lot in the hopes she could cut through some back alleys and lose this guy.

"Over there." Brent pointed to the railway line running along the southern edge.

Anna heard the low rumble and whistle of a train.

"We'll make it if you're fast," Brent urged.

Was he nuts?

"The barriers are starting to come down." Her heart hammered her chest. She flashed a look in the rearview and saw the jeep moving ever nearer. It was hard to judge distance at night, but the jeep looked a hell of a lot closer than the train.

Red lights flashed and the barriers were almost down. It was now or never.

"Do it."

She held tight to the wheel in case the tracks wrenched it out of her hands and pressed her foot to the accelerator. Brent braced his arm against the dash. There was a car in front of them and one approaching the crossing from the other side. Anna saw a lot of bright lights and felt the rumble of the locomotive through her clenched teeth. Accelerating hard, she pressed her foot to the floor, whipping past the compact in front and causing the driver to swing in her direction with a look of openmouthed horror. Her throat went dry as she crashed through the first barrier, the sound harsh and loud despite the roar of the train. She lost control as she hit the first rail and the car slowed to a crawl. She swung to face the locomotive. A train had killed her father just a few days ago and now she was staring into her own nightmare scenario. It was going much faster than she'd realized. Her heart thundered. Black spots danced in front of her eyes as she hyperventilated.

The train blew its whistle, brakes screaming through the night.

"Floor it!" Brent yelled. If she'd been in the passenger seat, she'd have gotten out and run.

The train wailed again angrily. She revved the car hard and finally broke through the barrier on the other side and shot away with only moments to spare. There was the sound of brakes squealing on the other side. But a quick glance in the rearview told her they'd lost their pursuers, and from the half-mile-long line of containers on the track, they were going to leave these guys way behind.

"Nice driving, slick."

She tried to talk but couldn't utter a word. Her skin steamed with perspiration.

"It's OK. They rarely give jail time for first offenders."

Anna tried to swallow but her mouth was too dry. "If you're trying to make me feel better, it isn't working."

Brent rested a large hand on her shoulder. It burned through the cotton of her blouse. "We need to get out of here before they send reinforcements."

Crap. Her pulse pounded and her skin grew clammy. "I want to go home." A deep longing rose up inside her. She wanted to return to her normal life.

He looked at her as if considering. "It might not be such a bad idea. We can be in Minnesota in a few hours. But you can't actually return *home* until this is over."

"We could check the mail at school and at my house." These were the most likely places her father would have mailed the evidence, and damned if she'd let these people find that envelope and get away with murder.

"We can swing by and hole up somewhere else in the city. Figure out our next move. There sure as hell isn't anything at your dad's place."

The need to regain some normality swelled inside her. "Let's do it." She longed to see her white picket fence and rambling rose. Talk to people she knew and trusted. See places she was familiar with. And if she didn't find the envelope, she was going to the cops. She was done being chased by killers.

It was early in the morning. Rand got out of the shower and toweled off. He'd caught a combat nap. Tension and rage had racked up, before condensing into a solid core of anger. He'd dumped the redhead in the bush—more or less alive—and driven to Victoria, then retrieved his and Marco's belongings from the motel. Then he'd stolen a small plane from a man who wasn't going to report it any time soon and made his way back to the mainland, heading across the border into Seattle and catching a commercial flight.

It sure felt good to be home.

Cops were saying Marco was dead. Kudrow had gotten a phone call asking if he could help identify the corpse. Kudrow had been real sorry he couldn't help. But it raised the question how they'd known to connect the firm with the aborted attack on Brent Carver's house. Anna Silver had blabbed to someone, but Rand doubted she'd told them the whole truth.

Assuming another of his false identities, he'd decided to retrace his steps.

Last night Kudrow had called to say Anna Silver and an unknown male—probably Carver—had turned up at her dad's place in Chicago. Vic had compounded a litany of fuckups and lost her. But her turning up there meant she hadn't found the envelope yet, because if she had, she'd either turn it over to the cops and they were all fucked, or she'd disappear with all their hard-earned cash. Sixty million was a lot of money and he'd bet—if someone hadn't stolen all his frickin' money—on the latter. She was still looking for it, just the same way they were, and now he wasn't just pissed. He wanted retribution.

It was Wednesday. Given the snail pace of the postal service, it could still be a few days until the damn thing arrived, but with two dead cops, they were running out of time before law enforcement started asking the tough questions. Petrie was looking at other angles to figure out where Davis might have funneled the money, but Rand wasn't holding his breath.

He got dressed. Pulled on a knit cap. Walked the six blocks to a sweet little ranch house with its white picket fence and sweet scented garden. Checked the mailbox before heading around the back with a handful of shit. Fucking flyers.

Cauldwell Lake was nothing more than a subdivision serving the Twin Cities. Anna's house had been around since the fifties and the city had finally encroached on its borders.

He pulled on latex gloves and removed his lock-picking kit out of his back pocket. It took all of thirty seconds to let himself in, and thanks to the mature, leafy garden, none of the neighbors could see a thing. The kitchen was bright white with oak counters. Nice, classy. He looked around. Examined the quality of the silence, every sense on high alert for a surprise party. Sensing nothing, he searched each room carefully before allowing himself to relax his guard. The first time he'd been here, he'd done a quick search for obvious bolt holes. Now he knew she was smarter than that, plus she had help. He needed to delve deeper to see if he could figure out what made her tick and where she might go. He started in the bedroom. A big-ass painting hung over the bed. Pretty perfume bottles lined the small dressing table along with a framed wedding portrait of her mother and father. He opened the closet and dropped to his knees as he began going through all her junk. Shoe boxes, shoes, jewelry, paperbacks. Nothing.

He rose to his feet, took a walk to her office, and eyeballed the books on the shelves. A lot of self-help books and how to survive abuse bullshit. A small smile curved his lips—at least she'd be well ahead of the game after he finished with her—except, of course, she'd be dead. He stared at the filing cabinet, opened the drawer, and found her banking details and credit card bills. Petrie already had this so he ignored it and dug deeper. Everything was alphabetized and filed within an inch of its life.

No address book, though.

He put aside postcards she'd sent to herself from various places around the country—sad—and a few from friends. He noted their names. Next on the list would be checking into their phone records and see if they'd received any calls from burner cells.

Time was running out and the team would need to get out of Chicago ASAP. The game was over as far as the charity side of things was concerned. In the past, the IRS and Treasury Department had steered clear of probing too deep into the charity's books. The government used their services often enough that they didn't want their dealings to become public knowledge. But, with the bodies piling up, there would be an investigation. He could almost hear the feds crunching their teeth on subpoenas and warrants. When they figured out who else Rand & Co had been working for over the last eighteen months, the whole team would be fucked six ways to Sunday. And Rand sure as hell didn't intend to be extradited to the Middle East to face criminal charges if the administration of the day decided they wanted some political leverage. He knew how to disappear, but he wanted his damn money first.

He sat back on his heels and eyed a stack of color-coordinated boxes. *Holy crap.* Pain shot through his jaw as he clenched his teeth. For all her organization she still kept too much shit. Why did people do that?

There was a sound at the front door and he drew his weapon.

"Anna. Anna! I know you're in there. I'm sorry. Please, can we talk about this?"

A smile curled Rand's lips. *Romeo, Romeo. Oh, fucking Romeo.*

"I messed up. I'm sorry, but I've never dated a girl like you before and I'm…I'm out of my league."

Rand twitched the curtain in the living room. *You've got that right, pal.*

"I'm on my way to work, but I'm not going anywhere until we talk this through. I'm staying right here."

Persistent little prick. Noisy too.

Rand thought about it for three whole seconds and then opened the door. The guy blinked as he hauled him one-handed inside, closing the front door with his foot.

"Who the hell are you? Where's Anna?"

Rand stuffed his gun in the back of his waistband and leaned down until they were nose-to-nose. "She's already forgotten you, asshole."

The little toad started scrambling, legs seeking purchase on the ground and not finding it.

"OK, this is what we're going to do." Rand took Romeo by the scruff and marched him into the kitchen. He shoved him into a chair and closed the blinds.

The guy made a break for the door and Rand brought his elbow across his face and heard the bone snap. The guy screamed and Rand grabbed him in one hand, the dish towel in the other. Blood poured down the man's crisp white shirt. Rand stuffed the towel in his mouth, shoved him face-first on the linoleum, and gagged him. He used another tea towel around the wrists. The guy struggled uselessly, wriggling like a worm on a hook.

Once he had his wrists and ankles secure, Rand climbed to his feet. Scared eyes met his from the kitchen floor. Rand extracted the Ka-Bar knife from the sheath strapped to his leg.

"You're going to tell me where Anna might be, and if I think you're telling the truth, I might leave your dick attached." He crouched next to the guy. "What's your name?"

The guy grunted and Rand pulled the gag out for a second.

"Peter," the guy gasped.

Rand replaced the gag and nodded. "OK, Peter. Here's what we're going to do." Peter tried to scoot across the pristine floor but it wasn't happening. "I'm going to cut you every time you don't answer a question truthfully. Got it?"

Peter's eyes bugged. Rand smiled. "Too slow." He swiped the knife across Peter's cheekbone and watched him bleed. "Got it?"

Peter nodded fast and furious.

Having someone at your mercy was a hell of a high. No wonder there were so many serial killers roaming the world. But he wasn't doing this for fun. He thought about the redhead and grinned. That had been fun. Anna was going to be fun too.

"Where's Anna likely to go?" He lowered the rag but already knew the guy didn't have a clue. Peter shook his head and Rand held his jaw closed with his hand as he skinned the top of his ear. "Now you might not think you know but dig deep, OK, Peter?"

The poor guy nodded frantically, blood and snot dripping down his face.

Rand wiped his knife on Peter's expensive pants. "Just tell me what you know, all right?"

Again the frantic nodding.

"How long you and Anna been dating?"

"Six months."

"You doing her?" Rand asked.

Peter's spastic head shaking made Rand still the knife. "Six months and you haven't fucked her yet?"

Peter gasped for a decent breath. "She doesn't like being touched. She won't let me anywhere near her."

Rand replaced the gag. The idea of Anna being frigid was an unexpected turn-on. The thought of how desperately she'd fight him…shit, he shifted uncomfortably, he'd need another redhead if Anna didn't show up soon.

He smiled. Maybe he'd let Peter live, poor bastard. "She has something of mine." Sixty million—split five ways now Marco was dead—and a shedload of battered pride. "I need to find her and get it back." Rand lowered the gag to show his sincerity. Helped the guy sit up with his back against the kitchen counter.

"I don't know where she is."

"What do you know?" asked Rand.

"She works at Oakwood School. Has a couple of girlfriends, I can tell you where they live. Works out at a gym three times a week two blocks from here."

Sold out only five minutes into a new relationship. Such was life.

He nodded encouragingly. "Keep going, Peter. You're doing great. But give me some names and addresses now. Details."

Blood covered the guy's shirt front, lower face, and neck. Rand was beginning to feel a little sorry for the guy. Six months dating and no action? *Christ.* He'd have dumped her after the second date—somewhere wild and remote. The woman was a goddamned prick tease.

Fear churned in Brent's stomach for both Anna's safety and his own freedom, because even the idea of prison was like a noose around his throat. Brent drove. Hell, he'd been driving for hours. They hadn't checked out of the hotel in Chicago. In fact, they'd booked the suite for the whole week and left the rental in the parking garage—just in case anyone tracked them to that hotel. Let them think he and Anna were holed up, having marathon, dirty-old-man-doing-his-PA sex. Instead, they'd grabbed their stuff, hired another vehicle, and hit the road.

The foreign landscape hadn't improved his mood. He missed the ocean. This vast expanse of land felt too static, claustrophobic. How did anyone stand it without going nuts? Plus there were all these cars going in every direction. Cars on both sides of him, pressed close, front and back. His stomach started to churn.

What sort of pansy-ass was scared of fricking driving?

Gritty eyed, he signaled and pulled into a drive-through for coffee. Glancing quickly at Anna dozing in the passenger seat, he couldn't help thinking that this was the sort of future he'd denied himself when he'd killed his father.

Too bad. Get over it.

He ordered them both coffee at the window and Anna woke up, blinking widely. "Where are we?"

"Thirty minutes out. You want to drive?"

"Sure, you must be exhausted."

He wasn't tired. His brain felt like it had been hotwired, and until this thing was finished, he didn't feel like closing his eyes.

But a mental break would help, and she knew her way around the city.

Pansy-ass.

They swapped seats, and before long they pulled up in a neighborhood of bungalows and swing sets. He frowned. "Where are you going?" They'd agreed on finding a motel and contacting some of her friends and colleagues from the school.

Her back was straight. Jaw set. "It's early. We should check the mail at my house before there are too many people around. And I can grab some stuff from my house."

"What stuff?"

"Work, for school." Tendons shone white through the skin on her knuckles. This was her way of gaining control of the situation. He got that, but…"It'll take just a couple of minutes. I have everything on an external drive and in a single box file. That's all I need." Her eyes were hard, determined. "We grab it, the mail, and get out of there."

His heart turned into a stone that rattled around his chest. He should have known she'd do something like this, and with her hands on the steering wheel, he was powerless to stop her without crashing the damn car. Although maybe it was better to get this over with. A quick in and out early in the morning. He ran his hand through his short spiky hair. "Fine. Don't pull up outside your place. Do a drive-by, we'll see if anyone is camped out front, then park around the corner." He grabbed his hat and put it on her head. "Keep it on," he ordered when she went to jerk it off.

"But the car windows are tinted." She scowled but left the hat in place. They pulled into a quiet street lined with mature trees. He saw the white picket fence ahead on the right and immediately knew it was hers.

"Don't slow down."

She drove past and Brent checked it out. Pink roses nestled in green leaves, looking like some idyllic grotto. It wasn't his beach, but it was pretty. He hated it, and didn't know why.

There didn't seem to be anyone watching the place from the street. "Pull over up ahead." They were far enough away to not be noticeable.

The silence was intense. "They can't watch everywhere, right?"

"They tracked you all the way to Bamfield. Putting someone on your house seems like a no-brainer."

She went white, but these guys were not playing games. He wasn't going to sugarcoat reality just so she could get herself killed. It was early. The neighborhood was quiet. That perfect morning light filtering through the leafy canopy.

"It's a nice spot," he conceded.

"I know it isn't a million-dollar home, but I like it." There was longing in her eyes as she stared toward her home and his heart shriveled a little. He understood exactly what it meant to love a place. Just another reason things would never work out between them, even if he wasn't a convicted killer and she wasn't on the run.

"How long do we just sit here?" Anna asked after a minute's silence.

Brent laughed. "Well, an hour would be sensible but I figure you have thirty seconds tops."

He could feel her energy growing, sparking off her skin in invisible waves. Her hand slid to the door opener.

"And we're done." Junkies craving a fix had more patience than Anna. Hell, mental patients on a psychotic break had more patience than this woman. He blew out a massive breath and climbed out of the car. Stretched his back as cool morning air swept over him. Anna came around the front, still dressed in figure-hugging black with the cap on her head. Hot, even after a night sleeping in the car.

Shit.

He took her hand so she didn't disappear on him. Instead of walking up to the front door he cut along the street behind her property. He felt exposed out here on the asphalt. The desire to carry a gun was overwhelming but he knew he was going to run into the cops eventually, and didn't want to be armed when he did. Deportation held no allure if he ended up back in prison. Even being with Anna was dangerous if she was implicated in Davis's misadventures. But he gripped her fingers tighter and she squeezed back. It shocked him almost as much as that kiss.

Don't think about the kiss. It had been one of the most innocent kisses of his life and had seared his feet to the floor.

"Let's cut through the neighbor's garden," he said.

"I don't think the Radmundsens are going to enjoy two people sneaking through their yard."

"The whole point about sneaking is they don't find out."

She laughed quietly. *God.* Was that the first time? He wasn't exactly known for lightening the moment.

They cut through the neighbor's neatly trimmed lawn, strewn with kids' bikes and balls. Goalposts against the rear fence. He held out his hands to give Anna a boost over the fence, ignoring the feel of her body against him.

Too good for you, pal.

He vaulted the panel and dropped beside Anna, who was staring at her back door with a frown.

"What?" he whispered.

"Something looks different..."

"What?"

"I don't know."

"Blinds? Plant pots? Length of the lawn?"

"I don't know," she snapped.

"Don't get your panties in a twist."

Those green eyes narrowed into a death glare.

"You do wear panties, right? Because I've heard stories about you schoolteacher types—"

Her elbow struck his solar plexus and he stopped talking.

She got to the back porch just ahead of him. He stopped her with a hand to the shoulder. "Let me go first." He took the keys from her fingers and took a step forward.

She gripped his arm. "Be careful." She was getting a vibe and he was getting it too. A frisson of danger, an undercurrent of warning.

He opened the door onto carnage. The smell hit him first. A man lay in a pool of crimson. His ears had been mutilated, face sliced, shallow cuts all over his body, marked by bloodstains. Red smears across the floor that suggested he'd spent a lot of time writhing in agony and trying to escape—drag marks showed he hadn't gotten far.

Anna gasped. He tried to grab her before she went inside, but hell, she was slippery.

"Peter? Oh, no, Peter!" Her hands went to her mouth.

"He's dead," Brent said roughly. His skin prickled with something that felt a lot like fear. He grabbed her hand, intending to drag her away from this scene of violence when the tiniest sound made him whirl.

The guy from the subway station photograph stood in the kitchen doorway with a smile on his face and a knife in his right hand. He wore gloves and a wool hat. And had the coldest eyes this side of death. "Anna."

Brent launched himself at the stranger. He had the advantage of size, surprise, and twenty years in one of the toughest survival situations in the world. "Run!" he yelled at Anna.

He hit the guy hard and they flew through the doorway. The fucker twisted and they crashed to the floor and rolled, taking out half of Anna's living room furniture with them. He jabbed the guy's nose, blood gushing over his jaw.

"That's your DNA all over your crime scene, buddy. You're done." Brent punched him again.

Black eyes hardened and Brent got flipped in the air. "Not. Unless. They catch me. Asshole." The other guy had the advantage of military training and the desire to not end up where Brent had spent most his life. Anna stood in the doorway as the killer got to his feet. She screamed—which wasn't real useful when it came to getting the hell out of there. Brent roared and he was back on the floor with his arms wrapped tight around the bastard's neck while that knife flashed way too close for comfort. Adrenaline primed his body for action. Heart drilled. Lungs bellowed. No way was this guy getting through him to Anna.

A fist to the balls had white-hot agony flashing along every nerve, but he didn't let go. Knew, if he did, both he and Anna were dead. Where was she? Why the hell wouldn't she get out of here?

Jesus.

He had the guy's knife arm pinned under his leg. They were so close he could smell the guy's sweat and soap. They grunted, muscles straining as they wrestled for supremacy. With a bullish grunt the other guy bucked free and twisted around to face him. Both on their knees facing one another, the knife flashed and Brent hissed with pain as the edge nicked his chin. The force was enough to throw him on his back. The guy loomed over him, aiming to shove that blade right through his gut, but there was a loud crash and he collapsed limp on the floor as wine and glass rained all around.

Brent climbed to his feet, dripping alcohol and green shards.

"Is he dead?" Anna's eyes were huge. She held the broken bottle in her right hand. She dropped it and it rolled on the floor.

Brent checked the guy's pulse. Felt it flutter. "No." Then he picked up the unbroken neck of the bottle and wiped the fingerprints off with his T-shirt, dropped it. "Just in case," he said, catching her eye. No way was she doing prison time for saving his ass. Then he heard sirens. "One of your neighbors must have reported the noise. Let's get out of here." He acted on instinct. He wasn't sitting around to be questioned by cops and stuck in a cell for God knew how long. Dread rammed his heart into overdrive. He dragged Anna out of the house. Both of them battered and covered in dark stains. Blood. "Are you hurt?" he asked as they hopped the fence and jogged toward their rental.

She shook her head. Peter's blood then—whoever the fuck Peter was. Poor bastard. She tripped but he kept her moving.

"Keys," he demanded.

She was fishing in her pocket but the sirens were getting too close. He slipped his hand in her pocket, got the keys. Put her in the passenger seat and then got in, started the car, and turned and drove slowly away. "Which way?" he asked.

Anna sat in stunned silence as he searched the neighborhood for a clue of which way to head. He wanted to get on the highway and take them as far from here as possible. "Which way to the freeway, Anna? Or a mall?" They needed to get cleaned up, buy supplies, and regroup. They needed to get the fuck out of here. He needed Holly's help to get Anna into protective custody. That was the only place she'd be safe. He was done with these pricks. Davis had managed to poke a stick in the wrong fucking hornet's nest.

Anna had hit zombie land. He passed a squad car speeding toward her house. Checked his speed. Saw signs to the 494 and Mall of America. Now *there* was the place to get lost. They needed to disappear, to get off the grid until the cops got a goddamn handle on this shit. Hopefully finding that asshole unconscious in Anna's house with a dead guy in the kitchen would speed things along.

"Who was Peter?" he asked.

Nothing. No flicker of reaction. She'd shut down and wasn't coming out anytime soon.

He followed signs and buried the car among thousands of others outside the giant mall. He grabbed their bag from the backseat, changed shirts. He undid the buttons of Anna's black shirt and pulled it over her shoulders. She sat there unmoving in a pretty navy bra and he could think of nothing except how vulnerable she looked. He dragged a plain blue T-shirt out of the bag and pulled it over her head. He put the ball cap back over her long hair and adjusted it so her face would be hidden, hair pulled up.

He climbed out of the car, slung the bag over his shoulder as he got Anna out of the car, and guided her into the mall.

He'd just left the scene of a crime and it was enough to put him back inside indefinitely.

Time to run.

An ear-shattering noise pulled Rand out of the fog, and he was on his feet and out the back door before he'd even figured out what it was. Cops. He vaulted two fences and tore off his hat and wiped the blood off his face. He stank of booze and there was a lump on the back of his skull that throbbed like a grenade.

He'd had the big guy and had been about to gut him when that bitch had nailed him. The situation had turned into another shitfest and he needed to get the fuck out of Dodge and figure out where Anna Silver had run this time.

Peter had been a waste of time. The guy really did know nothing and the idiot had twisted at exactly the wrong moment and a harmless jab had ended up pricking the guy's kidney. Bye-bye Peter. Poor schmuck. She'd strung him along. Hell, Rand had done him a favor putting him out of his misery.

He'd dropped his knife in the house. *Shit!* And bled all over the living room. Cops were going to be all over him for murder if they found him.

They weren't going to find him.

He had more false identities than Jason Bourne. He made himself stop and buy a newspaper. Changed his gait from leaving a crime scene to taking a morning stroll. Kudrow was going to be pissed. There was so much heat right now he didn't even want to talk to the guy, but he didn't have a choice. He got back to his motel room and climbed into the shower, fully clothed. When the water ran clean he stripped off and shampooed his hair. Once he was thoroughly clean he got out, dried off, and punched in the number.

"She's in Minneapolis," he said.

"You have her?" Kudrow asked.

"No."

Kudrow started swearing.

"She's still looking for that envelope. Got a guy in tow—Carver."

"I've got two dead cops. A private investigator in the ICU. Marco's dead and the fucking RCMP are sniffing around." Kudrow sounded like he was about to stroke out.

"Cops might want to talk to her now. There was a murder at her home..."

Kudrow growled. "You're fucking this up, Rand."

"It's been fucked up from the moment it started and you know it." Anger swelled inside him. He was the one chasing across continents and fighting for his life, and this guy was criticizing him? He hung on to his temper. Just. "The guy helping her is an ex-con. He's got to be connected."

"We're running out of time," Kudrow said quietly.

Rand heard the subtle edge of desperation in the guy's voice. "You *are* working on an alternative plan, right?"

"We're sorting things out at the office." Code for packing up and moving out. Kudrow's voice dropped lower. "You need to find that girl."

That I do.

"We need that money, Rand." Kudrow knew it was only a matter of time before the feds caught up to them.

"Got any cop connections in Minnesota?" asked Rand.

Kudrow thought for a minute. "No, but Petrie claims he can hack into any police database in the country. Let's see if he can live up to his big-mouth boasting for a change. Sixty million dollars. It's a lot of money."

Sixty frickin' million. No kidding.

"Mail service can take a week for a letter to get anywhere." Rand stood naked, looking out of the motel window, trying to think.

"We don't have a week."

"They're going to need transportation. Somewhere to stay. She can't run on cash forever." And he wanted to be there when she stopped running. He clenched his jaw thinking about how close he'd been to her. He'd seen her pupils flare, seen the flush of rose on her skin. Smelled the slight musk of her sweat. He'd had her within arm's reach. So close. So damn close. No way was he letting her win. But his first priority was getting his hands on that money because he could always come back for his revenge another day, when she least expected it. A thought suddenly struck him. "We're going about this all wrong."

"No shit," Kudrow snarled.

Rand smiled. "But I know how to do it right." Finally.

CHAPTER 11

Anna followed Brent in a daze through the brightly lit aisles of another big-box store. Peter. Dead. Blood all over her kitchen floor. The images revolted her. The look of excitement in the killer's eyes when she'd met his gaze like he knew her, like he owned her. She shuddered. She recognized that predatory glint.

Tears welled in her eyes. Poor Peter. She'd treated him dreadfully. He'd gotten nothing for his trouble except the dubious pleasure of her company, and the first time he kissed her, she'd dumped him. Now he was dead. She wasn't worth that. No one was worth that.

Brent had kissed her. She touched her lips.

Why had she reacted so badly to being kissed by a nice guy like Peter, but enjoyed the touch of Brent's lips against hers? Had Peter just tasted wrong? Or was she still punishing herself for the past by being attracted to someone so completely unsuitable?

"Snap out of it, Anna." Brent clicked his fingers under her nose. "I need you with me until we get out of the city."

She blinked. Brent. They were in danger. *He* was in danger. She swallowed and nodded. They both wore ball caps and had changed shirts. She frowned. When had they done that?

He picked up a large box from the shelf. "Hold the cart."

She grabbed the handlebar. He dumped the box and strode to grab sleeping bags off a shelf, and a first aid kit. He got the biggest one on the shelf and then she remembered all the blood.

"I think I'm going to be sick." Her hand flew to her mouth and he grabbed her wrist and strode down an aisle that led to the bathrooms. He didn't even hesitate, just strode into the ladies' room and held her hair while she vomited into the toilet.

Thankfully it was early and no one else was there.

He wrapped her hair around his hand and stroked her back.

After a moment she got herself back together and wiped her mouth. He flushed and maneuvered her to the sinks. She shied away from the mirror. She looked like crap, but that wasn't what bothered her. The expression in her eyes reminded her of a time she'd spent years trying to forget. Being lost. Defeated.

He let go of her hair, smoothing it down her back as she rinsed out her mouth with cold water. Then he leaned over the sink and washed his face, paying particular attention to the cut on his jaw. He dried off and turned to face her. The expression on his face suggested he didn't want to talk about it, but she couldn't help herself.

"Did I kill him?" Her voice was rough as a saw blade. "That man back there?"

He shook his head. "He had a pulse. Hopefully the cops got him."

She gripped her stomach as the nausea threatened to return. She'd hit a man over the head with a bottle. Exactly the same thing Brent had done to his father. His father had died and he'd gone to prison—could go back again if the cops caught him now. Fleeing a crime scene was illegal, even she knew that. She grabbed his arm. "You have to get away from me. Head back across the border—"

He shook his head. "I'm not leaving you to deal with this alone, Anna."

"But if they catch you now..."

His grip firmed. "Let's make sure they don't catch us."

She blinked. He wasn't leaving her. He'd put the thing he valued most highly—his freedom—on the line for her. Damn, he'd even put his life on the line as he'd wrestled that monster back there. "But—"

"No." He smiled and he looked so tender, emotion welled up but she wasn't about to start bawling like a baby. He wasn't leaving her. The thought left her full of both relief and terror.

She remembered those pitiless black eyes. "We need to go to the cops." Revulsion crept over every inch of her skin. She knew what he'd do if he caught her.

She was surprised when Brent nodded. "But not here. We need to meet Holly, and head north across the border." She didn't think they should wait that long, and a plan was starting to form in her mind.

Her teeth rattled. "I'm scared," she admitted.

He pulled her to his chest. Rested his chin on her head. And damn, it felt so good, so right she just held on tight for a minute. When was the last time she'd relied on anyone? Before her dad had gone to prison, that's when. And look how well that had turned out.

Voices outside the door made them jerk apart.

A woman came into the bathroom pushing a stroller. Her mouth dropped when she saw Brent. He wrapped his arm over Anna's shoulders and smiled. "Morning sickness," he lied easily. He got her moving out the door. "She can't go more than an hour first thing without tossing her cookies."

The woman's expression turned sympathetic, but Anna's heart thumped uneasily as she thought about the idea of being pregnant. *Kids.* She'd always thought she didn't want kids. She had pupils she loved, but her own baby? Being responsible for an entire life? She'd thought she hadn't wanted that, but now...the brush with death had her realizing that having a baby was something she actually thought she could handle one day. Being a parent was something she'd like to try. If they got out of this mess alive, she was going to readjust a few of her life goals. That was the one good thing about near-death experiences: they made you figure out what was really important. Friendship. Loyalty. Looking after the people you cared about.

So how was she going to get Brent out of this mess?

They found their cart where they'd left it in the aisle.

"I'm going to grab some clothes," she told him, careful to keep her voice upbeat even though she felt miserable inside. "I'll meet you in the men's department in fifteen minutes. Then we'll get some food and head out of the city."

Dark eyebrows rose, but his gaze never wavered from hers. "OK—fifteen minutes. But don't think about ditching me and turning yourself in. I'll just follow you right to the nearest cop shop."

Oh, heck. Was she that transparent?

Blue eyes pierced her. "I don't need any sacrifices, Anna. I don't deserve any. Going to the cops without that evidence just makes your father—and possibly you—look guilty."

Gooseflesh crept over her. "Me?"

"Your father 'stole' their money—I'm guessing a lot of money—otherwise, these assholes would have cut their losses and moved on. He said he sent *you* the details. What if they went for some accessory angle? Without the evidence we can't prove squat about Davis's good intentions. And in jail you're vulnerable to whoever they can buy off."

Not to mention she'd be in *jail.* "I'm sorry I ever got you involved in this mess."

He tipped her chin up and her heart took a tumble. "You didn't. Davis did."

She blinked away the stupid tears that wanted to fill her eyes. She was starting to fall for Brent, a guy who was as dangerous to her well-being as her father's love had ever been. Love was an unstable, volatile emotion she could never trust.

She'd been alone her entire adult life. Sure, she had friends, colleagues, but she never really opened up. Never trusted. After the physical and emotional abuse she'd endured as a teen, the barriers she'd built had become an invisible fortress. But sometime during the last week, Brent had breached those walls and got closer to her than anyone else ever had.

Now those blue eyes darkened with something she recognized. Something that echoed deep inside her. Her heart gave a painful twist. *Great. Just great.*

They were in deep shit.

Parole violation? You bet your fucking ass. But he couldn't throw Anna to the wolves and assume the system would save her. It didn't save people. It locked them up and threw away the key. In the meantime, these assholes were getting away with murder. He and Anna were off the grid for now, camping in the boonies and hopefully falling off the face of the planet long enough to catch a break. But he was no closer to finding that evidence, or clearing Davis's name than when he'd started this. Jack's PI company was still investigating, but with Jack out of action...*shit.*

What the hell was going on? Who were these people? What had Davis stumbled on?

He was praying these guys hadn't linked Brent Carver to B.C. Wilkinson. He'd buried his identity deep because people were nosy and he didn't want a bunch of ex-cons turning up at his place hoping to rip off a few canvases or put a hole in his head. And although the reasons might not have been saintly, it was all working in his favor right now. But if his shithead parole officer heard about any of this, he was headed straight back to maximum security, and even the thought brought a low hot bolt of nausea slamming into his gut.

A week ago he'd been worried about turning up at a show. Now he was trying to avoid appearing on *America's Most Wanted.*

Plan A and B had both fucked up and now they were trying something new. Flying completely under the radar. He wasn't taking any chances.

He'd called Finn and told him what was going on and where and when he hoped to cross the border. Then he'd dumped everything electronic and paid cash for a couple of new prepaid cell phones. They'd ditched their bloody clothes in the trash, left their rental car at the mall—e-mailed his agent to get it delivered back to the company—and got a bus to a car lot. Using his alter ego's credit card he'd bought a two-year-old jeep and they'd headed west into the Dakotas. Theoretically he still had to show up in NYC in a couple of days' time. Chances of that happening were about as likely as the guy on Anna's kitchen floor getting up and walking home.

Who the hell was Peter anyway?

They'd traveled for hours, zigzagging across three states. Now light was fading fast and Brent felt like a zombie. He took his frustration out pounding in a tent peg. Anna sat in a canvas chair watching him. She wore dark glasses that covered hollowed-out, exhausted eyes, and looked so close to breaking it was killing him.

They'd eaten junk food and grabbed a few basic camping supplies—coffee, instant pasta, bread—but neither of them had the energy to do more than swig from water bottles.

"I did exactly what you did." Her voice was hoarse. "You got twenty years in prison."

So this was what was bothering her. "I killed someone. You didn't." He looked up. "There were extenuating circumstances in your case."

She lowered her glasses to reveal bloodshot eyes. "You had extenuating circumstances too."

But no one had listened, which was exactly why he'd gotten her the hell out of her house this morning. The thought of sitting in a holding cell while the cops sorted this mess out was akin to having electrodes attached to his balls. No, thank you.

"The guy's alive. Quit beating yourself up." The fucker had had the edge on Brent. If she hadn't hit him when she did, chances were he'd be dead and she'd be...

So far he wasn't turning out to be such a great bodyguard.

"Is the line that thin?" Her voice was as soft as the mist that hung over the nearby lake.

"Between good and evil?" Brent paused. He didn't try to make light of his crime but..."No. But the line between being branded a criminal versus upstanding citizen? You bet your sweet ass."

Even if the sonofabitch was dead, Anna Silver did not deserve to go to jail. She was running for her life through no fault of her own and that bastard deserved it.

The longer the day went on, the more she looked like she was about to snap. They needed sleep and this campground off Route 94 was the last place anyone would expect them to stay. Place was packed with families, but there was just enough space to squeeze in a two-man tent into a secluded bay near the water. It was quiet down here. No RVs. A couple of large family tents were barely visible through a thick stand of trees.

"Who was Peter?" he asked, tightening guylines.

"Oh, jeez. I'd almost forgotten about Peter." She lost the little color she had left. Her hands dug into her scalp. "We dated for about six months, but I broke up with him Friday night after he kissed me." There was something in her voice and his stomach clenched.

"He tried to force you?"

"No." She shook her head. "I just didn't like it." Her breathing hitched. "He must have come to my house to try and make up. I barely gave him a thought since I last saw him."

"You've had other things on your mind," Brent reminded her gently.

"Shit!"

The profanity shocked him. He hadn't heard her swear before. She was about to lose it, and they really didn't want to attract any unwanted attention. He spoke fast. "A kiss tells you a lot about someone. You know that, right?" He took her by the shoulders. Christ, she felt so tiny and small and goddamn perfect. "I read whole books on kissing when I was inside." Just to torture himself. "And it's not just about touching lips—it's a connection, maybe some sort of genetic litmus test. Peter"—*poor bastard*—"failed the test. It was him, not you." He shook her slightly.

"But he's dead because of me—"

"Hush now." He pulled her against him, rocking her for comfort and hoping to keep the volume down. "He's dead because some bastard likes hurting people." She flinched, but he held tight. "No one does that for money. They do that because they enjoy it." Gina's smile flashed through his mind. Finn had sworn to him she hadn't suffered, but sometimes his imagination conjured up the worst images.

He let go of her and stood back. She needed to rest. He grabbed two thin air mattresses and the sleeping bags and tossed them inside. Tidied up while Anna went off and used the restroom. He was just getting antsy about her when she came back. He held the tent flap wide.

"Bed," he said firmly. They climbed inside, not even bothering to get undressed. The air mattresses were shoved next to one another and there was barely enough space for him to maneuver without climbing all over Anna. *Christ.* Given that he was attracted to her, this was not going to be easy, but he wasn't an animal. He took off his belt and shoes. Put the single flashlight near the door. Lay down on his back and stared at the canvas stretched overhead.

It was a warm night. They both lay on top of their makeshift beds. Their arms brushed one another in the tight space. She didn't balk or freak, which told him how exhausted she was.

He hadn't forgotten the incident in the hotel room—half a millennium ago—when she'd gone white as a sheet and backed away from him like he was going to smack her. There had been raw panic in her eyes as she'd flashed back to something terrifying.

Brent had a short list of possibilities. None of them were good.

He could hear her breathing in the darkness. Quiet. Awake. Aware.

As a young guy in prison, he'd spent a lot of time protecting his ass. Literally. After the first shower incident, where he'd half blinded a guy who thought Brent would be easy pickings, he'd gained a reputation for not being worth the trouble. He'd been lucky. His first cellmate, Ian, had been a lifer who'd taken him under his wing and helped him learn the rules. Ian hadn't wanted anything from Brent except a tidy roomie who didn't yap. Not a problem for Brent. The guy had been fatally knifed four years later, in some altercation over fried chicken of all things, but by then Brent had learned how to take care of himself. Not everyone was so fortunate and he'd witnessed plenty of abuse.

It sucked being in prison, but some people didn't know how to live on the outside. He did. He'd been doing just fine until a week ago. He clenched his fists in the darkness. Now he was risking everything because of a promise to a dead man. Trouble was it was more than that, and no matter how much Brent wanted to pretend he was doing this for Davis, he was actually doing it for Anna—or maybe, if he were really honest, for himself.

He closed his eyes against the memories that were still sharp across his brain.

Ever since Gina had been found murdered last year, he'd been trying to redeem himself in some small measure. He'd spent his whole life pushing people away to keep them safe, but it hadn't worked. Now he was keeping Anna close and hoped it would be enough to protect her.

The night air cooled.

He turned on his side and moved as close to Anna as he dared. He rested his hand on her waist, and her muscles froze beneath his touch.

"You ever going to tell me about it?" he asked, finally.

Her breath caught. The silence got heavier, and for a moment Brent thought she wasn't going to answer—maybe even pretend she was asleep, though it was obvious she wasn't.

"I was raped," she admitted quietly. "But I think you'd already guessed that, hadn't you?"

Regret clawed at him with angry talons, regret for things he couldn't change. His chest tightened painfully. He wanted to shout and pound his fists against something, but that wouldn't help Anna so he calmed it down. Shoved it into a corner where he could deal with it later.

"Do you want to tell me what happened?" he asked gruffly.

She twisted onto her side and he withdrew his hand, but she groped for it in the darkness and squeezed. "I never told anyone. Ever."

All those years of bottled-up emotions, the degradation, the humiliation. For the first time, he felt anger at Davis, for putting her in danger. For not taking better care of his daughter. He ran his palm over her jaw, anchored his fingers in her hair. "You need to talk to *someone*, doesn't have to be me—"

"I want to tell you." Her palm rested against his heart. "It might help explain why I'm so screwed up. Or some of it, anyway."

Anna rolled onto her side, facing away from Brent. She'd spent years in denial, as if by never talking about the rape she could pretend it never happened. But without realizing it, that decision had tainted all her subsequent relationships because, subconsciously, she was always waiting for the rules to change and to get raped again. By denying the reality of what happened to her, she'd denied the extent of the trauma and impact it had had on her life. She was through with denial.

Who moved first she didn't know, but suddenly Brent's arms were wrapped around her and his chin rested in her hair. Anna leaned back against the solid wall of his chest and absorbed some of that strength. They were spooning, his chest pressed tight to her back and, despite the shimmer of sexual awareness between them, it felt safe and reassuring.

How was it possible to feel safe after everything that happened? People were trying to kill her, but they hadn't succeeded yet because this man was by her side. But how was it possible to feel protected by a man like Brent?

Her fear of him was gone—if it had ever existed. He'd blown her nice staid little life to smithereens, and despite the terrible situation she now found herself in, she was enjoying letting go of some of the rules that had guided her. Being on the run made it easier to remember what was important, and *living* topped that list. Strange that it hadn't before. Now she was ready to blow this particular demon from her past and move on to a better, freer life. Assuming she got the chance.

Her heart thrummed uneasily, but she clenched her fists. She could do this.

"Do you remember any details from my letters about my high school prom?" she asked.

"I know your asshole boyfriend dumped you two days before it." His rough voice ruffled her hair. "And you tried to commit suicide not long after." His warm arms tightened around her, perhaps already making the connection.

"I dated Sam for a couple of years and he claimed to love me. Then Dad got arrested." She could hardly blame Sam, because she'd have done anything to escape the situation too. He'd been a sweet kid. She'd given him her virginity but it hadn't been enough to get them through the scandal. "He put up with the teasing and taunts for a while and then he couldn't take it anymore. I was a social pariah. Maybe his parents forced him, but when he dumped me, I wasn't surprised. I was more surprised we lasted as long as we did."

"Spineless weasel."

"He was just a kid." She could tell Brent wanted to object again, but he kept silent so she carried on. She'd been spat on, slapped, bullied. Getting dumped by Sam and her girlfriends had hurt at the time, but paled into insignificance with later events. "So, this other guy asked me to go to the prom with him instead."

"Who?"

"Doesn't matter." She shivered as a cold memory blew over her skin. Brent pulled her closer, his skin as hot as an open fire.

"Matters to me."

"Why? So you can spend another twenty inside for something that happened eight years ago?"

"You think you're not worth it?" he demanded.

"He's not worth it."

"What if I promise to just beat the shit out of him?"

The venom in his voice scared her. "I never told Dad because I know he'd have gone after him and I didn't want that. You have to promise you won't touch him either." Her breathing grew choppy. "I don't want to have to worry about you…" Her voice broke and she buried her face in the sleeping bag. What sort of admission was *that*? That she cared. Too much.

Whatever happened, they weren't going to live happily ever after. They lived separate lives in separate countries. Thinking of what had happened to poor Peter, they'd be lucky to live through this mess, period.

When she went to pull away, he held her and murmured, "Fine. I won't touch the bastard." His breath brushed her cheek and she shivered. The scent of him engulfed her, comforted her. So big. So masculine. No soft edges, but gentle and unexpectedly kind. She trusted him more than she'd ever trusted anyone else in her life. More than she trusted herself.

Her heart pounded, but she had to get this story out. Needed to expel the words.

"So this guy asks me to the prom even though it was obvious he didn't really want to." She flashed back to his expression.

Sullen. Angry. "A friend of my mom's fixed us up. We went in his car and I was just so grateful to be going—maybe dance, you know? Pretend everything was normal and that I still fit in."

The way Brent's fingers tightened on hers reminded her he didn't know. Age sixteen he hadn't gone to the prom. He'd gone to jail and his childhood sweetheart had waited a lifetime for the boy she'd lost, and then she'd been murdered. It was a much sadder story than hers. Darkness gave her strength to finish this. That and the fact he'd gone through far worse. She started to tremble.

"You don't have to tell me." His voice rumbled through her back.

A lump wedged in her throat because she did. For the first time in her life, she needed to get this out. It was like a tumor trapped inside her and she had to get rid of it before it took over her life and destroyed her forever.

"We started driving toward school but then he changed his mind. Said we were supposed to meet two of the guys on the beach first. I guess I was a bit nervous. I was so desperate for everything to go back to normal. To talk to my friends. Maybe to win Sam back when he saw me with another guy." The memories kept coming, backfilling the empty void of her life. The cool breeze off the water, the grit of sand against her bare skin. "When we got there, the beach was empty so he suggested we dip our feet in the ocean. I thought it was a cute idea—being all dressed up and on the beach."

The weight of Brent's silence crushed her and made it difficult to breathe.

"I wore this blue silk gown and silver heels—to match my name." She'd bought them to try and cheer herself up and had known she looked good in them. "He opened a bottle of beer and gave it to me. I didn't know he put something in it. A roofie or something." Damn, she felt cold on the inside. Like her bones had been put in the deep freeze. All these years later and she couldn't stop shaking. "I only had a few sips—I don't like beer—but after that I could barely stand. I didn't even know what he was doing when he started unzipping my dress." She laughed but it came out garbled, like a choke, and she squeezed her eyes shut even in the darkness. "I think I thought we were going swimming, but it all got fuzzy after that." *Not fuzzy enough.*

Brent's arms tightened further, the force of the embrace almost painful, but it helped ground her in the here and now and kept her from floating screaming into the past.

"He folded my dress very neatly and laid it on the sand. I remember thinking that was nice of him. Folding my dress so it doesn't crease. Then he started messing with my panties and I realized I wasn't even wearing a bra because the dress didn't need it. I started to panic and tried to get up and run, but I was in my stupid heels and he caught me..." Her fingers went to her lips. "He ripped off my panties so I was naked except for the fuck-me heels—his words, not mine. Then he raped me in the sand."

She clamped her thighs together as if that would change the past.

It had hurt, a lot. Rough, brutal violence that defied society's conventions, and overpowered her weak attempts to fight.

She could hear Brent's breathing, feel his chest expanding. He rocked her gently in the circle of his embrace. "When he was done, he threw my dress at me and stuffed my panties in his pocket. Told me he was going to show the guys, tell them he'd fucked me on the beach because I'd begged him to and that no one would believe me and no one would care even if I told them the truth." Her lips curled in remembered horror. "And then he told me I wasn't even any good anyway.

"I believed him."

Brent rubbed her neck with his chin. Kept silent. But she could *feel* his rage.

"He drove to school and left me in his car like a piece of garbage. I walked home barefoot." She'd snuck in, told her mother she'd had a headache. Then cleaned up in the bathroom as if water and soap could wash it all away. She'd wanted to burn the dress, but hadn't had access to a fire. She'd stuffed it in a box in the attic instead.

"You never told anyone. Never reported it?" His voice was a dark rasp.

"No. He was right. Everyone hated me and I wasn't about to go to the police." Terrified he'd attack her again, she'd locked herself in her bedroom and had been more alone than she'd ever imagined possible.

A long pause. "What about your mother?"

"She didn't hate me, but she was a wreck. I couldn't tell her." Her mom had already been devastated by her husband's betrayal, finding out her daughter had been attacked would have undermined all the progress Katherine had made. Anna hadn't been able to deal with the idea of coping with all that on top of everything else.

She tucked the tangled mess of her hair behind her ear. She still needed to talk to her mother about Dad. Needed to figure out a way to repair their tattered relationship.

"And two days later you tried to kill yourself." Brent's voice was rough as that long-ago ocean.

It had been the blackest period of her life, and thinking back on it now, it was a miracle she'd survived. "He bragged to his buddies that we had sex and they believed him. Everyone was whispering and pointing at me, only this time it was even worse than when Dad was arrested because none of it was true, and it *hurt* so much. It was...God, it was awful." Her insides scrambled just remembering the shame and disgust. And the fear it would happen again. "I went back to the beach trying to figure it all out, and then the storm came." Her tears dried up. "I just wanted it all to go away.

Brent's quiet support boosted her.

"As soon as I got in the water, I knew I'd made a mistake. I didn't want to die, and I fought hard to survive." The words came fast now. She'd been lucky to have spotted by a fishing boat. Beyond lucky. "Everyone assumed I'd tried to commit suicide because of Dad. I know that's what he believed." What he'd died believing. Another painful regret she'd take to her grave. "In the hospital they kept telling me how 'well' I was doing and it made it harder to tell them what had really happened. In the end it was just easier to let them think it was Dad's fault…"

There was silence for a long time—nothing but the sound of the wind in the trees and their own quiet breathing. Did he hate her for that deception, for that weakness? It all seemed so petty now.

"I'm glad someone pulled you out of the water, Anna."

Not judging, or condemning the mistakes she'd made. He rubbed his hands up and down her arms and something flickered in their wake. Something exciting. Something unfamiliar. Something good.

Her emotions jumbled and jolted. The pain from the memories diminishing. The desire to move on from the past, growing stronger and stronger every second, despite the fear and uncertainty surrounding the future.

She turned to face him, cupped his cheek, and reached up to kiss him softly. She'd been a coward for so long. He'd given her so much over the last few days. Sacrificed so much. But that wasn't what this was about. Brent Carver made her ache with ravenous lust and gritty desire and it was so new, so unexpected, so precious, she had to explore it. For a few seconds he remained unresponsive beneath her. Then his lips moved gently over hers, shattering something deep inside, something that had held her prisoner for a very long time. The ice in her blood turned to steam. Uncertainty turned to need that crawled through her belly and arrowed lower with sharp arousal. She traced her tongue along the seam of his lips and felt something change as he let her inside to slowly taste him.

Strong, powerful male. Gentle protector.

A low growl rumbled through his chest and then he was kissing her hard and deep, his tongue tangling with hers in a searing dance. Hunger exploded along her nerves. Her heart hammered. Breath coming in gasps. Her fingers slipped beneath his shirt, sliding over taut hot skin. She felt him shiver even though he made no move to touch her. He was letting her take everything at her speed, giving her the sort of control she usually craved.

Curious, she slipped her hand lower, the back of her knuckles grazing the flat abs and smooth skin, her own nipples responding by tightening into sensitive peaks that she wanted him to touch. Cautiously, she cupped the bulge at the front of his jeans and his hips surged forward. She stroked him through the denim, intrigued by the length of him growing bigger and harder, straining against her palm. The idea of having him inside her didn't scare her. It made her hot. His fingers dug into her hip bone, holding her in place. Not pulling her closer.

Which was a crying shame.

Her whole body pulsed at the idea of making love with Brent. Before the rape she and her high school boyfriend had messed around and had sex a few times—it hadn't been her smartest decision but, with everything that came after, she hadn't regretted it. She knew sex could be fun, even enjoyable. A few years ago she'd bought herself some sex toys, determined to figure out what the hell was wrong with her—it turned out there was nothing wrong with her, it was guys she didn't trust. She *knew* there was pleasure to be had. And she'd spent years imagining how a man might touch her with desire and how she might respond like a normal woman. But until this moment it had never happened.

She wasn't going to be put off by fear or inexperience. There had been so much death recently she knew there was no guarantee of tomorrow. She might never get another chance to be with this man the way she needed to be. A low sound of want came out of her throat, her hands moving to the button of his jeans, the low rasp of the zipper. But he pulled away and she was flipped fast so she was facing away from him and then jammed tightly against his body. She tried to twist but his arms were bands of steel.

"We're not doing anything you might regret tomorrow," he gritted out.

"W-why not?" The tremor in her voice betrayed her arousal. She pressed her legs together but her sex still throbbed.

"A lot has happened over the last week and you're not thinking straight." His body was shaking. He wanted her. Judging from the impossible-to-ignore erection pressed against her butt, he wanted her a lot. "I don't want you confusing gratitude with lust."

She almost choked on outrage. "What!" The pissed-off exasperation in her voice made him laugh and she felt it with her whole body. "I know the difference between gratitude and lust, Brent. And between rape and sex. The fact I'm about thirty seconds away from my first orgasm in months is making it all very clear to me."

"Dammit." His lungs were heaving. "Why did you have to mention orgasms?"

"Isn't that the point of what we're doing?" Or trying to do, in her case. Although there were other reasons she didn't want to think about—bonding, connection, intimacy, love.

She reached back to touch him, but he caught her hands and held them tightly clasped in front of her. "We're not doing this, Anna."

"I finally get the whole mindless lust thing and you aren't interested?"

"I never said I wasn't interested." His voice was rough in her ear. With one hand, he deftly undid the button of her jeans and slipped inside her panties. She arched back against him as he pushed one finger deep inside her. "Oh, God." She spread her legs wider. Trusting him. Wanting him. It had been so long since anyone had touched her and it had *never* felt this good.

His heart pounded against her back. "You are so small and tight." His voice was rough as he stroked in and out, spreading her wetness over her folds, making her breasts ache. She was so turned on it was going to take about ten seconds for her to climax.

"I want you to touch me, Brent. I want you inside me."

"I am touching you." He was annihilating her. He let go of her wrists and shifted one hand to torture a beaded nipple. "And I am inside you." His teeth grazed her neck. Two big fingers plunged deep, the heel of his hand pressing against her clitoris just hard enough to make her explode from the onslaught of sensations. Every nerve blasted like a firework, white light blinding her, and she opened her mouth in a silent scream as it went on and on and on. He slowly brought her back down to earth. Her heart was still galloping and his fingers were still deep inside her. She trapped his hand with her thighs when he went to withdraw, enjoying the aftershocks, wanting more. But after a moment he readjusted her clothing, and pulled her back against him, wrapping her in his arms.

"What about you?" Damn stubborn man.

"I'm not willing to take the risk you might be making a big mistake."

"Isn't that my problem?"

He held her against him for one long second and then eased back. "Not tonight. Tonight it's mine."

"I don't think you'd be a mistake," she said.

His silence said he believed otherwise.

Gradually her heartbeat returned to normal and a languid feeling of exhaustion stole through her relaxed muscles. Her eyelids drifted shut. She gave a peaceful sigh when he finally pulled her snug against him. Then she slept.

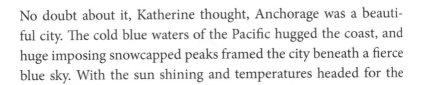

No doubt about it, Katherine thought, Anchorage was a beautiful city. The cold blue waters of the Pacific hugged the coast, and huge imposing snowcapped peaks framed the city beneath a fierce blue sky. With the sun shining and temperatures headed for the seventies, today promised to be perfect. Not to mention the feeling of solid ground beneath her feet. She hurried along the sidewalk toward the log cabin visitor center. She wanted information on the Alaska Botanical Garden and knew Ed wasn't interested. He wanted to take a helicopter trip over a glacier, but the thought of doing that made her queasy. Helicopters scared the bejesus out of her. She was hoping he'd go with the Montgomerys and leave her to her own devices for one day.

He'd always been involved in everything she did. Some might say *over*-involved—she thought of Harvey. It usually didn't bother her. Most of her friends had ditched her when Davis had been arrested, and although she now moved in those same circles again, she'd never forgiven that betrayal. It meant she had no close confidantes. She pressed her lips together to force back a sudden onslaught of emotion. She wasn't even close to Anna and it was her own fault. Their relationship had changed when Katherine had married Ed, and in the process she'd lost a precious piece of herself, but hadn't even known it at the time.

Now, she realized fiercely, she wanted it back.

Harvey was right, damn him. She wasn't in lust with her husband, but they shared a life together, companionship, and security. And maybe that wasn't the most romantic attitude, but romance had gotten her nothing but grief and heartbreak and she was never going there again. *Darn it.* She drew her fleece around her shoulders.

She was unsettled and confused about these feelings she still had for Davis, which had taken her so by surprise. She looked up and came to an abrupt standstill, charmed by the sight of the log cabin with its wildflower roof. Flowers bobbed bright in the breeze and insects darted throughout the gorgeous scene.

A van pulled up to park at the curb beside her.

"Katherine!" someone called her name and she turned to see Harvey hurrying after her.

"Dammit."

Suddenly the side door of the van rattled open and someone grabbed her and pulled her inside. What on earth was happening? Her hip hit the metal rim of the door and pain shot through her body. Something dark and heavy smothered her face and she started to struggle as she choked on the musty scent. Her heart contracted hard and fast. Panic shot through every nerve and vein. Then the door was slammed shut on a male shout and she heard a series of scuffles and bangs as someone tried to crush her.

Harvey. She heard Harvey.

There was the sound of the door opening again. The thud of a body hitting steel. *What's going on?* The pressure eased and Katherine lay on the hard floor as someone tied her hands and feet with zip ties.

Oh, my Lord. *I'm being kidnapped.* This didn't make any sense. She wasn't rich. But Harvey was. A sharp prick of pain made her flinch. Then blackness rolled over her in a solid wave.

CHAPTER 12

Anna woke but Brent was gone. She sat up and then flopped back. Yesterday had been the stuff of nightmares but last night had been amazing. The relief of sharing her bitter history with Brent, followed by the hottest make-out session ever, meant that when she'd finally dropped off, she'd slept like she had a head injury. She grinned like a loon, hoping Brent had gotten some rest too.

A robin sang in the tree. Children laughed in the distance. The tent smelled of warm canvas and sunshine. She breathed deeper and another scent tantalized her nostrils. She threw back the covers and pushed out of the tent. Brent was hunkered over the stove he'd bought yesterday, frying bacon on a skillet. He'd either showered or been for a swim because his hair was wet.

"I'm starving, and you are a lifesaver."

He shot her an amused look from under his brow. Her mouth watered and it had nothing to do with the broad shoulders or lean muscle. She was so hungry her stomach started making begging noises—a bit like she'd made last night. She didn't regret it, though. Not even for a moment. She sat on the picnic bench with wild hair, wearing yesterday's clothes, and held out her hands. He stood and brought her coffee.

"It's hot," he warned as he slid the mug into her grip.

It was instant, but tasted fantastic. She met his vivid blue gaze. "Thanks." For the coffee. For the orgasm. For holding her together and believing she was worth helping, even if it was only because of a promise he'd made her father.

"You're welcome." The words buzzed over nerve endings that felt stripped of their usual armor.

He turned back to his bacon and she forced herself to stop watching all that male perfection and take in the other scenery. They were surrounded by trees and hidden to the south by the jeep. There was a path through the poplars to what promised to be a small lake. The sun had the feel of promised heat in its early rays.

"Do you think we're safe?" she asked quietly.

Brent looked up. "For now." He snagged three pieces of crispy bacon and stuffed them in a fresh white bread roll. She was drooling by the time he brought it over. She bit into it and the salty heaven made her eyes cross with bliss. She smacked her lips as flavor flooded her mouth. "Where did you learn to cook?"

He was watching her mouth, but he cocked an eyebrow.

"Prison," she guessed.

"No. Though I'm not sure frying bacon counts as cooking." He took a bite of his own roll. Chewed. "When Mom left, things got a little lean in the kitchen department," he admitted. "I figured out the basics."

"No one ever tried to get you kids into social services?"

He gave her a look that suggested she was crazy.

"How old were you when she left?"

"Six. Finn wasn't even out of diapers—he was slow that way." He shot her a grin.

"You don't hate her?"

He shook his head. "She was a battered wife. A victim."

"She was your mother," Anna said fiercely. "She should have taken care of you."

"The way yours took care of you?" he pointed out.

OK. It *had* been hard when she'd effectively been abandoned by both parents at a time she'd desperately needed them. But she'd been a teen and ultimately it had taught her to stand on her own two feet. "There is no comparison. If your mother had taken you boys with her, then your father wouldn't have been able to abuse Finn and you wouldn't have killed him. You wouldn't have spent twenty years of your life in jail."

"If she'd taken us with her, he'd have never have stopped looking for her. He was an asshole." Brent grimaced. "I am not blaming my mother for what I did. That's chickenshit."

"Fine, I'll blame her for you."

"Too late." He finished his roll and licked his fingers.

Anna's eyes widened. "You know where she is?"

"Was."

"She's dead?"

Brent nodded, stood, and threw out the dregs of his coffee. "Cancer. Three years ago."

"Did you go and see her?" Her heart pounded.

He shook his head but refused to meet her gaze.

"What, then?"

At first she thought he wasn't going to answer. "I hired Jack Panetti to track her down. By the time he found her, she was in a hospice."

"And?" Getting information out of Brent was like wringing out a rock, but then she remembered how much he'd opened up to her over the last few days, and strove for patience.

The flatness of those blue eyes belied the emotion that shimmered through the air. "She had a new family. Why would I want to remind her of all the bad times?" he said simply. "She was dying."

Her hand went to her mouth.

"I'd planned to let Finn know where she was in case he wanted to contact her, but..." He jerked his shoulder. "She died."

"So you didn't tell him?"

He shook his head. "We weren't exactly talking back then."

"Because?"

He laughed, some of the tension draining from his face. "Because I'm a jackass."

Aspects of Brent's life were so tragic and yet he never blamed others. He always took full responsibility. Emotion bombarded her from all directions. A crying jag would help, but she needed to put on her big girl pants and help get them out of the situation she'd gotten them into. "So," Anna began as she cleared up the breakfast stuff, "where do we go today?"

"I don't want to risk crossing the border unless I know Holly's in the same province. I'll contact Finn later." He looked toward the lake. "This is a good spot. I think we should just lay low for now."

"Are you serious?" The idea of not running for a few hours, of pretending everything was normal and they were just on holiday sounded wonderful. "What if the police are after us?"

His lips thinned. "They're looking for you." He handed her a paper. Every drop of blood drained to her toes and she swayed. She was on the front page, her passport image, grim and unsmiling. There was a picture of her home, with a body on a stretcher being wheeled out. No mention of anyone being arrested at the scene, only that no one had seen her since last Friday night. The cops didn't know if she'd been murdered or if she was the killer. Her insides twisted. The reporter had managed to dig up her father's dubious past, and his recent death. All her friends and colleagues would know her family's dirty secrets, but that was the least of her problems.

Laughter moved closer as kids played in the trees. She ducked her head. Brent rummaged inside the nearby jeep and pulled out a large bag of toiletries and towels before slipping the ball cap gently over her dark hair. "You and I are off to the shower block for a little beauty work." A mischievous glint sparked in his eyes. "You might want to grab your bathing suit."

Ten minutes later she stood in a T-shirt and panties because they hadn't planned a beach trip when they'd bought their supplies. Brent squinted at the hair dye package. "Why'd they have to write everything so damn small?" he grumbled.

The place felt warm and damp from the previous occupant's shower.

"Let me see."

"I've got it." He held the box high above her head. "You did me, now I'm going to do you."

It felt like someone had just lit the flame under them as his eyes flared and she swallowed hard. His jaw clenched as he went back to reading the instructions. He'd stripped off his shirt and just wore board shorts that clung to his narrow hips and strong thighs. Every muscle was covered by tanned skin, bleached hairs sprinkled over lower arms and legs. Rugged male perfection. All her female parts sat up and drooled.

"No tattoos?" She was trying to get them back on neutral footing, but it wasn't working because her pulse kept skipping and her hands kept wanting to reach out and touch.

"How do you know I don't have any tattoos?" His eyes laughed as she grinned at him.

"I saw you naked, remember?"

He frowned and then remembered how they'd first met. "Not my finest moment. *Among other things*," he mimicked her words from that night less than a week ago and laughed. "Prison tats aren't my kind of artwork."

God, he was handsome and unexpectedly good humored. For an ex-con. Even the label felt like a betrayal. He shouldn't have served life, he shouldn't have been convicted. And now she was the one wanted by the cops and he could be arrested for just being with her. But he'd already told her he'd turn himself in if she went to the police, and she didn't trust them. At least with Holly, she had a chance of telling her story before they locked her up and threw away the key.

"Whatever you're thinking, it isn't going to happen," said Brent.

Her eyes flashed to his.

"Come here." That dimple cut into his cheek as he smiled.

She found herself taking a step closer in the cramped space. He pulled on the plastic gloves, wrapped the towel around her shoulders, and moved her a little closer. He mixed the hair dye and started applying the thick cream to her hair from the roots down. "The great thing about going blonde is you don't have to pretend to be smart, it's just an unexpected bonus." He smiled, his own blond hair darkening in the humidity. His fingers continued to massage her scalp. Once he'd gone over every strand, he covered her hair in the plastic bag provided and stepped back.

Jeez, she felt ridiculous, standing here with a gorgeous man while wearing a plastic bag on her head. But even now, the awareness that fired between them at all the wrong moments sprang to life. Remembering what had happened last night, Anna started trembling.

Brent turned away to wash his hands in the little sink beside the shower stall. "Cold?"

As an active volcano. "A little," she said, because she was a coward and didn't know where they stood, or what he wanted.

Brent got his towel off the peg and wrapped it around her waist. His fingers brushed the sides of her breasts and they both jumped.

"You'd better take it from here." He took a step back into the shower curtain. His voice deepened and those board shorts were telling their own story. There she was covered in a T-shirt and two thick towels, with a plastic bag on her head, and he was still turned on?

She didn't know whether to be flattered or terrified. Maybe his sex life was as screwed up as hers. As he'd spent twenty years in prison, that was probably a given. She sat on the tiny wooden bench. After a few moments, Brent checked his watch and sat beside her. The wood groaned.

His arm touched hers. Shoulder to elbow. The connection would have made her bolt a week ago. Today she let herself relax into it and imagined how normal people lived their lives. "I don't suppose you brought a Sudoku puzzle?"

Brent shook his head and closed his eyes, leaning back against the bare wall.

"How long do we have left to wait?"

"Twenty-five minutes and eighteen seconds." He hadn't even looked at his watch.

She fidgeted. The silence seemed to bounce around the brick walls. "Anything you want to talk about?"

He blew out a soft laugh. "No."

"You sure?"

"I'm just sitting here, trying not to think about sex."

Her mouth went dry. "How's that working for you?" Her eyes automatically dropped to his shorts.

He linked his hands and draped them over a rather impressive bulge. Shivers ran over her body that had nothing to do with cold. She was turned on. So turned on, she was having to work hard to not squirm in her damn seat. No one else had ever affected her like this.

He kept his eyes closed. "Actually, for the first time since I was an adolescent boy, the idea of sex in the shower doesn't terrify me." Those bright blue eyes caught her watching him and glimmered. "So even though I feel like a dirty old man because you're, like, ten—" His lip curled. *Badass.* "I'm still feeling pretty damn good."

She was twenty-six years old, and he thought the age gap between them was their biggest problem?

"We're both consenting adults." She raised a hand to touch his face.

"Don't." He grabbed her hand.

"Why not?" she asked softly.

"I'm not the sort of guy that a girl like you should mess around with." A rogue trickle of moisture ran down his temple.

"A girl like me?" Her spine stiffened and she tried to pull her hand away, but he wouldn't let go. "What sort of girl would that be?"

"A good girl." His knuckles skimmed her cheek. The energy in his eyes burned. "A woman who recognizes trouble and is smart enough to avoid it."

"In the normal world, you'd probably be right." Hurt flickered across his features, but he hid it. He hid a lot of things. "Because in the normal world, you wouldn't have even let me in the door. But you did. Now you're stuck with me."

He raked his hair with his fingers, making it stick up on end. "I'm not just some 'guy,' Anna. I'm a fucking killer. A *lifer.*" Anger emanated from him in waves.

"You served your time—"

"I will *never* finish serving my time." He stared intently into her eyes as if trying to impart some important secret.

And then she got it. "This is all about punishing yourself? You pushing me away physically when I know you want me, because it's part of some self-imposed payback for killing your father?"

His lips curled into a cruel sneer. "Maybe I don't want you."

Christ, he should have terrified her, but she knew he'd never hurt her.

Anna pressed her mouth to his before he could move away, determined to prove he was wrong. She slipped her tongue along his upper lip and felt a tremor move through his shoulders and down his spine. He held still, but if he thought he was fooling either of them, he was nuts because desire swarmed the air so thick she could barely breathe.

And suddenly she was crushed to his chest, his mouth angling across hers and diving deep. Big hands gripping her shoulders, her hips. The towel slipped away, leaving only the thin cotton of her T-shirt and panties covering her.

Her nipples bunched tightly against his chest. She rubbed against him, desperate to touch him, skin on skin. He pulled back, eyes as dark as indigo, and she thought he was going to stop, to tell her he really didn't want her. Then his gaze lowered and he stretched the thin cotton of her shirt taut across her breasts. A sharp piercing bolt of desire made Anna hold her breath in anticipation.

He lowered his mouth, teasing her through the wet cotton, abrading sensitive flesh until she squirmed and panted and almost ended up on the floor. He pulled her across him so she straddled his thighs. The narrowness of the bench stopped her from getting as close to him as she wanted and she moaned in frustration. Strong hands clamped her hips as he feasted on her breasts, drawing out a sensation that pulled all the way down to her core. She held on tight to his shoulders, wanting to touch him, but knowing if she let go, she'd fall, and if she fell, he'd stop touching her.

She did not want him to stop.

One of his hands moved south and eased inside her panties. Her back arched up as he slid one finger inside her. "You're so fucking hot."

"For you," she gasped, and let her head fall back as he moved his finger inside her, then added another, the fullness testing her. She dug her nails into his shoulders. "I want *you,* Brent."

They could have been anywhere and she wouldn't have given a damn. He had her completely at his mercy and it didn't terrify her.

In fact, she wanted more, she wanted all of him. Then she was flying, spinning out of control, her inner muscles clenching around his fingers in a long rolling explosion of pleasure. She collapsed against him and he wrapped both arms around her and held her tight. She could feel his heart pounding alongside hers, his erection pressed against her stomach.

She reached for him but he grabbed her hands and held them still. His eyes were haunted.

"I think we both know you want me." She leaned up and drew his earlobe between her teeth. With a shudder he picked her up and set her purposefully away from him.

"Maybe," he said, "but I learned a long time ago, you can't always get what you want."

He let himself out of the shower cubicle, running as much from himself as from her. How ironic that she'd finally found a man she truly wanted to make love to, and he was as screwed up as she was.

"Where the hell is she?" Ed said to Barb as he looked at his watch for the millionth time in the last three hours. They'd both searched the enormous ship for their respective spouses but there was no trace anywhere. He headed back to their cabin to check that Katherine hadn't taken her cell with her. How dare she take off like this? He knew she'd been feeling a bit down lately. That's why he'd booked this cruise, to cheer her up. But to go off without a word? That level of selfishness was maddening and totally out of character. Fury pounded through his blood. The fact Harvey Montgomery was also AWOL set his teeth on edge. He'd seen how the other guy looked at his wife. Katherine was the real deal when it came to natural beauty and everyone wanted a piece of it. But Ed didn't share. He never shared.

Ed had lost his first wife to cancer when his son was a teenager. It had been a terrible time, but they'd gotten through it. She didn't know it, but Katherine had stopped him from making a colossal mistake when Eleanor had lain slowly dying. He'd almost run away. Almost crumbled under the staggering pressure of watching the woman he'd sworn to love waste away into a skeletal shadow. But once he met Katherine, he knew he could get through it and come out the other side as a better man. So he'd helped her and her daughter through Davis's arrest and imprisonment—more than happy to pick up the pieces.

Goddamn Davis Silver, ruining their holiday. He and Davis had worked together, although they'd never really gotten along. Even after all these years, the imbecile was making his life difficult. What the hell Katherine had seen in him was beyond Ed. The guy was a total fool. Idealistic and stupid. Now Davis was dead—someone from work had called to tell him the news. Ed gritted his jaw. He wished the bastard had died in prison a long time ago. Someone must have told Katherine, probably Anna. That was why his wife was acting so uncharacteristically uncooperative.

He wasn't worried about Katherine straying. Even the thought of causing a scandal made her break out in a rash. But it didn't stop men from trying to gain her attention.

"Maybe she and Harv ran off together." Barb smiled her snarky smile, but it looked strained. She'd followed him in his search, and usually he enjoyed her company and her pithy attitude. She flirted with him, and he wanted his wife to know other women found him attractive. Barb was fun and energetic, but right now he wished she were somewhere else.

Like making sure her own husband didn't stray.

"Did you call Harvey?" he asked Barb.

She shrugged a delicate shoulder, the lines on her neck revealing her age. "I left him a voice mail. I expect he chartered a helicopter and went up some mountain somewhere. We had a tiff."

The back of Ed's neck grew hot. Harvey was rich as Crusoe, which Barb loved to remind everyone within shouting distance.

Well, he'd better not have taken Ed's damn wife with him. Anger and resentment grated at him. What had Harvey Montgomery ever done to deserve his cash? Not a damn thing. Born with a silver spoon in his mouth. Suddenly a wave of jealousy hit him. What if Katherine *was* with him? What if she was having an affair and he was too dumb to realize it?

Christ. He felt dizzy and his knees went from under him and he collapsed to the bed, sinking his face into his hands.

He felt fingers in his hair. "Don't worry Ed, darling. I'm sure it's nothing serious."

He thrust her hand away. His phone rang and he snatched it up. It was Harvey fucking Montgomery. "Where the hell are you and where is my wife?"

A stranger replied, "Funny you should ask that, Mr. Plantain."

Ed pulled back for a moment in surprise, then he put the phone back to his ear. "Who is this?" he demanded.

"Shut up and listen. I have Katherine." The voice was low and calm. Unease hit Ed dead center in the chest. "If you want to see your wife alive again, you need to do the following. Get Anna Silver to Vancouver Island by 1400 hours tomorrow. If you fail to produce your wife's daughter, I will kill Katherine." No inflection, no emotion. "If the cops find out, I'll kill Katherine. If for a moment I think you're trying to screw with me, I will kill Katherine."

Who the hell was this? Were they serious? Was it a joke? "Can't you just go to Anna's house?"

"Yeah, I think I might have already tried that, Einstein."

Oh, my God. "Is Harvey there too?"

A small huff of amusement. "I'll call you again with instructions of where to take Anna when you get her, alone. And I suggest you keep this to yourself, Ed, because I'd sure hate for you to make a mistake you can't fix."

The man hung up and Ed stared at the phone, shaking, wondering if it was a sick joke. Then he got another incoming message with a photo attached. He opened it and flinched as he saw Katherine and Harvey lying next to one another, bound hand and foot.

Barb looked over his shoulder. "Dear God. We need to call the police."

"No cops."

She stuck her hands on her hips. "Look, Ed. Harvey and I are probably getting a divorce. In fact, I'd be far better off financially if I pretended I never saw that photograph. But they've been kidnapped—you can't just run around thinking you know how to handle this."

Her sharp features were locked on his, showing more compassion and understanding than he'd ever imagined her capable of. He nodded. He knew exactly what he had to do.

Fire radiated across Jack Panetti's back, but what he noticed first was that god-awful smell. Antiseptic and sick people. His stomach rebelled. There was a constant irritating beep. Where the hell was he? He squinted at pale blue walls.

"He's coming around," someone yelled. *Too damn loud.*

He turned his head away from the noise and closed his eyes. *Damn.* His insides felt like jelly and his brain so drugged he could barely lift his eyelids. He tried again. Saw a stranger leaning over him. He knew the guy was a cop from the cheap suit and excess baggage under his eyes.

"How you feeling, Mr. Panetti?"

"Like I've been shot. Again." He lifted his head long enough to wriggle his toes. Thank God. Being paralyzed was what he'd most feared when he'd slipped in and out of consciousness in the ambulance and his lower body had gone numb. The fact his legs worked made him want to dance, though he wasn't quite up to that yet.

A half smile tugged on the detective's lips. "Third time according to the docs."

Jack nodded and then held still, waiting for the world to stop exploding. "Twice as a cop." Probably the unluckiest cop alive. Or maybe the luckiest, depending on your perspective. Jack had always been a glass-half-full kind of guy. He saw his secretary and the Denver office's computer guru, hanging around the doorway. He shot them a concerned look, and tried to mutely apologize for causing them grief.

"What happened?" he asked. His tongue was thick with the taste of anesthetic.

"We're hoping you can tell us."

A swift image of a uniformed police officer jerking on his feet flashed through his brain. Oh, God. All of a sudden he was grateful for the pain in his back because it meant he wasn't dead. Jack closed his eyes. "The cop?" he asked. The heaviness in his brain wasn't all drug related.

"Dead." The detective's voice was quiet with the knowledge that he could have been that cop. Jack could have been that cop too. The guy had never stood a chance. "What can you tell us?"

He sucked in a deep breath, but maybe he had a punctured lung because it didn't seem to be helping. "I was staking out the home of the head of security for the Holladay Foundation." He reeled off the address. The cop exchanged a look with someone across the bed standing behind Jack. He didn't have the energy to turn and look. "I was about to call it quits when some guy climbed in the backseat, put a gun to my head, and told me to drive." Shame welled through him. "I couldn't believe how lucky I was when that patrol car came up on the highway. I sideswiped him to get his attention."

He'd gotten the man killed and every person in the room knew it.

The detective was writing in his notebook. "You see a face?"

Jack frowned. "Maybe. It was dark." He needed to get in touch with his client. Brent Carver was up against something bigger than either of them had imagined. Hell, he hoped the guy was still alive.

"Why were you watching these guys?"

Jack's face distorted as he tried to smile. "It was just a hunch. A guy died under mysterious circumstances on the subway last week—"

"The guy who claimed he was stealing their money?" The detective perked up.

Jack nodded. "I was just trying to make sure it was an accident, is all. You need to talk to their security people."

"The death was deemed accidental, if I remember right."

It hurt to talk but Jack was grateful to be alive. That cop was dead. "You need to look harder."

"Yeah, try telling that to the state attorney's office," the young detective muttered under his breath. "Did you see the shooter come out of that house?"

Jack shook his head. "Did he have a family? The uniform?"

The detective stared at the white sheets of Jack's bed. "Wife and two boys."

A sharp clawing pain was reflected on the heart monitor.

"Who's your client?" This voice was harder, condemnation in every word. It was always the quiet ones you had to watch. He turned his head carefully. A female detective stood by the window. A tall woman with short-cropped copper-colored hair. All angles rather than curves.

"Can't tell you that."

The woman leaned over him and Jack got a face full of bitter disapproval. "We've got a dead cop—"

"And your client could be in danger," the younger guy said with more tact.

Jack pressed the call button for the nurse. He never revealed a client. "If I think it'll find the bastard who murdered that cop, I'll tell you. In the meantime I'll see what my team can dig up."

The witch's eye twitched. "Interfering with a police investigation is a criminal offense—"

Jack's temper spiked. "You think I don't know that? You think I don't want that bastard *more* than you do?"

"Keep us informed if you get any solid leads, OK?" The younger guy was obviously the peacemaker and the brains of the organization.

"Sure." Jack held the redhead's glare as she backed to the door. "Have a nice day, Detectives."

From the way her eyes shot daggers at him, he figured it was a good thing he was already flat on his ass. When they were gone, his secretary, Ramona Stone, and his technology guru, Trace Maddox, came into the room. "Thanks for rescuing me from the ballbuster."

"Hey, you should have stayed asleep. That detective is a bitch on wheels." Trace's fervent words suggested they'd shared some quality time.

Ramona put her hand on his forehead and then kissed his cheek. "Glad you decided to rejoin the living."

"Me too." He leaned his head against the pillow and smiled at the nurse who approached. Then he faced Ramona and asked, "Did you speak to the client?"

"He called a few times, but…" Ramona held up a newspaper, and there was Davis Silver's daughter on the front page. *Shit.* "Her boyfriend was found dead in her house. Cops are asking for any information on her whereabouts."

She was supposed to be with his client.

"See if you can contact the client. We need to keep working his case."

"No work for you," the nurse told him sternly.

"We're on it," Ramona told him softly. He caught her hand.

"Low profile. No following these cowboys around." He glanced at Trace. "No offense."

"None taken." Trace tipped his cowboy hat.

"These people must have left some kind of online trail."

Trace smiled. "I'm on it, boss. Relax." He winked at the nurse. "Enjoy the view."

Her hair wasn't so much blonde as honey brown. The shade made her dark eyes and brows stand out, and it suited her. Brent had just grunted.

Since that burst of desire in the shower, they'd managed to find a place to coexist between the scorching attraction and blind fear. An unspoken time-out, detached from the reality that had become so terrifying over the last forty-eight hours. But Anna wasn't finished with Brent Carver. Not by a long shot.

They wandered down to the campsite shop and Brent found cheap watercolors and a sketch pad. He looked like a kid on Christmas morning, but she doubted he'd ever had a real Christmas. She remembered the boys in that photograph in Brent's home and compared it to her own idyllic childhood. The memories seemed far away, but still inspired a wistful sense of longing.

She found a paperback and they picked up sunscreen and a cheap bathing suit for her and a couple of beach towels. She also grabbed a big floppy hat and plastered a smile on her face, because she didn't want anyone to recognize her from the grim portrait on the front of the newspaper.

They strolled slowly to the beach, not holding hands but in step and almost touching. They headed through the woods by their site and found a quiet spot on the warm sand. There were people around, loads of kids, and the occasional dog, but no one paid them any attention.

"Do you think we're safe?" She spread her towel and dropped to the sand with her book.

"This is the last place a bad guy is going to expect to find us. Hell, I can't believe it myself."

He went down to the water and filled a small plastic cup. Then he sat beside her and started sketching. She watched him doing a wash of the sky. Even a few brush strokes revealed his incredible talent. He wore those same board shorts and a T-shirt they'd picked up yesterday with a zebra on the front. Didn't matter what he wore, he always looked good. The muscles in his arms flexed as he painted. He set one picture to dry while he started another, almost feverish in his intensity.

"You've missed it."

He caught her eye briefly. "It's my drug of choice." The calming satisfaction of getting a fix relaxed the tired lines of his face.

Anna felt bad. She taken him from his home, put him in danger, *and* deprived him of his passion. A lucrative passion. His livelihood. What would happen if he ended up back inside? The thought squeezed her lungs so tight she could barely breathe.

It wasn't a game. This was life and death and years in prison.

She buried her nose in her book and tried to read, but as the sun rose she drifted off to sleep. When she woke, Brent was standing next to the water's edge throwing a stick for a chocolate Lab that danced around his legs, making the water splash and both of them grin happily.

She wandered down to join him, the sand hot against the soles of her feet.

He launched the stick and the dog leaped into the water.

"Who's your new friend?"

"Just some mutt." But he didn't fool her.

"Why don't you get a dog? You obviously love them."

One mile-wide shoulder curled up.

Then she got it. "You deny yourself all the things that make you happy. And you're scared you'll have to abandon it if anything happens to you."

He shot her a scowl, but kept his mouth shut.

The sound of excited children's voices bounced around the lake and a bunch of them ran out of the trees.

"There he is! Boomer. Boomer!" one kid called.

Anna noticed Brent's mouth tighten with disappointment, though he tried to hide it.

"You're denying yourself some basic companionship in the unlikely event—"

"It's not *that* unlikely."

Because of her. Her stomach cramped and she folded her arms over her waist as the kids and dog converged.

"This your dog?" Brent asked the kids. He held the stick hostage as the dog danced around.

"Yes, sir, we've been searching for him all over the camp," the eldest, a boy about twelve, piped up. The dog kept wagging his tail, mouth open, eyes hopeful as he eyed the stick. The boy wrestled the dog into its collar and started jerking the leash.

Anna winced.

"Next time he escapes, check out the beach first," Brent called. "He's a water dog." His voice trailed off as they dragged the poor animal away.

Anna reached a hand around Brent's elbow. "You should get a dog. Finn would watch it for you if anything happened—"

"I don't want a damn dog," he snarled, back to being the bitter man she'd first encountered.

She searched for something to say, but Brent had withdrawn and locked himself behind those big stone walls. He jerked off his T-shirt. "I'm going for a swim. Want to come?"

She shook her head. "I haven't swum in years. Not since the night I almost drowned."

He stared at her for a long moment but didn't say anything. She'd made the mistake of reminding him of the person he usually showed the world and he was rebuilding his armor. He handed her the car keys from his pockets. "I'll be back in an hour. Don't go anywhere," he warned.

Anna watched him walk away and then dive into the gentle lapping water. This was how he got all those muscles, she realized. Swimming. He cut across the surface of the lake, never seeming to tire. After a few minutes of standing there gawking at him, she went back to her towel. His sketch pad was closed but she saw a page edged in blue sticking out. Eyeing the distant swimming figure, she eased the paint box off the top and opened the pad.

The first four paintings were of the lake, each similar but different. The fifth picture was of her, dozing beneath her oversized hat. It shocked her. He'd drawn someone tranquil, serene. Soft lines, long slender legs that belied her short stature. His view of her was unsettling. It wasn't how she saw herself—uptight, meticulous. His painting showed someone she wanted to be: relaxed, beautiful.

She closed the pad and tried reading her novel. But when he came back, wet shorts clinging to every powerful inch, she couldn't concentrate.

That body made her realize she'd always dated boys. Boys who did as they were told. Boys she could control.

Brent Carver was no boy.

And he was determined to hold her at arm's length even though they both knew the time they had together was short. She doubted she'd ever meet another man like Brent. The question was, what was she going to do about it?

CHAPTER 13

Katherine groggily opened her eyes and rolled her head to see where she was. *Ugh*. On a hard concrete floor that made her feel every one of her fifty years. A curved tin roof arched overhead and someone watched TV about thirty feet from where she'd been dumped.

She tried to move her arms, but they were tied behind her back and her ankles cinched close together. The position and lack of blood flow was excruciating.

"Katherine," someone whispered.

Harvey.

She twisted the other way, trying to ignore the pain in her bound wrists.

"Are you all right?" he asked.

"Yes," she whispered back. "Are you?"

He nodded, but he sported a ripped shirt and a bloodstained swollen nose where someone had either punched him or introduced him face-first to a wall.

"Why are they doing this? What do they want?" Hysteria crept into her voice and her heart lunged.

He shook his head, but made the movement small as he kept one eye on the guy watching TV. "I don't know."

"*I'm* not rich," she hissed, and it came out like an accusation.

He raised one brow. "You're the one they stuffed in the van. They just grabbed me because I was drawing too much attention to them."

She frowned. It didn't make any sense.

"I told Barb I wanted a divorce last night." He looked around the warehouse. "But I don't think she had time to organize this."

Katherine opened her mouth in shock. He'd actually done it. Left his wife. And thought she might kidnap him for money. That was not a happy marriage. "I'm sorry," she said quietly. She knew she'd had something to do with his decision, although she didn't know exactly what.

"Don't be." His eyes were warm. "It's been on the cards for a few years. I just never had the guts to do it before."

And it did take guts, Katherine realized. To walk away from a life you'd made, in the hopes of finding a better one. She was trying not to think about her life with Ed. It had been fine. For the last nine years, Ed had taken care of her, gotten her through heartbreak and betrayal, but…

But was the problem.

For the longest time, she'd been a weak broken creature. Pathetic and nervous as a doe. Davis's betrayal had undermined every belief she'd had in herself. After years of telling herself she didn't care about him anymore, his death had hit her hard. And lately Ed's rigid control had started to feel suffocating. Stifling. But those feelings made her feel ungrateful, which was why she'd been ignoring the problem. *What problem?*

She was done living that way. Davis's death reminded her that life was fragile and temporary. There were no second chances. "Why were you following me?"

His eyes crinkled. "I saw you leaving the ship. I wanted the chance to apologize for upsetting you last night. It was never my intention to try and get you into bed. I was actually just enjoying the fact I could talk to you so freely—about anything, which was really rather stupid and highly inaccurate, given how you ran out of the lounge like I'd molested you under the table."

If she hadn't been bound and lying on a concrete floor, she might have blushed. "I'm sorry." She held his gaze. She was sorry for everything. For overreacting last night and getting him mixed up in this today.

Harvey seemed genuinely nice. He talked to her as if he valued her opinion, something Ed never did. Oh, and he'd tried to stop kidnappers from carting her off in a van, which was a pretty big deal as they were both now tied up on this floor.

They were close together, so close she could feel his breath on her cheek. It felt intimate, and yet she was glad she wasn't alone. And that made her very selfish indeed.

"What do you think they want with us?" The nerves were back and there was nothing she could do to lose the image of cut-off ears or missing fingers.

"Does Ed have any enemies?"

"No," she said, and then it came to her. "But my ex-husband died last week—"

"The thief?"

She nodded. Grief morphed into anger. "If anyone was involved in something dubious, it would be Davis." Bitterness tasted acidic on her tongue. God, she'd been such a fool to believe all his lies and then mourn for him. She put him out of her mind. Someone would rescue them if they just stayed alive long enough. "What are we going to do?"

He leaned closer. If he hadn't been here, she would have gone out of her mind. "See if you can find anything sharp to cut these goddamned ties, but don't let them know you're awake."

He closed his eyes and looked like he'd suddenly nodded off. Was he sick? Then she felt a presence loom behind her and turned her head. Obviously she wasn't very good at this kidnap-victim business, but she did know how to keep her dignity. "Could I have a drink of water, please?"

The guy was bald and muscular, and looked like a cleaned-up biker. He shrugged and turned away. A moment later she heard the tap running. He came back and helped her sit up. The glass he held to her lips looked murky. She decided this was a time in her life when she couldn't afford to be fussy. She swallowed the water greedily. Her mouth was bone dry. The water slid down her throat and down her neck with delicious satisfaction.

Harvey pretended to sleep.

"Thanks. Can you tell me why you've taken us?"

Baldy shook his head.

"You can't just grab us off the streets and not tell us why!" Her voice rang out in the open space.

The big guy squatted closer beside her and she got a strong whiff of unwashed male. She forced herself to meet his gaze. His eyes were intelligent and sympathetic, but they were also resolute. No way could she talk him around. He stuck a pistol in her face and her heart started drilling through her chest as he swung the gun at Harvey. "Your buddy here volunteered for this mission and we don't need him."

"Please don't hurt him." The idea of anyone being murdered for trying to defend her was unbearable.

"Behave yourself and no one will get hurt."

"He's worth millions," she nodded toward Harvey, who started coughing. "His family will pay to get him back."

The bald guy didn't look impressed. "Unless he's got sixty to spare, it's no dice."

"Sixty thousand?" She eyed Harvey with a hopeful smile. His eyes opened and lit up.

"Sixty *million*," the guy sneered.

Harvey's expression fell and Katherine pursed her lips.

"It would take a few days," Harvey said as if mentally tallying his assets. "Let Katherine go and I'll start making the arrangements."

Katherine gaped. He had to be bluffing. The bald man's gaze narrowed, considering.

She didn't know if that was good or bad for their chances of survival, so she decided to change the subject. "Why would kidnapping *me* help you get sixty million dollars?" And suddenly she knew, and if Davis hadn't been dead, she'd have killed him herself.

"Like I said, behave yourself and no one will get hurt. You're just here to provide a little incentive to someone else."

The only people who cared about her were Ed and Anna. *Anna*. Sweet Jesus. "If you touch my daughter, I swear to God—" He braced his dirty shoe on her shoulder and pushed. She fell hard against Harvey and he tried to cushion her fall with his body.

Their captor smiled. "We just want our money, lady. No one has to get hurt."

He turned and left them in a tangled heap. She felt Harvey's heart beating against her ribs and absorbed some of his heat while she tried to get her emotions and limbs back under control.

"I didn't know you had a daughter," Harvey said mildly.

Katherine gave a small laugh. "I don't see her very often." And then she burst into tears.

Brent heard the kids before he saw them, and watched Boomer rocket out of the woods and into the lake like a torpedo. He grinned. Life didn't get much happier than a dog chasing a stick in the water.

Maybe he *should* get a dog. Hell, if he survived the next week without going to jail, he'd adopt a whole damn pack. They'd be good security.

When he'd come back from his swim, Anna had been dozing, and when she'd woken up, he'd made her a ham roll for lunch out of the supplies they'd brought with them. A meager peace offering, but a necessary one.

He'd been an asshole and she deserved better. He didn't know how anyone calling himself a man could force himself on a woman, but he knew plenty of animals who liked to take advantage of the vulnerable. He wasn't an animal and he had no intention of taking advantage of Anna, no matter how much he wanted her. She'd been through hell and he was determined to get her through this mess and out the other side, alive, intact, and ready to move on to a better life. The trouble was, Anna had other ideas.

They'd both relaxed and caught some sun. They were about to head back to the tent for the night, having stayed on the beach for as long as they possibly could—avoiding the intimacy of the small canvas shelter because he didn't know how long he'd last if she started kissing him again.

"Wait up," he ordered. Anna stopped, hands full of towels and books and the bag of bare essentials they'd brought with them in case they'd had to flee.

She stood in front of him with her light honey-colored hair glinting in the dying rays of the sun, those intelligent green eyes hidden behind film-star sunglasses. He squeezed out a tube of sunscreen and slathered her nose to protect a burn that was starting to form. She just shook her head at him and started up the beach again.

"Can I see your pictures?" A high-pitched voice squeaked loudly from behind him. *Shit.* Where'd she come from?

The little girl barely reached his thigh. She looked up at him with massive brown eyes. He cleared his throat. "Sure." Kids usually avoided him, not that he saw that many on his private beach.

He dropped down to his knees and spread the paintings out. They were just loose sketches. More a reminder of color and form. He might work up something bigger when he got home. *If* he got home. He released a deep breath.

"I like that one." She pointed to one that had a tiny picture of Boomer dancing beside a figure by the water. He knelt down, found a pencil, and signed it. "Here. It's yours." He held it out but she refused to take it.

"Mommy says I'm not allowed to take gifts from strangers."

Great, now he was going to get busted as a pervert. He heard the other kids come up to where he knelt in the sand. The eldest boy continued to throw the stick for Boomer, who splashed like a lunatic. A fickle friend. Brent grinned though. The dog's enthusiasm for living in the moment was contagious.

"I like that one." Another girl, an older sister judging from the matching brown eyes, pointed at a picture that he thought was technically the best, but lacked emotion.

"I like that one." The little boy pointed to a picture that showed the rocks off to the side of the lake.

Brent signed them all. Added a fourth for the kid on dog duty.

"Are you an artist or something?" the older girl asked as she admired the picture he'd given her.

"Or something."

Her eyes were bright and captivated. It was kind of cool to see their reaction to his work. A million times more satisfying than any New York gallery opening.

"You should keep them safe," he told the kids. "Hold on to them." *They might pay your way through college someday.* He gathered his other paintings, including the one of Anna he'd never part with, and picked up his stuff and turned to find her watching from a seat on a fallen log.

"Your girlfriend looks funny with that stuff on her nose," said the youngest girl who'd started all this.

The idea of Anna as his girlfriend twisted something up inside him, but this was Pretendland, so he smiled and hoped the kid didn't notice it skipped his eyes. "I think she's beautiful anyway." His heart gave a nasty little clench. What he was feeling didn't feel like pretend, it felt like warm longing and desperate want. And he didn't deserve a woman like Anna. He never would.

As he jogged up the beach, he forced himself to cool it. He just had to get through the next couple of days and then maybe he'd get home with some measure of redemption for all the mistakes he'd made in the past. Anna's life was in the States teaching little kids. Even if they got out of this alive, he was poison to her life and career, and he had no intention of dragging her down to his level.

That evening they skirted around each other politely, as if they both realized their relationship had shifted but neither knew how to deal with it. Anna went to bed when it got dark, but he stayed outside until he was sure she was asleep. Then he lay there on the sleeping mat, mesmerized by the sound of her breathing so close beside him.

He woke and immediately knew Anna was gone. He groped around in the dark. The flashlight was missing. His pulse drummed. He struggled with the zipper trying to get the stupid tent flap open. *Don't panic.* She'd probably just gone to the bathroom.

Sure, don't panic, asshole. People were trying to kill her, and Anna wasn't exactly thinking straight after everything she'd been through. He poked his head outside the tent, the fresh breeze whipping across his face. *There.* A flash of light down by the water. A feeling of dread reached inside his chest and pummeled his heart.

He stumbled out of the tent, tripping over the guyline. Bright moonlight guided him, though he jarred his ankle running on the uneven ground. He vaulted the fallen log onto the sandy beach. A small pile of clothes were folded neatly in the middle of the sand, the flashlight dumped on top. His heart stopped beating. She was upset. Her father had died and he'd rejected her. He was such a fucking asshole.

She'd said she hadn't swum since the night she'd almost drowned. He scanned the dark water, but there was no sign of her.

She can't do this.

He ran, blood pounding so hard it formed a terrifying roar in his ears. He wouldn't let her give up. He tore off his shirt and ran full speed, diving into the water. His body cut through the surface and he ignored the blast of cold that stunned his senses. He saw a flash of pale skin. Swimming fast, he reached out and grabbed her arm. They broke the skin of the water in a confusing spray.

"Let go of me!" She fought and kicked and, when he wouldn't let go, she struggled so frantically they both went under.

When they bobbed back to the surface, he pulled her against him. "I'm not letting you do this." They went under again.

"You're going to drown me," she spluttered when they surfaced again.

She was naked. He knew this because his arm was clamped around her chest, her skin like slippery silk. Her nails weren't quite so sensual as they bit into his arms as she tried to dislodge him. He wasn't letting go.

He dragged her, kicking, swearing, onto shore. Her legs tangled with his and they both went down in the shallows. He pinned her beneath him, so furious, so mad that she'd do this to herself, to him. Like life was nothing to her. *He* was nothing.

"Why would you throw it all away, Anna? Why would you just give up?" He gripped her shoulders and her eyes morphed from anger to sudden understanding.

She touched his face, her expression softening. "I just went swimming, Brent." Her thumb touched his lips and a shiver of heat shot through him at odds with the coldness of the lake. Her hair floated in the water. Eyes, colorless in the silvery light, glistened with memories. "I needed to wash off everything that happened, get back into the water, and prove I'm not afraid anymore." She thrust her jaw out at him. She had good reason to be afraid.

Shit.

He closed his eyes. He'd seen she was gone and panicked like a fool.

They lay for a moment on the shoreline, straddling water and sand. Then his mouth went dry as he figured that not only was she naked, he was planted in the cradle of her hips like a man on his way to heaven. That intimate connection was all it took for someone who'd gone a year without a woman to become fully aroused.

She froze. He went to roll off her, but she kissed him. She was like heat and moonlight as she tasted his lips, his tongue. He banked the terror he'd been feeling and let her play with his mouth. Lust and want rammed his bloodstream as their tongues met, but they weren't doing this. He wasn't penance. He was just another mistake, another way of punishing herself.

Who was he kidding? He was the one punishing himself, and it was killing him not to just take what she offered.

Her hands touched his face, and he cradled her lightly in his embrace. Desire heated his body, his skin hot enough to singe, and he wanted to crawl all over her and drive himself deep. Her hands slid over his chest. Lower.

Finally she came up for air. "So, if kissing tells you so much about a person, then why does kissing you feel so good?"

Her question was a punch in the gut. He forced himself to pull away, to climb to his feet. Kissing Anna did feel good, it felt great. He didn't know if her response to him was ordinary or not, but he sure as hell enjoyed how she'd unraveled in his arms. Some people might consider him worldly and experienced, but when it came to women, he was anything but. He'd been with Gina. That was it. Women had written to him in prison, but he was of the belief that anyone who wrote to a stranger serving a life sentence for murder had more than a screw loose—they were nucking futs. Or lonely. And he might be alone, but he wasn't lonely. At least he hadn't been until he'd met Anna.

She moved closer, her breasts brushed his chest, and his blood took a nosedive. He knew how to back away, to say no, and shut someone down. Despite his brain screaming warning signals, none of that was happening right now. Her arms wound around his neck and she stood on tiptoes, every inch of her small perfect naked body rubbing against his and making lust snake through his blood like red-hot whiskey.

"Anna." His voice dropped to a rough growl. "You don't know what you're doing."

"For just one night, I want to be with you. I want to forget about everything else. It doesn't have to mean anything. Couldn't you just lie back and let me make love to you so I can remember what it's like to be whole and undamaged?" She couldn't reach his lips and he refused to drop his head. His little head was already giving him enough trouble for both of them, telling him to stuff his damn conscience and get fucking laid for a change. He let out a small breath of relief and despair as she moved away an inch. Then her hands gripped his shoulders and she hoisted herself up, wrapping her slender legs around his waist before pressing her lips to his.

He clamped one hand to her naked ass, the other around her waist as he staggered under the onslaught of her mouth. The heat and fervor of her obliterated his defenses and he kissed her back, itching and desperate to get inside her. He was done with being noble. Who the hell was he trying to kid anyway? "Let's go back to the tent," he urged.

"No." She didn't stop kissing him, his lips, neck, ears...*fuck!* His toes curled. "Here," she demanded, "on the sand."

"But—"

"I want to erase the memories, Brent."

Erase, not forget. She ran her tongue over his neck. *Fuck*. She must have known if she took her mouth off him, if she gave him a chance to think, he'd remember why they couldn't do this. She was fourteen years his junior, a pure sweet brilliance that he had no right to be touching. But with her lips on his skin and her hands tracing the muscles on his back, his two brain cells were toast.

His fingers kneaded her ass and his erection strained against his zipper, instinctively trying to get closer to her hot core pressed up against him.

"It's just sex," she said, and kissed his lips again. His hands started to move over her curves, the smooth sleek muscles. The idea of "just sex" blew his brain. He didn't want emotional entanglements. Didn't want a wife. Couldn't be trusted with that sort of responsibility. And pushing Anna away was impossible, so they'd try it another way.

She was petite, but not fragile. Strong as iron and pure as the silver she was named after. Having casual sex didn't fit with his image of her, but what the hell did he know? Maybe this was what they both needed. Although deep down he knew this was anything but casual on his part.

She must have felt his reluctance. She unwrapped her legs and slid down him, causing a thousand nerve endings to spring to stunned attention. Then she unflicked the button on his shorts, drew them down. Oxygen disappeared and he swayed as she took him in her hands.

He fell to his knees because he was toast. There was nothing damaged about this woman. Frustrated, he kicked off his shorts, and when she crawled over him, he pulled her up his body so she straddled him. She rocked against him and his eyes crossed. It was too dark to really see but she felt like raw silk as she rose over him. She stroked him and he just wanted to kiss her all over. A blast of cold hard reality hit home. "I don't have a condom," he gritted out.

"I do." She scrambled over to her pile of clothes until she found her shorts and pulled one out of her pocket.

"When did you buy those?" he asked.

"In the store. Earlier."

She'd thought about this.

She'd planned it.

Sex. With him. His mouth went dry. Blood punched.

Hell.

Sweat ran down his temples. He grabbed her hips and held her still for long enough to bite out, "I'm clean." He needed her to know. "I haven't been with anyone in over a year."

She rocked against him, and he rolled her on her back, then hesitated, worried he might have hurt her. She lay on top of their clothes and he could just make out her body in the moonlight.

"You're so beautiful." He touched his fingers to the tips of her breasts and she arched off the ground. He followed with his lips, drifted over the hollow of her collarbone, the swell of her breast, back to the sensitive curve of her neck. He touched the sweep of her hip and then the secret depths between her thighs. He eased one finger inside her and slid it very gently backward and forward over sensitive flesh. Every time he touched her, he wanted it to go on forever because she reacted with such startling force. She bucked and writhed beneath his hands, making whimpering sounds and thrusting her hips in gentle demand. He slipped another finger inside her and eased her wider. She felt incredible. Then he couldn't resist anymore. He wanted more. He inched down her body and spread her thighs, felt her stiffen.

"What are you doing?" she asked, an uncertain edge entering her voice.

"Do you trust me?"

She laughed softly. "You think we'd be having this conversation if I didn't?"

"I know we wouldn't." He was frustrated he couldn't see her, but *Christ*. "I want to taste you. Can I taste you?" He didn't wait for her answer. He put his mouth on her and kissed her, drenched in her flavor and her heat. There were no complaints, no resistance. Her body went lax, her hips rising off the sand and he held her steady against his mouth and feasted.

She tasted like spice and sin and sweet, sweet heaven. Her tightly bunched nipples called to him and he stroked them, flicked them, rolled them until she was panting.

She was incredible, like quicksilver in his hands. But she was so tiny, he was terrified he was going to hurt her, or crush her, especially after everything she'd told him. Then she draped her legs over his shoulders and her heels dug into his back as she threw back her head with a silent scream as she came. And he realized she wasn't delicate or fragile, she was strong and supple and resilient.

Unbroken.

She pulled away from him almost immediately and sat up, looking shocked, breathing hard. He tried to quiet the fervor in his blood. Figured they were done, and he could deal with his raging hard-on in the cold lake. Then she pushed him onto his back and once more straddled his thighs.

"You don't have to do this." He deserved an A for effort. Maybe Olympic gold. "I'll give you as many orgasms as you want."

Her hand wrapped around him and he couldn't stop the instinctive thrust of his hips.

"I just want to return the favor."

"It isn't a contest," he gritted out. "I'm not keeping count of how many times you come."

"Brent." She sounded frustrated and a little bit pissed. He liked it. He liked the way she was acting all bossy and in control in a situation that should have unnerved her. Come to think of it, she'd never exactly been shy and retiring in his company. He didn't scare her. How the hell could a woman who'd suffered the way she had not be terrified of him?

"I've never felt like this before," she said. "I have never burned from the inside out or wanted a man as desperately as I want you. This is all new to me and I feel fabulous."

She did feel fabulous, and he knew all about burning from the inside out. "I don't want to hurt you," he confessed.

"You won't."

She stroked him until he was so hard and throbbing he thought he might pass out. Her touch might be inexperienced but, hell, he was easy. He could barely think past the idea of getting inside her. He felt like an animal, all desperate and feral, denying himself a basic need. For what?

"If you don't want to come inside me, we can find other ways," she said. "I won't force you, but I'd like to share this with you. I want you."

He met her gaze in the moonlight. Saw the raw need and ragged lust. She was naked and *begging* him to have sex with her.

Obviously he'd lost his frigging mind. He ran his hands up her back, scraped his fingers down the lean muscles. "Fuck. I want you. I just shouldn't have you."

She fumbled with the foil package and then slid the condom over him, her expression a tight frown of concentration. Every muscle in his body shook. Then she positioned the tip of him exactly where he wanted to be, he gave up pretending this wasn't going to happen as she slid slowly over his length.

Lord, have mercy.

He gripped her waist and she squirmed, getting used to his size, internal muscles spasming around him. She rocked her hips and went deeper. Then she added a twist to the movement and he felt that spine-tingling, ball-squeezing, mind-blasting animalistic need, building and building inside him. He didn't dare touch her because there was no control left for anything except wanting it not to end—never to end.

"Am I doing it right?" she asked hesitantly.

"Are you fucking kidding me?" He gritted his teeth and stared at the stars, spotted the Milky Way as lust spiked through every vein, popped each nerve. Then she started rising up and sliding down and he thought he was going to black out. He couldn't stand it anymore and gripped her hips and drove deeper, deeper, harder. Grinding against her, wanting to get more inside her so she could swallow him whole. Then she cried out in those small gasps that curled around him and squeezed so tight he couldn't breathe. He let himself go, the hard release catapulting him to the moon as a nuclear explosion of white-hot ecstasy burned his mind, obliterating every thought in his head except this. Except her.

She collapsed on top of him, skin slick with a mix of sweat and sand and sex. Their hearts pounded each other as the breeze cooled their overheated bodies.

Holy motherfucking hell.

She moved just slightly against him. Twitched her hips and he found himself growing hard again. He smoothed the hair off her cheek. What the hell had he done? He clenched his jaw.

"We're going to need another condom," he said. He was going to burn for this anyway, so he might as well go up in flames.

She leaned over and found her shorts, searched through the pockets once more. He lay there, admiring the view. She pulled out two condoms and dropped them on his chest with a flash of a grin in the darkness. He protected them both and pulled her back over him.

He didn't know what *this* was between them. But maybe he shouldn't worry. Sex was a great stress reducer. She rocked against him and his vision went blurry. *Christ.* His hands sought hers in the darkness and he rolled them so she was on her back, with him planted deep within her. He paused, knowing this was how she'd been raped—on her back in the sand. "Is this OK?"

She nodded. There were no shadows of pain or anguish in her eyes. Just liquid lust and bright feverish want. And maybe this wasn't about him. Maybe this was all about Anna, and he could certainly live with fixing one broken part of her life. Her knees drew up, giving him a better angle, and then he slipped his hands beneath her, raising her up as he thrust hard, harder and couldn't stop. Sand was everywhere, adding another fine layer of friction. There was nothing gentle this time. No holding back as her body demanded more, fingers biting, ankles digging into his ass. *This* was therapy. A way of getting off and getting some sleep. It was raw sex on a deserted beach and they both needed it.

He drove her to another orgasm and followed her over the razor's edge, resting his forehead in the curve of her shoulder as he shattered. Then he carried her into the water and they did it again.

CHAPTER 14

Anna had just spent the most incredible night of her life, making love with a man who'd not only been gentle and giving, but—once he'd gotten over thinking she might break if he pushed too hard—also ruthless and demanding. They'd stumbled back to bed in the early hours of the morning and finally fallen asleep. They'd woken up to warm sunshine and the soft scent of canvas and made love one more time before reality intruded.

She ached in unusual places and each twinge brought a wave of awareness, a reminder of what they'd shared and done to one another. She felt free. Liberated. Not only had she buried a lot of old pain, she'd figured out she could have a fantastic sex life too, a fact that had remained hidden from her all these years. She didn't need to be repressed or in control. She just needed the right guy.

Could Brent Carver be that guy?

The idea seemed crazy, and yet…she didn't have time to ponder. They couldn't stay here, playing make-believe forever. The rising sun had brought with it an escalating need to act.

"I'm going to the restroom," Anna told Brent as he finished packing up the tent.

He grunted without turning. He hadn't said much this morning. Anna didn't know if he was tired or just having second thoughts about being seduced. He wasn't a man who liked to get close to anyone, and she'd battered down his walls last night. From the look on his face, she'd have to batter them down again next time.

She needed to get through to him that he was a decent human being who deserved good things in his life. Good people. Assuming they ever got themselves out of this mess.

She walked along the paved road to the nearby washrooms. In her stiff new jeans and baggy T-shirt, she couldn't have felt less feminine or attractive, not that she cared right now. But it was a long way from the pretty skirts and sandals she usually wore and emphasized how dramatically her world had changed. She was wanted by the police for questioning, and traveling under a false identity. Clothes no longer mattered. Respectability and image no longer mattered. All that mattered was finding whatever it was her father had sent her, keeping Brent out of jail, and not dying. She'd discovered last night that she really, really wasn't ready to die.

She'd tried to keep some sort of guard on her emotions, but there was a huge difference between telling yourself not to get emotionally involved, and not doing it. Especially when you were both naked. After what they'd been through over the last few days, it was hard not to feel something. And after the way he'd made love to her last night and burned away her demons, she'd be lying if she said she wasn't already halfway in love with him. But maybe that was just gratitude and postcoital glow.

She used the restroom and washed her hands, letting the water flow coolly over her wrists.

Their plan was to cross the border and meet up with Brent's future sister-in-law at Emerson. It was only a few hours to the border, but Brent was worried the border was going to be watched, so they were going to wait until it started to get dark again, during which time Anna would go insane. Hopefully Holly would be there to meet them and no one would get hurt or arrested. A huge icy claw slid inside her. She couldn't bear the thought of being responsible for getting Brent sent back to prison. She wouldn't let that happen, and between her and Finn and Holly's RCMP connections, they'd fight to keep him safe.

Was *this* love?

How did you even know? How did you put faith in that sort of nebulous emotion?

Walking back from the restrooms, she passed the office and noticed the computer they had for customer use was free. She bit her lip. They were leaving anyway. What harm could it do to send her mom a quick e-mail telling her not to worry? She didn't even know if she'd received the first message about Dad.

She walked inside and sat down. Should she?

No one was around as she opened up her webmail. Seven messages marked URGENT caught her attention. All from Ed. She opened one up. All it said was "call me" with Ed's cell phone number. Her heart tripped in her chest. She and Ed weren't close, but they got on OK. Why was he e-mailing her and not her mom? She spotted a pay phone. Dug ten dollars out of her purse and got change from the guy behind the desk. She dialed her mother's cell first, but it was turned off. So she tried Ed. He answered on the third ring.

"Hello?"

"Ed, it's me, Anna."

"Thank God, Anna. I've been trying to reach you."

From the desperation in his voice, she wondered if the cops were using him to track her down. If that monster who'd killed Peter had escaped, then they might consider Anna a suspect…

"Your mother is sick." His voice shook in obvious distress and he sobbed. Ed wasn't that great an actor and her mother was the center of his universe.

"I thought you were on a cruise?"

"She took ill in Anchorage and we flew back to the island. You have to come now. They said she might not make it more than a few hours." He broke down, completely undone.

Her mother was sick, dying. *Oh, God.* Coming on top of her father's death a week ago, she felt like her world had shattered.

"Which hospital?"

Ed gave her the name of the hospital where she'd been admitted all those years ago, and told her to call him when she got into Victoria. She hung up the phone, and something made her look up. There was Brent, watching her. His eyes were hooded, cold even. None of the lover and all of the ex-con.

"What are you doing?" he asked.

"Change of plan," she told him as they walked back to their cozy little campsite. It was packed up now. All trace of their stay here folded and stored in the back of the jeep. Except she'd never pack away the memories. They meant more to her than all the money in the world. Her hands shook and she tried to steady them by putting them on her hips. "I spoke to Ed. Mom's seriously ill. She's been taken to the hospital." Her voice broke as she climbed into the jeep. "I need to fly back to Victoria straightaway—"

"Holly can't meet us until later today."

She swallowed the ball of fear and anger that lodged in her throat. "There has to be another way. Ed said she might only have a few hours." Reality hit her hard in the chest. She wanted to cling to him, but from his expression, that wouldn't be a good idea. "She might die."

"It's not safe." He sat poised to turn the key in the ignition and she wanted to yell at him to hurry.

"What about paying someone to take us in a small private aircraft like we did last time?"

He closed his eyes and seemed to be trying to rein in his temper.

"I'll pay you back—"

"I don't want your damned money!" he yelled. He ran his hands over his face. "I don't know anyone here. I have no connections. Crossing the border with Holly is the safest way to get you into protective custody." *And make sure I don't end up in jail* hung silently in the air.

He started the car and they started driving. North. Toward the border.

The image of Peter dead on her kitchen floor whirled inside her mind, along with that of the man with the cobra-cold eyes who'd looked at her like she was naked and his to do with as he pleased. Her insides turned to ice. But what if her mom died while she was hiding from these people? What if she never saw her again, never had the chance to say she was sorry for being such a crappy daughter? Because, with a clarity she hadn't known before, she realized she'd had a big role in how far they'd grown apart. Her mother had tried to reach out to her over the years and she'd pushed her away for fear of getting hurt. And that distance had also been a weapon that she had wielded with cold precision to keep people away.

It had to stop.

She had to make it stop. "You have other connections. There must be other ways of fighting these guys. People like them who can find them before they kill us..."

He froze, and then shook his head. "Those are not the sort of people I want to deal with." He swallowed. "All they need is one asshole who's trigger-happy and we're looking at conspiracy to murder charges. I won't prove everyone right about me being a cold-blooded killer." The tightness of his features made his mouth look harsh. "I'd die for you, Anna. But I won't kill for you. Not unless there's no other choice."

Inside she was quaking. She couldn't believe she'd even considered it, much less asked Brent. Shame filled her. What did that make her? A liar and a monster. A hypocrite and the worst sort of human being on the planet. But she was running out of options and these people had no moral compass about fighting fair. Keeping Brent safe and staying alive were important, but if her mom died before she had the chance to see her, she wouldn't be able to live with herself.

"It's just a few hours more until Holly can meet us—"

Her stepfather's words came back to her. "I can't wait that long. Drop me off at the nearest airport and I'll go on my own. They won't expect it." She was doing this one way or another. And at least this way would get him out of her orbit and keep him safe.

Brent was quiet for a long moment. "You'd put yourself in danger for a woman who forgot you existed? Who didn't even notice you were raped and suicidal?"

The words hit like a physical blow, but it said a lot about her inner resolve that she was able to answer him. She raised one brow. "Wouldn't you?"

He swore and looked away from her. Five minutes later he pulled over and made a call. Fifty-three minutes later, they were airborne.

Jack hated hospitals. He hated doctors, stethoscopes, X-ray machines, hospital food, and, did he mention, doctors? The nurses weren't bad though, especially the little blonde who'd offered him a sponge bath earlier. He'd refused on medical grounds, but got her number.

"Jerkoff," he muttered as the latest overeducated, egotistical specialist walked out the door.

"Because he told you to rest?" His secretary crossed her legs and he found himself distracted for a moment. Who knew Ramona had legs? She was usually behind her desk whenever he saw her.

"Because he wants to cut me open again," Jack grumbled.

"I'm not sure wanting to remove bullet fragments lodged near your lung makes him a jerkoff," Trace said without looking up.

"Although the whole god complex sure does." He sat in a corner with three laptops up and running.

"I thought he was nice." Ramona pressed her lips together to hide a smile.

"He was hitting on you as I lay here dying."

"You're not dying," Ramona chided. "God isn't that kind to me." Her prim smile told Jack she was joking. He hoped.

"You going to use that number he gave you?" Jack asked her. Not that he cared, except his secretary dating his surgeon was a worst-case scenario he fully intended to avoid.

Her lips quirked. "Maybe it depends on that raise you promised me."

"Blackmail. I'm dying and she's blackmailing me."

"You're not dying." Ramona's voice grew louder. Jack grunted and Trace slid him a slow smile.

"You got anything yet?" he asked the cowboy. They'd met through Trace's sister, whom Jack had dated for a couple of months. The relationship had fizzled out, but he still sent her flowers on her birthday for setting him up with her brother who was a freaking online wizard. Jack had just about figured out IP addresses and… yeah, that was about it.

Trace pressed a finger to each temple. "A headache from trying to track money through so many different banking systems when someone went to a lot of trouble to wipe the trail clean."

"How did Davis Silver set up the accounts last time he stole that money?"

Trace flicked him a glance. "He set up three separate private bank accounts in his name and was pretty damn sloppy about moving the money. A child could have followed that trail. Or even you," he said pointedly.

"Anyone notice I'm the injured party here? That I was shot?"

They both made rude noises and he laughed, but it hurt. "So, either Davis learned a hell of a lot more about money laundering in the past decade or…"

"Or someone else moved the money this time." Trace nodded. He'd already figured that out.

"You've run other bank accounts in his name, right?"

Trace raised one brow. "It's only because you got shot that I'm not punching you for that."

"Don't let that stop you from trying, sunshine." Jack grinned. It felt good to joke. It felt damn good to be alive.

"Davis Silver always maintained his innocence." Ramona's hand went to her chest and she spoke softly. "What if he was never guilty? What if someone set him up nine years ago too?"

"Then he's the unluckiest bastard ever." Jack groaned as he lay back against the pillow. He was worried about his client. And now he was worried about a man he'd never even met having been framed for a crime he hadn't committed. Those were the worst cases. Miscarriages of justice ate him up inside.

"Any chance you can find out the IP address that was used to create those accounts nine years ago?"

"Nice thinking, boss, but they actually did that in court using Windows's Primary Domain Controller's SID—Security ID—which can identify both the individual computer and the user. It was a generic computer in the department where he worked."

Brent had asked if there was any way of proving his friend's innocence. "Did the cops look to see if any other accounts were ever set up from that same machine?"

Trace blinked at him. "Wow, that's actually a real good suggestion."

Jack felt smug and tried to sit up straighter, but ended up curled over in pain.

Ramona fussed over him. "You need that bullet fragment removed. Before it does real damage and gets into your brain or something."

"You worried about me, Ramona?" He tried to smile, but fuck if it didn't hurt. "Fine. Call the damn doc and tell the butcher he can operate." Ramona buzzed the nurse.

Jack turned to Trace. "Do the search, even if it takes all night." The pain in his chest was getting worse, nearly overwhelming—and he'd actually thought he'd be getting out of this death trap soon. "If you find anything at all, call the client ASAP. If you can't reach him, call a woman named Holly Rudd. She's in his file." Jack's vision was starting to fade. That couldn't be good. "If you can't reach anyone else, tell the goddamn Chicago PD, but do not reveal our client's name..." And then he was gone, sinking under waves of faltering vision and screaming machines as people rushed around him.

The first thing Katherine registered as she drifted back into consciousness was a deep, bone-biting chill that penetrated the light fleece she wore. Then pain. Her hands were swollen and numb, the hard plastic cutting into her wrists, but at least her hands were now in front of her. Her ankle bones rubbed against one another with bruising pressure. Her hip throbbed every time she tried to shift or get comfortable.

Had she been in a car accident?

There was a gentle rocking motion that made her feel nauseous—not a good idea while wearing a gag. It was dark except for a small strip of light beneath a door. The room felt small, like a closet, the floor felt hard, but not concrete hard.

Where's Harvey? A short sharp burst of panic shot through her and she thrust her legs sideways, desperately searching. She connected with something warm and solid and immediately quieted. Was he breathing? She wriggled closer, pressed her body against his back to feel whether or not his chest was moving. *Yes. Thank goodness.*

Her touch must have woken him because he rolled over. Even though they couldn't see one another's faces in the darkness, he reached out and took her icy fingers in his, massaging them gently. He shuffled closer, offering his warmth and comfort. She squeezed his hand in gratitude. What a mess.

Harvey managed to spit out his gag and then she felt his fingers against her lips as he eased her gag down over her chin. "We're on a boat?"

"I think so," she whispered. The last thing she wanted to do was attract anyone's attention by making a noise. And that was the crux of her whole life, she realized. That's what Davis had taken from her, and now these animals were trying to do the same.

Katherine managed to turn around so she could peek beneath the door, but all she could see was what looked like a narrow corridor. And then a pair of black boots appeared and she cringed away from the light as someone opened the door. She found herself staring up at the hard handsome face of a man wearing mirrored sunglasses. He squatted, expression devoid of emotion. He lowered his glasses, and his eyes were the scariest thing she'd ever seen—far colder than the mirrored lenses. She scooted back next to Harvey and the guy grinned, but it still didn't warm his eyes.

"You planning something stupid?"

Katherine shook her head vigorously.

"Because there are all sorts of ways to make you compliant." The suggestion in his eyes scared her to death. She wedged herself tight against Harvey.

His dark gaze shifted between the two of them and whatever he saw must have convinced him they'd behave.

He closed the door and both she and Harvey let out matching sighs of relief.

"Who was that?" Katherine asked.

"I don't know." Harvey rubbed his chin against her hair. "But the devil comes to mind."

A shiver ran down her spine. "I'm so sorry I got you dragged into this."

"I got myself into this mess chasing after you."

When was she ever going to be anything but a liability?

"But I wouldn't change a damn thing, Katherine. The thought of you going through this alone makes me ill."

They lay side by side, pressed together for warmth and support. Ed would hate this. He'd probably hate the fact she was with Harvey as much as the fact she'd been kidnapped. Katherine didn't know what to make of that.

They were slowly taxiing along a runway in Victoria. Anna was shaking from a combination of nerves and lack of food. No matter how hungry she was, she couldn't force herself to eat until she'd seen her mom.

They'd made it through customs in Vancouver with the help of a tall, square-faced man who'd worn plainclothes but had an RCMP bodyguard and whom not a single person had questioned. Turned out Holly's father was a big deal in the RCMP. A *very* big deal.

She'd overheard Brent agree to deliver her into protective custody as soon as Anna had seen her mother. Anna fidgeted in her seat, unable to relax. Even before the seat belt signs were off, she'd grabbed her meager bag of belongings from under the seat, and was on her feet. Brent had left his new jeep and all their camping gear in a barn in North Dakota. She'd make sure he got it back if she had to drive it all the way here herself.

Right now he was still mad at her. Her assumption that he was OK with people dying was selfish and insulting. Now that she was thinking rationally, she knew she'd meant to suggest finding bodyguards rather than hired guns, but her mouth had opened before her brain had engaged. The results weren't pretty. Plus, he was worried about her for coming out of hiding and rushing home—although since she'd planned to go into protective custody anyway as soon as she'd seen her mom, she didn't really know what the problem was.

His features were set in tight, angry lines. He certainly wasn't acting like he remembered a damn thing about last night.

The airplane doors opened and they were striding along the flight tunnels into the small airport. Finn had arranged for them to pick up a car. He and Holly were en route back from Winnipeg and, apparently, not exactly the founding members of the Anna Silver fan club.

Brent and Anna went to the rental desk and then tracked down their car in the parking lot. Anna got in the passenger side and placed her belongings in the backseat. She shifted in her seat and shot Brent a look from under her brow. He wasn't talking to her. She'd screwed up.

"Thanks."

He glanced at her sharply.

"For everything, but especially for last night."

His brows crunched over those incredible blue eyes, but he still said nothing. The silence was full of brooding menace. Why was she forcing this issue? Her stomach rumbled and she placed her hand on it. There was a drive-through up ahead and he signaled. They pulled up at the window and he ordered coffee and muffins.

"It helped," she said when the server disappeared. Still he didn't speak. Just placed the coffee in the cup holders and drove off. She wanted him to know how much it had meant to her. It hadn't been just sex for her, and as they might have to go their separate ways in the near future, she needed him to know that.

She'd expected a flippant "anytime" response. This moody quiet unnerved her. She turned and looked out the window, caught a glimpse of her reflection. God, she looked like crap. She pulled a face.

The countryside was rugged, the trees a lush healthy green. A few miles farther down the road Brent pulled into a turnout that overlooked a vast stretch of ocean. His skin was pale, jaw locked so tight it could have been superglued.

Then he spoke.

"Next time you need a therapy fuck, find someone who doesn't give a shit."

He got out of the jeep, slammed the door, and went to stand by the guardrail and stare out over the bluff. Anna sat stunned. She tried to steady herself with a sip of coffee, but her hand shook so much it spilled. She wanted to go after him, to comfort him.

She made herself sit in the damn seat and not move a muscle.

It was better this way. She was bad for him. It was better that he started to hate her, because there was no way they had a future together and he'd already sacrificed too much.

So even though she wanted to go to him, to wrap her arms around him, and to tell him it hadn't just been therapy, it had been amazing, she sat there. It would just drag him further into the mess of her world at a time she needed to push him away—for his own good. He finished his coffee and got back in the car, not looking at her. His admission that he felt something for her seemed to embarrass him, and that shamed her. Because he wasn't alone. But she needed to make a clean break, and telling him how she felt about him would only make the parting even harder than it promised to be.

It didn't take long to get to the hospital.

"Just drop me off at the entrance." She forced the quaver out of her voice.

He looked like he wanted to argue and then decided against it, as she already had her door open. "What ward is she in?"

"Ten," Anna said. She didn't want Brent's obvious disapproval to mar her reunion with her sick mother. She didn't want Brent upset or angry. She should never have gone to him for help, although if she hadn't, she'd probably be dead. "If you'd rather, I can get a taxi into RCMP headquarters while you pick up your truck. You could still make your exhibition…"

Holly had impounded the truck in a fit of fury.

He shot her a look of blue fire, but didn't bother to answer. He pulled a burner cell out of his jeans pocket and tossed it in her lap. No touching. She felt like a leper and knew she deserved it.

"Your father asked for my help. Until Holly has you safely under her wing, I'm sticking." Whether he liked it or not. Which he clearly didn't.

She tried to not let it hurt. "OK, just give me a few minutes to talk to Mom alone first." She slipped his cell phone into her jeans pocket. He didn't say anything. Just waited for her to get out.

Her legs were unsteady as she walked through the large glass entrance of the hospital building. The last time she'd been here, she'd been in the ER and then locked up in the psych ward for a week. She shivered. That hadn't been any fun.

"Anna!"

She whipped around at the sound of her name. Saw Ed standing near the coffee shop and hurried toward him. He looked like he hadn't slept in a week. "Thank God you're here." He grabbed her arm and started tugging her toward a fire exit.

She slipped out of his grasp but hurried beside him. "Is Mom OK?"

"I transferred her to a private facility that has better doctors." He wouldn't meet her gaze.

Panic clutched at her chest. Oh, crap, that had to be bad. Whatever else she thought of Ed, she had never doubted his devotion to her mother. They strode out the side door and into the parking lot. She looked around for Brent, but didn't see him anywhere.

"What exactly is it that is wrong with her?"

His white sedan was parked three rows over. He steered her toward it.

"Wait. I need to call someone and tell them where we're going." She pulled out the phone Brent had given her and dialed his number. Ed looked impatient enough to grab the phone from her hands. His skin was ashen and his lips were bloodless. Things must be bad with her mom. Brent's cell was busy so she left him a quick voice mail. "What's the name of the place?" she asked Ed.

"St. Catherine's."

Apt. "Never heard of it." She told Brent to Google it and to meet her there. The space would do them good.

She braced herself for bad news when she got in the passenger seat. "So what's wrong with her?"

"Breast cancer, so help me God." He ground the words out like he was in physical pain.

Not cancer. Please not cancer. Her mother had always been the picture of health.

Ed's hands were shaking. His first wife had died of breast cancer and now her mom? It wasn't fair. Emotions bubbled in her throat, too terrible to deal with. She refused to believe her mom was going to die, although from the look on Ed's face...

And she wanted to reach out and lean on Brent, let him help her through another terrible moment in her life. Because she was selfish and a coward. Like he needed more trouble or anguish brought to his doorstep. She straightened her spine. She could deal with this. She'd dealt with plenty of bad things and she was stronger now. Strong enough for others to lean on her.

"I need a coffee." Ed sounded like someone had taken a saw to his vocal cords. They pulled into a Tim Horton's and Anna looked around, the area familiar because it was near where her grandmother had lived. When she'd been growing up, she'd spent a lot of time here. Most of the shops had changed—a florist and coffee shop stood where the hardware store had been. The post office was still there, though.

Her heart stopped beating for a moment, everything suspended. Then it raced triple time. Everything fell into place as she stared at the Victorian façade of the heritage building. Her father's horrible apartment. Her old letters in that battered red box. The cryptic message from her father, "*You'll know.*"

She did know.

And all of a sudden, she wanted it to be over. Then she could be with her mom, nursing her back to health, because she *was* going to get better, and they were going to have a proper relationship. Anna was done with living a life in small, unsatisfying pieces. She was going to talk to Brent too, because she had fallen for him and, assuming she lived through the next few days, she wanted to be brave enough to tell him that without any expectations. Maybe it would go nowhere. Maybe it was one of those crazy connections based on intense circumstances, but she finally wanted to find out. She'd hurt him and there was no excuse for that.

God, she'd messed up so badly.

To push away a man like that after he'd given her so much? Because she was scared. A coward. Well, she was done being a coward. She was done running away.

She got out of the car as they lined up in the drive-through. Ed shouted at her. She ignored him and crossed the street and walked into the old building with its rows and rows of post office boxes. Retracing the steps of her tortured teen self when her mother couldn't bear even the thought of a letter from her former husband coming into her reinvented life. The PO box key hung on her key ring where it had been for so many years, she'd almost forgotten what it was for. Her grandmother had died at the end of January, and she'd probably renewed this PO box automatically every year. Anna would get the paperwork at some point, but she hadn't seen it yet.

There were people everywhere. Students with backpacks, seniors clutching checkbooks. The atmosphere was hot and stifling, making her light-headed and woozy. She braced herself against the wall of metal doors. *Please let this be it.* Anna slipped the key in place and opened the box. Inside sat a manila envelope with her name scrawled across it in Papa's handwriting. A lump the size of an apple lodged in her throat.

This was the last thing her father had sent to her, and would prove his intentions when he'd moved that money. Had he been telling the truth? Because if he had, maybe he'd told the truth about all the other stuff too, but no one had ever believed him. No one except Brent.

Her head started to pound with an incoming headache. Her hands shook as she reached for the letter. There wasn't time to read it, and maybe she wasn't ready to face whatever was inside that missive. Maybe she should give it to the RCMP or at least wait until Holly arrived so she could open it in front of witnesses? That actually made a lot of sense.

She folded the envelope three times and slipped it into the front pocket of her new jeans, which were loose, probably because she'd dropped ten pounds over the last week from stress.

She locked up the box and weaved her way around three students carrying backpacks, and wished her life was that uncomplicated. But even back then, Anna had had a way of making everything somber and serious. A bitter laugh escaped. No matter how emotionally bleak Brent's life looked, hers wasn't much better. She'd lost her father and been raped, and even though she pretended she'd dealt with these issues, she hadn't. Anna had just packed everything carefully away and tried to forget. She'd never been brave or strong. She'd just done denial and aloofness until it was so much a part of her character she didn't even know who she was anymore. Maybe now was the time to find out.

CHAPTER 15

Outside, the fresh breeze hit her with enough force to jerk her into the present. The envelope crinkled against her hip, reminding her that the worst of the nightmare was over. This would hopefully help identify the men who'd killed the police officers and Peter, and shot that poor guy in the back. They'd stop chasing her, and both she and Brent could go back to their lives, and maybe think about pursuing what they had, slowly, from a distance.

Why this didn't bring her happiness was probably because her mom was fighting for her life. She curled her fingers into fists as she strode to where Ed had illegally parked on the curb. She opened the door and climbed in.

"I thought you'd run away," he said simply.

Because that's what she did. "No." Not anymore. She crossed her arms over her chest. "I didn't even know there was a medical facility out this way." Her voice was rough. She didn't want to lose her mother. Not now. Not when she had so much to say to her for the first time in years.

"It's not far."

"Do you want me to drive?" she asked gently. He looked like crap. Pasty skin and a sheen of sweat across his brow.

He shook his head and wiped his eyes with the heel of his hand. Her phone started ringing and it jerked her back into the present. Brent. Her heart gave a little trip. She needed to tell him about finding the envelope, but she really wanted to tell him in person. Or maybe that was just an excuse because she wanted to see him again. *Next time you need a therapy fuck, find someone who doesn't give a shit.* Not exactly the most romantic words, but at least now she knew he cared even though he didn't want to. She went to grab her cell, but suddenly she was facing the black barrel of a gun.

"What...?"

"Give me your phone."

"Ed, I don't understand—"

"Just give me the damn phone!"

She dug into her bag, pressing the answer button as she handed it over. Ed narrowed his eyes and then rolled down the window. Anna watched him openmouthed as he tossed the cell out of the window. It landed with a crash on the sidewalk.

"They have your mother," he said gruffly. His eyes were red rimmed, lips disappearing into a mouth pressed firmly closed.

"Who? Who has Mom?" she asked, but instinctively she knew. "So she's not sick?"

"She could be dead for all I know, Anna. Dead, because of that stupid father of yours and your own damned stubbornness."

Anna shook her head and edged closer to the door.

"Oh no, you don't." He locked her in. He kept the gun trained on her, and somehow managed to throw some plastic strips at her.

She picked them up and stared at them. Zip ties. Blood drained from her head, leaving her dizzy and clueless. Hell. She'd made another mistake. A big one. A deadly one. And she was going to have to deal with it alone.

"Put one around your ankles. Make it tight. I don't want to crash the car, because if I do, your mother's dead and I honestly don't know what I'd do without her."

"We need to call the cops. They can help us get her back safely—"

"No. *No* cops." Spittle came out of his mouth. "You didn't hear his voice when he told me what I had to do. He said you owed him. He'll kill her if I don't do exactly what he wants."

Anna knew precisely who he'd been talking to. The man with no soul. The man who'd murdered Peter in her pristine white kitchen. The man she'd hit over the back of the head with a bottle of pinot grigio. In a flash she also realized she could never go back to that house. Her life had changed irrevocably—whatever she did next, it wouldn't be there.

"Do it," Ed insisted, pointing at the ties.

Anna wound one around the bottom of her jeans.

"Tighter." Ed's eyes were fierce. No trace of sympathy that he was driving her to her death.

"They'll kill you too," she told him quietly.

"No. They promised." Ed shook his head. "I'm going to get your mother out of there. We'll escape. Now your wrists, either side of the seat belt so you can't run away again."

I don't do that anymore. She cinched the tie with her teeth. "What about me?" she asked quietly.

"I've always done my best by you, Anna. Paid for school, sent Malcolm away to the States for college. Don't say I wasn't good to you."

"You knew?" Her mouth dropped open as Ed's gaze shifted uncomfortably away from her. "You knew your son raped me?"

Ed's eyes flashed wide and he shook his head. "I know you two had sex. I figured you weren't in a great place to be making those kinds of decisions so I sent him away—"

"Bullshit, Ed! That's fucking bullshit." Her stepfather looked enraged by her language, but she didn't care. "He raped me, and that's why I tried to commit suicide—because of your vile, horrible son."

"Don't say that."

"Why not? You are about to deliver me into the hands of murderers. Mom might already be dead. What exactly do I have to lose from telling the truth?" She should have told the truth years ago. Even if no one believed her. But the past didn't matter. The thought of her mother in the hands of that monster made her go cold. "We need to go to the cops and make a plan. Not wander blindly around, trusting the word of men who've already killed at least three people that I know of."

"Shut up." Ed's hands gripped both the gun and the wheel so tight she was either going to get shot or die in a high-speed collision. She tipped her chin. She wasn't cowering from Ed or the people who'd kidnapped her mother. Brent couldn't help her right now, but she drew on some of the lessons he'd been trying to teach her. She was tough, she was smart, and she could damn well learn patience.

Brent would be proud of her sticking up for herself, and that thought left a huge gaping hole in her chest. Letting herself love him had been akin to forgiving her father. Just a week ago the thought of that had been impossible. But somehow she'd finally found the strength to absolve not only her father, but herself too. The knowledge gave her strength at a time she desperately needed it.

It had taken her a long time to understand that happiness had nothing to do with respectability or pretty surroundings. External trappings meant little if you weren't happy on the inside. For a woman who'd surrounded herself with beauty and cared way too much what others had thought of her, it was a bitter realization. It wasn't houses, or jobs, or flowers that mattered. It was personal connections. The photographs on the mantel. Putting yourself out there. She thought of Peter and how she'd settled for such an insipid relationship because it had been safe. Yes, she'd had her reasons for living that way, but she was sick of them. Sick of the fear. The restrictions. Anger burnt away the layers surrounding her heart. She didn't want to be that shallow any more. She wanted to have the courage to be honest about her emotions. To really *feel*. To fall helplessly in love, even if that person didn't love her back. But she thought Brent might. She remembered his tender lovemaking last night. He just might.

Brent had thought he'd known her through her letters to her father, and she knew suddenly he was right. He did know her. And she'd known him—from the painting that hung over her bed and lulled her to sleep every night. He'd been there for her the same way she'd been there for him, before they'd even met. It meant something. She just needed the chance to prove it.

Ed turned left and started down a winding road. She braced herself, then saw a chopper on the ground, rotors winding up. Until Brent she'd been damaged goods. Now she felt heartbreakingly whole, but it might be too late. She might never get the chance to tell Brent how she felt about him.

Ed slipped his pistol into his jacket pocket, but he was a fool if he thought they wouldn't find it. A big bald guy pulled him out of the car and frisked him, relieving him of the weapon. While he was patting Ed down, Anna wriggled to get the envelope and managed to slide it inside the front of her panties, just above her pubic bone.

The bald man came around to her side of the car and opened the door. Cut the plastic ties and pulled her out of the car. She searched his gaze, but his eyes were hidden behind dark sunglasses. "Is my mother OK?"

"She's fine. If your father hadn't been such a dick and if you hadn't caused us so much trouble, your mom would still be enjoying her cruise and none of this would have happened."

This was her fault? She opened her mouth in astonishment. He replaced the zip tie with another set of plastic cuffs. He ran his hands over her shoulders, chest, waist, thighs, back, and ankles, miraculously missing the envelope that nestled low against her crotch. "She's clean," he called out.

Anna scanned around to see who he was talking to, then realized he was speaking into a headset. Where was he taking them? He bundled both her and Ed into the chopper, him sitting opposite, a semiautomatic resting on his thigh.

Crap. How on earth could she get them out of this?

Ed looked genuinely distraught, but she wasn't feeling real empathetic toward him right now. Yeah, he loved her mom, but he'd probably just gotten all three of them killed. He'd known what had happened to her as a teen but he'd never told anyone. He'd actually used the situation to insinuate himself closer to her mother, and pry her further away. The worst thing was, she'd let him. She'd imploded on herself and the only person who'd suffered had been herself.

She made a vow right then and there to never let the bad guys win again. She eyed the gun. Maybe it wasn't the best time for that sort of revelation, but she had nothing left to lose.

Brent walked slowly across the parking lot of the hospital. He didn't know much about women, but he did know he didn't appreciate being a stud service for women with issues.

He'd known having "just sex" was going to be a disaster. *Christ.* He raked his hands down his face. Yes, it had been fantastic, out of this world, but…*dammit.* He gritted his teeth and pushed all thoughts of her away. So they'd had sex. Big fucking deal. Except it had been a big deal, for both of them, and it wasn't happening again. He liked his life quiet and his women at a distance. Just needed to figure out this disaster Davis had left them in and he could go back to painting his ocean in solitude, which right now sounded as appealing as a cavity search.

He stopped walking and dropped to his haunches with his hands clasped over his head. What the hell had he been thinking?

That he could make love to Anna—the girl he'd spent half his life "in love" with—and not fall for her completely and irrevocably? Did he enjoy torture?

Obviously he did.

Because he was going to torture himself with the memories of last night for the rest of his stupid life. He blew out a massive breath and realized someone had stopped to stare at the spectacle he was making of himself. He straightened, gave them the stink eye.

People had been staring, for one reason or another, his whole life.

He carried on walking, through the main doors, following signs for Ward Ten. He was supposed to be in NYC by tomorrow night. He found the elevator, forcing himself to ignore the claustrophobia as the doors closed and the walls pressed in on him. When Anna was in protective custody, he'd take off to the Big Apple. He didn't want to be the center of all that fuss, and no way would he reveal his true identity to a gallery full of press people, but he wanted to get off the island. Maybe on the way back, he'd pick up the jeep in North Dakota, and he and Finn could road-trip back, a final bond of brotherhood before the poor bastard got married.

He strode down the corridor, but when he got to Ward Ten, it was geriatrics. Davis's ex-wife might have lost her mind years ago, but she wasn't that old.

"Excuse me." He stopped a nurse who gave him a thorough once-over before she smiled.

"What can I do for you?" The words combined with the look were suggestive. *Very* suggestive. Brent was flattered, but his body didn't respond.

Good girls, every goddamn time. It was a curse.

"I'm looking for a patient by the name of Katherine Plantain. I was told Ward Ten, but it looks like I'm in the wrong place." Brent used charm that felt rusty as old nails. He leaned over the desk and showed off his dimples. "I don't suppose you could help me out?" A bad feeling had wormed its way into his gut.

"Are you family?" Her eyes twinkled.

"Favorite nephew."

"I just bet you are." She glanced at his ring finger then her nails tip-tapped on the keyboard. Frown lines appeared next to her eyes. "I don't see anyone of that name booked in."

He turned the monitor which earned him a sharp "Hey!" from the nurse, but he was already running back down to the elevator, pressing buttons to get him to the main entrance where he'd last seen Anna, his heart scrambling in his chest. *No, no, no.* He put his cell phone back together, battery and SIM card, and dialed the number of the burner cell he'd given her as he strode past the coffee shop, kicking himself. It rang and rang and finally was answered but there was nothing but silence and then a rush of air and a crash as if someone had tossed it.

Brent froze in his tracks, then whirled around in a circle, not knowing what the fuck to do. "No!" he yelled. Security headed his way, but he swung away from them and outside into the fresh air. His heart pounded.

Where was Anna? How could he have let her out of his sight, even for a minute? Sure he was angry, but he knew how dangerous these guys were. *Stupid, stupid fuck.* He called Finn.

His brother answered with a pissed-off, "We just landed. And don't think I've forgotten that stunt you pulled on me the other day. You and I still need a little *chat.*"

"I can't find Anna," Brent interrupted another verbal ass-kicking.

"What do you mean? I thought you were going straight to the hospital."

"We did. I dropped her off at the entrance to park the car and she's vanished. Worse, there's no record of the mother being admitted."

Finn swore. "Stay there. I am coming to get you."

Brent clutched his head to keep it from exploding all over the sidewalk. "I can't stand here doing nothing."

"Holly's going to call her dad"—the deputy commissioner—"and we'll set up extra security at the airports and seaports. They'll want somewhere quiet." Not hard on an island the size of Scotland, but with just a fraction of the population. "But they need Internet access if they're doing what we think they are doing, and they'll want weapons." Finn was thinking out loud, using his ex-Special Forces background to figure out what the bad guys might do next. "They won't travel through public channels. They'll find a different way." The same way Brent had.

"Anna was carrying a cell phone but I think they tossed it." Brent gave Finn the number and heard Holly in the background, then the sirens went off.

"Use your contacts and I'll use mine," Finn shouted above the din. "Call everybody you can think of who might see or hear something about these bastards. I'll be there in fifteen minutes. Wait for me."

Finn hung up and Brent just stared at the phone. He'd spent most of his adult life trying to push his brother away because he'd told himself he didn't deserve family, didn't deserve happiness. He'd killed their father and had never forgiven himself, no matter how many years he'd served in prison. But he hadn't meant to kill him. And the drunken fuck hadn't given him much of a choice. He'd been protecting a kid too small and injured to defend himself, and if he hadn't lashed out, Finn would be dead.

It was time to accept that he'd been punished enough and maybe, just maybe, he deserved another chance.

But Anna had been taken…

Shit, he felt sick.

He'd once again let down someone he loved—and he didn't even bother pretending he didn't love her with his whole heart, even if she'd probably never feel the same way about him. The last few hours he'd spent in her company, he'd been back to his bitter distant self, because that was how he dealt with things. Because in the past, showing any sort of emotion was a weakness that could get him killed. But he wasn't in prison anymore—he was supposed to be free, except he was trapped by his past as surely as he'd been by those iron bars.

It was time to give himself a chance, but first he had to find Anna. He started dialing. He called two old "friends," then got a call back. But it wasn't from his contacts. It was from Jack Panetti.

"Sorry it took a while to get back to you."

Christ. Brent closed his eyes. The poor bastard was in the hospital because of the people who were after Anna. They weren't fucking around.

"But while I was lying around doing nothing, I managed to help prove your boy, Davis Silver, in most likelihood was set up for fraud by a guy called Ed Plantain."

"What?" Brent lowered himself to a nearby bench, feeling like he'd had his brain smashed in. "Tell me."

"One of my guys did a search for any other bank accounts that had been set up using the same PC that was used to create the bank accounts Davis supposedly set up nine years ago." Brent's brain hurt. "My computer guy went back fifteen months prior and hit the jackpot. He found another cluster of private bank accounts set up in the Cayman Islands, but the only money ever deposited in them was the opening balance."

"And they were set up in Ed's name?"

"Correct. He set them up in the April, his wife died in May."

"And you think what?" Brent's brain was too screwed up to deal with this information. Anna was *missing.*

"I think he planned to steal money, either to pay for his wife's treatment or to get the hell out of Dodge and leave her to it. But she died. I'm just speculating here, but I'm guessing a year later he set Davis up for the fall, although I don't know his motive."

The wife, *Katherine.* She was the motive. "Ed Plantain was there to pick up the pieces when Davis's wife's life went to hell."

"There's something else…"

Pain clutched at Brent's chest, but he didn't have time for a coronary.

"Last Friday, Davis Silver deposited over sixty million dollars into those old accounts of Ed Plantain's." *Holy fuck.* "Trace is tracking the money, but I'm pretty confident the trail is going to lead us back to the Holladay Foundation. Given the setup and the players, I'm thinking some sort of illegal mercenary operation."

These guys were killers, that was for damn sure.

"So Davis knew it was Ed who'd set him up," said Brent. When had he found out? Why hadn't he told someone?

Because he hadn't wanted to upset the woman he still loved with all his heart.

Christ, love sucked. "I'm going to rip that asshole apart." Ed Plantain had stolen Davis's life. Brent could hear sirens and stood up, waving his hand in the air as the cruiser came into view. Holly pulled up with a screech of brakes and a rush of exhaust fumes. Finn climbed out. Holly carried on talking into her radio. The sirens went quiet.

Jack was still talking to him on the cell. "I want these bastards, Brent. Personally I don't give a shit about Plantain, but I sure as hell give a damn about the guy who shot that cop in front of me and then put a bullet in my back. Whatever is going on, I want them held accountable. You understand me?"

"I understand." Something ugly tightened in Brent's gut. "These guys are going down for what they've done."

Finn's blue eyes pinned him as he waited for him to end the call. "Holly just spoke to the captain of that cruise ship Anna's mother and stepfather were on. The steward went down to the Plantains' cabin to check on them at her request, and discovered another woman tied up and locked in the bathroom. She claims Ed Plantain locked her up when they discovered their respective spouses had *both* been abducted. She wanted to report it and Ed didn't. He got violent when she told him she was going to do it anyway."

"Sonofabitch." All these lives disrupted for sixty million dollars. Hard to believe it was worth it.

"Airline records say Ed Plantain flew back alone and landed back in Victoria early this morning."

Easy to guess the scenario. The bad guys had had enough of chasing Anna around the country and had instead taken Anna's mom as leverage to draw her to them instead. And Ed had lied to Anna to make sure she didn't suspect or back out. Brent couldn't believe he'd let her meet the weasel alone, but his feathers had been ruffled by the fact he'd fallen for her after telling himself not to. He'd taken his eye off the goal. *Fuck.* This was all his fault.

"Holly already put out a be-on-the-lookout for Ed and his car, which has GPS tracking. They're trying to get a trace on those phones, but it can take a few hours to get warrants and the phone companies onboard."

"Meanwhile, they could be doing anything to Anna." *Christ.* He remembered the guy he'd tackled at Anna's home. The thought of her being abused or killed drove a spike through his heart. "My PI found the money Davis moved. Figures they're mercs." Holly heard him and held up her finger to tell him to wait one minute. "The cops need to freeze those funds." Although that still might not keep Anna safe. *Shit.*

Finn grabbed his arm and lowered his voice. "I know what you're going through, Brent. I was there last summer and it feels like someone is ripping your heart out with needles, but I'm here for you."

Brent hadn't forgotten, though he'd been numb from losing Gina at the time. He didn't know what the hell he'd do if he lost Anna too. Finn hugged him hard and Brent closed his eyes before finally wrapping his arms around his brother and squeezing tight. Even after everything he'd done, Finn was still there for him. He'd never fully accepted it before, but he did now.

"Keep reaching out to those contacts of yours that Holly likes to pretend don't exist. Don't give up hope." Finn dug his fingers into his shoulder. "We'll find her. They need somewhere quiet. Somewhere with computer access. Somewhere they can disappear."

"Could be anywhere."

Holly joined them, looking scarily official, armed, and in her uniform. Thank God she was on his side, although he hated having to follow the rules.

Finn's phone rang and he checked the display with a frown. "It's Laura Prescott from Bamfield." His brother's face turned hard as he listened to whatever Brent's neighbor had to say. "Laura, I want you to listen to me very carefully. I want you to go to Thomas's over at the marine lab *right now*. Get the hell out of there, but make it look like you're just going to the store. No nosiness, got it? No heroics."

Finn hung up on her. "Big-ass boat moored at your dock. A couple guys she doesn't recognize patrolling your grounds."

Holly went back to her radio. Brent turned ice cold inside. Would they be *that* bold? Why not? They'd already committed kidnap and murder. "It's remote and has Internet access. But it could be a diversion or a coincidence."

"Not likely. It's a good spot. Last place we'd look as the cops only just finished processing the crime scene in the woods there. And hell, it would be a bonus if you and Anna just showed up unexpectedly."

Brent shook his head. He couldn't get his mind around this. "Anna hasn't had time to reach the cabin yet."

"Unless they had a helicopter," Finn said quietly.

Brent was backing away from Finn. Finn watched him with that steady blue gaze.

"I've got a police chopper on standby," Holly shouted through the open window. "And people checking for any unauthorized helicopter activity in the Alberni Valley area."

Finn opened the front door of Holly's police cruiser and motioned for his brother to get in. "I'll sit in the back for a change."

Brent stopped moving. Christ, he hadn't realized how badly the thought of getting in the back of a cop car scared him. But his brother knew. His brother had always known.

"Let's go," Holly ordered.

Brent climbed in the front seat and held on as Holly whipped out of the parking lot. Sirens blaring, lights flashing. His heart was pounding but his mind was starting to focus. As long as they didn't know where there money was, Anna was safe. Of course *safe* wasn't the same as unharmed, but he pushed those thoughts aside so he could function. With luck they wouldn't be too far ahead of them. With *luck* this wasn't some giant wild goose chase. But right now they didn't have anything else to go on.

Anna had been through hell before and survived. That's all she needed to do—survive—and he'd take care of the rest.

Ed shivered in the corner of the helicopter, clinging to the firm belief that fate was on his side. He hadn't slept since he'd gotten that phone call to say his wife had been taken. When he'd failed to get in touch with Anna, he'd been ready to walk into RCMP headquarters and beg for help. But she'd finally gotten her head out of her ass long enough to check her e-mail, and by pretending her mother was near death, he'd gotten her on the island before the appointed time. He'd kept his side of the bargain. These bastards better keep theirs.

Anna's eyes had drifted shut a few minutes ago. How could she sleep? Didn't she care about the woman who'd given her life? Ungrateful wretch. Saying Malcolm raped her? Maybe he shouldn't have forced his son to take Anna to the prom, but the boy would never have taken anything that wasn't freely offered. Girls had fallen over themselves to go out with the former high school football star.

But a guy's reputation didn't suffer if he slept around, whereas a girl's did. Maybe Anna had convinced herself she'd said no just to save face. Ed didn't think it was necessarily fair, but that was life. And life was not fair.

Katherine. Just the thought of his delicate wife in the hands of these monsters made fury pound through his veins. If they'd so much as *touched* her…He clenched his teeth around the thought. Harvey Montgomery better keep his hands off her too.

This was all Davis's fault; maybe it was his way of getting revenge. Setting the guy up had been child's play, but maybe he should have just had him killed instead. It would have been easier in the long run.

When Eleanor had been sick, he'd set up bank accounts in the Caymans, planning to rescue what remained of their savings before it was all wasted on medical bills. Then he'd sell the house, and build himself a new life in paradise. Eleanor wouldn't have cared. She'd barely recognized him, she was so pumped full of drugs. Malcolm could have joined him after he finished high school, and Eleanor would have been taken care of in the hospital.

Then one day, when he'd been at his lowest, Katherine had comforted him to her breast and he'd known everything would turn out OK.

So he hadn't followed through with his plans to leave, and Eleanor had died quickly. A blessing, everyone said, and he certainly hadn't argued. And he'd been gifted the tools and knowledge of how to get the life he was destined to have with Katherine. Fate. With a little cunning thrown in.

Sure, he'd waited a year to put his plan into action, using the time to sink Davis further and further into the mire, but it had been worth it.

Ed eyed the guard. A man who wanted to rip away the life Ed had worked so diligently to build. He was obviously just a grunt, not the brains of the operation. Ed needed to deal with whoever was calling the shots and convince them he could help, just as long as his wife was safe.

The pilot kept his eyes averted, and Ed had noticed when getting onboard that the identifying numbers on the helicopter were all covered with masking tape. They flew low, avoiding radar. *Damn.* Up ahead there was a flash of the coast, and a small clearing just visible to the left, among the endless stretch of pines. The chopper banked toward it and the pilot set the machine down as gently as a sleeping baby in a crib. The bald guy got out of the helicopter and pulled Anna down beside him. She stumbled to her knees and he dragged her back to her feet.

Ed rapidly unclipped his belt and scooted after them. "We had a deal. Where's Katherine?" he shouted over the noise of the rotors. The pilot didn't wait for them to be clear, he took off and the three of them ducked away from the dangerous tail blade.

"Where's my wife?" Ed yelled.

The bald guy raised his gun at him. *Oh shit.* Ed threw himself to the ground. Anna shoved the guard and the shot went wide. Then she took off. What the hell did she think she was doing?

"I just need to talk to your boss," Ed shouted after the man who gave chase to Anna as she ran through a slim path among the fireweed.

Ed jogged after them both. Part of him wanted to run and hide, but he wasn't a coward. He'd proved that all those years ago when he'd stood by his dying wife. He'd proved it by fulfilling his side of the bargain with these people.

Up ahead, a man stepped out of the woods and Anna stopped dead. The bald guy grabbed hold of her arm.

"I've been looking for you, Anna Silver," the new man said.

The hairs on the back of Ed's neck stood up. This was the guy he needed to talk to.

"Where's my mom?" Anna demanded with enough attitude to make Ed scowl. Did she want her mother dead?

"Feisty," the new guy said with relish. "I like that in a woman."

"Let her and Ed go and I'll tell you everything you want to know," said Anna.

A bolt of shock ran through Ed that she'd try and save him after he'd sacrificed her this way.

"I kept my part of the bargain," Ed raised his voice. "You promised me my wife in exchange."

The new guy seemed amused, and his lips twitched.

"I can help, you know. Whatever it is you do. I'm an accountant. Please, I'll do anything to help you, just let my wife go." Ed knew he was begging, but he couldn't help it.

The scary newcomer looked amused. "We already have an accountant." He raised his gun and pointed it at Ed's face.

Anna screamed, "No," and it echoed around the clearing before the bald guy put a gloved hand over her face and smothered the sound.

The man was bluffing, but Ed felt his bowels turn to water. "You promised…"

"I lied." And he squeezed the trigger.

CHAPTER 16

Cops crawled over every square inch of the Coast Guard station and right over Brent's skin. They were staging here, and trying to do it as quietly as possible, but in a town as small Bamfield, even one stranger was conspicuous. Thankfully, the officers had arrived in plainclothes, lugging heavy equipment bags. Now there were twenty hulking, black-clad individuals huddled around a map, which made it look like a terrorist attack was imminent. Holly was arguing with the head of the Emergency Response Team about their next move. Whatever was going down, the guy obviously didn't give a shit that her father was his boss.

Coast Guard Captain Cyrus Kaine eyed Brent across the upstairs lounge. His expression was a thin veil of contempt, and the feeling was entirely mutual. Kaine was an ex-cop from the big city and thought he knew everything about everything. The world was black and white. No gray allowed. They'd hated each other on sight.

There were so many badges in this room, Brent was starting to feel nauseous from that alone. Grinding his teeth to stubs wasn't helping much either. He stuffed his hands in his jeans pockets and watched them programming GPS units. Then they pulled out the plans of his house—the house he'd helped build, but did the cops ask for any input from him? No. They fucking didn't. Which was a shame, because those plans only told half the story.

It was almost full dark outside. The cops had night vision goggles, but he could walk this island blindfolded and still find his way home. But he'd discovered he couldn't say dick without someone telling him to shut the fuck up. They didn't trust the ex-con. Again—with the exception of Holly and her father—the feeling was mutual.

No doubt these guys were hungry to take down the bad guys. To punish cop killers with as much force as necessary. Which didn't save Anna. If anything, it put Anna in the line of fire between two sets of people who didn't give a shit about her except as collateral damage. This wasn't good. None of this was good. His insides twisted with fear and agitation. Holly checked him every thirty seconds to make sure he hadn't done anything stupid, and that pissed him off. He hated when people had him figured out.

"What the hell is taking them so long?" he growled under his breath. Finn glanced at him and then stood to go see what the plan was. Brent watched Finn open his mouth to say something, but the commander of the team shut him down. Six years in Special Forces looked about as popular as being an ex-con. *Figured.*

Anna's life was at stake here. It wasn't just some operation to catch bad guys. The bad guys could walk, as far as he was concerned—for now. Anna was all that mattered. He'd finally figured out that, for all he'd been out of prison these last four years, he still hadn't been free of shackles until he'd made that decision to help a virtual stranger.

Brent stood up and stretched out his back, and wished he hadn't given up smoking six months ago.

The head of ERT was going at it with Holly in a way that was making his brother bristle, even though he knew better than to interfere with his fiancée's job. He caught Cyrus Kaine's dark gaze.

For once the guy didn't look like he wanted to punch him. He looked like he knew exactly what Brent was thinking. Brent froze, and then breathed out again as the guy deliberately turned away and added his voice to the growing argument the cops were having.

Brent poured a coffee from the urn by the door. Added sugar, stirred, and sauntered down the stairs and out the door. Once there he ditched the coffee and jogged up the lane toward the lodge. Then he slipped into the trees that rimmed the northern edge of the peninsula and paused.

The irony didn't escape him that he could now end up back inside for disobeying police orders, but he didn't care. He'd messed up, broken his promise to keep Anna safe. He would rather rot in a cell for the rest of his life than let her down. A noise behind him made him spin.

"Go back," Brent told his brother.

"You're not doing this alone."

Brent shook his head. "Holly will kill you."

"Holly knows me better than anyone."

"I don't want you to get hurt," Brent muttered angrily. Finn might be a grown man, but he was still his little brother.

"I can look after myself, especially if you have a few weapons stashed away the way I think you do." He gave Finn a faint nod, just perceptible in the twilight. "And I don't want you to get hurt, either."

A massive knot formed in his throat, but he didn't have time to get emotional over something they both already understood implicitly. They struck out through barely visible paths, moving silently through the forest, avoiding the officers spread too thinly to cover so much ground. Avoiding the sleeping bear who'd been snacking on huckleberries in a nearby thicket, and the cougar who sat in a tree watching the twilight.

The bay where they'd grown up was secluded. Barkley Sound to the north and west, with its surging, unpredictable swells. Rugged untamed cliffs to south and east, forest obscuring every detail. They worked their way to Laura's property, spotting one man keeping watch on the back road from his house, but no other obvious guards. Brent had no idea how many people were involved in this, but sixty million was enough to fund a small army. Except they didn't have sixty million. They had squat, thanks to his friend Davis.

Brent led Finn to his mini arsenal. It wouldn't take out an army, but he hoped they could find and defend Anna until the troops arrived. Who knew where the mother and stepfather were. The SIG Sauer was in the cabin, in one of his specially built hidey-holes. Assuming the bad guys were downstairs, he could get to it without them knowing he was in the house. He had three more handguns—two liberated from unwelcome "visitors" to his property. He also had a shotgun and a hunting rifle, for dealing with the likes of that bear they just passed. Wildlife was fine outside, but Brent didn't want to have to share his house with anything hairier than he was.

He handed Finn a Beretta and a Smith & Wesson. Pocketed a Glock for himself.

"Do *not* get caught with that," Finn told him grimly.

Brent nodded and led him to the cache of ammunition. They packed what they could in their pockets. Finn took the rifle and started loading it. They squatted beside a giant spruce. "There's a hatch into the attic space on the roof," Brent said. "If we can get through it without them knowing, then we're inside."

"Didn't see that on the plans," Finn murmured.

"Plenty of stuff not on the plans," Brent whispered back. "There's also a trapdoor in the utility room, through to the crawl space. There's a panel that comes away on this side of the house, left of the chimney."

"One thing," Finn said quickly. "They might have stashed Anna on the boat. That would make sense if they wanted to make a quick getaway. If we stake out the house and they take off in the boat, we're back to square one."

"I don't think they are planning on taking Anna with them."

"Unless she doesn't tell them what they need to know."

True, but Finn hadn't met the guys they were dealing with. Or gone hand-to-hand with the man who'd slaughtered Anna's ex-boyfriend in her pretty little kitchen. That guy could turn Anna into a living breathing zombie if they didn't hurry. He might have already done it, but Finn was right. They couldn't afford to give them an easy escape route.

"How long would it take you to check out the boat?" Brent asked.

"Five minutes. I can make sure it isn't going very far if any of these fuckwits try to escape. *Wait* for me."

Brent couldn't see his brother's features, but he could hear him thinking.

"We don't know how many people are in there or where Anna is—or if she's even here. We need to stick close and see what information we can find out by covert observation." His hand gripped Brent's shoulder. "That means you don't rush in there like a fool if you see someone manhandling Anna." Those fingers bit deep. "You won't save her life if we give our position away. It means that unless she's in an immediate life-or-death situation you have to keep your cool."

He nodded. "I'll try." It was the best he could do, and he wasn't making any more worthless promises. Brent and Finn both chambered rounds, the noise sounding loud in the night, but hopefully they were far enough away not to be heard over the surf pounding the beach with a little Pacific fury. If the boat was the bad guys' escape plan, they'd better have packed survival suits.

Finn picked up the rifle and some bullets. Neither of the brothers had been great students in school, but both had been naturals when it came to sports of all varieties. In the army, Finn had taken shooting to a whole new level.

They crept forward and then Finn told Brent to stay put while he went off and dealt with the boat. Brent didn't want to stay still, but he'd more or less promised. So he hunkered in the bushes, thick with summer berries. He scanned the windows of his house and was rewarded with a glimpse of the sonofabitch who'd attacked them in Minneapolis. Relief filled him. They were in the right place. He made his heart calm down. Until the guy pulled someone to their feet and slapped them.

Holy fuck, that was Anna! He looked around frantically, but Finn wasn't back yet. OK. He held his ground, even though it went against every instinct. Then the fucker ran his knife along Anna's jaw and she flinched. Brent couldn't wait any longer.

Anna jerked away from the knife but kept her chin high. The man who killed Peter—Rand, she'd heard him called—turned away from her at the command of an older, distinguished-looking man with military-short gray hair and a barrel chest. She assumed he was the boss of this whole nightmare.

She looked around Brent's beautiful house, unable to believe these people had chosen this place to do their dirty work. And yet, as Brent had told her that first night she'd arrived—just a week ago—it was remote, and no one would hear you scream. Two men hunched over two laptops set up on the kitchen counter and another was on guard duty, watching the road. Baldy had gone upstairs for a quick nap. Apparently he'd borne the brunt of kidnap duty and was all tuckered out. Poor soul. Her mother sagged on the couch. Anna gave her a grim smile.

"I'm sorry, Anna," her mother whispered.

"This isn't your fault, Mom."

"I mean about before…about everything…"

The feelings of resentment that had clung to Anna for years drifted away. Maybe she hadn't been aware of it, but she'd blamed both her parents for abandoning her during her hour of need. She'd been filled with bitterness and secret loathing no one had been able to penetrate. "It was my fault too," she admitted, though emotion wanted to squeeze her throat closed. This might be her last chance to tell her mother anything. "I shut you out. I pushed you away. I regret that more than I regret anything else since Dad was arrested."

Her mother opened her mouth to say more, but Rand shot them a glance and they both froze. *Christ.* He was scary as hell.

Her mom looked pretty good, considering—she was uncomfortable from being bound for hours and possibly days, she had a bruise on her cheek, and her hair was a mess, but there was no real damage. Yet.

Anna didn't mention Ed. Not the oddly gentle "pop" of the gun as it took his life. Not the horror of watching him crumple slowly to the ground. Katherine wasn't the strongest person in the world. Anna needed her not to fall apart.

"Let her go and I'll tell you everything you want to know," she called out.

"So you found it, did you?" asked Rand. "The envelope?" The way his eyes moved over her made her skin recoil. She made herself not think about the envelope pressed against her bikini line.

"Where was it?"

"He sent it to a friend of mine in Minneapolis. We went there after we...saw you at my house." She swallowed but didn't look away.

"I owe you for that." He rubbed a spot on the back of his head. "Peter said you were frigid and didn't like sex."

She tried to block out the words and the images that bombarded her, but he was right there and she knew her survival depended on paying attention. "You killed him. You killed a man who was half your size."

He shrugged. "If you hadn't run, I wouldn't have had to kill him, now would I?"

"You're saying this is my fault?"

He leaned down until they were eye to eye. She could smell his skin. "Actually, it's your father's fault, stealing our money."

"You were trying to set him up—"

"No, we weren't. We just used his access codes to cover our backs. If he'd left it alone and kept his nose out of it, nothing would have changed. Petrie would have erased the activity records and none of this would have ever happened. The money was ours, earned fair and square."

She didn't believe him. "If that money was legit, you'd have gone to the cops when it went missing."

"Legit? We risked our lives for that money. Just because today's government didn't sanction it didn't mean the last one wouldn't have—or the next one for that matter." He touched a finger to her hair and curled it around her ear. Revulsion sifted through her. "I *served* my country. You live in your pretty little house surrounded by pretty things like it's a God-given right, not something men like me have to pay for with blood."

She associated blood with her home all too keenly. But he truly saw himself as some valiant soldier getting what he deserved.

She looked at her mother, helpless against such brute force. "Now you're just a coward, only serving yourself."

He took a sharp step back as if she'd spat on him, then raised his hand as if to slap her.

"Enough bickering. Give us whatever Davis sent you and we'll let you both live," the older boss man snapped.

"Let my mom go and I'll do everything you want. As fast as you want."

The gray-haired guy exchanged a look with his hired killer and she couldn't contain a shiver. Rand took her T-shirt in one hand and drew the knife up. She flinched away as it tore through the neckline and narrowly missed her chin.

"Is this how you get off?" she asked him calmly. "Forcing yourself on women who don't want you?"

That cold smile again. It wrapped its way up her spine and tied a knot in her bravado. "Sometimes."

Her mom tried to stand, but was struggling with her bindings.

Rand took a step and shoved her mother facedown on the couch. "Don't be in such a rush. Momma, you'll get your turn next."

"Rand," his boss said impatiently.

Anna noticed the way the monster's lips tightened. "Do as your boss tells you or you might get in trouble," she goaded, hoping that if she could get them fighting among themselves maybe she and her mother could find a way to escape.

The pulse in his neck throbbed visibly for a couple of beats, but the chill in his gaze never wavered.

"I'm going to search you, Anna. Very thoroughly." He walked around her slowly. "Make sure Vic didn't miss anything." Vic was Baldy, she'd found out. She didn't think it was a good thing that they were using their real names in front of them. Mr. White and Mr. Black would have been fine with her.

He flicked his knife between her breasts and nicked her skin before he slit the fabric of her bra. Deliberate. She stood there with her breasts exposed and blood trickling down her front, and realized she didn't care. She thought about Brent. His smile. His eyes. His warm solid support. Whatever happened to her body wouldn't break her. Not this time. She just needed to figure a way out of here. Because as soon as they found that envelope, she was surplus to requirements.

"You kissed my photograph at my mom's house."

His eyes flickered in surprise.

"The cops have your DNA from there and in my house in Minneapolis. They know who you are. You're not going to get away with this."

"It only matters if they catch me. They aren't going to catch me." His lips curved cruelly. "Take off your pants."

Anna licked her lips, fear getting to her despite herself. But her hand went to the button of her jeans. She didn't fight or argue. She didn't want him to do this himself because he'd not only enjoy it, he'd also find the package. She undid the zipper and pushed the envelope down into the pile of denim at her feet. She was in her panties and socks. Her shoes had been taken from her on the boat. Rand put his knife back in the sheath on his belt but her relief was short-lived as he pulled his gun. He seemed distracted by her legs, and she stood there trembling, praying, he wouldn't notice the small corner of beige peeking out of the blue.

He stood in front of her, ran his hands through her hair, over her ears, neck. He pulled her tight against him and ran both hands over her back, his gun scratching her skin as it went. She could feel his arousal and avoided his gaze even though he stared straight into her eyes. He started to spread the cheeks of her buttocks and she braced herself when the old man said, "For fuck's sake, Rand. That's not how I want you to get the information—"

Rand swirled and nailed the guy between the eyes. The bullet barely made a sound with its professional-looking suppressor, and there wasn't much blood.

"About goddamn time." The guy wearing thick glasses didn't even look up from the computer. But then he did, and his eyes traveled down her body with appreciation but no real heat, and then landed in her pile of clothes. His slow grin made her flesh go cold. "I think you missed something." He pointed at her jeans and Anna closed her eyes. *No.*

Rand's jaw was tight and then he glanced at the denim and pulled out the folded envelope she'd tried so hard to conceal. "Fucking schoolteacher." And then he slammed the butt of the gun into her temple and she dropped like a stone.

Brent found hand- and footholds in the massive logs and pulled himself up the side of his house with more brute force than skill. The roof was metal, so he slid carefully across it and went to open the hatch. A firm hand stopped him.

"Let me check it isn't wired, first." Finn. Quiet and calm, without recrimination. The guy moved like a goddamned ghost and almost gave him a heart attack.

Brent nodded. They eased the hatch open a fraction, Finn using a small penlight to sweep the rim. "Clear," he said.

They dropped silently into the tight attic space, which was empty of everything except insulation.

They sat unmoving for a moment, ears strained as they listened to the silence. They slowly lifted the flap, which opened into a spare room that housed a bed and nothing else. Brent didn't exactly get a lot of visitors. He didn't even know why he'd built a house this big except that it was the opposite of prison.

It *was* a smart place for the bad guys to hole up.

The cops had left, but the area was still officially a crime scene. It was remote, but had everything from a fully stocked kitchen to wireless Internet. They just hadn't counted on the small community's inability to keep their noses out of other people's business. And they hadn't counted on the Carver brothers.

The bedroom door was slightly ajar and a thin sliver of light gave them some illumination, revealing a bulky shape on the bed.

Brent swallowed the fear and panic for Anna's well-being and concentrated on not making a sound as he dropped to the floor. He might not be military, but he'd grown up tracking animals in the bush and all his survival instincts had been honed in an abusive household and then in prison. He aimed the Glock at the unmoving shadow and took the rifle that Finn lowered to him before his brother landed like a cat beside him.

The lump on the bed didn't move. He and Finn went to opposite sides of the bed and squinted at the gray tuft of hair that stuck out of the bedclothes. Not Anna's mother, and her stepfather was bald. Finn raised a handgun as Brent eased back the blanket. An older guy's eyes were wide open, a gag stuffed in his mouth. He looked exhausted, dirty, and terrified. One eye was swollen shut. Finn checked his back and ankles. "Cuffed," he breathed quietly.

Brent lowered the gag but placed a finger to his own lips. "Who are you?"

"Name's Harvey Montgomery. I was with Katherine when she was abducted in Anchorage."

He and Finn exchanged a glance. That fit with the information Holly had gleaned.

"You guys the rescue party?" Harvey whispered as Finn cut his ties. Brent removed the covers so Harvey could flex his arms and legs to get the blood flowing again. It must have hurt like a bitch from the look on his face.

Brent grimaced. "I'm a friend of Katherine's daughter, Anna. This is my house." And damned if these bastards were killing the woman he loved in a place that meant so much to him. Damned if they were killing her anywhere.

"Cops are on their way," Finn reassured the man. Finn went over to the bedroom window and opened it up.

Brent pointed to it. "If you can get out of there without making a sound, do it. But if you make a noise, I'll shoot you myself."

Harvey shook his head. "I'm not about to abandon a woman to these maniacs. Give me a weapon. I'll help you."

"You know how to use a gun?" Finn asked.

"US Marine Corps, soldier." He obviously pegged Finn as part of the pack. Brent's lip curled. Another clique he didn't belong to.

Finn handed Harvey the Beretta and a handful of ammunition. "Don't shoot the ladies." He slung the rifle on his back.

There was a cry from downstairs and Brent went for the door. Finn grabbed him. "Softly," he whispered. "Let's not prove the assholes from ERT correct, OK?"

Finn was right. He nodded. "How many bad guys?" he asked Harvey in a low whisper.

"I've seen three but heard two more since they stuffed me upstairs. I'm rich, which is why I'm still alive. I'm the backup plan."

"Where are they keeping Katherine and Anna?"

"Katherine was in here with me until about fifteen minutes ago. They came and took her downstairs when the others arrived."

Harvey's eye was swollen shut—from the look of his face, he'd tried to stop them and failed. "I didn't see her daughter."

People could do a lot of harm in fifteen minutes.

Brent eased onto the landing, keeping below the solid oak stair rail. They knew one guy was watching the back door. Downstairs was pretty much open-plan, except for the laundry room. There was a heated conversation going on that he couldn't make out. Finn tapped his shoulder to tell him something when someone opened the bedroom door behind them.

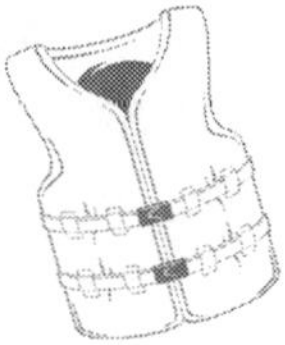

CHAPTER 17

Fuck.

The guy was blinking sleep out of his eyes, which gave them a split-second advantage. Finn caught him in a headlock, smothering any sound the guy made with his hands and arms, driving him smoothly back into the room. Brent and Harvey swept in behind and closed the door quietly behind them.

"Keep lookout," he murmured to Harvey, who nodded and cracked the door, peering out.

The big guy slumped in Finn's arms, sagging to his knees, unconscious. Finn hoisted him onto the bed. "We need to tie him up."

They were in Brent's bedroom so he grabbed the SIG Sauer out of a secret panel in a false beam. Finn raised his brows. "I didn't see that."

"Me neither," murmured Harvey appreciatively.

"Got any duct tape in there?" Finn asked.

"No, some in my studio though. Want me to get it?"

Finn shook his head. "Ties? Belts?"

Brent went over to his wardrobe that was mainly full of worn jeans, board shorts, and faded T-shirts. He pulled three ties from next to a tailored jacket he'd worn for his parole hearing. The clock was ticking. Anna was in danger. He grabbed a pair of woolen socks from his top drawer and stuffed them in the guy's mouth and secured it tightly with the first tie. Finn bound the wrists together and Brent took the ankles, tying the shoelaces in a knot for good measure. Brent grabbed a couple of leather belts and they trussed him across the bed and attached him to the bed legs.

"How long will he be out?" Brent asked.

"Not long enough," Finn answered.

"Shit." Brent did not want this guy to start to bang around up here and raise the alarm.

"I'll watch him." Harvey came to stand beside them. They all kept their voices barely a whisper. "I'll keep him covered and shoot anyone who comes to find him. It would be my pleasure."

"Just make sure they aren't cops," Brent said. "And if cops turn up or if someone throws a flash bang in here, you put the gun down and stick those hands as high in the air as they go."

With his luck Brent would get an RCMP bullet through the skull, although he wasn't sure it would be termed "friendly fire."

"Cops'll be here soon," Finn agreed. He turned to Brent. "I can't get a clear shot from inside. I'm going to take the rifle outside and find a position where I can see the living room. You sit tight. Only interfere if Anna or her mom are in imminent danger, and whatever you do, keep the fuck out of the line of fire." And then he was gone. Brent nodded to Harvey and slipped out after him.

There was a gunshot from downstairs, and Brent's blood turned to ice. Maybe he was already too late.

Anna came awake in a pile of limbs on the floor, her head feeling like it had been cracked open like a raw egg. Her vision was blurred, but she realized her mom was snuggled up beside her. Slowly everything clicked back into place. Like why she was lying on the floor wearing only an open shirt, a tattered bra, panties, and socks.

She sat up, woozy and unbalanced. She gripped her mom's hand and tried to loosen her ties so she'd be more comfortable, but her mom seemed out of it, as if she'd been drugged or had just given up. The men at the kitchen counter flicked her a glance, but ignored her as no real threat. And really, she wasn't. She couldn't even see straight and her head pounded.

The men were whispering. She strained to hear.

"What's the name associated with those accounts?" Rand asked.

"Plantain. Ed Plantain." The geeky guy shot her another glance. But she concentrated on her mother's eyes and willed her to come out of the fog. She watched the men out of her peripheral vision.

"So he set Davis up?"

The accountant's brow's rose. "I don't know, but yeah, it looks like it. Sly bastard." *What did that mean?* "It'll take me thirty seconds to move our money back..." His hands hovered over buttons and then he frowned. "Hmmm. I think someone's onto us." The guy tapped faster and then grinned. "They locked down one of the accounts, but I've moved the rest. And," he said archly, "we are all cosigners on each other's accounts, so let's not think about getting rid of anyone else."

Anna eyed the dead man on the floor. One of their own. Murdered. *God.*

"Browning was a liability." Rand was chillingly reasonable for such a cold-blooded killer. "Get Kudrow. We're gone in ten minutes." They both looked at her and her mom huddled on the floor. "I've got a little unfinished business with the schoolteacher."

Ten minutes. Well, at least it would be fast.

Her throat was tight, but she had something she really needed to know. Something more important than his plans for her.

"What did you mean? *Who* set Davis up?"

Rand's lip twitched. He nudged her mom with his foot as she lay almost comatose on the floor. "Seems your stepfather set your dad up so he could be there to pick up the pieces for your sweet mama. That's a lot of trouble to go to for some ass. Bet you're glad now I shot the fucker."

Her mom's eyes widened infinitesimally, but she didn't meet her gaze. Anna's mind wouldn't stop spinning. Her dad had been innocent. Everything he'd ever said had been true, but no one had believed him—except Brent.

Oh, Jesus. It was awful. She'd let him down, thanks to that creep Ed. Her heart crumbled inside her chest, that they'd hurt him that way. Her mother would never forgive herself. Anna would never forgive herself. But if she wanted to survive the next ten minutes, she needed to do something drastic and that didn't involve going off to la-la land like her mom. Anger surged through her body.

Rand grabbed her wrist, his iron grip bruising flesh as he hauled her to her feet.

She fought him, stumbled forward. "Let go of me!" Despite the pain, she twisted and jerked against his hold, his fingers biting ruthlessly into her skin. She grabbed at the heavy couch but struggled to find purchase in the thick navy fabric. Her nail tore and she bit down on a scream. He had a hundred pounds of pure muscle on her, but she refused to let go. Coming to a halt, Rand gave a savage jerk and almost pulled her arm out of its socket. She cried out and he laughed. Tears burned her eyes, but she wasn't about to let them fall.

She wasn't going to let him destroy her. She'd rather he shot her than raped her, so pissing him off didn't matter. It was all going to hurt. She certainly wasn't going to curl into a fetal ball and give up.

At the bottom of the stairs, she hooked her flexed foot on the end rail and refused to budge. The hard edge of the gleaming wood cut into her ankle. She gave a silent scream as the agony of being violently stretched tore through her. Rather than the pain, she concentrated on not letting go. If she could slow him down, maybe he wouldn't have time to finish what he started. Maybe a miracle would happen and she'd be rescued. For a long time she hadn't believed in miracles, but right now she was willing to give one a chance.

Rand let out a furious bellow and heaved her sideways. She crashed into the opposite wall, screaming with shock and frustration. He gave a satisfied growl as he dragged her up the torturous risers. Every step raked the fresh bruises on her body until she writhed in agony, every hard edge inflicting new injuries as he unceremoniously yanked her along like a sack of flour. Her flexed feet caught against the edge of the last stair and she dug down hard as he swore with anger and frustration. He was going to hurt her anyway, so she had nothing to lose. Which brought another shocking realization. The life she'd made for herself in Minneapolis meant nothing anymore. She wanted Brent—not just to save her, but to love her.

God, could the secret of happiness be *that* easy?

Brent didn't want a live-in lover. But so what? She could change his mind, or they could keep separate homes. She'd travel a lot. She could even teach in Canada, and move back to the island. For the first time in her life, Anna wanted to fight for a man. For a life with someone. And he might not go for it—hell, he was stubborn—but he'd already admitted he cared. Something unfurled inside her chest. From a man like Brent Carver, "care" was tantamount to a full-on proposal.

"Let. Go. Of. The. Fucking. Step. Bitch." Rand jerked her forward, anger penetrating that emotionless gaze for the first time. She yelped as he freed her from the step and she plowed straight into the wall. She caught a sharp blow to the nose, which made her eyes sting. *Dammit.* Rand looked amused. He dragged her across Brent's highly polished floors. Frantically she flailed around, but there was nothing left to grab on to. The monster was going to rape her and then he was going to kill her. Then he was going to kill her mother, and chances were Brent would find their bodies when he came home.

Damn it! That was almost the worst thing of all.

She staggered to her feet and launched herself at him, scratching at his face. A ridiculous amount of pride surged through her when she connected and blood bloomed on a scratch across his left eye. He slapped her and her ears rang. She tried to knee him in the balls but he controlled her easily, every attempt to hurt him fueling his amusement and the homicidal gleam in his eye. She hated his smug smile, wanted to rip that smirk off his ugly face. He shoved her into the bedroom she'd used when she'd stayed here last week. Her suitcase was open at the bottom of the bed. She slapped him in the face and he punched her in the mouth, a sledgehammer of force knocking every thought except pain from her body. She landed stunned on the bed. Tasted blood.

"Don't bother moving, honey. It'll just be a waste of energy." Then he closed the door and grabbed her ankle.

Katherine's mind was shrieking in silent agony. Ed had set up Davis? Davis had been innocent? All this time. All these years. Pain banded her stomach and she wanted to roll into a ball and scream. But Anna was being dragged upstairs and her daughter needed her now more than ever. Dear Lord, how she'd let that child down. Let Davis down. Been nothing but a poor excuse as a wife and parent. She dragged herself across the floor to the body of the man she'd assumed was the boss. The fact they'd shot him so callously suggested she'd been wrong about that too. Her hands throbbed with pain. Her feet were in agony. How could Ed do that? Huge sobs wanted to engulf her but she forced them back. And even though it was only the word of these evil men, she knew it was true because suddenly her whole life made sense.

Was Ed really dead? She couldn't believe it. It turned all her anger upside down and inside out, although she would never have been able to forgive him.

The guy tapping keys was mumbling to himself. Sitting behind the enormous kitchen island, he couldn't see her where she lay on the floor. And the man dragging Anna didn't consider her a threat because she hadn't been. She'd been useless. But now the only person who mattered to her was in danger, and she didn't care if she died saving her—she *was* going to save her.

She found what she was looking for even as she heard Anna cry out again. The dead man had a small penknife on his keychain. She grasped the keys in numb fingers and sawed at the plastic holding her feet together. They snapped apart and she held her breath at the noise, but the man just kept typing. *Probably stealing his friends' money*, she thought bitterly.

She maneuvered the keys upside down between her palms and found an angle to attack the thin white plastic. It took longer, but after about twenty seconds of frantic movement, the cuff snapped. Pain rushed through her extremities along with an awful utter silence. The man on the keyboard had stopped typing. Her heart thumped. She lunged for the dead guy's gun, still strapped to his leg, but found herself face-to-face with a shiny silver revolver.

"I don't think so, lady," he said.

"Why are you doing this to us? You could just walk out the door," she implored. "Take the money and run."

He snorted. "And have Rand, Kudrow, and Vic after me for the rest of my life? No thanks." He cocked the gun and Katherine closed her eyes. So angry with herself for failing Anna. Angry with Ed, even angry with Davis. She tilted her chin and drew in a last breath. And then came a gunshot, followed by the instantaneous crash of the enormous windowpanes, glass shattering everywhere. She opened her eyes as the man who'd threatened to kill her toppled over. The other man, Kudrow, came running into the room as she ducked behind the kitchen island, grabbing the computer nerd's revolver with fingers that were suddenly steady. Another shot, and a man's dying grunt as a bullet smashed into flesh. And then there was a man she didn't recognize with a rifle at her side, helping her up, half pushing her out the back door. "Go. Run," he said.

"My daughter!" she cried, dropping the gun.

The stranger's eyes hit the stairs. "You first. Go!"

She grabbed his arm. "There's a man called Harvey too. I don't even know if he's still alive."

"Harvey's fine. I saw him earlier. Let's get you out of here."

He'd heard the sonofabitch drag Anna upstairs. Her cries of pain ricocheted inside his brain and exploded like deadly shrapnel. He'd wanted to step in so bad that forcing himself to simply stand here behind his bedroom door almost stopped his heart. But he also knew the bastard was holding a gun and until he put it down, Brent couldn't risk a confrontation.

In approximately thirty seconds, that gun would be the last thing on the fucker's mind.

He had to wait for the advantage, but that advantage put Anna in ever greater danger and the thought of that bastard touching her clawed at him with frenzy.

He heard Anna smack him, and the return punch and her scream of agony.

His nails bit into the wooden frame of the door. Five more seconds.

Brent had known rage before. Childhood rage when his mother walked away and left them with their father. Adolescent rage every time his dad used Finn like a punching bag for his pleasure. Adult rage in prison when someone tried to demean or degrade him because they thought they had the right.

Nothing compared to the white-hot anger that sang like fire through his veins and obliterated all thought, all feeling, and all memory.

He walked swiftly out of his bedroom and into hers. The bastard was poised over her, one hand clasping both of hers above her head, the other ripping off her panties.

Brent took the slack off the trigger.

"No!" Anna cried.

What?

"Don't kill him. He's not worth going back to jail."

He dropped his jaw. Did she really think he gave a fuck about prison right now?

The guy's hand started to reach for the pistol on the nightstand. "Move another inch and I'll blow your head off," Brent told him. Christ, he wanted to damage him. Wanted to stick a bullet right between his eyes for daring to hurt Anna.

The hand stopped moving. Instead the guy rolled to his feet, but took Anna with him so she was a human shield. *Fucking, fucking fuck.*

Anna's eyes beseeched him with apology.

Damn, he couldn't believe he hadn't just shot the fucker on the bed, but the bullet might have hit Anna too and he couldn't risk it. There was a massive crash of glass downstairs. Shots fired. Brent smiled grimly. They were at a standoff. They all listened for the running feet of a swathe of cops, but nothing happened. Brent knew it was Finn, but this guy must be wondering what the hell was going on.

Brent kept his eyes on the soulless black gaze and his gun didn't waver. Anna's eyes were huge green pools of what should have been terror but looked a hell of a lot softer than that. She smiled at him and his heart threatened to blow. God, he loved her.

"Let her go and I'll tell you how to get out of here without the cops seeing you," Brent offered.

The eyes flickered.

"I don't give a shit about anything except Anna." Brent edged closer to the door. "There's a trapdoor in the roof. You get to it through a hatch in the next bedroom." Brent tilted his head.

The guy kept eyeing his handgun. Brent braced himself just in case he decided to dive for it. He didn't want to risk shooting Anna, but the guy could not get that firearm or else they'd both be dead.

"Put the gun down or I'll break her neck." The bastard changed the angle of his grip. It was no idle threat. The way he moved his hands to exactly the right spot proved he'd done it before. Probably too many times to count.

"He'll break my neck anyway. Don't let him escape, Brent. You already stopped him from raping me." A firestorm of relief swept over him, but they were still in deep shit. Anna was struggling to breathe as she balanced on tiptoes, clutching at the guy's hips. "Rand here deserves to spend his life in prison. *You're* the good guy."

She was bleeding and naked except for a flapping shirt and she was trying to make him feel better? He wanted to snarl but didn't dare let his attention shift for even a second. In his peripheral vision, he saw a movement in the trees outside. A shadow that didn't belong. Brent moved so he wasn't in the line of fire and prayed like he'd never prayed in his entire goddamned life.

"I love you. Please don't think this was your fault," she said.

Damn. How did that even happen? A woman like her loving a man like him?

"Aw, how sweet." Rand laughed, and shifted his grip to make that final fatal twist.

As Rand's arms tightened painfully around her neck, Anna knew she was about to die. He'd win, and Brent would be destroyed. *No!* She made a last frantic lunge for the knife sheathed at Rand's waist. Her heart almost seized when she finally snagged the handle and pulled it free.

She adjusted her grip and drove the blade deep into Rand's solid thigh. He howled in pain and released her. She leaped for the bed and Rand's gun. He'd been seconds from raping her—the knowledge gave her a hunger for vengeance she'd never experienced before.

But he grabbed her foot and she hit the mattress face-first.

"Let her go, asshole." Brent raised the gun and aimed it at Rand's chest. But Rand let go of her foot for a moment to fling the nightstand, one-handed, at Brent and it knocked the gun out of his hand.

Grabbing at the sheets, Anna tried to drag herself across the bed. She didn't care that she was nearly naked. She just wanted to live. Rand grabbed her foot again with bruising force. She turned her head and watched him rip the knife from his thigh, a look of hatred blazing from those black depths as he raised the knife to slash her. Memories of Peter flashed through her mind and she kicked hard.

Brent launched himself, connecting his solid fist to Rand's nose, which burst with blood, and he let her go. The fact Brent had already risked everything for her made him a hero. The fact he'd been willing to kill for her showed her his love and devotion. She didn't need the words and doubted she'd ever get them. A barrage of blows knocked Brent back a step, and her heart lodged in her throat as Rand lunged after him with the knife.

"Get out of here," Brent yelled at her.

No way was she leaving him. *The gun.* She scrambled across the bed and grabbed Rand's gun, but her hands were shaking so badly and the two men were so close together she couldn't risk shooting.

Brent clearly needed all his wits to fend off the enraged man coming after him with a bloody knife clutched in his fist. He dodged to the left and kicked at Rand's knee. Rand grunted in pain but didn't go down. Brent grabbed a towel off the radiator and wrapped it around his left arm for protection as he tried to keep between Anna and the man who'd tried to destroy her, who'd treated her like she was a piece of trash.

He was protecting her again. Protecting her from what it felt like to take a life.

"You think you're some sort of badass because you killed your old man?" Rand swiped blood off his chin with the back of his hand and sneered at Brent.

"I protect what I love."

The admission stunned Anna and she swayed. Finally, he'd recognized the instinct that was programmed into his DNA. She wouldn't change him for anything.

"I'm going to take her from you, Carver. You won't be able to stop me." The flat tilt of that cruel mouth said he believed it too.

"Not as long as I'm breathing, cocksucker," Brent said. "Get out of here, Anna. Let's prove we're a lot smarter than this dumb-ass."

Anna edged toward the door. It made sense, but the idea of leaving Brent alone with this animal didn't sit easy. And where were the others? What if she ran into another of Rand's gang and they ended up back at square one?

The gun shook in her grip. "I'm not leaving you, Brent."

Brent jumped out of reach of six inches of honed steel.

"She's just waiting for me, Romeo." Rand cupped himself and jeered. "I've got something you can't give her."

Not what to say to a woman who'd already been raped once. A woman you'd beaten and stripped and humiliated. Shaking with rage she pointed the gun at Rand's penis, and the guy sucked in a sharp breath and took a half step back. Finally showing her a little goddamned respect.

"Anna," Brent warned.

God. It ripped at her. The desire to just hit back harder, to hurt and inflict pain. To force him to value her as a human being. But Brent knew the cost and he was trying to help her. She recognized that even as she rode the wave of fury.

So she aimed lower, at his feet, and pulled the trigger.

Nothing happened.

She pulled it again, but got the same thing. Anna's jaw dropped and everything started happening in slow motion. She dropped the gun. Rand grinned and went to slam that honed blade into Brent's gut, but a shot ripped through the glass and a gaping hole appeared between Rand's eyes. He went rigid, suspended in the air for a long second before toppling onto the bed. She shuddered as blood and brain matter sprayed the room.

Brent snatched Anna into his arms and squeezed her tight, turning her away from the bloody mess of the dead man.

She couldn't believe it was over. Rand was dead. Her legs barely worked, but she didn't need them with Brent holding onto her like a parachute in free fall. That's what her life felt like right now—free fall, and she needed Brent if she ever hoped to land safely. "I can't believe you found me."

"I can't believe I let you go." He ran his hands over her body, as if reassuring himself she wasn't injured. She burrowed closer, wanting to crawl inside his skin.

"Are you OK?" he asked.

She laughed at the dumb question. "Yes. No. I'm sore all over. Bruised and battered," she shivered in his arms, "but I'm alive and he didn't rape me. Thankfully, he was saving that for the finale."

"He got his own goddamn finale." He rocked her against him. Then he pulled off his T-shirt and pulled it over her head. It hung almost to her knees, but she still trembled in reaction to everything that had happened. She pressed up close to his warmth, knowing this man was her hero, the same way he'd been Finn's hero. And she loved him so much it hurt.

"I was a jackass earlier," he murmured into her hair. "There's a good chance I'll always be a jackass."

She shook her head and winced because the headache was coming back, stronger than before. "I was awful to you. I tried to push you away so you'd be safe from them but I was stupid—"

"If I hadn't been a prick, these guys wouldn't have taken you." Lines of anguish cut into his face. He sure did like to torture himself.

"Ed might have just shot you and I couldn't have coped with that." Anna dragged his face down to hers and kissed him.

He raised his head. "I don't deserve you but I want you. I really want you—to be with you." He gently kissed her. *Ouch*. Her lips throbbed and her head pounded, but she never wanted him to stop. "I can't believe I let that fucker get his hands on you."

"Ed tricked me into his car but I finally remembered where Dad would have sent the envelope and found the evidence." She met his gaze, a fresh wave of anguish moving through her. "Ed set up Dad and we all believed he was guilty. Everyone but you."

Brent nodded. "Jack Panetti figured it out too. Your dad knew it was Ed. I'll make sure the world knows Davis was an innocent man. Your father deserves that."

Anna nodded, her grief still new and heavy. Now it was heightened by the fact she'd let him down so unforgivably.

Brent's arms tightened around her as if he knew what she was thinking. "He loved you. More than anything else in the world, he *loved* you."

"I just wish I'd been a better daughter, a better person." But regrets were worthless without change. Now was a good time to make those changes, and Anna was determined to cling to this new chance of starting over. She looked up at the man who'd risked everything for her and ran a fingertip over his jaw. "I feel like I barely know you, and yet…" she whispered.

"I feel like I've known you my whole life."

She felt it too. An inexplicable, unbreakable connection. They held each other's gaze, and then her jaw dropped as she suddenly remembered. "Oh, God. My mom." She pulled away. "We have to get my mom."

CHAPTER 18

There was another loud crash downstairs, voices, and the pounding feet he'd been expecting. "That's the cops now. Better late than never."

Anna's eyes widened. "Where's your gun?" He spotted it beside her suitcase and scooped it up.

"They can't find you with that." Her eyes went wide and frantic and she went to grab it. Desperate. Because she worried about him. He stepped over to the corner wall, hidden from view, and ditched his weapon and ammo into another secret wooden cubby that was invisible to the naked eye. Two seconds later, cops burst into the room.

He put his hands on his head as the cops made them both lie down on the floor and frisked them for weapons.

They checked that the bad guy was actually dead and then, when Brent couldn't stand it for moment longer, he growled, "Get this woman a medic and a fucking blanket." And he realized with sudden clarity that he didn't care about what people thought of him. He wasn't a bad person. He'd been forced to make an awful decision and he'd paid for it. But nearly a quarter of a century later, he was finally willing to forgive himself and move on. To give himself a second chance, to have a better life, a normal life. Assuming his ass didn't get thrown back in jail…which wasn't looking so great from this angle.

Someone removed their jacket and helped Anna to a standing position as they wrapped it around her.

Black shiny boots entered the room. The head of the Emergency Response Team and Brent's future sister-in-law. He grinned. "Hi, Holly. I've been meaning to ask what I'm supposed to wear to the wedding. I hope you don't mind stripes."

She pursed her lips, not impressed by his attempt at humor.

"Who took those first shots downstairs?" asked the burly police officer with the pissy attitude.

"I assume it was one of your guys." Brent shrugged from his uncomfortable position on the floor. "I was busy having the snot beaten out of me." *Again.*

"Where's your boyfriend?" the tactical cop asked Holly in a tone that made her bristle.

"Right here," said Finn, coming in the room sans weapons. *Thank Christ.* "I was helping Anna's mother to safety."

"She's OK?" Anna choked out.

Finn nodded and smiled. "She was about to stage her own rescue when I found her. Harvey's fine too."

Anna's face transformed. "Oh, thank goodness."

"The guy who took out the kidnapper said you were armed." Head of ERT pointed a finger at Brent. "Where's the weapon?"

"The guy's seeing things. The only gun belonged to that fucker." Brent eyed Rand's body with disgust.

"Possession of a firearm is a parole violation, Mr. Carver." The guy nodded his head to one of his officers.

Shit.

"You can*not* be serious!" Holly argued. "He doesn't have a weapon and he just saved this woman's life."

"Interfering with a police operation? You bet your ass I'm serious. And I'll find that weapon."

Suddenly Brent heard the familiar sound of handcuffs, and his whole body clenched when someone slipped them around his wrists.

"No," Anna screeched. "You are not arresting the man who just saved my life."

Although Brent figured technically he hadn't saved anyone. Finn went to open his mouth. Holly was about to step in when they all heard the familiar strident tones of his neighbor.

"I demand to see my client *immediately*." Laura.

Hallelujah. "How'd she get here so fast?" Brent asked no one in particular. She was downstairs, but he could hear every word of her exchange with the cops.

"Someone must have called her." Holly's expression was impassive.

And he closed his eyes, because Anna was safe and nothing else mattered. He suddenly remembered what she'd said to him when she'd thought she was about to die. He rolled on his back, a mixture of fear and excitement churning in his gut. "Did you mean it?"

Huge green eyes regarded him with absolute certainty. "I love you," she said in front of everyone.

Brent grinned.

Holly tapped him with her foot. Harder than strictly necessary.

"What?" he snarled.

"You don't just leave a girl hanging when she tells you she loves you." She glared at him, as if this was the biggest problem they currently faced.

"I said it already." Technically speaking. "How would you like an audience every time something important happened in your life?" He shook his head. Then he laughed, which wasn't comfortable when handcuffed and lying in shards of broken glass on his own highly polished hardwood floor. He looked up at the woman who'd shown him exactly why freedom was all it was cracked up to be. "I love you, Anna Silver. I will do anything for you. But don't put your life on hold for me. Do *not* wait for me." He groaned as some big bastard hauled him to his feet. "I might not be around for a while."

"You need to get ready, Brent. Your life is about to change," Anna warned him.

That didn't sound like much of a promise. The woman never listened to him anyway. They marched him out the door in handcuffs. Finn too. Laura was going to *freak* when she saw that. He grinned. "Bring it on."

Twelve hours later, Katherine sat on a bench seat inside police headquarters. Out front, members of the press were prowling like hungry dogs in search of scraps. They'd gotten hold of this story involving cop-killing mercenaries, millions of dollars of stolen money, kidnappings, a shootout, and an almost decade-old miscarriage of justice. The place had exploded, everyone wanting an exclusive. Katherine had been released from the hospital with a few minor bruises. Most of the damage wasn't physical, and she knew she was going to need some professional help to get through the guilt.

Guilt for not believing Davis. Guilt for Anna getting hurt. Guilt for dragging Harvey into this mess. Even guilt for getting Ed killed. She hadn't wanted that. She'd never wanted that. She drew in a shaky breath, feeling like she'd been physically beaten. Every muscle ached and it still didn't touch the mental anguish.

Police had questioned her for hours, showing her various mug shots, including one of the nice young man who'd saved her. She'd seen him led away from the house in handcuffs. She'd been confused and then realized that whatever he'd done to save her life probably hadn't been legal, and her opinion of the justice system had slipped another notch. Her memory had grown pretty fuzzy about the details after that. All she knew for sure, or so she'd told the police officers who'd questioned her, was that she couldn't remember whether or not the young man had been armed when he'd come and whisked her to safety. Then she'd questioned them, on why they hadn't worked harder to believe Davis's story. If they'd just dug deeper—if *she'd* just had a little faith in something as extraordinary as true love.

She didn't blame the police for her part in Davis's betrayal. That was all on her. And how he must have hated her. But they'd botched their investigation and needed to admit it, to make sure they never did anything so destructive again.

Harvey came out of an interview room. The look on his face when he saw her was one of relief. "Thank God you're all right." He sat heavily beside her. Almost touching. Odd to be so hyperaware of him now sitting so close, when they'd spent hours holding hands and holding each other together.

"Are you OK?" she asked quietly.

He nodded and rubbed his eyes. "I don't think the Mounties bought my story about overpowering the guy and getting that gun off him, though." Harvey shrugged. "I think those men are in serious trouble for saving our lives and I've made sure they know they have my attorneys at their disposal."

"I think Anna's in love." Katherine hoped her daughter dealt with it better than she ever had. She wrapped her arms around herself, cold to the bone. Her clothes had been taken by the crime scene people, so she was in scrubs from the hospital. Harvey was in a borrowed sweat suit and looked a little ridiculous. He didn't seem to care.

"From the look on Brent Carver's face, I'd say the feeling is mutual. I wonder who he is. See the art on his walls?"

Katherine had been too scared to notice pictures. She shook her head.

"Barb's on her way here," said Harvey after a brief moment of silence. "Ed tied her up in your room. She seems pretty worried about me."

"Do you think you two can work things out?"

Harvey shook his head. "No, but we can part ways amicably and with dignity."

Katherine felt an uncomfortable knot tighten in her throat. Dignity. That would be nice. Her life was constantly being dragged through the gutter and newspapers. She had to find a way to get past it all. To move on.

"I'm about to bury two husbands in one week. I think that might be a record."

"Christ. I can't believe what you've gone through." He scrubbed his hand through short gray hair. Neither of them was young anymore. "I'm glad you didn't have to go through it alone."

She smiled and patted his hand. "So am I. Thank you."

They sat in silence for a little while. The clock ticked and people moved around them, but it was like they were together in this odd little bubble. She was going to miss this man who'd accidentally become her friend.

"Maybe," she said cautiously, "when this is all over, we could go away on a trip. A *platonic* trip," she added.

"I'd like that." His eyes crinkled at the edges. "Where to? Sun, or sand?"

She looked down at the floor and thought about all she'd done with her life and all she wanted to do. "Maybe we could go wherever the whales are," she said quietly.

He swallowed thickly and then stood. "I'd like that." And then he walked away.

Anna came out of the interview room to intense bright sunshine. She blinked at the light and rubbed her eyes. She didn't know the last time she'd slept, and worry for Brent gnawed at her brain. She couldn't believe they were holding him, that they could revoke his parole whether he'd committed a crime or not.

She was so furious she wanted to hit something, but so tired she could barely keep her eyes open. She wasn't going to let them do this. She wasn't going to let Brent suffer because he'd saved her life.

Her mouth was dry, so she begged a coffee off the cop behind the desk. He seemed friendly enough, but she refused to be charmed by anyone in a uniform, even one with Italian good looks. She still wore Brent's T-shirt, along with some borrowed pants, and looked like she'd been dragged through a forest of thorns backward by her hair.

"Where's Brent?" she asked for what felt like the millionth time.

"Still being held," the officer told her as he handed her an RCMP mug. He looked worried, which couldn't be a good sign. "Holly told me to tell you to stay strong. She was ordered in for questioning. Finn's being held too, but he's not on parole so he'll be released soon, I think."

"Is Holly here?" Anna needed to lean on those connections of Brent's if she hoped to keep him out of prison.

He nodded. "But they're making her and her father take a backseat on this investigation. They are both too involved, and there's a lot of media exposure on this one."

Crap. She'd hoped those links would smooth Brent's way. "None of this is his fault."

The officer was quiet for a moment. Then he leaned closer and said quietly, "You need a bargaining chip."

She frowned as his dark eyes probed hers. She didn't have any bargaining chips. She had nothing.

"Hey, Chastain. I need you to go out on patrol," someone shouted from four desks over.

"Right."

"Your mother's in the waiting room," the man, Chastain, said.

Anna stared at him in shock. "She's here?"

He gave her a dark-eyed smile. "She's been here all night, waiting for you."

Anna nodded and bit her lip. She'd thought she'd be sedated in the hospital.

"If you don't want to see her, I can sneak you out the back," he offered.

"Why are you being so nice to me?" The kindness almost broke her. She wanted fire and rage and some rigid law enforcement persona she could hate.

"Because you and your mother have suffered enough following a grave miscarriage of justice." He pointed in the direction of the waiting room.

Anna braced herself. She'd spent a lifetime running away from emotion, and now it was time to face it. When she got to the room, her mom was laid out across four chairs, fast asleep, wearing green scrubs. She went over and knelt beside her. Stroked her hair.

Her mom's eyes opened slowly, but they weren't cloudy. They were sharp and clear.

"Anna," she said on an exhale.

"Mom." Anna smiled.

Katherine sat up, a little wobbly. "Are you all right?"

Anna sniffed and nodded, but her eyes filled. Katherine dragged her into her arms and Anna bawled like the world was ending. All the grief for her father, Brent, her past, poured out of her and her mother just held and rocked her in a way she hadn't since Anna had been a little girl.

"I'm so very sorry, sweetheart." She kissed her hair and squeezed her tighter. "I've failed you." She sniffed. "And Davis. I let you both down so very badly."

"We both let Dad down. Ed fooled us all," Anna said quietly when she was able to speak again. Then she braced herself. "There's something else I want to tell you. Malcolm raped me before the prom."

Katherine had been pale before, but now she went sheet white. "That's why you tried to kill yourself?" Her lips were bloodless. Anna worried she was going to pass out.

"Yes." Finally, it was out. It was done.

"Oh, my Lord. That animal. That perverted little disgusting swine." Katherine shuddered. "I never liked him, but I never dreamed he'd…did he attack you at home?" Her mom's eyes were wide.

Anna rubbed her mother's cold hands. "He probably would have, but after I tried to kill myself he backed off. Plus, I told him I'd written a letter to Papa and that, when he got out, he was going to kill him." It had felt good to scare the crap out of her attacker. Malcolm had a healthy respect for his own hide.

"But you didn't tell your father, did you?"

Anna shook his head. "I should have. He died thinking I tried to kill myself because of what we thought he'd done. Even though he was innocent, it must have torn him apart."

Katherine covered Anna's hands with her own. "You were right not to tell him—it would have eaten him up with grief the whole time he was in prison. If he'd known about Malcolm, he would have killed him. *I* want to kill him. The revolting freak."

"Do you think I should press charges? It's just my word against his, and it happened so long ago."

"It's not about that, Anna. If you can bear to do it, it's about standing up in court and getting it all out there in the open. Even if they don't convict him, people will know. And there may be others."

Anna had thought of that too.

"The same way I'm going to stand up in court and shout from the rooftops that the police officers who investigated that theft from the city were incompetent." Katherine's voice got louder. People were starting to look their way. Anna bet at least one of the voyeurs was a reporter. Katherine got up and paced. "I'm going to sue the city until that measly million dollars looks like chump change."

That was it! Excitement sparked inside Anna and she kissed her mom's cheek. "Keep making a racket, Mom."

Her mother grinned. "I'm enjoying it, actually." This, from the woman who'd been avoiding the spotlight her whole life. "Where are you going?"

"To find Brent's lawyer. And see if the threat of a long, drawn-out, and *very* expensive lawsuit is enough to get the man I love some good old-fashioned justice."

The Mounties held him for three days, then suddenly—inexplicably—he was free to go.

Laura claimed she didn't know why, but he didn't believe her.

Anna had been forced to return to the States and answer questions about finding Peter's body. It had been nine days since he'd seen her. Nine days since the shooting. He clenched his fists. What he wanted was to get on a plane and fetch her back. But they wouldn't even let him in the country and she'd told him during several phone calls that they both just had to be patient.

Pah! Him? *Patient?*

He could be patient.

Maybe.

The last few weeks had taught him many things, and one of the most important things was how to trust again. He had his brother and Holly. Brent would never doubt their loyalty again. And he had Anna. Just as soon as those assholes in Minnesota figured out she was nothing but a victim in the whole crazy saga.

Something else he'd learned over the last few weeks was self-forgiveness. Not only for his father, but for Gina too. They hadn't been right for one another. He'd loved her, but not with passion. Not enough to make a life together. He'd never lied to her. Never wanted her to get hurt. And he'd have done anything to save her. The fact she was dead wasn't his fault. The ache in his chest was beginning to ease, along with the guilt and age-old feeling of self-disgust. Eventually, with time, that too would heal.

Jack Panetti had identified the one surviving mercenary as the guy who'd carjacked him and then shot him in the back. That fucker was going down on federal charges of murder of a police officer, kidnapping, and attempted murder. He'd fessed up to a whole lot of bad, from the charity being a cover for illegal mercenary activities, to Davis catching them moving their ill-gotten gains, and them trying to find Anna to get it back. Illinois had abolished the death penalty, so the guy was going to get a taste of many, many years in prison. Brent hoped the guy enjoyed it as much as he had.

With a little help from Jack Panetti's IT guy, the cops had found all the money. Now the US and Canadian authorities got to fight about who kept it. Davis had been wrong about them stealing money from the charity—they'd simply been using the foundation as a smoke screen to obscure their dirty dealings. Feds had just linked a recent assassination of a high-level American diplomat in Yemen back to Rand and his crew, and the shit was hitting the fan. Thankfully, Davis's name had been cleared, both in this investigation and the one that had put him inside in the first place. His record was going to be expunged.

Brent had received notification that his parole officer had changed and he was back to reporting every two weeks, which went in the plus column. But somehow his identity had been leaked to the world, which was a pisser. He'd missed his NYC exhibition, but got an e-mail from a woman in South Dakota asking if he'd recently given some watercolor paintings to her four children. He'd had his agent write back to prove provenance and tell her to insure them for at least ten grand each. His agent was pissed with him, but all the publicity and his apparent "hero" status in the media had increased the value of his artwork, which had mollified the guy slightly.

Hero status. That was a kicker. He'd never pretended to be a hero.

He stared at the water.

The waves fizzled to a stop at his toes.

Thankfully the cops hadn't found his weapons or hidey-holes. After he got back, he made sure all guns were dumped far off-shore, never to be seen again. He was done with all that. He just hoped it was done with him.

He looked at his house. The bodies were gone. Glass cleared up. He'd had a professional cleaning crew come in as soon as the cops were finished, removing blood and guts and pretty much every stick of furniture that might have a bad association for Anna. The windows were still out—they had to be custom-made and replaced. And the place was looking pretty damn bare, but at least it was still standing, bullet holes and all.

He looked around at his beautiful wedge of the Pacific Rim and tried to feel contentment. But it wouldn't come. Inside, misery swirled with a total lack of appetite for life, in a way he hadn't felt since those early years in prison. He'd tried to paint. Tried to get drunk. Ended up just sitting here, watching the water, wanting Anna more than he'd ever wanted his freedom. The fact he suddenly needed more from his life was both terrifying and exhilarating.

"Hi."

Her voice had him spinning. His heart gave a big kick before it started beating again. "Anna." He felt like he was dreaming.

She was dressed in a pretty pink camisole and tight black jeans. The bruises had faded and she looked recovered from her ordeal, on the outside at least. "I'm sorry it took so long to get back here. I didn't call ahead because I wanted to surprise you." She held a small urn in front of her. "And I needed to fetch Dad…"

Davis. His eyes smarted.

"I thought this would be a good place for his ashes." Her moss-green eyes were huge as she raised them to his. "The best place."

"It isn't the best place when you're not here," he said quietly.

"No?"

He shook his head.

"I've been doing a lot of thinking—" Anna began.

Brent didn't like the sound of that.

She looked around. "I know you love it here but"—Hope shrank inside him—"I don't think I can live here full-time. I mean weekends, for sure." She bit her lip. "I'm moving back to Victoria, to my grandmother's home. To be closer to Mom. And closer to you." Her gaze clouded, looking troubled at the enormity of the challenges they faced. "How are we going to do this?" she asked uncertainly.

"One day at a time," he told her, never looking away.

One side of her lips twitched. "Sounds a bit like prison."

He moved closer. "Better food. Better company." He opened his arms.

She placed the urn carefully in the sand and leaned into him. He wrapped his arms tight around her, so tight she squeaked. She wasn't a dream. She was here in his arms and he never intended to let her go.

"I want to be with you, to live with you, wherever you are." He buried his nose in her hair and inhaled a sweet citrus scent.

"I love you, Brent Carver." She smiled up at him, eyes shining, her chin rubbing his chest. Tiny, stubborn, and perfect. "But it's not going to be easy."

He laughed. "After what we've been through, it'll be a piece of cake."

"Yeah, but this is for the long haul. Living together, sharing space. I haven't done that in forever."

They were alike in so many ways it was startling. "We'll figure it out. I can always retreat back here when either one of us needs solitude. I'll give you space if you need it." He hooked her hair behind her ear. "You set me free, Anna."

Those eyes of hers saw all the way through to his soul. "You're a good man, Brent. You deserve to be free."

"What do you think your dad would have made of us being together?" It bothered him. Hell, being part of the human race bothered him. It had been easier when he'd been alone. Easier, but not necessarily better.

She grinned and leaned back in his arms. "You're the son he never had. He loved you. You *know* that."

"Do you think he'd have loved grandkids?" A loaded question. He watched her very carefully.

Her eyes widened and she swallowed. "Not straightaway, but one day." Her eyes searched his, looking for answers, but he was giving nothing away because he wanted to know how *she* felt. "One day, yes, he'd have loved grandkids."

A feeling of relief and joy burst through him. He hadn't known he held a deeply buried desire for a family until he'd asked that question. And if Anna didn't want kids, he'd be content. He'd always be content with Anna. But suddenly the idea of making babies with her filled him with a weird sort of hope for the future, because if she trusted him enough to be a father, she must really trust him. But how in the hell would he tell his children about his dark past? He had no fucking clue, but he wanted kids. He really wanted them.

All his insecurities would worm their way to the surface eventually, Anna's too, but they'd deal with them later. All he needed right now was in his arms. He went to kiss her but she stopped him.

She laughed. "I think you're turning out to be a big softy, Brent Carver."

"Wrong." He slanted her a suggestive look and a wicked half grin.

"Wait." Her expression turned serious and she pulled away. "There's one more thing I need to tell you first." She dug for something in the back pocket of her jeans. Held up a thick envelope. "I spoke to an attorney about pressing charges against Malcolm Plantain." She chewed her thumbnail. "There is no statute of limitations for rape in British Columbia. You guessed it was him who attacked me?"

"I figured it out." He'd put the clues together, and gave himself big marks for not having the sonofabitch taken down a back alley and beaten within an inch of his life. He massaged his hands over her shoulder. "You sure you want to do this?"

She shook her head. "No. I don't. But I have to. People have to pay for their crimes."

That made it sound easier than this was going to be. Taking someone to court for rape often hurt the victim just as much as the accused.

"I don't want you to get hurt."

"I got hurt a long time ago. I'm over the hurt now, and it's about time I was brave enough to stand up to my past," she said.

He intended to stand with her. "Did you tell your mother?"

She nodded. "She took it hard at first, but she's dealt with everything so much better than I anticipated. She's been a rock and we've grown a lot closer. She said she'd support any decision I made." She gripped the envelope tighter. "She got you released."

He snorted, then realized she wasn't kidding. "How the hell did she do that?"

"By threatening the city and the cops with massive litigation over Dad's wrongful arrest and conviction."

"She *should* sue them."

Anna shook her head. "She told them she'd drop the lawsuits and even stop talking to the media *if* they did the right thing by you. You didn't do anything wrong. You saved my life. Believe me, she's more than satisfied with the results." Anna reached up and touched his lips. A ripple of desire shot through his body at the contact, but he controlled himself.

Her fingers gripped his. "I'm going to need your support to take Malcolm to court. I don't think I can do it alone."

"Always." There was no hesitation. Hell, there was nothing he wouldn't do for this woman.

"I want to be with you. I want a chance of happiness with you while we figure out the shape of our future," she said.

"It can be any shape you want." He couldn't believe he was lucky enough to have this shot at a real life, but he was taking it and he didn't intend to fuck it up. "I don't think you understand exactly how much I love you."

Her throat worked and her eyes shimmered. "I do, Brent. I was there, remember?"

And now she'd made his eyes water so he blinked hard to get rid of the tears. Men like him did not cry.

She handed him the envelope, bent down, and picked up the urn. Stood in the surf as she let her father go. He waited for the sadness to come as he watched the breeze disperse the ashes of his best friend, but there was a feeling of intense peace instead. Davis's name had been cleared and Brent knew this would have made the man happy. He hoped the fact he and Anna were together would have made his friend smile.

When she was finished and they'd both said their good-byes, he scooped her into his arms and strode toward the house.

She tensed.

His hold tightened and he stopped moving. "We don't have to stay here. I can sell the place—"

She touched his mouth again but this time with hers. "Take me to bed or lose me forever," she said against his lips.

"I'm not losing you. Not ever."

"Just keep telling me you love me."

"Every day. Every single moment of every single day." He lifted his head. "And I want a dog."

She smiled. "Let's get two in case they get lonely."

He nodded and then forgot what they were talking about when she kissed him again.

He came up for air. "I need a date to my brother's wedding in September. I'm the best man." The thought brought with it a bolt of terror. All those cops in one room. *Shit.*

A smile curved those pretty pink lips. "We're going on a date?"

He huffed out a laugh as he started up the steps. "We're going on many, many dates. I'm done hiding out from the world. Just as long as there aren't too many other people involved." He shuddered.

Those green eyes of hers sparkled. "I'm done hiding too. But right now all I want to do is make love to you in a real bed without people trying to shoot us. Think you can concentrate on that?"

He grinned. "Yes, ma'am."

"Hmm, I like the sound of that."

"Yes, *ma'am.*" Goddamn good girls. Got him every single time. Or maybe it was just one particular good girl, he amended a few moments later as he laid her down on his bed and stripped her down to bad-girl underwear. Maybe it was just Anna. Good or bad, she was the only woman for him.

ACKNOWLEDGMENTS

Writing can be a lonely business, and I rely heavily on my writer loops, Facebook, and Twitter friends, to connect me to the universe and help keep me sane. "Thank you" to all my online friends. My critique partner, Kathy Altman, is a paragon of patience and common sense as she helps me polish each manuscript; I couldn't do it without her.

Also, thanks to my family, who put up with odd working hours and weird mutterings as I worked through various drafts of this manuscript. My husband and kids really *are* the best. Thanks to my wonderful in-laws for their constant sales pitches back home in the UK. The retirees of Killearn don't know what's hit them!

Big thanks to Holly, my furry companion, for our daily walks and the constant updates on the local rabbit and squirrel populations.

And, finally, special thanks to my agent, Jill Marsal of Marsal Lyon Literary Agency, LLC, and my editor, Kelli Martin, and the whole team at Montlake Romance who are so wonderful to work with.

ABOUT THE AUTHOR

JAMES HARE, © 2012

A former marine biologist who completed her PhD at the Gatty Marine Laboratory in St. Andrews, Scotland, Toni Anderson has traveled the world with her work. She was born and raised in rural Shropshire, England, and, after living in five different countries, she finally settled down in the Canadian prairies with her husband and two children. Combining her love of travel with her love of romantic suspense, Anderson writes stories based in some of the places she has been fortunate to visit. When not writing, she's busy walking her dog, gardening, and ferrying the kids to school, piano, and soccer games. She is also the author of *Storm Warning*, *Edge of Survival*, and *Dangerous Waters.*